D0606798

RESIST

Also by Ilima Todd
Remake

Todd, Ilima,
Resist /
[2016]

sa   10/24/16

RESIST

ILIMA TODD

SHADOW
MOUNTAIN

To my parents,
me ke aloha pumehana

© 2016 Ilima Todd

All rights reserved. No part of this book may be reproduced in any form or by any means without permission in writing from the publisher, Shadow Mountain®, at permissions@shadowmountain.com. The views expressed herein are the responsibility of the author and do not necessarily represent the position of Shadow Mountain.

All characters in this book are fictitious, and any resemblance to actual persons, living or dead, is purely coincidental.

Visit us at ShadowMountain.com

Library of Congress Cataloging-in-Publication Data

Names: Todd, Ilima, author.
Title: Resist / Ilima Todd.
Description: Salt Lake City, Utah : Shadow Mountain, [2016] | ©2016 | Series:
    Remake ; volume 2 | Summary: Having been rescued, remade, and returned to
    Freedom, Theron chooses to be a healer and falls in love with a captured rebel.
Identifiers: LCCN 2015044859 (print) | LCCN 2016004252 (ebook) |
    ISBN 9781629721040 (hardbound : alk. paper) | ISBN 9781629734125 (ebook)
Subjects: | CYAC: Healers—Fiction. | Liberty—Fiction. | Government, Resistance
    to—Fiction. | Love—Fiction. | Science fiction. | LCGFT: Science fiction.
Classification: LCC PZ7.T5665 Rh 2016 (print) | LCC PZ7.T5665 (ebook) | DDC
    [Fic]—dc23
LC record available at http://lccn.loc.gov/2015044859

Printed in the United States of America
Publishers Printing, Salt Lake City, UT

10 9 8 7 6 5 4 3 2 1

ASSEMBLY COUNCIL SUMMIT
Location: Freedom Province #17
Meeting Minutes for 28 March 131.8

Attendance
All Prime Makers present excepting
Isra, Freedom 7
Rigg, Freedom 22

Call to Order
Summit host, Prime Maker Voss, opened the meeting at 8:45 AM. Minutes of 26 December were read and approved.

[Motion to accept: Jyler, Freedom 11; Seconded: Kopin, Freedom 3; Approved: Unanimously]

Prime Maker Report
• Final details of proposed Freedom 27: approved with majority vote. Potential locations to be investigated and presented at the next summit meeting.

• Transition of Casian to Prime Maker in Freedom 19 completed without incident. No reports of population uprising or complaint. Satisfactory leadership conversion on record.

• Concerns regarding Prime Maker Eridian, Freedom 1, reviewed, including: unsatisfactory use of rebels within the province, further reports of escaped citizens, and inconclusive results regarding test subject [Batch #1372, Member #9 aka "Nine"]. Eridian to present definitive results of experiment Nine at next summit meeting in three months' time where final vote regarding status of Freedom 1 will be taken.

Adjournment

Assembly Council to reconvene 23 June in Freedom Province 1 to coincide with biennial conference and research facility proposals.

PART ONE

CHAPTER ONE

The world fell apart when she left. As though it, like me, mourned her absence. But while I find temporary measures to numb my sadness, Freedom fuels its sorrow with desperation, turning that grief into something that looks a whole lot like madness.

Like tonight.

I'm in the middle of my first cage fight when the sirens sound, an hour earlier than normal.

"Is this a joke?" I stand straighter and drop my fisted hands, glancing toward the street and the line of Seekers that patrol it on foot. The guns strapped to their chests are held at the ready. Armored vehicles follow close behind.

Those are new.

A pain shoots through my gut, making me double over. Then a knee to my face. I fly backwards into the metal cage walls, ricocheting back into my opponent's fist before I finally collapse on the floor.

"What the . . . ?" I curse and rub a hand over my mouth, coming away with a fresh streak of blood. "That was a cheap shot, Gray."

He shrugs, a smile forming on his lips. "Sorry, Theron. I couldn't miss an opportunity to knock you down. It happens so rarely." He offers a hand, and I take it, stumbling a moment to steady my feet.

"It's not my fault you're so slow. I can see your fist coming at me years before it gets here." I smirk. "Usually."

Gray's tall, like me, but looks like he weighs twice as much. All muscle, too. He'd reduce me to Theron-soup if I didn't move so quickly. I'm faster than most fighters I go up against, even with my limp.

I test my jaw, shifting it left to right. Nothing's broken. "Guess it's a draw tonight." Spectators are already leaving the area, their bets on our fight forgotten.

"You're the only one bleeding, my friend. That would make the winner . . ." He taps the cleft in his chin, as though thinking hard about which of us should be crowned victor.

I smack the side of his head and raise my fists, sending a jab his way but stopping before contact. "Let's make it official." I lure him with a bent finger and a grin, but Gray's face falls.

"I can't risk it." He glances to the street, and I know he's not talking about the fight. It's this cracked curfew. It started three months ago, along with the extra border patrols, the random apartment searches, the tracker scans. The Prime Maker's gone paranoid, but I'm the only one who knows why. The only one who knows what—or who—she's looking for.

Funny thing about Nine—she's a thief, a free-breaker. She

stole our freedom with her choice to leave, yet we're the ones paying for her crime. I don't know why Eridian needs her so badly, but sometimes I think she's more obsessed than I am about finding Nine. At least that's the lie I tell myself every night, when my spare hours are spent either fighting in the cage or drinking in the nightspots. Both have a way of making me forget about the girl I lost, though buzz drinks work faster. It looks like I chose the wrong method tonight, thanks to this early curfew. I'm too awake to head home now. Too aware.

Gray opens the cage door and stomps down the stairs. "I'll see you at work tomorrow, Theron."

I give him an affirmative grunt and throw on my shirt. At the street's edge, I pause and watch the Seekers make their way through Freedom Central. The sirens continue to blare through the province, background music to the Seekers' march. They scatter citizens out of the brothels, question the drunks stumbling out of the nightspots, and test the trackers of anyone who stares at them two seconds too long. You'd think those little plastic tracker guns had bullets in them considering how people cower when the gun latches on the tiny nub behind their ears. I'd take the pain of a tracker replacement over the pain in my chest any day.

I weave between two armored vehicles. I've never seen them before. They're rusted and worn—ancient. I wonder where they came from. They make deep, guttural sounds like some growling beast gearing up for a fight. A predator ready to attack.

The Seekers up top sit behind massive firearms that look like they could take down an entire building in one shot. What in Freedom's name does Eri plan on doing with these things? She's going to kill us all in her childish game of Tracker Seek. Except Nine's already won this game. Eri just doesn't realize it yet.

As I turn the corner onto my street, I see a familiar Seeker hovering outside my building's entrance. Bron. He yells orders I can't hear clearly to the half dozen guards surrounding him. Something about *Prime Maker*, *time running out*, and *you idiots*. He waves a yellow piece of paper in the air. Probably more of that propaganda that makes Eridian throw a tantrum every time her Seekers find it posted throughout the province.

I've never read the flyers—they're always torn down before I have the chance—but people talk. I know the flyers say something about how we aren't really free. Not really equal. There was a time I would have balked at that. With the freedom to choose who and what we are, choose what we do, I can't think of how we could be more liberated. But the way things have become these last few months? Yeah . . . if this is freedom, it totally sucks.

I should ignore Bron, but I can't help myself. When I reach the front doors, I salute. "Greetings, gentlemen. Out for a leisurely stroll this fine evening?" The sun hasn't set yet. I've no idea what prompted the early curfew, but even these guys have to admit it's ridiculous.

"Watch it, Theron." Bron crumples the yellow paper and stuffs it into a pocket. "I suggest you head inside. I can't protect you out here once the sirens stop."

"Protect me?" I narrow my eyes, daring him to tell me what to do one more time. "Since when have you ever protected me, Bron?" While I've been summoned for questioning by Eri too many times to count, Bron has "questioned" me in his own way a few times—methods involving swollen eyes and broken ribs.

"Just because you're the Prime Maker's pet," Bron says, flicking a bug off his arm, "doesn't mean you're *my* pet. The day will come when she won't need you anymore, and you'll wish you exercised a little more restraint with that tongue of yours."

8

It takes everything in me to not stick my tongue out at him. "I'm not the one with a leash around my neck." I bark like a dog and make to reach behind his ear to scratch it.

He swats my hand away and flares his nostrils.

I've pushed my limit. "Whoa. Down boy." I grin and slip into the building before Bron decides to hold an impromptu interrogation. He's right about one thing, though. Eri lets me get away with mouthing off and pretending the rules don't apply to me because I'm her most valuable commodity right now. I'm live bait. She believes I'm the strongest reason Nine has to return to Freedom. Me. I can't let her know the truth: Nine is not coming back. Not for me. Not for Eri. Not for anyone.

The elevator's been broken for a week, and I'm already used to making the trek up four flights of stairs. Strange it hasn't been fixed yet, but then again, strange seems to be the theme of recent Freedom. A forgotten elevator is probably the least of Eri's worries.

I walk down the dimly lit hallway to my apartment, pausing just outside. There, on the opposite wall, is another yellow flyer like the one Bron held. I scan through the words and phrases on the paper. *Freedom, equality, oppression*—things I expected. Halfway through the document, I freeze on one word. *Family*. I've no idea what it means, but that doesn't mean I haven't heard it before.

Nine used that word once.

I close my eyes and try to remember. It was the morning she left. We were in my apartment, eating breakfast. I told her what happened after the crash and about my Remake. How I decided not to change anything about myself because I wanted to be the Theron she remembered. I wanted her to recognize me if she came back.

You are more than a handsome face, Theron. You're kind and sure and brave. You are love and sacrifice.

You're family.

My eyes open, focusing on the word again. *Family*. Nine made it sound like a good thing. Like by being family, I was important to her. But it obviously wasn't enough to keep her with me. Maybe it's the reason she left.

I rip the flyer off the wall and crumple it in my hand like Bron did. Whatever the intent of this propaganda, I want nothing to do with it.

"Hey, Theron," Jadyn says from behind me. Her familiar scratchy voice bears a hint of irritation.

I stuff the paper into my pocket and turn to face her. The last thing I want is to get caught with questionable material. I don't need another interrogation right now.

"Hey, Jadyn." I step backwards toward my door, reaching for the handle.

"What do you think about this curfew?" Her short dress swishes with every movement, the large black poof of material scraping against my arm.

I shrug one shoulder. "I think the Prime Maker must be afraid of the dark."

She laughs then leans in conspiringly. "But the dark is the best time to party." She points over her shoulder. "A few of us are gathering at my place. Making our own nightspot tonight . . . if you want to come."

I'd normally jump at the chance to distract myself, to feel anything besides my normal misery, but I suddenly want to be alone. "Maybe next time."

She grabs my chin between her thumb and forefinger, pouting. "All right," she says. "But if you change your mind, you know where I live." She winks and heads down the hall. After she pounds on her own door, it swings open, music blaring from inside.

When I'm alone again, I take the flyer out of my pocket and smooth it against my door, skimming through the rest of the document until I find what I'm looking for. *The Rise*. It's the name of the group behind the propaganda. No contact instructions, location, or hint at something more to come. Just a name. I rip the paper into tiny pieces and deposit it into a trash receptacle at the end of the hall.

Once in my apartment, I head for the washroom mirror to examine the damage Gray did to my face. I stare at my reflection, startled by the man who greets me. His blue eyes are dull, empty. Like a storm washed away every trace of color, and the sun forgot to come back out. The circles beneath his dead eyes are as dark as the lashes above. The splotchy growth of hair on his face and neck is a sorry camouflage for the misery beneath. A tormented corpse, a shadow of a life.

I lean forward and press my forehead against his so that his image blurs and all I can see are indistinct shades of light. No corners or lines or curves. Just an ill-defined cloud of fog. I breathe out, the condensation on the mirror obscuring his image more. I don't want to see him, but I can't look away. He is a stranger, yet the only companion I have. I pull back, turning my face away before he fully reappears. I don't want him to see me either. Not like this.

I'm relieved to find a half empty bottle of my favorite fluorescent-green buzz drink in my cupboard. Maybe my nightly journey to forgetfulness isn't a wash after all. I drag the bottle with me to the far side of the room and open a window. Sitting on the ledge, I swing my legs around so they dangle over the street below. A few minutes later, the sirens finally shut off, and the silence left behind leaves a ringing in my ears that hurts more than the noise.

I lean against the side of the windowpane and watch the sun set over the province. I squint and try to see what's past the walls, outside our borders. The crop fields are just beyond the red bridge, but the distant landscape that's a shadowy mass of color during the day is just a shadowy mass of dark now, so I give up.

Whenever I pull the bottle from my lips, Freedom looks a little darker, a little less distinct. I can't tell if it's from the buzz drink or the setting sun, but it doesn't matter, because soon every part of me feels numb. It's the closest thing I've felt to happiness in the last three months, though I can no longer remember why.

CHAPTER TWO

*A*nother overdose." Iden rolls her eyes and flicks her finger my way. "This one's yours, Theron."

I look out through the glass panel embedded in the wall and spy the next patient in line. His hair has been replaced with some kind of reflective material, a hundred tiny mirrors covering his head in a strange mosaic. He paces the trauma station lobby with arms folded, periodically swatting at his elbows as though they're covered in spiders.

"Are you sure?" I wrinkle my forehead, feigning confusion. "He looks like one of your people." I point to the metal studs embedded in Iden's left cheek. It creates a spiral pattern that matches the style of her long peach-colored hair, which has been molded into the shape of a giant seashell. "Add an antenna, and I bet the two of you could make contact with your home planet. You could finally go home, Iden."

"Ha. Ha." She drops the portable drill in her hand. She uses it to make accessories for her clothes, hair, toes—whatever. Every day she wears something different, new. Like she's a living piece of original artwork. She stands from her desk and opens the door to the lobby. "Oz?"

The pacing man shakes his head, but somehow I know he means it to be in the affirmative.

I lead him to a nearby Healer room. The trauma station itself is rather large, though the low ceiling makes it feel small. With several stories above us that can be utilized in the case of an outbreak—one that might require a lockdown and quarantine—we've a lot more space than we need. Most days we only use these front rooms, though. The natural light coming in through a series of reflective skylights makes it a pleasant place to work during the day.

After three attempts to get Oz to sit on the bed, I give up and check his vitals the best I can while he's in motion, scratching and pacing through the small room. I slide my finger across my portable screen and log into the Healer records. He slides his finger on the screen when I ask, and I briefly glance through his records. He's been in twice before, but not while I've worked at the trauma station, which is nearly six weeks now. Oz's records show Opax abuse. It's a painkiller that, when taken in high doses, induces hallucinations.

"What'd you take, Oz?"

He pulls at the skin of his left elbow and leans his head back, staring at the fluorescent light in the center of the ceiling. "Little orange pills."

"How many little orange pills?"

"Mm." He stops next to the door and taps his right foot repeatedly. "Mm."

I grab a small flashlight and lean against the door, shining the light into one of his eyes, then the other. "Do you remember how many?" I ask.

He holds up five fingers, then three. I'm not sure if he means eight, can't decide between five or three, or is oblivious to what I'm asking. Doesn't matter, though. I know exactly what's wrong.

"Well, you didn't overdose, Oz. You're having Opax withdrawals. This patch will release smaller and smaller amounts of the drug into your system to help you step off more comfortably." I lift the back of his shirt and place a letdown patch between his shoulder blades, out of reach. Hopefully that will keep him from removing it until all the drugs have been released.

Oz leans his head against the wall and rotates it side to side, shaking his hands while he does. I find an atomizer and insert a healthy dose of Apreline into the vial.

"Put this tube into your mouth and inhale," I say, giving him the open end of the tube. When his breathing levels out, I let him hold the vial the tube is attached to. "This will help with the anxiety. You'll feel relaxed in a few minutes."

This time he nods and squeezes my shoulder, still inhaling the calming drug. It's his way of saying thank you, and I smile, glad he's already getting some of his sense back.

A loud metal clattering comes from the hallway. I open the door to see a table crash into the wall and loose papers fly through the air on the other side of the room. Gray is struggling to restrain a man out of control.

"Theron!" Gray shouts. "A little help, here?"

"Iden," I say as I rush out, "watch my drug patient?"

She nods her shelled head and checks on Oz while I jog over to Gray and the new patient. I grab the man's arm and help Gray maneuver him onto a bed. Setia, the other Healer on duty, tries to shout above the man's ruckus, her bright orange hair flinging wildly around her face.

"He wandered in like this. By himself." The lisp from her pierced tongue sounds funny at high volume. "No idea what's wrong."

I tilt my head toward the metal rails of the bed. "Strap him down, Setia." I secure my hold on the man's arm while Gray secures the other; Setia gets the straps in place. All three of us do our best to avoid the patient's flailing legs. I let Gray and Setia restrain his legs with more straps while I examine the patient.

He's much older than I am, probably twice my age. Shorter and stockier, too, with his hair completely shaved off. Which is strange. After seventeen years of monthly shearings, it's not often citizens choose to be bald after their Remake. But stranger than that, though, is that he looks . . . plain. Simple clothing and clean, accessory-free skin, no ink that I can see. He reminds me of . . . me. I rub the back of my neck, my fingers tracing my tattoo there. Even in the midst of an emergency, Nine finds a way into my thoughts.

"Can you hear me?" I ask the man. His eyes dart around his head, the edges of his lips turning a bluish color. "We need to get a dose of B.C.D. into his bloodstream. Now." Patches and dermastraps are too slow, and there's no way I'll get him to cooperate with an atomizer. After filling a needle with the meds, I attempt to find a vein, but he won't stop thrashing. If I wait for his oxygen to cut off and force him still, it'll be too late. How else can I get the meds into his blood—fast?

I drop the needle and run to Iden's desk, grabbing her portable drill. Racing back to the patient, I feel for a spot just below his knee, placing the drill bit against his bone. "Gray, get me a thick needle. Like the ones we use for emergency kidney flushes."

He opens his mouth to say something, then darts to the fallen cart on the other side of the room, rifling through the mess on the floor. Files of paper are scattered among medical supplies, most of them from Setia's desk. She insists on keeping paper records of her work though everything's recorded on the province-wide network. It's a weird quirk with her.

I look at Setia. Her files are probably the last things on her mind right now, her eyes trained on the drill in my hands. I don't know if she realizes what I'm thinking, but she covers her mouth anyway, as though I'm crazy. She's about ten years older than me and Gray, and I'm sure she's never seen anyone do this before. It might not work, but I have to try. It's better than letting the patient die.

After a deep breath, I begin to drill. I feel the moment the drill bit hits soft material beyond bone, and I remove the tool. Gray hands me the thick needle, and after getting the meds in place, I slide the needle into the bone marrow. I pull on the depression knob, extracting a small amount of the soft tissue into the needle to make sure I've hit the correct depth. Then I depress the B.C.D.—now mixed with marrow—into his bone.

Within seconds the patient relaxes, and we're able to assess his condition better. He continues to struggle with breathing, his face is flushed, and his tongue appears swollen.

"It's an allergic reaction," Setia says, finding an adrenaline vial and administering the drug immediately. I attach two anti-infection patches to the patient's chest and let Setia and Gray finish with him. After washing up and taking off my bloodied Healer shirt, leaving me in just a tank, I check on Oz, then help Iden clean up the mess our mystery patient made in his grand entrance.

"So," Setia says when she and Gray are done. "That was fun."

I'm sprawled on a seat in the trauma station lobby. One side of my mouth rises as the two of them settle on either side of me. We're usually the only three Healers on duty, along with Iden. "That's the kind of thing that made me choose the trauma station after my Healer training," I say. "Doing wellness checks or administering blockers to the Batchers all day long—no thanks. I'll take excitement and the unknown over that boring mess."

Gray elbows me in the side. "I've never seen anything like that."

I shrug. I don't know if he means the patient's condition or what I did to help him.

"Seriously, Theron." Setia sighs, brushing back her orange hair. "You're like a crazy Healer genius. How did you know to do that?"

I don't answer, because I don't really know. "Is he okay?"

"He's stable," Gray says. "But we're keeping him under until the meds take full effect. Another hour or so."

Setia's tongue darts in and out of her mouth, the studs clacking against her teeth. It's a habit when she's tired. Gray cracks his knuckles one by one, first by bending each finger backwards, then by pulling each one out of its socket. I'm sure other people would consider both sounds annoying, but I like it. It grounds me, and I feel like here, in this moment, is exactly where I'm supposed to be.

There's a peace you feel when you know you're doing what you're meant to. It's as though the path you've chosen and the path intended for you have converged, at least for a moment, and everything feels . . . right. That's how I felt with Nine. She was my purpose, the reason behind every choice I made. She was my source of peace, and she stole it from me when she left.

The closest I've come to regaining that peace is here in the trauma station. People come in sick, injured. Sometimes panicked. Always afraid. If I can find a way to help them, heal them, a calm settles over me, letting me know that what I'm doing is important—that it means something. They are only moments, small slivers of time, but it's enough to keep me going. Enough to push me forward with the hope that I'll find my intended path again someday and feel that peace in its entirety.

After Oz is discharged, I administer fluids to a woman who comes in dehydrated and run scans on a man with chest pains that, in the end, are just bad heartburn. Setia's called away for some project she's been working on at the research facility. I've no idea what it's about, but she's working there more and more lately.

The rest of the afternoon is quiet, and I eventually find myself in the room of our earlier patient. He's just sleeping now.

As discreetly as I can, I slide one of his fingers across my portable computer screen and settle into a chair next to his bed. His name is Catcher. Thirty-nine years old. Male. He lives one street over from me—not far. But there's no Trade listed for him. Strange. Not much of a medical record either, except for one bout of depression twenty years ago. And now an allergic condition, the allergy source unknown.

Catcher stirs, then sits up in bed, rubbing one side of his shaved head as he yawns. "You the guy who saved my life?"

"It wasn't just me," I say, laying the screen on my lap. "Our entire Healer team worked to get you stable."

"Funny." He chuckles, but it turns into a cough, his throat likely sore from struggling to breathe this morning. In a quieter voice, he adds, "I didn't peg you as the humble type."

I narrow my eyes at him. What's he talking about?

"Setia and Gray couldn't stop talking you up—told me about your performance under pressure. Quick thinking. Experimental procedure. Drilling a hole into my leg?" He raises an eyebrow.

I stand and pull the sheet back to look at the damage. He'll have a nice circular-shaped scar when the swelling goes down, but as long as we keep any infection away, he should be fine.

"It feels like you poured a vat of acid into my leg, by the way."

"You're welcome."

He smiles. "How long have you been a Healer?"

It's none of his business, but I think he asks because, like Gray and Setia, he's impressed with what I've done. He's not questioning my ability; he's praising it.

"Not long." I turn and reach for my screen, ready to call Iden in to discharge him. "You sure you don't know what caused the reaction?"

"Nope," he says too quickly.

I glance at him, but he runs a finger along the metal bars of his bed, distracted.

I scan through his file once more, making sure I haven't missed anything. I'm about to ask him why his Trade isn't listed—it might provide a clue as to what caused the allergy attack—but he speaks before I have the chance.

"What does Nine mean?"

My hand flies to the back of my neck. I forgot I'm only in my tank, the tattoo easily seen. I look at Catcher. His expression mirrors the rest of him. Simple. Genuine. Real. No malicious intent or morbid curiosity. Just kindness, perhaps gratitude. And something else I can't put my finger on. He's . . . different.

I clear my throat. "It's the number of toes I have."

Catcher's laugh bursts out of him like a clap of thunder. Loud and unabashed and happy. No, not happy. Something more than happy—joyful. I can't imagine anyone feeling that way, especially after facing death a few hours before.

It's like he has a secret tucked away inside of him. Hidden. But always there so when he needs to find something to smile about, he remembers it, and the joy seeps out of his skin so others can catch glimpses of it too. Maybe it's his form of peace. The converging of his paths.

His laugh turns to a cough again, and he falls back onto his pillow, exhausted. "It's a girl, isn't it?"

My bum leg falters beneath me, and I manage to trip over myself though I hadn't been moving.

Catcher nods, a wide grin on his face. "I knew it. It's always about a girl. It's like they give these females a magical power when they're first Made. Power to love us. Power to drive us to the edge of madness. We're useless against that power, and we'll never understand it."

You have no idea.

"Yep," he says, more to himself. "Females. They'll get you every time." He looks up at me and winks. "Where is this girl?"

I don't know what makes me say it, but I feel like I can tell this stranger anything. "She left a long time ago." I pause. "And she's not coming back."

His face turns serious, and I wonder if I said the wrong thing. If I said too much.

We're both silent for a moment, and as I'm about to leave, Catcher asks, "Are you happy, Theron?"

"Excuse me?"

"Are you happy? With the life you've chosen?"

I feel tears gather in my eyes, and I will them to stay there. With a voice I can barely control, I say, soft and low, "I didn't choose this."

I expect Catcher to ask me another question, but he just nods and presses his lips together into a sympathetic smile, as though he knows exactly what I mean.

CHAPTER THREE

When I walk into the trauma station the next morning, I hear a loud banging noise, followed by Setia cursing in the back lab. The door's ajar, so I carefully stick my head through and force my bottom lip out in a pout. "Why so sad?"

"Theron!" She jumps away from the counter and brings a hand to her chest, calming her quick breaths. "You startled me."

I open the door wider and step inside. "Sorry. Are you okay? It sounded like you stepped on a hot needle."

"Close," she says, forcing a laugh. "This cracked machine keeps shocking me." She points to the centrifuge on a wheeled cart.

I rub my forehead. "You trying to separate a blood sample?" We don't usually do lab work in the trauma station, though we can if the lab staff upstairs is too busy.

Setia shrugs. "It's for my research." Her eyes dart to the floor, her face turning pink.

"You don't have a centrifuge in the research facility?"

"I do, but this particular sample . . ." She sighs, impatient. "Will you help me?" She looks up at me, her chin trembling. Why is she afraid?

"Of course." I smile reassuringly, hoping to calm her. A part of me wants to ask about her secret project, but I don't press her. "First, let's make sure it's balanced." I lift the cover and check that the collection tube has a proper counterweight. "It looks good."

She taps her tongue piercing against the roof of her mouth. "Why does it keep shocking me?"

"The spinning mechanism causes a lot of static electricity." I make sure all the cords are secured to the wall. "If it's not grounded properly, you'll feel a jolt when you touch it." I shove the machine to the center of the cart. "This one's old. Sometimes I have to slip a gauze pad or two under the front left corner to level it out."

She points toward the machine. "Is that why it keeps knocking into the wall or shifting toward the edge of the cart when I turn it on?"

"Yup." I lean over to glance at the back of it, checking that everything looks good.

Setia steps back and rests against the wall. "The one at the research lab is completely hands-free. I never have to worry about troubleshooting."

"Must be nice," I say, standing straight again. "I put in a request for a new one a few weeks back, but who knows how long it will take. Ready?"

She nods.

I stand close to the machine and turn it on. It hums as the interior unit spins. The centrifugal force it creates will force denser substances to the base of the collection tube, separating the plasma proteins from the red blood cells. At least that's what's supposed to happen, but instead something sparks, and a puff of smoke rises from the back of the unit. I quickly turn off the machine while a string of curses falls out of my mouth, rivaling Setia's earlier ones.

She covers her smile. "What now?"

"Want me to send it to another lab?"

Setia tenses. "No. I—I'll think of something else."

I press my hand to her shoulder. "Hold on," I say. "I think I've got something that might work." I grab a screwdriver from one of the drawers and walk out to the line of beds against the wall. After disconnecting one of the hand cranks from the side of a bed, I return to the lab and remove the front panel of the centrifuge. I disconnect the drive motor and adjust the rotating arm, then rig the hand crank to the device. "This should do it."

Setia steps to the machine and turns the manual handle. The unit rotates freely, successfully spinning the blood sample. "You're something else, Theron. This is perfect." She looks up at me, eyes wide. "How'd you think to do that?"

"I used to manipulate the wiring around the automatic doors in the Batch tower as a kid." I grin. "Nine and I would sneak through the halls at night when we were supposed to be sleeping. I got really good at using whatever I could find to get those doors open."

Her face freezes for a moment. "Nine?"

My face falls. Did I say her name?

Setia must sense my discomfort, because she squeezes my arm and changes the subject. "Well, that explains why you went for Iden's drill yesterday."

"I guess." The transmitter at my waist buzzes. It's a message from Eridian; she wants to see me right away. My shoulders slump. I do *not* want to talk about Nine anymore today. And I'm definitely not in the mood for a scolding. I wonder if Bron reported my attitude during the curfew sirens the other night. "I have to run," I say.

Setia lifts a hand in farewell. "Thank you, Theron. For helping me."

"Any time." After closing the lab door, I tell Iden what's going on and head back outside. The Core building is next door, so I don't have far to walk.

The centralized location of our trauma station is ideal, easily accessed by citizens during emergencies. The main Healer building is in the southern part of the province near the Batch tower and is used for more serious ailments and surgeries that require specialized care for patients. There are also several wellness stations spread throughout the province for minor illnesses and checkups. But ours is the only trauma station in all of Freedom, and it rises several stories, towering over several smaller structures nearby.

But it's nothing compared to the Core building.

Square reflective panels cover each of the four walls of the building, rising dozens of stories high. The panels slope inward toward the top and end in a sharp point, as though sealing off any sort of entry except the one you're forced to take on the ground level. The front entry is framed by giant triangular molded glass pieces in gold, red, and black. The whole effect makes it seem as if the entrance is a blazing fire that will consume you the moment you've passed the threshold.

I walk through the front doors with my breath held, a throbbing in my limp. No matter how many times I come through here, it still makes me feel as if I'm walking past the giant teeth of a shark.

I stride to the center of the building's lobby and give my name to the man stationed at the front desk.

"Go on in." He points over his shoulder to Eri's office, and I enter on my own. Something I've done too many times to count.

Once inside, I head straight for the chair in front of her desk but freeze before sitting. Eri isn't alone. A large man in a black jumpsuit stands beside her, his arms folded across his chest. A red star inside a white circle—the symbol of our Freedom province—is stitched onto his shoulder. His medium-length blond hair is pulled into a short ponytail at the base of his neck, and a scar runs through his left eyebrow, so no hair grows in that sharp line above his eye. He's a Seeker, but one I've never seen before.

He looks me up and down and frowns. I've disappointed him, but I've no idea why.

Eri drums her fingers on her glossy black desk. "You can go, Odell."

He waits a moment before nodding and walking out of the room, not bothering to drop the bitter expression on his face as he passes me.

I finally take my seat, and Eri follows suit, relaxing into the chair behind her desk.

"Everything going okay for you, Theron?"

She knows things aren't okay. She knows things haven't been anywhere near the vicinity of okay since Nine left. But I don't think that's what she means.

"Just fine." I grip the armrests and wait for her rebuke. Wait for her to tell me a Seeker's job is hard enough without me mouthing off to those who should be shown respect and obedience and that for the safety of our citizens, I should avoid putting others at risk and consider our precious freedoms when I decide to blah blah blah.

But she doesn't say anything.

So I don't say anything either.

26

She finally stands and walks around to the front of her desk. "I have a proposal for you."

I shift in my seat. I've no idea what she's going to say.

"We've had a special Healer position open up, and I think you're the perfect fit for it." She pauses. "Actually, the head of this special Healer division thinks you're the perfect fit, and after a long conversation, he's convinced me."

"I'm content at the trauma station." Maybe this is why she asked if things are going okay. She's trying to gauge if I'm satisfied with my Trade. "In fact, I much prefer it over working in the Healer building or wellness stations." *Please don't ask me to work in the Batch tower.* Administering hormone suppressants to Batchers is not only the most boring work in the province, but that place reminds me too much of Nine. I'd go crazy.

Eri's transmitter goes off, and after glancing at the message on her screen, she angrily shuts it off and tosses it not-so-gently onto her desk. Impatient, she turns back to me. "You'd work on the Maker level."

Wait . . . what?

"It's two stories down, here in the Core building. The commute would be the same for you, and—"

"But I'm not trained to be a Maker." I scrunch my eyebrows together. "I'm a Healer."

She leans back on her desk. "And this is a Healer position. You'll just be doing your duties alongside the Makers."

"What sort of duties?"

Eri wavers for a second, thinking carefully about her answer. Gauging, despite her impatience, how she should phrase it. She really wants me to accept this position.

I wonder why.

She hasn't answered my question, so I ask again. "What

duties? Do the Makers hurt themselves Making the Batches?" I force a chuckle, trying to lighten the conversation, but stop when I realize she's frowning.

She paces in front of me. "I can't divulge any details about what specific skill sets will be required for this special Trade. It's not secretive so much as . . . high priority. Need to know." The clicking of her heels is unnerving, and I wish she'd stand still.

"Why me?" Given my recent behavior and indifferent attitude toward Seeker authority, I should be last on the list for something "high priority." Maybe this secretive assignment is just another way to control me.

"Because you've shown exceptional aptitude in your Healer performance," she says, matter-of-fact.

How would the Prime Maker know anything about how well I perform in the trauma station? Did Gray or Setia say something to her?

"And," she continues, "because I think you can be trusted to keep the confidential information you learn, well, confidential."

Like how I don't tell anyone about Eri's desperate attempt to find Nine. That the entire reason our province has been turned inside out is because of one lost girl.

"And this Trade," I say, "I take it I can't tell anyone about it."

"You don't have many friends, Theron. Surely keeping this to yourself won't be too difficult."

I don't take offense. In fact, I pride myself in being solitary. If I don't let myself become attached to anyone, I can't get hurt. I've learned that lesson already.

"No," I say. "It won't be difficult."

"There are other Healers," she says. "It's not like you'll be the only one. They've all taken vows of secrecy, and if you choose to do this, you can tell no one about what happens. About what you do and . . . see."

"I understand." I can't deny the thought of working at something so hush-hush is intriguing.

"No, Theron." Eridian leans forward. "I don't think you do. What the Makers do is vital to the liberty of our society; it's vital to our equality." She lowers her voice to a whisper. "You have to choose this. It has to be *your* choice. But if you do, you must understand if you talk to anyone about what happens on Sublevel Two, you will be considered a free-breaker and will receive the harshest punishment."

There have always been rumors of free-breakers being taken away by Seekers to some hidden prison and never coming back. But it isn't until recent months that I've actually seen it happen. Traitors and criminals, torn from their homes and escorted away—or killed. It probably doesn't matter which because we never see them again either way.

The trauma station is one of the only places I feel like I belong. That gives me peace. I don't want to risk losing that. I take a deep breath. "How can I choose something I don't know?"

Eri taps her foot one-two-three times before continuing to pace. "It's a valid question. I can tell you it will be more exciting than the trauma station. Life-altering. Eye-opening. Mind-blowing." She finally stops in front of me and holds my gaze. "But the best answer I have is: How could you not choose it?"

She's got me hooked, and she knows it. No other Trade has to undergo such extreme measures for secrecy. I remember that long-ago morning when Nine told me what she wanted to do for her Trade. I realized then that I'd never met any Makers before. Whatever high-priority stuff they have going on here must be intense—as in "able to distract and consume all my wandering thoughts" kind of intense.

Another way to forget Nine.

"Can I think about it?"

Eri's mouth turns down. "No."

A sour feeling spreads through my middle—part curiosity, part terror. I wrap my arms across my stomach as though I can hide the sensation. I pretend I know exactly what to choose, but the truth is I'm not sure. I'm not sure of anything anymore.

And it's all Nine's fault.

"I'll do it," I say, hoping I won't regret it.

Her arms clutch her chest in a moment of surprise. "Really?" she breathes.

"Yes," I say, nodding hard. I don't give myself a chance to reconsider.

"Good. You start today."

*   *   *

The blond Seeker is waiting for us as we exit Eri's office.

"Odell, please escort Theron downstairs." She turns to me. "I'll notify the trauma station of your immediate reassignment. Do you have any questions?"

I give Odell a sidelong glance, chancing he's in on this secrecy thing and it's okay for him to hear my words. "I have a feeling most of my questions will be answered by the end of the day."

"Yes," she says with a sigh. "Or you'll have several more. Good luck, Theron." She motions for Odell to take me toward the elevators, then rushes back into her office.

I walk into the elevator behind Odell. He pulls out a set of keys, flipping through several before settling on one and slipping it into a keyhole under the panel of floor numbers. He presses his palm against a small monitor and turns the key at the same time. A green light flashes beneath his hand, and he pulls away and presses a button marked "SL2." Sublevel Two, I assume. Unlike the other floors—Seeker headquarters on L3, Techies on L7—SL2 doesn't have any description.

After we descend and exit the elevator, I notice the same keyhole and scanning pad outside the elevator doors. Whatever goes on down here, they don't want just anyone waltzing in to find out.

Odell leads me past a series of doors embedded in the wall, then to the right through an unmarked door. He pulls out a card and swipes it through a slot near the door handle. A clicking sound pops the door open, and Odell presses on my shoulder, forcing me into the room.

"Wait here." He points to a plastic chair with chrome legs.

"What?" I ask, turning to face him while I walk backwards toward the lone chair. "No good-bye kiss?"

The door slams. Nice.

The room is small and white. A tiny window is installed in the door at eye level, but it's been blacked out with paint or fabric on the other side. The room bears no distinguishing marks, just the natural signs of age. Scuffed cement floors, dingy gray walls, a fluorescent light that buzzes every three seconds. I wonder what this room is or was used for. If it's a permanent reception room, these Makers need to learn a lesson in hospitality.

I wonder again about why Makers would need Healers on hand. Nine wanted to be a Maker. If she'd never left Freedom, if she'd gone through with her Remake, would she be down here with me? We could be living together in my apartment, like we always planned. Walking to work through Freedom Central. Stopping at the hot food vendors along the way. Holding hands and . . .

I jump from the chair and shove it to the corner. I came here because I thought it would help me forget Nine, but so far the opposite is true. I lift my fisted hands, station them in front of my face for protection. Then I go through several kick routines to keep my mind off that girl.

Front kick, front kick, side kick, back-side kick. There's just enough room for me to do a four-kick combination before I have to turn around and head the other way. Roundhouse kick, sliding side kick, double punch. Back and forth I move, every movement precise and controlled. Every kick fast and powerful.

I hear the faint sound of someone whistling a tune I don't know. Dropping my hands, I try to level my breathing, my chest heaving. The whistling stops outside my door. I lean against the wall, waiting for whoever's so cheerful to open it.

I hear a card slide into the slot and the door clicks open. Someone with a cane hobbles into the room, a wide grin across his face.

"Theron!" He brings the cane to his chest in a gesture that is partly a salute, partly a sign of humility. "My hero."

I step forward. "Catcher?"

CHAPTER FOUR

Is this what you do?" I ask, stunned to see him. "For your Trade, I mean. You're a Healer on the Maker level?" After Eri's big speech about secrecy, I understand now why Catcher didn't have a Trade listed in his file.

"Guilty," he says, his smile still wide. How can he be so happy all the time?

It suddenly comes together. Eridian said I was recommended based on my job performance. It was Catcher, because of what happened yesterday in the trauma station.

"You're the Healer in charge down here?"

"Guilty again." He moves to the chair in the corner and sits down, using the cane to help him get there.

I motion to his leg. "How is it feeling?"

"Fine." He pulls up his pant leg to let me see. A large bruise surrounds the area, but the wound itself is clean and healing nicely. "Just a little sore."

"Guess I forced it too hard," I say. "I'll do better next time."

Catcher's smile twists, and he watches me a moment, thinking about something. "You've never done anything like this before, have you?" He points to his knee.

I shake my head and step back.

He lowers his pant leg. "That's exactly why I chose you. I need someone who not only thinks fast under pressure, but performs fast as well."

"What exactly will I be doing down here?"

Catcher stands and hobbles to the door, motioning for me to follow. "I thought you'd never ask."

Down the hall, we walk through a set of double doors and enter a large white reception area. Several more doors branch off from this brightly lit room. A woman sits at a desk behind a computer, the glow of the screen turning her face an eerie blue shade. She doesn't look up as we stop in front of her.

Catcher points to the doors as he spins in a circle. "From this room, you can access every sector in the Maker division. Later today, I'll fill you in on what you'll do in particular as a Healer. But first . . . first you need to know where we come from."

There's a shift in his words, in the way he holds himself. He's nervous about what he's going to show me, as though unsure how I'll take it or if he can trust me. Eridian said Catcher convinced her to let me down here. So who convinced Catcher?

He leads me through a door on the far side of the room, left of the woman's desk.

"How long have you worked here?" I ask as we walk through endless hallways.

"A long time. Longer than most. I've been working here since my own Trade training."

I remember his age from his file. "You've been healing people here for over twenty years?"

"Yes. Healing *people*." He says it slowly, like he's not sure it's the right word.

He must have chosen his own Trade. Same as the rest of us. Same as me. But despite his endlessly cheerful nature, something tells me he doesn't enjoy his work.

Catcher leads us through another door with the sign FERTILIZATION LAB out front. There's one other person in the large room, a man with his hair styled forward so it covers the right half of his face. Like the woman at the desk earlier, he ignores us as we walk in. He opens some kind of package and sorts through the contents. Along one wall is a series of glass doors with steel borders. I can barely see what's on the other side, but the condensation on the glass indicates it's some kind of cold storage.

Stationed throughout the center of the room, almost like columns rising to the ceiling, are freestanding units also with glass doors. But I can see inside these. Tiny glass tubes sit in rows and rows on the shelves.

"What's in the tubes?" I ask.

"Ingredients for madness." Catcher ignores the columns and cold units and leads me through a plastic barrier, using his cane to push aside a heavy curtain that seals off this room from a smaller one in back. The smaller room is much colder but still comfortable. Metal cylinders sit along one wall, each one about three feet wide, waist high. Labels on the side read EMBRYOS, whatever those are.

Catcher pulls a microscope from a high shelf and sets it on a lab table. "I'm not going to tell you how the Makers do it. I'm not going to tell you what they use to do it." He takes a deep breath. "All I'm going to tell you is Makers Make embryos." The way he says it tells me it's not that he doesn't know; he's just choosing not to tell me. Not yet, at least.

"And what's an embryo?"

"A beginning. A seed. Life. Existence."

I raise my eyebrows. I'm not in the mood for riddles.

"It's us, Theron. Who we are at the start of life. A human in its earliest stage of development." He opens one of the metal cylinders, and a gust of ice-cold air escapes. He pulls out a clear plastic, circular dish and slips it under the microscope. After adjusting the lens for a minute, he steps back and asks, "Want to see?"

I hesitantly step to the microscope and press my face against the eyepiece. The sample tissue is circular, but besides that there are no distinguishing marks. "This is a human?"

He nods. "Just a few days into development."

"And this is what the Makers do? Make these . . . embryos?"

"Yes. They Make them and then cryogenically freeze them until they're ready for the embryos to mature."

Catcher removes the sample from the microscope and returns it to the metal cylinder, sealing the top when he's done.

"At that point, they implant the embryos into"—he pauses, as though trying to find the right word—"incubators. The embryos remain in these incubators for nine months—the process is called pregnancy—after which their development reaches maturity and they're removed. The Makers remove them, and Healers assist in that process."

I remember the joke I made with Eri, that the Makers hurt themselves while Making people. I'm starting to wonder if it's true. Why else would they need assistance unless the process was somehow physically demanding?

Catcher continues. "At that stage the embryos are called

infants, or babies, and are handed over to the Fosterers. I think you know the rest of that story."

Yes. They are destined for the Batch tower where they will grow with the others in their Batch, taught and cared for by Fosterers and Teachers and every other Trade that rotates daily for their care. They will be equal. Free.

"What's the deal with the incubators?" I ask. "How complex a machine is it, that the Makers need our help to remove the embryo—I mean, infant?" I've never actually seen an infant before, but I know they are just tiny versions of children. From what I remember as a child, they can't be hard to handle. Not for any capable adult, at least. "And what does any of this have to do with Healing? I'm trained to be a Healer, not a Maker's assistant."

"I'll show you." He glances at a clock on the wall. "Let's go see those incubators."

Once we're back in the main white reception room, Catcher leads me down another hallway. After walking through a maze of passages, my leg starts to throb. Catcher's must be hurting like crazy.

We finally enter a dark room with several chairs on tiered levels. It reminds me of the cinema, except instead of a screen in front, there is a large glass window that opens onto another room on the other side. We take a seat in front and sit in silence.

The room beyond the glass reminds me of those in the Healer building. White, clean, stark. It's fairly large, with metal tables, instruments, and a series of machines that would normally connect to a patient to determine heart rate, brain activity, and blood sugar levels.

"Is this a surgical room?"

Catcher nods. "We're here to observe the implantation of an embryo into its incubator."

Just as he says it, a set of double doors open into the surgical room, and three people, whom I assume are Makers, roll in a metal table with someone—a female—lying on top. She's unconscious, probably from anesthesia, and I watch in confusion as they hook her up to the machines. I open my mouth to ask something, but shut it because I don't know what to say.

Catcher folds his arms across his chest and answers the question I didn't know how to ask. "Theron, meet the incubator. Or as we more commonly refer to her, the surrogate."

I whisper under my breath. "They're implanting the embryo inside of her?"

"Yes."

This is incredible. I had pictured a machine of some kind—not this. "Where do they implant it?"

"In a cavity within her abdomen." He watches me for a moment. "It's a simple procedure, and the patient doesn't have to be unconscious for it, but it's easier if . . ." He doesn't finish.

I sit up in my chair. "She will carry it for nine months? Within her body?"

"Yes."

"Is she the only surrogate? Or are there others?" What am I asking? Of course there are others. Twenty Batch members are Made every month. That would mean—I mentally make the calculations—hundreds of surrogates.

Catcher nods. "Yes, there are many others."

We watch as the Makers wash up and dress in surgical clothing. I stand and walk to the window, engrossed by the whole idea of us starting life *inside* another person.

"And she will live down here on the Maker level, for nine months?" I say. "Along with the other surrogates?"

He frowns. "They usually live down here for years. After

gestation—the period of time it takes for one embryo to mature—the surrogates can carry another one, then another, again and again. Of course, not all embryos thrive, and if a surrogate goes too long without a successful implantation, she is . . . replaced."

I touch my stomach and wonder how it would feel to have something growing inside you. It sounds so—alien. Considering how little room there is, the infants must come out very small.

I feel Catcher's eyes on my hand and stomach. "All of the surrogates are female," he says. "They are the only ones who can carry the fetus. Once established, that's what we call the embryo—a fetus."

"Why only females?"

He clears his throat. "It's just part of their anatomy."

I can tell he doesn't want to explain further, and I don't push him. I've got enough to think about for now anyway.

The Makers remove a fabric sheet that had been covering the female, leaving her body exposed on the surgical table. As they proceed with the implanting, Catcher describes each step, telling me how they actually insert a few embryos for maximum probability of survival and not just one. And how the embryos are embedded into the side of a cavity called a uterus. The Healers watch a screen as the Makers operate, to make sure placement is ideal. I watch in silence, partly in shock, partly in awe.

When they're done with the procedure, the woman is taken from the room.

"In a couple of weeks, they will examine her to see if the embryos are thriving," he says. "At that point, they are handed over to us."

I turn around and intake a sharp breath, wanting to slam my palm against my forehead. "That's what the Healers are for," I say, finally understanding. "We take care of the surrogates, don't we? They are our patients."

Catcher rises to stand by me. "Yes, we monitor their health, and the health of the growing fetus."

"And we help with the removal of the fetus," I add, remembering what he told me.

"Yes, we help with the birthing process."

Birthing process?

"I'm sure you need time to let all of this sink in." Glancing into the empty surgical room, he adds, "But there's something I need your help with right away. And in order to do that, you'll have to meet the surrogates."

CHAPTER FIVE

I silently follow Catcher to the central white room then through another labyrinth of halls. He points out a path to the Healing facility where he says we'll do most of our examinations of the surrogates, but we don't stop.

"I'm taking you to the surrogate housing first," he says. "To see one female in particular. The one I need your help with."

I nod. "These surrogates—are they female Makers? Is that part of the duty of the Makers?"

He frowns. "No, they aren't Makers."

"I've never heard of surrogates until today. How does anyone know that Trade is an option?"

"Because it's not an option."

"I don't understand. Where do the surrogates come from?"

Catcher turns away and quickens his awkward pace. "I don't know."

"Aren't they from Freedom One?"

41

He shakes his head.

"From another province?"

"I don't think so."

"Then where?"

He stops and turns to me. Looks back and forth between my eyes. He drops his head and rubs his thumb and middle finger across his own eyes, as though drying tears not there. He finally glances up with a worn look on his face. "Do you ever wish the Remakers could erase our memories too? Things we've seen. Things we've done. I wish I could get Remade again, you know? Because sometimes what I know is too much of a burden."

I know exactly what he means. I've wished the same thing hundreds of times. I don't like who I have been, who I am, and who I'll most likely become—a shell of a person, stuck in the sands of Freedom. Stuck in a place I hate because it reminds me of Nine. And stuck with the parts that don't remind me of her—I hate that more.

He didn't answer my question, but I don't push him. I follow him down the hall again, this time in silence. This morning, Eri persuaded me to choose this Healer position on the Maker level. Maybe these women are persuaded the same way. It's not like they can be forced into a Trade without any choice at all. Not in Freedom.

I wonder what Nine would think about this surrogate stuff. If she'd feel different about having once wanted to be a Maker after learning what it entails. Or what she would think about carrying an embryo inside of her.

We come to another set of double doors. The female guard nods at Catcher in recognition and opens the left door for us. I didn't realize how quiet it'd been on our walk over, our brief conversation and click of shoes on the floor the only sounds, but

42

as soon as we pass through the door, a loud buzzing fills my ears. Not a heavy thumping like in the nightspots, but the bustling sound of conversation. The voices of dozens of females blending together.

Another guard opens a door for us, this one made of iron bars. Catcher removes a small vinyl bag from a side cabinet and leads me deeper into the room. A wall of bars extends down a hall and into a maze of paths, and behind the bars, in about ten-foot sections, is housed a female.

I pause in front of one section and step closer to get a better look. The woman behind the bars has short curly hair and light brown skin. Dark freckles spread across the bridge of her nose, reminding me of Nine, of course. It doesn't help that she wears a white tank top and gray sweats—Batcher clothes. She's no Batcher, though. She's a mature female. She's been Remade. But Catcher said the surrogates aren't from Freedom, so what would a Remade citizen be doing behind bars?

"Come on," Catcher says. "Keep moving."

I'd hoped these women were in some kind of temporary holding cell, awaiting transport, but the farther we walk, the more I can see behind each set of bars. Beds. Toilets. Washbasins. These women live here. Without any real space or any form of privacy. They are prisoners.

I lean my head down toward Catcher. "This isn't the prison housing, is it?" Prisoners are kept on the third floor alongside Seeker headquarters. I know he told me he was taking me to the surrogates, but I can't fathom why they would be treated this way. Why they would choose to live like this.

He looks up at me, the corners of his eyes pulling down with the weight of a thousand years. That's all the answer I need. This is why he was upset. He knew what we'd be walking into, what we were about to see.

What kind of cracked insanity have I gotten into? I feel nauseated, my stomach tumbling over itself. It's like these women aren't people but animals in cages. How can this be the start of life? It's supposed to be free and equal and full of choice. This is the complete opposite. And now I know this must be why things are so secret here on Sublevel Two. Because if word ever got out about women living in these conditions, Eri would have a rebellion on her hands.

You are a prisoner.

You are not free.

I shake the words of the flyer out of my head.

We turn a corner, and Catcher talks with a Seeker stationed there, telling him we're there to see one of the new surrogates. As they talk, I spin slowly in a circle, taking in the scene while trying not to meet the eyes of any of the females. Like if I don't really see them, I can pretend they don't exist. Because that's exactly what this is—not existing.

They shackle your wrists.

They cut you to your knees.

"You okay?" Catcher whispers, leaning close. The Seeker he'd been speaking to is gone.

My hands feel sweaty, and I wipe them on the side of my pants. "Do all these women have embryos inside of them? Growing?"

"Not yet." He pulls me with him down the hall. "This group arrived last week."

"Arrived?"

Catcher clears his throat. "We finished examining them a few days ago to make sure they're healthy enough to carry a fetus.

They'll undergo the implantation process soon." Catcher gives me a pointed look, as if to say, *I'll explain the rest later.*

I sigh with relief. If they just got here and are awaiting implantation, then this probably *is* a holding area. Not where they'll permanently live. Still, I wonder why such high security measures are needed.

We turn the final corner and come to a dead end. A brick wall extends several feet above me, painted gray. Lightbulbs hang from cords suspended from the ceiling; dust and cobwebs gather in the high corners. Catcher steps toward the bars of the last cell and drops the vinyl bag to the ground.

"Pua?" He reaches one hand between the bars and waves it, as though getting someone's attention. The woman inside the cell stands and walks tentatively to Catcher. She glances at me, then back at Catcher. I stay a few feet behind.

She's ridiculously good looking, black hair extending below her shoulders. Her skin is dark; her eyes are big and brown. And she's young. She can't be much older than I am, but her hair is unusually long for someone who should've been a Batcher not long ago. It makes me wonder again where these surrogates came from. Like the other women here, she wears a white tank and gray sweats.

Catcher points back toward me with his cane. "Pua, this is another Healer, like me. He's . . . a friend."

Pua looks at me again, and I suddenly feel self-conscious. I run my hand through my hair, my fingers lingering on the tattoo on my neck. I should have shaved today. Paid more attention to my clothes. I stand straighter, hoping she doesn't notice the odd way I always put my weight on my left leg. Ugh. What is happening to me?

Catcher grasps one of the iron bars. "I'm sending him in with you."

"What?" Pua and I say at the same time.

Catcher grins. "I'm going to let him examine you while I check on a few other patients." He glances back at me, then adds, "I want to see if he can figure out what's wrong with you."

"There's nothing wrong with me," she says, almost spitting the words.

There's a strange accent in her speech, as if she's from another place entirely.

Catcher's expression warms instantly, and he places a hand on Pua's shoulder through the bars. "Of course there isn't. I'm sorry, that's not what I meant." He sighs. "I'm just testing the new guy out." He raises one side of his mouth in a small smile. "It took over a week for the rest of us to discover your . . . condition. I want to see if Theron can do it in an hour."

"Theron?" Pua's eyes go wide, and this time when she looks at me, she glances me up and down, slowly. Taking me all in. There's something new in her eyes. Hope? Relief? I feel my face redden.

"He's smart, this one," Catcher says. "He might be the key to getting you out of your current situation."

An exchange happens between the two of them, a communication not involving words, just shared thoughts—a secret interaction. Pua finally nods, steps away from the bars, and moves back into her corner.

Catcher pulls out a set of keys, unlocking her cell door. He hands me the vinyl bag.

"It's just basic medical equipment, if you need it."

I lower my head and whisper so Pua can't hear. "What am I supposed to do?"

"Figure out what's . . . Figure out why the Prime Maker has declared her unsuitable to carry an embryo."

"And you already know why?"

He nods. "This girl's good at hiding things, protecting herself. See if you can figure it out. And then . . . see if you can fix it."

I grab the bag and step in the cell, turning to face Catcher as he locks the door. My heart speeds up. "Where will you be if I need help?"

"You're not afraid of her, are you?" Catcher laughs. "You'll be fine. Pretend you're in one of your cage fights. She's just an opponent you need to figure out. Find her weak spot and take advantage of it. Get her to open up, Theron. She needs you more than you realize."

I don't ask Catcher how he knows I cage fight; I just swallow hard and face Pua, who is crouching in the corner like the caged animal she is.

CHAPTER SIX

I glance around the small space. Of the four walls surrounding me, three are made of solid cement. As I glance back through the iron bars, I can't see any other cells from this vantage point. I wonder how many people Pua has interacted with since she's been here. Besides Catcher.

I give her a small wave. "I'm Theron."

Pua stays in her corner, unresponsive. *She already knows your name, you scab.* I sigh and walk to her corner, stepping around the edge of her mattress lying flat on the ground. There are no chairs in the cell, so I settle on the floor in front of her, positioning my right leg carefully to the side.

"Mind if I sit here?"

She looks up at me. "I'm not taking my clothes off."

"E-excuse me?" I swallow hard. Did she just say what I think she said?

"When they examined me the other day, they made me take my clothes off. I'm not doing that again."

It's hard to focus on what she says when I'm so caught up in the way she says it. Some vowels are pinched short and small, others spread wide and linger for a bit. It all sounds like a song, like there's a melody playing every time she forms the harmonious words.

"Did you hear me?" She tilts her head and offers a tiny smile, her nose scrunching a little as she does.

"Yes," I say, high-pitched and nervous. After a quick cough, I try again. "Yes." This time I manage a more reasonable tone. "I heard you. And no, you don't have to take your clothes off."

Her tiny smile grows wider. "If you're the smartest Healer Catcher's got, then we're both in trouble." She laughs, and it surprises me. Somehow, even her laugh has an accent. Here she is, locked away in a cell, suffering from *something* medical that needs to be fixed, and she's laughing. It reminds me of Catcher's ability to find joy in a place where everything is sorrow. It must be contagious, because she's got me laughing too.

"I suppose you won't just tell me what I need to know?" I ask.

She presses her mouth closed and twists her fingers in front of her lips, like she's locking them shut.

"It was worth a try," I say. "Do you feel sick?"

"No."

"Does any part of you hurt?"

She shakes her head.

I take a quick visual inventory of her. Her knees are pulled to her chest, arms folded and resting on top. Her wrists are raw and bruised, as though she's recently been tied up. I reach for her hand and pause, waiting to make sure she'll let me touch her.

She carefully places her hand in mine, and I examine the front and back, doing the same with her other hand. When I press my fingers to her wrist, she grimaces. But I don't think it's from pain—more like a memory of what caused it.

"What happened?" I ask, unsure if these injuries have to do with the problem I'm supposed to decipher.

She doesn't answer for a moment, just stares at her hand in mine. Then she pulls back, folding her arms across her knees again. "I, um, wasn't exactly cooperative when they first brought me here."

I stiffen, wondering again why these women are being treated this way. The thought of Pua fighting back gives me a satisfaction that surprises me. There's a strength about Pua that mocks the bars surrounding her. The corner of my mouth curves a little at the thought.

She leans forward and rests her chin on her arms, her eyes focused on me—and my lips. Why is she staring at my lips? Heat crawls up my neck, and I yank on my collar.

"I have a feeling," I say slowly, her eyes still trained on my mouth, "if I were to examine you using every instrument in that bag, I won't find anything else." I push the bag Catcher gave me to the side.

She grins. "Maybe you're smarter than I thought."

I rub my bum leg, sore from walking through the endless hallways of Sublevel Two all day, and think. If whatever condition she has is preventing her from carrying an embryo, maybe it has to do with what's going on inside where we can't see. Catcher said all surrogates are female . . .

"Wait," I say. "You're not male, are you?"

Her jaw drops as she sits tall, obviously offended.

"Right," I mumble. "I didn't think so."

She covers her mouth, and by the way her eyes crinkle at the sides, I know she's hiding another smile.

If I can't diagnose her the traditional way, I'll have to be creative. Stretching out my right leg, I pull my pant leg up, exposing my ankle and calf along with the horizontal scar just below my knee.

"Look," I say, pointing at the old wound. "I'm broken too."

She reaches forward and runs her fingers along the scar. Quietly, head bowed, she asks, "What happened?"

"I lost my leg in an accident." I think about the day of the shuttle crash, me and Nine in the water. The shark that came and bit my foot off before I told Nine to swim away. "They gave me a new one in my Remake. It looks normal, but feels strange. Different."

Her fingers move down the length of my shin, stopping above my ankle. But her eyes stay trained on my face and words.

I swallow hard. "I can walk and run fine, albeit with a small limp. It's when I forget it's artificial, that it's not really me, that I tend to trip or stumble. That I forget to concentrate on making it function like it should."

Pua pulls her hand away and rests it in her lap. "I'm so sorry." Tiny lines gather above her nose in an expression of sorrow. Concern.

I don't understand why she's so distraught. She doesn't even know me. "It's not a huge deal anymore," I say to make her feel better. "I'm used to it." At least I'm used to living with the physical part of it. The emotional part? I'm not sure I'll ever be used to that.

Pua tucks a strand of hair behind her ear and looks over me again, taking in my legs and arms, chest and shoulders. Her eyes roam to my nose, my ears, my hair. She glances at my eyes and moves back down to my lips. It takes everything within me not to turn around and catch my breath.

"You're very brave, Theron." She says it so softly, I barely understand her words. "I'm sure it hasn't been easy for you. Since . . . since your accident."

"I manage."

Her mouth curves into a warm smile. "Yes, I suppose you do."

Catcher said to find her weak spot. That I should get her to open up. "This ailment of yours . . . How long have you had it?"

"Several years." She looks up at me from beneath dark lashes. "But I manage."

"Yes," I say, grinning. "I suppose you do." Whatever it is, it doesn't seem to be life-threatening. Maybe I'll need medical tools after all. I turn around and reach for the vinyl bag. "I'm stumped, Pua. I'm going to do a diagnostic check, starting with your heart rate and breathing." I pull out the instruments I need then turn back to her. She's chewing on her bottom lip.

"Don't worry," I say, thinking she must be nervous. "It won't hurt. And I won't make you take your clothes off." I smile reassuringly.

Her face falls, and she focuses on my lips again. "What won't hurt?" she asks, tentative.

"Did you not hear me? I said I'm going to do a . . ." I let my words trail away.

Wait a minute.

I press my lips together, thinking through something. She doesn't take her eyes off my mouth.

I raise a hand in front of my face, blocking my mouth from her view. Her eyes shoot up to mine, narrowing.

Slowly, but making sure my words are loud and clear, I say, "You can't hear what I'm saying, can you?"

She doesn't answer, just watches as I lower my hand. Her bottom lip starts to quiver. I don't know if she's upset, embarrassed, or sad.

I drop the medical tools and scoot forward, sliding my hand along the side of her face and cupping her jaw. Angling her head toward mine so she can read the words on my lips, I say, "Is it with every sound, or are there certain pitches you can hear?"

Her voice shakes as she answers. "It's the full range." She wipes at her eyes and gives me a small smile. "I can't hear anything except for a tiny amount in my right ear, and only if you yell right into it."

"That's why you speak so clearly," I muse. "Because most of your life, you've heard just fine."

She nods. "It's gotten worse over time. I don't think it will be long before it's gone altogether." Her frown makes my chest ache.

I lean toward her right ear, out of range of her eyes. "Can you hear me?" I ask in a normal volume. When I pull back, she shakes her head, somehow knowing what I asked. That I asked at all. I wonder how many times people have done the same thing, trying to test her hearing range.

I press my mouth to her ear, like she said, and ask it again.

"Just a vibration," she says, pointing to her ear. "It tickles, but no sound."

I lean back. I don't want to hurt her but I need more information. I yell into her ear. "Can you hear me, Pua?" She had to have heard me that time. I think the women several cells over heard me.

When I pull back this time, she cups both hands over her

mouth and nods, a few tears falling from her eyes. I reach out and dry her face. "Why are you crying?"

"Sorry." She sniffs and sits taller, taking a deep breath. "It's been a long time since I've heard my own name."

I shift back and wait for her to look at me. "It's a beautiful name."

She blushes, making her dark skin turn a beautiful shade of warm.

"And at least I've figured out why you're always looking at my lips." I smirk. "I was starting to think I had some leftover breakfast on my face." I mock-wipe the side of my mouth, which gets her to smile again.

"I've had one too many boys think I was interested in them because of that unavoidable habit." She rolls her eyes. "An unfortunate side effect, I suppose."

"Not so unfortunate," I tease, and this time she turns away to hide her blush.

Pua taps my knee, the one with the scar, and says, "Your voice is kind of irritating."

My mouth falls open. "What?" Is that a roundabout way of telling me she doesn't want me here?

"You sound like a pig, rooting in the ground," she says, matter-of-fact. "I know it's warbled because of my messed up hearing, but I will forever think of you as sounding like a common swine." She pinches her lips together and makes a grunting sound. "Pua." The word falls out of her mouth as though she chewed on something sour. "Can you hear me, Pua?" She mocks me, the sounds coming out in pieces, spluttering into the air, more beast than human.

I place my palm against my forehead. "Glad I made such a good impression." Ugh. I can't win today.

She laughs, and it makes up for any embarrassment on my part. I'd do it again to bring that out in her.

I rise to my knees and motion to her ear. "Do you mind if I take a look?"

She shakes her head.

I dig through the bag and pull out an auditory scope. I see nothing abnormal inside her left ear, but when I look in the right, I notice something unusual behind her ear. Or rather, I don't notice it. After tilting her head to get a closer look, I run my finger along the fold behind her ear a number of times, but I don't feel or see anything. I double check the left side to be sure, then sit back on my heels, surprised and confused.

Pua leans forward. "I don't have a tracker."

She most certainly does not. But she knows what a tracker is, or at least she knows that's what I was looking for.

"Why not?"

She hesitates. "Because I'm not from—"

"Any luck, Theron?" Catcher's question cuts her off.

I turn around to see him unlock the iron door and step into the room, cane in hand. He leans against the wall, and Pua and I rise and move to stand beside him.

"Well," I say, glancing between the two of them. "Either she thinks I have gorgeous lips, or she knows what I'm saying because she reads the words on my mouth. You can tell me which one it is, honestly, because"—I lower my voice to a whisper, though it doesn't make a difference to Pua—"she can't hear what we're saying anyhow." I wink at Pua and wait for Catcher's reaction.

He points a finger at her. "You told him."

With both hands in the air, defensive, she says, "I did not. I swear."

"Unbelievable," Catcher mutters. "You find a way to fix it?"

I shake my head. I've no idea where to start, or even if it can be fixed.

Catcher hunches forward. "The Prime Maker is afraid the condition may transfer to a fetus she carries. Infants have never exhibited traits from their surrogate hosts, but Eridian doesn't want to risk it."

Pua folds her arms and frowns. "I don't want to carry one of your Batchers."

I narrow my eyes, thinking again about where the surrogates are from, and why they're forced into this work. Could that be why the women are unconscious during the implantation? Because they don't want to carry the embryo?

Catcher rests a hand on Pua's shoulder. "I know you don't. But it's better than dying, isn't it?"

Dying? Are these females killed if they're ill or don't comply?

The light mood I experienced with Pua vanishes, replaced with thoughts of death and imprisonment, things which have no place in Freedom. At least they never used to. Of course, if Catcher's been down here for twenty years, then maybe these things have been a part of Freedom for a long time. I just never knew it.

CHAPTER SEVEN

*A*fter saying farewell to Pua, Catcher escorts me back through the endless white hallways to the main elevator.

"This place seems bigger than the space occupied by the Core building." With how far we've traveled down here, I'd expect this Maker level to span several buildings up top.

"That's because it *is* bigger. A whole lot bigger."

I don't miss his glance to the opposite side of the elevator— the side we didn't walk today. Another white hallway disappears around a far corner. Perhaps that's where they keep the surrogates after they've been implanted with an embryo.

Catcher takes a deep breath. "I'd like you to work with Pua for the next several days. See if you can find a solution to the hearing problem."

I nod. "I'll do my best, but I've never seen anything like her condition before."

"I know." He runs a hand over his bald head. "Batchers

born deaf are usually . . ." His words fall away. Catcher is lost in thought. Or a memory. "We've never had the chance to study or fix the condition before."

"Deaf?" That must be the name of her condition.

"Never mind." He forces a smile. "I'm hoping you can do what I haven't been able to."

"Otherwise . . . she'll be killed?"

He sighs. "We have a bit of time. The third-floor prison housing is filled; Pua is at the end of a very long list."

"Whatever she did to deserve this, it doesn't mean—"

"She's done nothing wrong." He shakes his head. "Nothing except be born at the wrong place at the wrong time." Then under his breath, he adds, "But in the right way."

I'm confused. He's speaking in riddles.

Catcher ignores me and places a card and key in my hand. "I've already programmed your access to the sublevel so you can come down here at will. I want you to work with Pua, but if anyone asks questions, tell them you've been assigned to conduct ready exams on the surrogates. That should keep any Seekers off your case."

"I take it Eridian would not approve of my working with Pua?"

Catcher bites his lip. "She's under the impression you're here to help with high-risk deliveries. But she's aware I'm starting you off with exams. You shouldn't have any trouble."

"Why doesn't Pua have a tracker?"

He sighs. "Those holding cells are temporary. Where the surrogates go after that there's no need for trackers. Leave it at that."

I nod, understanding there's only so much I can take in right now anyway. He shows me how to use the hand scanner and keypad to access the elevator. The key will get me into the surrogate cells, and the card will open any automated doors along the way, including the elevator.

As we ride up, Catcher whispers, "Eri give you the whole 'keep silent' speech?"

"Sure did." And now I understand why. I wonder if anyone's tried to reveal what happens down here, and if so, whatever became of them.

"Be careful," he says. "I don't drag people into this world unless I have to. Unless it's a matter of losing a life, or saving one."

"I won't say a thing." Eridian knows I can keep a secret.

He nods, satisfied he can trust me. Again, I wonder why. He doesn't know me beyond what I did to save his life.

Once we exit the Core building, I glance at the surrounding towers. Is the Maker level below each of these structures? I look at the trauma station and wonder what's beneath it. The surrogate cells? Embryo storage? The opposite hall Catcher didn't show me? We turned so many corners down there. With no windows for reference, I couldn't keep my sense of direction.

Catcher tugs on my arm and leans close. "I'm off work for the next few days, so you'll have to come on your own. You'll be okay?"

"I think so. How'd you get three days off in a row?" Most people work every day on ten-hour shifts. Days off accumulate over time, depending on the Trade, but I've never heard of anyone taking two days off, let alone three.

"The Prime Maker and I have an understanding. Twenty years down there and seeing the things I've seen—I've earned a little time off now and then." He drums his fingers on the side of his pant leg.

"What will you do for three whole days?" I ask.

He cracks a smile. "Sit and do nothing. Sleep. Absorb myself into the floor of my apartment. It all sounds pretty nice to me."

Sitting around doing nothing is exactly what I don't need or want. Because that leaves too much time for thinking about Nine.

Gray, Setia, and Iden step out of the trauma station half a block away. They see me and wave me over. I glance at my transmitter. The shift's over and they're headed to the nightspots. I could use a drink or two myself.

I turn to Catcher. "Want to come for drinks and dancing before your thrilling days off?" I ask.

He laughs, tapping his cane on the ground. "Not sure I'm up for dancing. And I never drink."

My jaw drops. "Never?" Who doesn't drink?

His smile grows wide. "Have a good night, Theron." He winks and hobbles off to the residential district. I've known the guy little more than a day and already I'm intrigued by his strange ways. How can he be unusually happy when things, especially in his own life, are dire? How can he keep up that kind of hope in the face of despair? How does he get through a day without relying on buzz drinks and cage fighting?

I wish I knew, because this numbing routine I've developed is starting to wear me down. And it doesn't work as well as it used to. As much as Catcher intrigues me, as different as he is from most people I know, I can't help but think he's a whole lot like me.

* * *

"What's up with you tonight, Theron?" Iden elbows me in the arm. Today her peach hair is pulled into a tight bun, spikes of silver feathers sticking out of it. Her dress matches with silver feathers covering a sheer fabric. The strobe lights reflect off the metallic gleam, making her look like some kind of electric bird, emphasized by the metal studs in her cheek.

"Nothing," I say, lifting one side of my mouth. "It's just hard to see past the glare of your dress. My left eye is starting to twitch. I think I'm going blind."

"There he is." Iden rolls her eyes and takes a sip of her drink. "That's the first dig you've made at me tonight. I was wondering if you'd been replaced by an emotionless robot Theron."

I've been distracted, that's all. By the surrogates. Pua. All the things I'm not supposed to talk about. About where we all come from. It looks like I've found another reason to drink tonight. Another reason to forget.

"Iden, for someone with such a dismal personality, I find your contradictory wild wardrobe choice quite hilarious." I raise an eyebrow.

"We all have our way of hiding, I guess."

"Well said." I take a long drink and grab another glass.

"So what fancy new Healer position are you working at now?" Iden asks. "All we heard is that you wouldn't be working in the trauma station anymore."

I shrug. "Just some private thing for the Prime Maker. Not a big deal."

"You her personal Healer now?" Iden laughs.

It seems like a safe explanation. "Something like that." I press my lips together into a smile, and Iden laughs again.

"You're not working with Setia are you?" she asks.

"No." I glance toward the restrooms where Setia disappeared to a few minutes ago. "I still have no idea what kind of research she does."

"Same." Iden shrugs. "There are too many secrets floating around this province."

Before I have a chance to agree, Iden pulls me to the dance floor near Gray.

There's a cloud of smoke in the air, and it makes me dizzy. I usually welcome the sensation because soon after the dizziness comes euphoria, shortly followed by numbing. All of it erases any stress I'm feeling that day. Once that's gone, the forgetting comes. And all I ever remember is bliss. Pure, unadulterated bliss. But for some reason, the smoke makes my stomach churn, and the dizziness isn't as nice as I remember. I leave Iden with Gray and head back to the bar.

When I get there, I see a couple of Seekers harassing Setia at the end of the bar. They're yelling at her, and Setia yells back, but I can't hear what they're saying because the music is so loud. I move closer to find out what's going on, and just as I get there, one of the Seekers yanks Setia's orange hair back, exposing her pale neck, and presses the barrel of a gun to the side of her head. It's no tracker gun.

"Whoa." I run up to the Seeker and get a look at him. It's Bron. "What's going on?"

Bron glares at me. "Nothing to do with you. I suggest you back away."

I raise both hands in surrender. "Just trying to help."

"This one's wanted for questioning. And she's going to come quietly, willingly." Bron's eyes widen at Setia, as though making sure she hears his heavy-handed suggestion. "She doesn't need your help."

I lean forward, and in sort of a whisper-yell, say, "You okay, Setia?"

"Does it look like I'm okay?" Her words are a whimper, desperate in her piercing-induced lisp.

Bron flips her around, shoves her face into the table at the bar, and pulls her arms behind her. "She's a free-breaker, Theron. Free-breakers aren't allowed the privilege of living in Freedom. You know that."

"You don't have to be such a scab about it, Bron." I angle Setia's face toward me, wiping away a line of blood dripping from her nose. I think it might be broken. What did she do? "She'll go with you," I say. "Eridian will talk to her, and then you'll let her go when everything is cleared up." It's not a question, but there's a part of me that hopes it's all they'll do to her. "That doesn't give you the right to hurt her in the meantime."

"Hurt her? Do you think your peace and kindness rules apply to people like her?"

I think of the surrogates held beneath the Core building. I have a feeling those rules don't apply to a lot of people anymore.

I rest a hand against the side of Setia's face. "You'll be okay," I say, reassuring her.

But the look she gives me is one of fear, of resignation. She's not going to be okay, and we both know it. Two Seekers aim their guns at me to make sure I don't do anything cracked, and Bron drags Setia out of the nightspot. No one else seems to notice her being hauled away; either that or they choose to ignore it. When did subjugation become commonplace?

I've no idea what she did or didn't do. I wonder if it has something to do with her secret project or the blood sample from this morning. All I know is things are seriously cracked in this province, and I can't tell anyone about it. Probably wouldn't matter if I could, though. No one would believe me.

Suddenly the lights flip on, the music stops, and the curfew sirens begin to sound. The clouded smoke looks strange in the bright light. Choppy and cold and a lot less mesmerizing than it'd been a minute before. Funny how some things don't change—they are what they've always been—but it takes seeing it in a new light to make you realize it's completely different than you once thought.

CHAPTER EIGHT

"Hold your arms out to your sides," I say, showing Pua what to do with my own. "Good."

Pua does as I ask, her dark arms outstretched.

"Now walk to the other end of the room in a straight line, turn around, and come back."

I watch her bare feet pad across the cold floor of the exam room. They don't give the females anything for their feet, and for a moment I wonder if Pua gets cold in her cell.

"Okay, now do it again," I say. "But this time, hands behind your head."

She walks again without difficulty, then sits on the exam table with her feet dangling over the edge.

"Do you feel dizzy at all?"

She shakes her head. "I never experience any balance problems."

I rub the back of my neck and settle onto a stool. While

shifting my feet to spin slowly in a circle, I make sure she still sees my lips when I say, "Let's talk history. First off, have you ever met or come in contact with anyone else with your hearing condition?" Maybe it's contagious.

"Well, no one else in my immediate or extended family is deaf, if that's what you mean. So I don't think it's genetic."

I freeze midspin. There are too many things in her answer that make me pause. What does she mean by *genetic*? Like maybe her Makers Made her this way? Did they do it on purpose when manipulating her genes? And there's that word again—*deaf*—the same one Catcher used. It must describe someone who can't hear; yet how is there a word for something that hasn't happened before? But that's not what I want to talk about.

"What's a family?" I ask, watching her reaction. That's the word Nine used to describe me. The same word written on the rebel propaganda. What do Nine, the Rise, and Pua have in common that they all use that word?

Pua opens her mouth then closes it. I can tell she is measuring her response carefully. "They are the people I care about most," she finally says. "People I would do anything for."

I knew it was something important. Pua's eyes tear up, and her lip begins to tremble. I stand from the stool and slide onto the exam table next to her. Wrap my arm around her. It feels silly, comforting someone sentenced to die. Like I shouldn't bother trying, yet at the same time, like I should never stop.

"I miss them," she continues. "I was separated from them, and they'll never know I died here, trapped beneath the earth. They won't know to mourn my passing."

"You're not going to die." The words come easy, but as soon as they fall out, they land on my chest like a heavy stone, weighing me down. Her life is in my hands, and I'm not sure how to keep it from being ripped away. "I'm going to find a way to fix you."

"I'm not broken." Her accent is strongest when she's upset, defensive.

I drop my arm and watch her, trying to understand.

"I'm fine with how I am," she says, wiping her face. "I don't need to be fixed."

"I'm sorry. I didn't mean to offend you."

Pua shakes her head. "You did nothing wrong, Theron. It's this place. This province. It's poisoned."

I think I know what she means. Some kind of disease has found its way here, seeping into the cracks, absorbing into every surface. I don't know what it is, or how to stop it.

"Well, until we find a cure for Freedom," I say, "we can find a cure for you in the meantime. Then, when this place is fixed, you'll be here to see it."

She gives me a small smile, but I can tell she doesn't believe it. Doesn't think she'll live long enough for this province to return to how it was. Or become something better, perhaps.

Maybe I'll have to prove her wrong.

Watching my face, Pua slides her hand across my shoulder to the back of my neck and traces her fingers along my tattoo. "Tell me about Nine." She says it as though she knows it's a person and not just a number. An important person.

"It's a girl," I say, not knowing why I'm opening up to her. Pua's eyes are big and kind, her smile wide and warm. I thought I was the one comforting her, yet it's the opposite. How does she do that?

"Nine," I say, thinking about her willingly for once. "She was my best friend. I . . . I loved her." It's the truth. The terrible, unfortunate truth.

Pua's hand stills on my neck. Keeping me in place. Anchoring me to this moment. "She was your family," she says, tilting her head.

"She was my family," I repeat. My voice shakes, but I don't care. "But she left me. She left me here. Alone."

"Not alone," Pua whispers. Her other hand rests on my chest. I wonder if she can feel my heart racing beneath her touch. "A part of her is still with you."

I want to break. I'm about to fall into a million pieces, but Pua cups my face and brings it in front of hers. She presses her nose against mine and closes her eyes, breathing in deeply.

But me?

I can't breathe at all; the air is frozen in my lungs. What is she doing? There's nothing sensual or romantic about this moment— not that I'd be against kissing this girl, she's amazing—but that's not what this is. It's as though she knows what it means to love someone and lose them. She knows what it means to be apart from the ones you care about. Be away from . . . family.

Pua finally pulls back, her hands falling into her lap. She smiles up at me, a bit red in the face. "I'm glad to have met you, Theron. And I'm sorry . . . so sorry about Nine."

I like the way she says my name, like she has to dig down to unstick the middle of the word: *Theerin*. I tuck a strand of hair behind her ear, not knowing what to say. She knows me so well, better than anyone else in this cracked province. How is that possible, when we've just met?

"Thank you." I tap my heels against the base of the exam table beneath us. "For being here."

Her mouth twists, confusion in her eyes.

I run a hand down the front of my face. "No. Sorry. I don't mean I'm glad you're here." I make a vague gesture to the exam room. "I just mean I'm glad to know you here. Like, if you're going to be here, I'm glad I could be too, and . . . oh, never mind."

Pua giggles then smooths out her expression. "It's her loss."

She's talking about Nine, but somehow, Nine is the last thing on my mind. Something sparks inside of me. A calling, a frantic need. I don't know what to call it; all I know is I want to help this girl more than anything. I want to save her, not just from being killed, but from her cell, from this level, from a life as a surrogate. I want to free her and reunite her with her family, whoever and wherever they are. I want to help her.

"I'm going to save you, Pua."

She folds her arms as though suddenly cold. "You can't save everyone, Theron."

My mind rushes to my time in the ocean, after the shuttle crash. I couldn't save Nine. Not in the water; not when she came back. I wasn't good enough to be her hero.

"No," I say, "maybe I can't save everyone. But I can save you."

And I will. I won't stop until I do.

The exam room door flies open, and a Seeker—the tall blond one named Odell—steps into the room. "What's going on in here?"

I jump off the table, hoping my face isn't as red as it feels. "I'm just conducting a physical exam." I flash him my medic card and key, proof I have permission to be here.

Odell glances between the two of us. His expression is torn at first, then his brows narrow, the scar above his eye shifting. "This one's already been examined. She's been declared unfit to carry. Why is she here?"

I can't tell him about my assignment from Catcher. "Simple mix-up," I say. "I'll take her back."

Odell clasps both hands behind his back, making room for

us to pass through the door. "I don't want to see her out of her cell again."

"No problem," I say. I grasp Pua's elbow and lead her to the surrogate holding area, hyperaware of Odell following us several feet behind. I don't dare risk conversation with Pua while a Seeker is in earshot, but I glance at her now and then, making sure she's okay. I catch her watching me a few times, a smile teasing at her lips.

Odell continues to follow us to the room filled with the surrogates and through the maze of paths until we reach Pua's cell. I unlock it for her, and she steps inside, turning to face me, her hands grasping a pair of bars between us.

I glance over my shoulder to see Odell waiting down the hall and turn back to Pua. Without making a sound, I mouth to her, "I'll see you tomorrow."

She nods, not taking her eyes off my lips. Does she realize how irresistible she is when she does that? I give her a smile, and she mirrors it, whispering, "Good-bye."

Reluctantly, I turn and walk to Odell, who watches my approach carefully. I know he wants to say something to me, so I stop in front of him. He crosses his arms and looks me up and down, eyes narrowed again.

"Do you ever worry it'll stick that way?" I ask.

"Excuse me?" His furrow deepens.

"That space between your eyes." I point at the skin above his nose. "What if one day it doesn't smooth out again? You'll look permanently angry. Or confused. Or constipated. None of which are a good look for you."

He seems unfazed, continuing to assess me, as though he hasn't quite made his mind up about me. And unlike Bron, he doesn't let my smart mouth get to him. Finally, he drops his arms, mumbles something about following him upstairs, and heads out of the surrogate cells without looking back to make sure I'm following.

After a tension-filled trip up the elevator, Odell has me stand at the back of a line forming behind a metal partition. Those in line are dressed as Techies, Healers, Teachers, and even a few Makers. It's strange seeing them out of Sublevel Two.

"What's going on?" I ask.

Odell gives me a sidelong glance. No forehead scrunching this time.

"Random tracker checks," he says gruffly before heading to the start of the line. He scans the finger of the first person in line on his portable screen, then another Seeker in an identical black jumpsuit tests the tracker. The Seeker attaches the gun to the tracker, pulls the trigger, and waits for a light. Then Odell types in a bunch of things on his screen before releasing the person. And the whole thing repeats with the next person. The two people in front of me have trackers that light up red; they are sent to another line to wait for a replacement. All the other trackers light up green.

I step to Odell and slide my finger along his screen. I watch as the screen goes blank and glowing red dots appear on a map. He zooms in on one area, and the entire screen fills with fifty or so blinking lights. One of them has an additional circle around it.

"Is that me?" I ask.

Odell doesn't answer, just waits.

I feel a gun snap behind my ear, and the Seeker pulls a trigger.

"Green," he says.

The secondary circle on the screen disappears, and Odell grunts. It's his way of dismissing me. As a Batcher, I saw the giant tracking board where everyone in the entire province is mapped out so Seekers can find who they want, whenever they want, but I didn't know they could use portable screens too. I wonder if that's a new thing. Like the armored vehicles. And the early curfew.

I rub the back of my ear as I head home. I've had my tracker replaced before and am grateful I didn't need it tonight. These random tracker checks are ridiculous. How is that supposed to help with anything? Are they afraid people will run away while sporting a faulty tracker?

I think of Nine. That's exactly what she did, isn't it? She must have, otherwise they would have found her. She'd still be with me.

"Up for a match?" Gray jogs up and walks with me along the sidewalk.

"Not tonight," I say. I want to get home and think of what other tests to conduct on Pua. Cage fights and nightspots—they seem so trivial compared to someone's life in my hands.

Gray nods and rubs his chin, his fingers hesitating on the small indentation there. "Heard anything about Setia?"

I shake my head. "She didn't show up for work today?"

"No." Silence for a minute. Then he adds, "She'll probably be back tomorrow."

"Yeah," I say, weary and worried. "I'm sure she will be." I can't help but remember the look in Setia's eyes when Bron took her away. Why haven't they let her go yet?

We pass several empty storefronts, and I can't remember what they were once used for. The windows have been boarded up, paint flaking off the front doors while dust cakes the grooves in the wood. It seems like more of this province becomes neglected and forgotten every day. It's how I feel inside. How I'm afraid Setia will end up too. The world will keep going as if she'd never been here at all.

Gray squeezes my shoulder and lets me continue on without

him. I don't think he was especially close to Setia, but she was a friend. As much as any of them are to me. How does a Healer become a free-breaker? It doesn't make sense. I have no idea what she could have done.

An armored vehicle sits in front of my apartment building. Strange. As I enter the lobby, two Seekers stand guard inside, their guns strapped across their chests. Are they looking for someone? I hurry up the stairs to the fourth floor, skipping stairs as I do. When I reach my hallway, I see Jadyn standing in her doorway, glancing down the corridor at something.

I playfully tug the back of her hair, careful to steer clear of the thick collar she's wearing around her neck. It looks as though it's made of clear glass tubes wrapping around her throat over and over again. I don't want to break it and hurt her, or myself. It looks awfully fragile.

"What's going on?" I ask as she turns toward me.

Her eyes widen when she recognizes me, then her face falls. "They've been here for twenty minutes," she says in her scratchy voice, pointing down the hall.

I follow her finger to my apartment door, where one Seeker stands guard outside. Which means . . .

Those scabs.

CHAPTER NINE

I jog down the hall and push past the Seeker on guard, entering my apartment. I curse. The whole place has been torn apart. Furniture upturned, cabinets emptied. Sheets ripped off my bed. Even the food from my food chiller spills along my kitchen counter.

Four Seekers are still searching my small apartment. One of them is familiar.

"Lose something, Bron?" It takes everything inside me to not start a fight, my apartment as the cage, and my opponent an ugly Seeker who doesn't know his boundaries.

Bron shrugs innocently. "Random apartment check. You're no exception." His words are cruel, but they hold double meaning. He's trying to prove a point—I can't hide behind the Prime Maker's protection forever.

"Did you arrange for Odell to detain me in the Core building, too? So I wouldn't be here to stop you from barging into my place?"

Bron stands straight, pushing out his chest. "You can't stop us from entering."

"You'll never know if you don't give me the chance. Next time, we'll see how long it takes you to get through that door."

"That's enough, boys." Eridian's voice floats in from the hall, and we both turn to her, surprised. "Did you find anything?" Her question is for Bron.

He shakes his head, sneering at me.

"You can leave." I don't know which of us she's talking to. She waves her hand to the door, her eyes never leaving mine.

Bron hits my shoulder with his as he passes, a show of dominance, leading the other Seekers toward my door.

"Don't worry," I call after him. "I'll clean this up. Thanks for offering to help, though." I glance around the apartment. This will take me all night.

"It's a necessary evil," Eridian says, hands on her waist.

"Interesting word choice."

"Watch it, Theron." She kicks at a piece of clothing that had snagged on her high-heeled shoe. After a moment of silence, me absorbing the damage and Eridian looking me over, she finally says, "Everything okay in your new Trade?"

I rub my chin. "Outstanding," I say, enunciating every syllable. "Dream come true. Really. I'm so glad I can add that place to my repertoire of things that royally suck in my life that I can't say anything about. I've become a master at it."

Eri shifts her weight to her other foot, assessing me. "You've obviously nothing to hide." She waves a hand through the air, pointing out my apartment. "I believe that you don't know where Nine is. And I believe that you'll keep silent about your new

Trade." She steps forward and lifts her chin. Though she is several inches shorter than I am, even in her heels, she has a way of making a person feel small. "But I've been known to change what I believe on the tiniest bit of evidence, so don't take my trust for granted. And don't abuse it. It's a privilege not many people earn. Do you understand?"

Oh, I understand. More than you realize.

I nod once, forcing my mouth to keep closed.

As soon as Eri shuts the door behind her, I turn one of my chairs right side up and slump into the seat, thinking of Catcher. I sure wish I could have a few days off.

* * *

"Shh." I hold a finger to my mouth, unable to stop my lips from turning up into a mischievous smile. "Keep close."

Pua grabs my hand and ducks behind me as I look down the hall. No sign of Odell, or any other Seekers for that matter.

"Come on." I pull her with me into the white hallway, hurrying as we go. My shoes are the only ones to echo on the slick ground; Pua's bare feet are silent on the floor.

I review the steps in my head as we go, trying to remember the way to the scanner room. Right turn, right turn, left. Through the double doors, another left, and there. I slide my card through a slot embedded near the door handle, and the door pops open. A series of lights flick on one by one, illuminating the room. A full-sized body scanner takes up most of the space on the right, while an observation room sits to the left behind glass windows. Two computers sit atop a long, narrow table.

"We should hurry," I say, "before anyone notices you're missing."

We easily got past the Makers and Healers in the hallways, but it's the Seekers—one in particular—I worry about. They're the ones who know she isn't a standard surrogate hopeful. She's a walking corpse who has no business being out of her cell.

Pua points to the scanning machine. "Am I supposed to climb in there?"

"Yes." I step to the machine. Though I've operated them several times as part of my Healer training, the last time I was in one was just before the shuttle flight to my Remake. That trip ended in disaster. I shake the memory out of my mind. "You lie down here, along the platform. It will slide automatically into the scanner. Hold still. It will only take a few minutes. Hopefully I'll see something in your ear that I can do something about."

"Sounds simple." She hops onto the platform and stretches her legs out in front of her. "It won't hurt, will it?" She watches my mouth for an answer.

"No." I hesitate, heat crawling up my neck as I realize what I forgot to tell her. "You, um . . . you'll have to take your clothes off first, though."

She laughs. When she sees I don't join her, her face evens out. "You're serious?"

I cringe and nod. "You can wear one of those, though." I point to a light-blue cotton gown on the table. Healers use them during examinations sometimes. It's short and wraps around her body, but it's the best I can offer.

Her mouth falls open. "Smooth, Theron. Real smooth. Let's lure the poor prisoner girl into a secluded, hidden room and make her take her clothes off under the guise of saving her life."

The hint of a smile on her face tells me she isn't completely upset. I sigh, grateful. "You know it's not like that," I say. "You can wait until I'm in the observation room—"

Her hands find a resting spot on her waist.

"—where," I add, "I will definitely not observe you getting undressed. My eyes will be glued to the computer screen. I promise." I hold a hand up as though pledging a formal vow.

She raises one eyebrow and mutters, "Fine." I have no idea what her deal is about modesty, but I admit it's kind of adorable.

"Since you won't be able to hear me or read my lips while you're in the scanner, let me explain what's going to happen." I point to the platform. "Once you're"—I cough—"uh, undressed, lie down on the platform and holler at me that you're ready. I'll start the program, and the platform will slide into the scanner unit. A light will move up and down your body. I'll do a quick full body scan then spend a few extra minutes near your head to get a good look at those ears."

Pua twists her mouth. "How long?"

"The whole thing will take about five minutes. If something doesn't feel right, let me know. I'll be able to hear you fine while you're in there."

She nods.

"The machine tells you when to hold your breath, but since you won't hear it . . . Just breathe normally and don't wiggle around too much."

"No wiggling," she says, eyeing the exit as though having second thoughts. After taking a calming breath, she looks at me and forces a wink. "Got it."

I hope she can't see my blush in the dim room. "Let's get this over with," I say, marching to the observation room. Once in my chair, I hover a finger over the start button and rest my forehead against the tabletop so I don't "accidentally" see Pua without her clothes. I start to count. One. Two. Three. . . . Seven.

. . . Fourteen. How long does it take to change from a tank top and sweats to an examination gown?

I'm this close to taking a peek to see if Pua's okay when her voice echoes through the room. "I'm ready."

I press the start button, sitting tall in my seat when I hear the hum of the shifting platform shut off. I watch the screens as the scanner moves up and down her body. Nothing unusual at first glance. I'll have to access her file at home when I have more time to look at it carefully. Maybe there's something affecting her hearing remotely.

"It's really cold in here," Pua shouts. I should have told her there's a microphone in the unit so she doesn't have to yell, but it's too late now. "You might want to think about a heater seeing as how the no-clothes thing seems to be a favorite among you Healers."

"Noted," I say to myself, my shoulders shaking in silent laughter.

"Or," she says, this time softly, as though to herself, "pump some air in here so a person can breathe."

She must feel claustrophobic. I hurry through the head scans, paying attention to the cochlear region. Her eardrums are intact; everything looks clean. Zooming in, though, I see what I couldn't with a handheld instrument. The auditory nerves are destroyed on both sides. Though sound is received, it's not reaching her brain to comprehend it. It's not something we can fix here, but at the Remake facility they should be able to fix it easily. That is a good thing, I think. Surely the Prime Maker will allow her to go and be fixed. It's got to be worth saving a life. Saving a surrogate, even.

"I'm letting you out," I say into the com connecting to the

scanner, then shake my head. *She can't hear you, Theron.* I press the button to release the platform.

"Aah!" she screams as the platform moves. "Don't look!"

I laugh and rest my head on the desk again, counting silently to myself. It'll probably take longer for her to put her clothes on than it did to take them off. The numbers trail away as I think about what to do next. I'll have to talk to Catcher. Discuss how to get Pua to the Remake facility. If that's not possible, I don't know what we're going to do. We've never done a cochlear replacement in Freedom. I doubt we'll find the right—

"Boo!" Two fingers jab me in the sides.

My head slips off the table, and I half tumble, half slide to the floor in surprise. I grunt as my bum foot folds beneath me, and I turn around in a flash to see Pua covering her mouth, though it does nothing to silence her laughter.

"I'm so sorry," she forces out. "I didn't mean to . . ." She extends a hand to help me up.

"So this is what I get for being so polite and considerate, for closing my eyes and not peeking. I'm attacked." I nudge her arm so she knows I don't mind.

Her hands fall to her side, smile wide on her face. "I said I'm sorry. I didn't think you'd cry out like a child. I won't tell anyone, I promise."

It's hard to feign offense when her accent is so adorable.

"Wow. Nice." I sit back into the chair. "I feel so much better. Really."

She sits beside me, motioning to the screens. "Well," she says, the humor gone from her voice. "What'd you see?"

Pointing to the auditory nerves on the screen, I ask, "Were you ever sick as a child? Like, really sick?"

She thinks for a minute, then nods slowly. "Yes. Around

twelve years old. I got a really bad fever for a couple of weeks. My grandfather was able to get it under control, but I was in bed most of that summer." She turns to face me. "You think that has something to do with it?"

"Maybe." I lean back. "What's a grandfather?"

Pua turns away again, drumming her fingers on the table. "He is part of my family."

I press my mouth closed. What is it with that word that creates a stirring in my stomach? I can't explain the feeling, or what it could mean.

She carefully rests her head on my shoulder. We stay like that a few minutes in silence. Not saying anything. Just sitting. Thinking. Maybe she's not ready to return to her cell, like I'm not ready to let her go—despite our earlier rush.

"Can you fix me?" she finally asks, softly. She doesn't face me, so I'm not sure if she really wants to know the answer.

I lift her chin so she can see my words anyway. "Honestly, I don't know."

She looks away, her jaw tight.

"But," I say, angling her face back toward mine, "at least I know what's wrong. Let me talk to Catcher and . . . we'll see."

"Okay," she mouths.

"Okay."

We hurry through the halls again, returning to the surrogate housing without incident. After I unlock her cell, Pua pulls me into a tight hug.

"Thank you," she whispers.

Her touch—this closeness—reminds me of Nine, and I'm tempted to pull back. But I settle into her embrace, forcing myself still.

I've no idea what she's thanking me for. I haven't saved her yet, but the idea that she has any kind of hope is a strong push for me to do something about it. To help her where she can't help herself. I rest my chin on the top of her head. I know she can't hear me, but I say it anyway.

"You're welcome." It's a promise from me to her that she'll really have a reason to thank me soon.

CHAPTER TEN

I don't care if Catcher still needs a break, this is more important than a day off. I need to find him and tell him what I found out about Pua. The problem is, I'm not exactly sure where he lives, only that he's one street over from me. I think for a minute about the tracker map on Odell's portable screen. I wonder if I could find him that way. But it would mean snagging a screen from a Seeker, maybe asking nicely. Neither of which sounds appealing.

I hurry out of the Core building and enter the trauma station next door. Knocking on the glass window separating patient from Healer, I get Iden's attention. She presses a button that unlocks the door and lets me through.

"Hello, stranger," she says, giving me her signature sullen look, though I know by the glint in her eye she's glad to see me.

"Miss me?" I ask, winking at her.

"Hardly." Today, her peach hair comes to a point in the center of her forehead, the back of it styled in short spikes. The pink and yellow makeup around her eyes form glittering starburst patterns. When she rolls her eyes, it's as though they're dancing under lights.

"Oh, please." I slide onto her desk and fold my arms. "I bet this place has gotten so dull you've succumbed to daydreaming about me walking in through the doors just to see my handsome face."

"You're right," she deadpans. "You make my life complete, Theron. How have I not seen it until now?" Her voice remains monotone, as though it actually hurts her to force the words out. But the way her lips twitch, I know she enjoys my teasing.

"I always knew you'd come around some day." I point at her computer screen. "Do me a favor?"

She rolls her eyes again but runs a finger across the screen, then looks up at me, expectant.

"The patient that came in the other day—the one with the allergic reaction?" I rub my fingers along the scratchy growth of hair along my jaw. "I want to, um, follow up with him. Make sure he's okay."

Iden begins typing on the screen. "You mean you want to make sure the poor man hasn't lost his leg after you drilled a hole straight through it?"

I shrug one shoulder. "Something like that."

"Hmm." She scans the records. "What's his name again?"

"Catcher."

"Here he is." She turns the screen toward me so I can see the familiar file. Name, age, missing Trade. That's the one. I quickly read his address.

"Perfect." I tap Iden on the tip of her nose. "Thanks."

"Yeah," she says, spinning the screen back in front of her. "Whatever."

I give her a frown as I stand from her desk. "Oh, don't feel so sad about me being gone. We'll always have Oz—the missing link to your alien kind."

She quirks a smile, which falls as soon as it came. Her face turns serious, and she leans forward, whispering. "Have you heard about Setia?"

I shake my head, not trusting myself to speak. Where did Bron take her?

Iden leans even closer. "Rumor has it, the Seekers took her." She glances to Setia's desk, piles of paper haphazardly strewn along the surface. "But all her stuff is still here. If she isn't coming back, don't you think someone would come get her files?"

I follow Iden's glance. Whatever's in Setia's desk is probably on the province network. Maybe no one but us knew she kept paper records. I doubt anyone will come for her stuff.

I'm afraid Setia has become another number, another citizen taken away for no apparent reason, or for a cracked reason no one will tell us about. Because Eridian answers to no one, right? Who keeps her in check?

I wave farewell to Iden and walk toward Catcher's apartment. It's nearing the end of the shift as I get there. Like every other residential building in Freedom, Catcher's is identical to mine. He's on the first floor, though, so I don't have to scale stairwells or take my chance on sketchy elevators. His apartment is the last one on the left, at the very end of the hall. After taking a deep breath, I knock on his door.

Nothing.

I knock harder, not caring if I wake him. This is too important.

Still nothing.

I knock again and call out his name. This time a door opens, but it's not Catcher's.

Several units over, a female with short white hair sticks her head out of an apartment door. "Keep it down, you scab. Some of us are trying to breathe in peace." She slams the door before I can apologize, and my eyes diminish into slits. If that woman heard me, Catcher should have. He's not here.

I glance at my transmitter. Only an hour before curfew. I decide to wait in front of his door. He'll have to return when the sirens sound, right? But after an hour of counting the tiles on the ceiling and memorizing every stain on the carpet as I pace the hallway, the curfew sirens begin, and still no Catcher. After a few minutes, I hurry out of his building and jog to mine, making sure to slip inside before any Seekers see me. As I turn in for the night, I wonder where Catcher could be, and more importantly, if he's okay.

* * *

I place my hand on the scan pad, turn the key, and press the button for Sublevel Two. The hum of the elevator drowns out the endless questions in my head—the ones about Catcher and Pua and the surrogates and Nine. Still, always about Nine.

When I'm through the metal doors of the surrogate holding area, I head straight for Pua's cell. Gripping a pair of bars, I rest my head against them and watch as she sleeps peacefully on her mattress, tangled in sheets. If she wasn't surrounded by metal and concrete, I would guess she was content. Relaxed. Anything but on her way to being executed. If only she could stay calm like this, asleep, until I figured out how to help her.

Since I couldn't find Catcher, I've nothing new to tell her today. And there's not much I can do in the way of testing to help her, but I can't resist coming to see her anyway.

She's become my project, my mission, my purpose. I can't abandon her. And I admit I look forward to seeing her. She's funny and beautiful and smart. She's also broken in a way I can understand, so in a way, I need her, too. I need her because she gives me faith in a place that is faithless, hope in a place that is hopeless.

She begins to stir, and I'm glad. It's not like I can call out to her. And walking into her cell while she's sleeping feels too invasive. But I also don't want her to think I've been staring at her like some creep, so I step back and fold my arms, spinning around to take in the other cells. The woman in the next unit is young like Pua. Short curly hair the color of honey. She leans her back against the bars, staring at the ceiling. Maybe imagining the sky outside. I wonder how long it's been since she's seen it. One week? Two? Ten?

In the cell next to her is a slightly older woman, around thirty years old. Her skin is so pale it's on the verge of transparency. I see another woman, one with bronze skin like Pua but with lighter eyes, and another so young I'd think she was a Batcher if she wasn't obviously Remade. On and on they go, trapped, imprisoned. Do they want to leave here? Do they want to escape? Or are they ready to carry infants for our society? Do they even understand what that will entail? Because I don't. Not really.

"Theron."

I turn to the familiar voice and smile, stepping back toward Pua's cell. "Good morning," I mouth without a sound.

"Good morning," she says. "Did you talk to Catcher?"

My face falls. "I couldn't find him. But I will today. I'm not worried."

She glances between my eyes and nods, accepting my words. "Okay. Then I'm not worried either."

I give her a tight smile. It's a lie—that I'm not worried. There've only been a few times in my life when I've been more worried than I am now. And it almost always has had to do with Nine. Am I destined to care about people I can't keep with me? It's a masochistic life I've tried hard to abandon. Why this girl? Why now? I wonder if I could walk out of here and give her up. Forget her. Because if she's taken away too, I don't want to be the one left grieving her absence. I've become a master at it, but it doesn't mean I like it.

The sound of boots echoes through the hall, and Pua steps away, retreating farther into her cell, staring at something, or someone, behind me.

"Step away from the bars."

I turn to see Bron's familiar ugly face. He gestures with his gun the direction I should move.

Narrowing my eyes, I do as he says. "What's going on?" I look past him where a group of armed guards line up along the halls.

Bron ignores me as he orders his Seekers to proceed. They unlock the cells and lead three or four women each toward the exit.

"Where are you taking them?" I call after him, but he doesn't answer. Pua is the only one left. She stares at me, frightened. Like I am. "Don't worry," I tell her. "I'll be right back."

I rush toward the exit where the last of the Seekers and women have left and march through white halls. I stop at the first door guard I see. "Where are they taking them?"

"They're getting implanted with embryos today," he says, like it's no big deal. "After that they'll move to the surrogate rooms. We've got a new group of females coming in here tomorrow, so the place will get cleaned up and prepped for them."

That's why Pua's still here. She's not going to become a

surrogate. "What's with the heavy military force? Do the females normally become violent or something?"

The guard shakes his head. "I've never seen this before," he says. "But I've heard rumors of prisoners escaping. Maybe the Prime Maker is increasing security measures to prevent it from happening again."

Prisoners. Are these surrogates considered prisoners? If so, how have some managed to escape in the past? It doesn't make sense. More than anything, it's probably a byproduct of Eridian's recent paranoia.

I walk back through the empty room, eerily silent now that the women have gone. Cell doors are left open, a mattress, bedding, and washbasin the only things left behind.

I turn the final corner and head for Pua's cell. "You said you were separated from your family," I say, fumbling through my pockets for the key. "What happened? Was it the Seekers? Did they do something to you?"

She lowers her head. "They came to our island. Attacked our homes. Singled me out and dragged me away from my family. I don't know what happened to the rest of them. I—"

"All clear!" someone shouts.

I drop the key in my hand and flip around to see a Seeker with blond hair heading our way, tapping something into his portable screen.

"Odell?" The name's out before I can stop it.

He slowly glances to me, then back down to his screen, unfazed by my presence. He's not surprised to see me. "All the women have gone, Theron. There's no reason for you to be here today."

I reach down for the key and clear my throat. "But this is my Trade. What am I supposed to do—"

"Take the day off." He seems agitated, but doesn't lose his cool. He walks over to a rolling cart, one the guards use to distribute meal trays to the females. After placing his screen on top, he continues to slide and tap his fingers on the surface. Without looking at me, he says, "You'll have plenty to do tomorrow with the new arrivals. They'll all need their basic exams. That'll keep you busy for a while."

"But . . ." But what? There's no way he'll let me stay with Pua. I step toward him and turn my back so Pua can't read my words. "But what about this one?" I tilt my head toward her cell. "How much time does she have?"

Odell sighs heavily before scrolling through records on his screen, possibly the execution log, I'm not sure. He pauses and looks up at me, his jaw tightening. "It's not a concern of—" His transmitter buzzes. He picks it up and listens to whoever's on the other side. After a few seconds, he says, "I'll be right there."

Odell returns his transmitter to his waist and quickly paces down the hall. Before he rounds the corner, he turns back and yells, "I better not see you here when I get back." Then he's gone.

Sighing in defeat, I return to Pua at the bars. "I have to go."

She nods, understanding. "I wish I could break out of here myself. Run away, somewhere they can't find me."

I swallow hard, a part of me wanting to steal her away and run with her. Somewhere we could both hide. But I won't get far with the tracker in my head, and there are too many obstacles in the way to escape this level unseen. We'd probably both be killed within minutes. I have to find a solution for her hearing problem. That will prevent her execution. That needs to be my priority right now.

"Don't do anything cracked while I'm gone," I say, worried about her desire to flee. "I'll be here tomorrow, I promise." I've made so many promises, I wonder if the word means anything anymore. To me. To her.

I have to find Catcher. Now.

Pua leans her head against the bars, looking up at me with wet eyes. "I don't want you to go," she whispers.

A surge of emotion rises in me, starting at my feet and moving up my legs and chest, crowding in my head. It's as though I can't contain it inside me, and my eyes well up with moisture from the pressure of it all.

I slip my hand through the bars and caress her cheek, then bring her forehead to my mouth. "I know," I say against her skin. She can't hear me, but I'm sure she knows what I'm saying. How could she not? "I don't want to leave, either."

She grips the sides of my shirt, her hands shaking. I can't imagine what it's like to be here, locked away. Alone. Even in a room filled with females, it's terribly isolating. And for someone who doesn't hear the sound of other voices, it must be unbearable. Yet now, knowing you'll be the only one until the new surrogates arrive, frightening too.

I pull back and lower my head so our eyes are level. "I can't stay." My words shake coming out, but I don't know if she can tell by looking at my lips.

"I know." She rests her hand on the side of my face for a few seconds, then drops it, stepping back from the bars. "I'll see you tomorrow."

Her forced smile is enough to make me fill with emotion again, this time spreading to the tips of my fingers. I long to reach for her again. I know right now, in this moment, I would do anything for this girl. I would do everything. Whatever it takes to make her feel safe again. Even risk my own life to do it.

"Tomorrow," I mouth to her, then I turn to leave. But

something in the corner catches my eye. The rolling cart. And sitting on top, Odell's portable screen. I rush to it without thinking, hoping I'm not too late. Instead of sliding my finger across it so it can recognize my print, I tap it once, hoping Odell is still logged on. Sure enough, the glowing screen appears, the execution records still pulled up. I find Pua's name and her assigned execution date.

Three weeks.

She has only three weeks.

I feel like my head is spinning, and something catches in my throat. It's not enough time. Not nearly enough.

Catcher will know what to do.

With that thought, I exit the program and search for the one I need. The tracker map. I find the icon and tap on it, opening a familiar map of Freedom with hundreds, thousands, of red lights dotting the screen. When I zoom in on a certain part of the province, the lights become more distinct. Individual. I don't have a lot of time, so I quickly scroll through the map to Catcher's street, and then to his building.

There it is, one light blinking within his apartment, the last one on the first floor. To be sure, I tap on it, and his name appears. *Catcher.* He's there now. I have to go.

I log off Odell's screen and hurry to the elevators.

CHAPTER ELEVEN

I pound on his door one, two, twenty times. "Catcher! I know you're in there, you scab. Let me in."

Silence.

What in Freedom's name is going on? I saw his light on the tracker screen. I didn't imagine it. Sure, he could have left between then and now, but it's doubtful. I'm tired of playing this game. I glance down the hall and hesitate, but no one's here. It's the middle of the day; everyone's working in their Trade. Everyone but Catcher. Either he's hurt, or there's something seriously cracked going on.

I take a deep breath and send a kick into his door handle, successfully breaking it open, and successfully sending a severe pain through my faux leg. *Brilliant job, Theron.* His door swings inside and bounces off the wall, flying back toward me. I stop it with my hand and hold it open, taking a look inside his apartment.

"Catcher?" I don't expect an answer. Not after bashing on his door for ten minutes, but it feels rude not to address him in his own place.

I laugh at myself. Because breaking in his door is not rude one bit. Nope. I hope he doesn't give me too much flak for this. I close the door behind me, though it doesn't latch into place. He'll have to get that fixed. Oops.

Catcher's place is a little bigger than mine. While my apartment consists of one giant room—my bed taking most of the space in the center with one door leading to a washroom—his has a short hallway to the right, leading to what I assume is a bedroom, while this main area has a few cushioned chairs in front of a wide, open window with a view to the street.

The whole room is much cleaner than mine. Not really lived in. No dishes in the sink, no papers scattered on the countertop. The only thing unusual is a raw piece of wood lying next to a small knife on a side table. The wood has been carved away, forming a rough human shape, small chips of wood scattered on the table surface. Must be a hobby of his. A quick glance in his bedroom reveals linens tucked in place, unused. Weird.

I limp through the apartment, my leg still throbbing from kicking in his door, and search in cabinets, under furniture, behind every door in this place. Nothing. What's going on? After pacing in pain for about half an hour, I find a pen and paper to write him a note.

Where are you? I need to talk to you. Now.

I sign my name and leave it on his kitchen counter.

Back in the street, I run my hand through my hair in frustration. There's this terrible, gut-breaking feeling you get when you know what's right, you know what you have to do, but due to circumstances out of your control, you can't do it. I felt it that night in the water. I needed to get Nine to safety, rescue her. I knew I had to. But I couldn't. So I sent her away. Except I pushed too hard, because when she finally did come back, it wasn't enough to keep her. The distance between us was too much. We'll never come together like we once were, and it's my fault. I wasn't strong enough, brave enough. I wasn't anything enough for her.

It's the same with Pua. She's right there. So close I can touch her, hold her. Breathing, alive, heart beating. I have her, but she's slipping through my fingers faster than I can get a grip. Three weeks. She'll be gone in three weeks. Not just gone—dead. Killed. I feel like I've already lost her. I know I have to save her, but I don't have the means to do it. Not without Catcher. But he's abandoned me too.

Maybe I'm not strong enough. Brave enough. Maybe I'm not anything enough for anyone.

The pain is crushing me from the inside. I think I might implode from it. My injured leg has nothing on this pain. But I know how to forget it. At least for a little while.

I run to the nearest nightspot and grab a buzz drink. I down the entire glass, and then another. The third goes down slower. I don't want to pace myself, but I don't want to throw up either. I want to be numb. I want to forget.

I smile when I lose count of how many drinks I've had. Because it means I'll start to forget other things too. Soon my head is filled with colors and lights, music and sounds. A heady, smoky feeling fills me, and I name it—

"Bliss," I say out loud. "Bliss!"

I stumble to the dance floor and shake my body to the pounding beat. Then stop.

Don't shake so hard, Theron. You don't want to—

Whoa. My stomach churns, and I think I might throw up. I make my way to the washroom and heave over the toilet. Yeah. Not so pleasant coming up as it was going down. When my stomach is empty, I fall to my knees. Tears fall into the basin. I tell myself it's a side effect of the drink, but deep down in my broken gut I know it's a side effect of being me. I can remember again, and now I'm sick on top of everything else. This is so cracked.

When I'm able to get to my feet, I head for the bar again, forcing myself to take another drink.

Slow, Theron. Go slowly this time.

It doesn't matter how fast I get there, as long as I get there without screwing it up again. I think I fall asleep for a bit, waking when some stranger drags me to the dance floor and gets me to move with her to the numbing music. Three dances. Twelve. I lose count, which reminds me of counting glasses, which pushes me to the bar again.

I've no idea how much time has passed, but when the music changes to something loud and grating, stinging my ears, I cover them and complain out loud. "Shut it off," I say, my words jumbled. "Next song."

I guess no one else likes the song either, because they begin filing out of the room, and soon I'm the only one left, crouched over, hands covering my ears. The lights flip on, and everything that was dark and comfortable turns bright and harsh. I don't want to be here, wherever here is. I want to be warm and dizzy again. I stumble to a chair and close my eyes, forcing out the bright.

I don't know how much time passes, but the annoying song finally shuts off, and I lower my hands. The noise is gone, but there's still a ringing in my ears that makes my head throb. Or is it the light? I think it's the light hurting my head. I need to get out of here.

I stumble to the exit, and though the streetlights shine like little stars in the corners of my vision, it's pleasantly dark outside. Night. I think that's what this is called—night. How long has it been since I've been outside at night? Too long. Though I can't remember why.

As I'm about to step into the street toward what I think is the general direction of home, a giant metal beast moves in front of me.

"Whoa!" I fall back onto my rear. "Ow." That hurt. I peer up at the beast—all hard edges and smooth sides. What kind of beast is that?

I hear the sound of a thousand boots stomping to my side, but when I look, there's only one pair of boots, nudging my waist.

"That hurts!" I say to the boots. "Stop it."

The boots are replaced with knees, leading to a waist-chest-head of someone who looks familiar, but I can't remember why. He's ugly, though. Dog ugly. Maybe he's the beast I was thinking of a minute ago.

"Gruff." I bark at him. Maybe that's the only language he understands—dog tongue.

"Get enough to drink tonight, Theron?" The dog speaks my language.

"How—" I'm about to ask him how he learned to talk, but I spew the contents of my stomach all over him instead. "Oops."

The dog curses, lifts me to my feet by my shirt collar, and pulls my hands behind my back. "It's past curfew, Theron. Know what that means?"

"Time to sleep," I mumble. Sleep sounds really nice right now. Where's my bed?

"Nope," says the dog. "Past curfew means it's time to wake up."

*   *   *

I see the needle in the dog's hand, and my mouth falls open. I didn't know dogs even had hands. He taps it to release any air, then moves my head to the side, exposing my neck.

"I'm not a Batcher," I say. I'm too old to be a Batcher. I've already been Remade.

"It's not hormone suppressant, you idiot." The dog growls. "It's Lucidate. To burn all that alcohol in you and get your brain cells working again. Fast."

The moment the meds are in my body, it brings new meaning to the word "burn," because that's exactly what it feels like—my entire body in flames. I scream, half expecting smoke and embers to fly out of my mouth. It's the worst pain I've ever felt, even more than getting my leg bitten off by that beast in the water.

Beast.

Nine in the water.

I blink my eyes open. I remember now. I went drinking to forget. Forget . . .

Pua.

She still needs me. She needs my help.

Catcher.

I try to stand from my chair, only to realize my feet are tied together, and two Seekers on either side of me restrain my arms. I look up to the dog that brought me here.

"Bron," I whisper.

"Welcome back, my friend." He pats me on the shoulder like we're old pals. "You passed out on our way here. Usually it's the

98

shot that wakes people up, but you came to just before I gave it to you so you got to experience the whole party. It was quite entertaining, actually." He chuckles.

"Lucidate," I say, finally understanding. I was drunk, and the annoying sound I thought was terrible music was actually the curfew sirens. I didn't make it home in time, and Bron found me on the street. "That stuff burns," I add. I've administered it to many patients but never needed it myself. I had no idea it hurt that much. Good thing it goes away as fast as it comes. I must have been really out of it for them to use it on me.

Bron tsks. "When you choose to get drunk and choose to miss curfew, well, you choose to get burned."

Clever. I roll my eyes. "So what now? I get a scolding, a lecture, and you tuck me in at home?" I tilt my head from side to side and blink several times. I'm wide awake now. Thanks to those meds, I doubt I'll get any sleep tonight.

"Don't you wish you were so lucky?" Bron walks away from me. I hear him speak to someone at the door, saying something about me being ready, then he exits, leaving me alone with the Seekers restraining me.

I look around. The room is run-down, dirty, like we're in a building abandoned years ago, left to scavengers and rodents. The walls droop against their supports, peeling layers of color and material revealing their history. Holes in the walls show there are several rooms connected to this one, all in similar disrepair. Maybe it's a part of Freedom left to rot because Eri doesn't want to keep it up anymore. Like the broken elevator in my apartment building. Or the storefronts along some sections of the street. Perhaps one day every structure in the province will look like this one—forgotten, abandoned. I wouldn't be surprised if this is what we all deteriorate into if Eridian doesn't find her precious Nine.

The door opens, and Bron returns with Eridian. Her standard bun has come loose, and her heels have been replaced with steel boots, a ridiculous combination with her gray blazer and matching skirt. A deep red stain runs up her left sleeve, and part of me wonders if it's her blood or someone else's.

"Hello, Theron." Her usual steady voice is rushed and frantic, even if her words are chosen carefully. "I'm surprised by your infraction tonight. I thought you were doing well."

"I *am* doing well," I say. "The new Trade is better than I could have hoped for. Really. And thanks to that lovely burn, I'm feeling myself again after a few too many drinks tonight. Innocent mistake."

"Innocent?" She motions to someone at the door who brings a large bucket and places it on the floor in front of me.

Water. It's filled to the brim with water.

No.

Anything but water.

"An innocent mistake would be drinking a little more than you could handle, yes," she continues. "But that isn't what happened, is it?" She motions to the Seekers holding me in place.

They immediately force me from the chair to my knees and shove my head into the bucket, submerging me up to my neck. I hold my breath for as long as I can, but my lungs begin to burn. My eyes burn. Why does everything have to burn?

When they finally pull me up, I take in a huge rush of air, swallowing some of the water dripping from my hair into my face.

"No, Theron." Eridian's words are still rushed, but calculated. "You drank yourself to the point of being sick. But instead of quitting like most would, you started over again, poisoning your already weakened body. Why?"

Before I can answer, I'm plunged into the water again. I wasn't prepared, and some of it runs into my nose, into my throat. It burns burns burns. I cough in the water, doing my best to not breathe any more in. But my best isn't good enough. It never is. I inhale a rush of water just before my head is yanked up again.

"Please," I say, feeling as though I'm spitting up gallons of water. "Stop."

"Stop?" Eri laughs. "You didn't stop. Is it because you were feeling guilty about something? Perhaps you were trying to forget you'd done something wrong. That you'd lied."

"What—"

Eri yanks on my hair with her own fingers so I'm forced to look into her cold eyes. "Where is she, Theron?" She shouts at me, specks of spit landing on my face. "Where is Nine?"

"I don't know," I sputter.

She releases her grip, and I'm prepared this time, taking a deep breath before going under. I count, trying to slow my pulse, calm my frantic heart. But as soon as I have no breath anymore, I begin to panic, remembering my time in the ocean. When I was forced under, pulled below the surface by another kind of beast. When I struggled to stay afloat in the dark after losing my leg. After losing my best friend.

I.

Can't.

Do.

This.

This time, I welcome the water as I breathe it in. Because maybe it will be my last breath, and I'll finally be at peace. Nine can't haunt me if I'm dead.

As I'm lifted from the water, I hear Eri yelling at me before my mind catches up to what she's saying.

" . . . that why you stole the screen from my Seeker?" She's screaming. Can't she hear how ridiculous she sounds?

I spare a glance at the Seeker to my left. His eyes are wide, face pale. Even he's afraid of whatever this thing Eri has become.

She slaps me across the face. "Were you trying to find her, or make sure she remains hidden? Where? Where are you hiding her?"

I start to laugh. My shoulders bounce, my mouth turns up, and my eyes squint. It feels good to laugh. To enjoy this show as if it were a worthy form of entertainment.

"Hiding her?" I say between chuckles. "Why would you think I'd be hiding her? I hate her. I hate Nine with every miserable part of my being. Look at what she's done to me." I'm yelling now, a worthy match to Eri's frenzy. "Look at what she's done to *you*. Do you know why? Because she hates us too. Why would anyone want her back?"

It's really a question for myself. Why would I want her back after everything she's done to me? But Eri mumbles her own answer.

"She's the key," Eri says, her voice trembling. "She's the only one who can save us all."

"She's *destroyed* us all."

I hate Eri. I hate this place. I hate Nine. She lied the day she called me family, because from what little I've learned about the word, family wouldn't do this. Nine is a liar and a thief. And I hate her for it.

I want the burning again. With the burning, there wasn't room for things like feelings or thoughts. Just fire and flame.

And maybe cleansing too. A thorough purging of my system of anything lingering from my hateful past.

I ready myself to be dunked again, ready to inhale the burn the second my head hits the water, but it doesn't come. Instead, Eri lifts the bucket and pours the contents over my head.

"He doesn't know anything." It sounds as though she's on the verge of tears herself. "Take him home."

CHAPTER TWELVE

*A*fter Bron and his goons unceremoniously shove me through my front door, I drag myself to the shower and sit at the bottom of the tub through three cycles before I have the energy to stand and shut it off. Exhausted to the core, I get dressed and fall into my bed, eager to finally get lost in my dreams. But sleep doesn't come. I'm emotionally exhausted—torture will do that, I guess—but the Lucidate's still got me wired. My stomach starts to grumble, so I head to the kitchen and find something to eat.

Sitting on the ledge of my windowsill, I watch the province, dead asleep in the early morning hours. So peaceful. So calm. It has no idea about the madness brewing. It can lay its worries to rest and start a new day, fresh and clean. How many sunsets will it take until I can bury all of my demons?

Around four o'clock in the morning I can't take it anymore and change into a pair of sweats and a tank. I grin, realizing I look like a Batcher. Or a patient, which is appropriate. I have some kind of disease—one without a cure. I'll forever be searching for that cure.

I reach the cages, though of course no one's there yet. Not this early. I run through my warm-up first, stretching my limbs and back muscles. Then I practice my kicks. Front and side, roundhouse and sliding kicks. Low, high. Combinations. I punch and slice through the air with my arms, twisting as I go, giving it as much power as possible. I wish I had something to hit, something to take my impact. After an hour, I'm covered in a layer of sweat, and though it hasn't been enough to make me forget, my mind has at least calmed down into something reasonably stable.

As soon as the sun begins to rise on the horizon, I hear the click of the cage door, and it swings open.

Catcher.

Wow. His timing is perfect. Where was he yesterday? Or the day before? When I needed him. When he could have saved me from a lovely torture exercise.

He pulls his shirt over his bald head and begins rotating his arms to stretch them out. "I got your note."

I grunt to let him know I heard him, but I have no intention of making this easy for him.

"You going to tell me what the big emergency is?" He tries to keep his voice calm, but I detect a hint of nervousness in it. Nervous about how I'll react to his absence, or where he's been, or that he's lied. Any of it. Well, he should feel nervous. Because I'm going to cream him in this ring.

"You really want to fight me, old man?" There'll be no audience for several more hours, but that doesn't mean we can't go a round or two. "We may both have a bum leg, but I've been working with mine a whole lot longer than you have." I hop once on my right leg to prove it.

A smile spreads on Catcher's face. "My leg's fine now. And I'm no old man, little boy." He signals me with one fist to call me over.

I've never seen Catcher in the cages before, but that doesn't mean he can't fight. He's shorter than I am, but thicker too. Still, I'm one of the best, and I'm about to prove it to him.

I jab at him, a soft blow, just to test him. He counters with a side kick that slides into a second, catching a small brush of skin. Before I can react, he twists and sends the back of his fist into my face, making my nose burn.

All right. My man Catcher can play. Let's play.

My jump front kick forces him deeper into the cage, but he twists away before I have a chance to make contact. He comes at me with an upper cut, but I'm fast, and I duck and send my fist into his stomach instead. Catcher's torso caves in slightly, a natural response to the pain, and I use that momentum to pull his head down. He stumbles to the floor but quickly recovers and gives me space as he regains his stance.

"You don't have to go on," I say, a smile teasing my lips. "I won't tell anyone you quit."

Catcher laughs. "I can do this all day."

All right, then. I circle around him, fists up, arms in front of my chest, bouncing on my toes. When he comes for me, I dodge his kick and spin, sending an elbow into his back. I expect him to stumble again, but instead he pulls a roundhouse and knocks me on the side of the head.

I half grunt, half shout in surprise, and I touch the back of my hand to my cheek. I'm going to have a bruise there.

"I won't tell anyone if *you* want to quit." Catcher grins, and I mirror it.

We alternate combination after combination, matching each

other's moves, strengths, speeds. Landing several decent hits, neither of us seems to pull ahead, and in the end we call it a draw, which, if you ask me, means Catcher won since he's twice my age, and I'm supposedly an expert at this.

"Why haven't I seen you in the cages?" I ask. It's obvious he'd do well here.

He shrugs. "Not my thing."

A lot of things aren't his thing. It evidently doesn't mean he can't, just that he won't. Catcher is a strange man, and from what I've discovered in recent days, more mysterious than I first thought.

His face goes serious. "Why the note, Theron?"

I know Pua's more important, but I can't help myself. "Where were you?"

Catcher steps up to me, his face inches from mine. "Why. The. Note?"

He's not going to give me anything, and I wish I could reciprocate. Keep silent. But Pua needs us, and Catcher's her only hope. "It's Pua. I figured out what's wrong with her."

His eyes widen, and he steps back slightly, waiting for me to continue.

I sigh. "It's a damaged cochlear. Both sides. The nerves are shot. A side effect from a high fever years ago, I think. There's nothing we can do from Freedom. She needs to go to the Remake facility and have them replaced."

Catcher's face falls. "Eridian won't approve that."

"We have to try."

"No."

"I can talk to her. Convince her." I try to think of something I might have on Nine I could barter with. After last night's torture session, it's obvious Eri's desperate for anything I might know about the girl we lost. It's our only chance.

"No."

"Why not?" My shouted words echo through the empty arena.

"I . . . I tried that once." Catcher looks up at me, tears in his eyes. "It's not going to work. We have to find another way."

"There is no other way!"

Catcher rubs his bald head. "We'll figure something out. If we mention it to Eridian, she's going to—"

He doesn't finish, but I can see his mind churning with thoughts he plans to keep to himself.

"She's going to what?"

"We. Can't." He stares at me for several seconds.

"I'm not going to stand aside and let her be killed. I won't." I begin pacing through the cage. "I'll sneak her out. Help her escape. Hide her. Whatever it takes."

"You shouldn't let yourself get attached," Catcher mumbles. "Be careful. It's harder when you get too close." His words feel like advice he doesn't believe in taking. "These surrogates, they . . . It's better to not let yourself care for them."

Well, too late for that. "They aren't animals. They're human beings. They have the same right to live that we do. Whatever cracked stuff the Prime Maker has going on is her problem. And one I don't agree with." I stop and turn my narrowed eyes to Catcher. "If you won't help me, I'll figure it out myself. I don't care if I die trying, I'm going to save her."

I march toward the cage door, but Catcher steps in front of me, blocking my way. I shove my shoulder against his, showing him I'm determined and don't care what he says.

"Is it true?" he asks softly.

I exhale in frustration. "Is what true?" I spit at him.

"Is it true you'd risk your own life to save those women? To save Pua?"

I measure his question carefully before responding. "Yes." There's no doubt in my answer.

He searches my eyes then nods. "I wanted to wait to show you, but I think you're ready. Meet me in the Core lobby in an hour."

"Why should—"

He presses his palm against my chest to stop my words. "I'm going to show you where I've been the last few days."

* * *

After a quick shower and breakfast, I head for the Core building where Catcher's waiting for me near the front desk. Without a word, I follow him into the elevator, and we descend to Sublevel Two. Once we're off the elevators, though, we don't head right. Instead Catcher goes left.

At the first set of doors, I see the same scanning pad as the elevator, and something new—a blood draw. At least that's what I think it is. Catcher presses his thumb against a small, depressed mold that holds his digit perfectly. I see a needle protrude through the clear plastic and prick his skin; a small bubble of blood is sucked into the unit. When the machine is satisfied, the door clicks open, and we walk through.

"Only a few Healers are allowed past the doors." Catcher's voice isn't just low, it's reverent. As though we're walking on hallowed ground. "All of them with my express approval. So you won't get in trouble for being here. Eridian trusts me exclusively to choose who I will for Healer duty in this section. She'll trust my selection of you for it too."

I haven't told him about my interrogation last night. If I do, would he change his mind about me being here? Realize Eri doesn't trust me as much as she once did? I don't want to risk it, so I remain silent.

After a few turns, we reach another set of doors. So far what I've seen looks the same as the rest of the level, though I think it may span a lot more distance underground than the other areas.

Catcher pauses before the double doors. "Once we go through here, we cannot speak our minds. They monitor everything in these rooms. Video and audio."

"They?"

Catcher doesn't answer, just gives me a look as if to say, *You know who.*

I suppose I do. Seekers. Eridian.

"Only say out loud what's necessary for the job."

"What job?" I ask.

"We're checking on the health of a young Batch." He brings out his set of keys again.

"There are Batchers down here?"

"Not the ones you think," he mumbles. "You'll understand in a minute. Again—we can't say what we want. Follow my lead, and we'll talk about it after we're up top again. Understand?"

I nod, and Catcher unlocks the doors. I follow him into a large room with gray walls. And cages. That's what I think they are at first. Tall fighting cages reaching a few stories into the air, as though this were some kind of arena for ultimate cage fights for giants. Except the smell that finds my nose isn't of blood or sweat or defeat, it's a stench of insanitation and uncleanliness. Like the place hasn't been cleaned for centuries, or like it's a holding area for animals. I wonder what stands above us in Freedom, because whatever it is, it conceals these cages. The ceiling is so high, it reaches far beyond the Maker level.

As I glance around, I see that the cages don't hold animals, but humans. Adult male humans. All of them are mature with skin different shades of brown, reminding me of the surrogates. But their heads are shaved like young Batchers, no matter their age. They wear rags and either scrawny pieces of leather on their feet or remain barefoot. I think the condition of their clothing and footwear may signify how long they've been here. As though nothing is ever replaced, and the necessities of life—clothing, shelter, food—are a luxury instead of a need.

Each pair of eyes follows us as we walk down the center of the room. I wonder if to them, it looks like we're the ones in the cage, forced along a path like cattle in a factory. Looking closer, I realize the cages aren't like the fighting cages at all, but have distinct pathways of doors with gates installed. The males file into separate cages one at a time through a one-way gate that locks automatically as soon as a certain number of people have passed. They're being sorted and divided. For what, I don't know.

I glance to Catcher, and he gives me a sad smile before his gaze falls to his feet. I have so many questions. Where are these men from? Why are they here? And why are they treated so poorly? But I remember what Catcher said about not speaking, so I keep my mouth closed. I have a feeling he's been here many times before. Twenty years' worth of times. If I'd seen this over and over through the years, I'd want to look away like he is. But for me, today, I'm too shocked not to look.

We come to the end of a branching path. None of the imprisoned males file into the cages on this side, because they're already full, having reached their quota, I suppose. We stop in front of a cage, the eyes of those within boring a hole into me. I want so desperately to talk to them, but I take my cues from Catcher.

"They are counted and sorted every morning," Catcher says, his voice flat and monotone.

A vertical rotating gate with protruding bars turns, allowing barely enough space for one man to walk through at a time. The first male in this group shuffles down a path similar to our own and into the dark where I cannot see. I wonder where it leads.

As if he can hear my thoughts, Catcher says, "Today, this group will work in the textile factory, making Batcher clothes."

So they have Trades like the rest of us. Although, like the surrogates, I doubt they chose this Trade. I ask what I think is a safe question. "Why don't they wear Batcher clothes like the surrogates?"

Catcher frowns. "The surrogates require a certain level of hygiene and health in their living conditions to guarantee the health of our Batchers." A pause. "These slaves do not."

Slaves. I don't know what the word means, but I'll have to ask Catcher about it later. He spares a look for me before continuing in his stiff voice.

"Other groups will go to the metal shops, refuse plants, food processing, or pharmaceutical center."

I swallow hard. They are factory workers. Every one of them. I assume they go up to the province level via elevators or stairs right into their allotted buildings in the north part of the province—the factory district. They must remain hidden from citizens in Freedom, always. I wonder if they sleep in these cages or have cells somewhere, like the surrogate holding area.

Eridian keeps so many secrets locked down here, and I wish I could forget the ones Catcher has shared. I don't want to know about the surrogates or these slaves. I don't even want to know about this Maker level.

What's the purpose of keeping it hidden? If our own citizens were to find out what's happening, would they fight against our Prime Maker and her cabinet?

I turn to Catcher, attempting to keep my voice steady. "Are we to perform our exams here, on the males?"

He shakes his head then leads me down another path. After a turn, we come to a pair of metal doors and walk through. This hallway has doors on either side with a window installed in each so I can see through to the other side. Each room is packed with people—young, old, male, female. There's not enough room for anyone to sit. They stand or lean on each other, their cheeks hollow, skin pale.

"This is the sick bay," Catcher says as we continue walking.

Sick bay? It looks like somewhere you come to die, not to get better.

I rub the tattoo on my neck, for the first time glad Nine is nowhere near this Maker level. Nowhere in the province. Anywhere is better than here. I squeeze my eyes tight then blink before asking, "How many Healers work in the sick bay?"

"None." Catcher's voice snags on the word. It's obvious these sick people, who are apparently never administered to, affects Catcher deeply. I decide to stop asking questions, to let Catcher tell me what he needs to when he needs to.

Another set of doors brings us to cells like the surrogates live in. A similar noise level echoes throughout the room, and I find comfort in the fact that at least this feels familiar. That is until I see them.

Children.

CHAPTER THIRTEEN

They crowd the cells, about ten per unit. Their heads are shaved like the adult males, and the few clothes I see are in the same state of raggedness. But many of them are naked. Do they get any kind of clothing from Freedom, or are they stuck wearing what they arrive in until it . . . falls away?

For the adults, I was able to stomach these conditions. They understand that what's happening to them is not right. And though they might not have means to fight or escape, they still know it's wrong.

But these children—do they remember where they came from, or will they assume this life is normal? That being trapped in a cell is the only way to live?

I clutch my hand over my stomach, nausea threatening to overflow. Catcher warned me about video surveillance in this place. Audio. I press my lips together to keep my body from giving away my true feelings.

Keep it together, Theron.

We walk slowly along a path in front of the cells. The children run and scramble to the bars, clutching them and peeking their faces through. And from so many of them come smiles and laughter. How can they do that? How can they find the smallest trace of happiness in a place like this? I blink my tears away.

"Are we examining the children, then?" I ask, cursing the shaking in my voice. This must be the young Batch he talked about.

Catcher looks me up and down and nods, his warm eyes sending me what little comfort they can. "Yes. We'll start on this end," he says, pointing, "and work our way down to the rest. As soon as we're done, they'll be taken to the fields."

The fields? The ones past the red bridge near the concert house? Do these children work there? My heart sinks.

Is that what a slave is, then? Someone forced to work against his will? And for the benefit of who? Freedom One? Eri? Me?

Talk about free-breakers. Our province, our way of life—we are the ultimate free-breakers of all. Where do these children have a choice? When do they get to choose their Trade or who they want to be?

I nod and turn my face away from Catcher, stepping to the first cell and unlocking it with the key Catcher gives me. The children here are both male and female, ranging in age from fourth to eighth years.

They scramble over each other to be first, not understanding what's happening. Catcher opens a cabinet against the wall and retrieves basic Healer equipment. Handing me a few instruments, I begin to examine the child closest to me. Eyes, ears, nose, and throat. I don't record results or really keep track of who I've examined, but when one child is done, they help push the next to the front, as though this were some kind of game and it's only fair everyone has a turn.

Catcher does the same next to me, one child at a time. They rub his head and pull on his ears and nose, as though they're familiar with him. He's probably seen this group many times before. They speak to each other in accented words—some similar to Pua's, some not—and even address me and Catcher sometimes, but I remain silent, following Catcher's lead. I smile and try to make my expression encouraging, though. Despite the children's cheerfulness, their general appearance makes me believe they'd welcome any positive gesture on their behalf.

When we're done with the children in this cell, we move on to the next. Then the next. In the fifth unit, Catcher carefully leads one child to me and turns to another.

"The purpose of the exams is to make sure they're fit enough to work," he says without looking at me.

As I examine this child, a male of about five, I wonder why we're declaring them fit. To think I'm sending a child out into the fields makes me sick.

Catcher continues. "If there are ailments of any kind, they are declared unfit for work and are sent to the extermination unit."

I cough to cover the painful sound that leaves my mouth. Catcher continues to work without a blink. I don't think these children know what "extermination" means. Has Catcher ever found one to be unfit? How could he send a child away to die?

With a shaky hand, I shine a light into one eye of the child Catcher gave me, then into the other eye. And I freeze. This one. His left eye. It doesn't respond to the light. He's blind in that one eye. At least partially. I lower the light and watch his eyes, then raise it again. If you weren't looking for it, you couldn't tell one eye didn't work.

I turn the boy to the side to look in his ear, but I'm not really looking. I'm thinking. This is why Catcher passed this one to me. He knows the boy has a bad eye, because he's seen it before. It's his way of telling me we don't report the ones who can continue to work despite a disability. At least if it's not obvious. Because when the alternative is death, it's the only way we have of helping them. I almost lose it, biting the inside of my cheek to keep myself in check.

I let the boy go and examine another child, and another, making sure each is reasonably healthy, reasonably strong. I wish I could take each one and hold them and whisper words of encouragement in their ears. Tell them everything will be okay, though I know it won't. I want them to have a small moment of hope, but I have to hold back. Maintain my composure.

I try to ignore the burning in my chest. One child holds my face between his hands and looks up at me with big, light brown eyes. His features remind me so much of Pua, I have to squeeze my eyes shut to prevent myself from screaming from the pain of it all.

When we've worked through every cell in the room, Catcher locks the final one, then stands before a small rectangular component on the wall. After lifting a plastic cover, he presses a button, and hidden doors on the far side of each cell unit pop open. The children scurry out—surely to the fields up top, and most likely through a path that keeps them hidden. Because otherwise I definitely would have heard about Batchers working in the fields at some point during my years in Freedom.

After the last ones are out, the doors close again, leaving an eerie silence behind. But it isn't the quiet that haunts me. It's the memory of those children burned in my mind. Their big eyes, their arms wrapped around my neck, their playful laughter— it's too much. I stand there, staring into the empty cells, unsure what to do. Up until this point in my life, I've had a goal, a purpose. Even if that goal was simply to forget about the girl I lost, it was something to guide my decisions, my actions.

But now, my life will never be the same knowing that down here, beneath the rest of the world, hidden like some kind of deadly disease, are these children. These men and these sick. These slaves. They are locked away and forgotten. I can't unlearn what I've seen and done today. I used to want to forget Nine, forget she left, forget the pain. But now there's something a hundred times more painful I want to forget. I want to forget this level, these people, this evil I've seen poured out on the innocent. But there's no way I will forget this. Ever.

So I stand, motionless. Helpless. I have no goal, no idea what to do next. I'm frozen in my thoughts. I can't move forward, I can't go backward, so I'm stuck not knowing how to help or fix or do anything for them. They need me. They need all of us. But how can I fulfill that need?

"Theron?" Catcher carefully steps in front of me. "Are you okay?"

I stare at him, blankly. I feel the blood drain from my face, and I open my mouth, but no words come out. What could I possibly say?

He presses his lips together, understanding in his eyes. "We're done here for the day, and this is what will happen next." He steps close to me and says, "We will head back to the elevators, return to the Core lobby, and walk out of this building, an honest day's Trade completed."

He waits for me to say something, but it's taking all of my

strength to remain standing. I don't have the energy or sense to form a response.

"Then we can head for my apartment for something to eat. Maybe visit for a few hours before curfew. Deal?"

He takes my silence as a yes and nods, leading me back through the sick bay, back through the now empty giant cages, and out the doors into the familiar halls of the Maker level. I follow him up the elevator, into the lobby, and out into the street. The sunlight brings some clarity to me, and I have the sudden urge to run. Away from this building, this place, this life. Run away from everything. But Catcher's hand on my shoulder keeps me in place, as though he can read my thoughts. So instead I maintain a steady pace the best I can, the pain in my leg feeling as fresh as the day I sustained the injury.

When we're in Catcher's apartment building, we head straight for his door, where he struggles a moment with the keycard, possibly from the damage I inflicted on the door—was it only yesterday? When he finally gets it open, I rush to the bathroom where I heave over the toilet.

My stomach is emptied within seconds, and I drop to my knees, holding onto the seat, trying to erase the images in my head. But instead of disappearing, everything I saw today in the north part of Sublevel Two becomes larger, more distinct. The images burn themselves into the recesses of my brain. I will never be rid of them for the rest of my life.

Catcher stands in the doorway, his arms folded across his chest. "Need a buzz drink?"

I shake my head. I'm done with the numbing. Done with the gambling and the fighting and every other lie that exists in this province. It's all a way to blind us and make us feel comfortable in our counterfeit lives. Because none of it's true, and I'm tired of pretending it is. Besides, I'll need my full strength and clear thoughts to figure out what to do next.

I finally understand why Catcher is the way he is. Why he doesn't party with other citizens. Why he keeps to himself and lives a different life. Because I am who he once was, and he's probably what I will become. Our minds and hearts are the same, and we don't have time to bother with buzz drinks and mind-numbing music when there are so many lives depending on us. Depending on me.

"I'm sorry you had to see that, Theron," he says. "I wanted to spare you from it for as long as I could, but we're running out of time. And you're not a young Batcher anymore."

No. Not anymore. I'm a fully mature adult, though I don't think I knew what that meant until today. I'm ready to do what needs to be done, and I look up at Catcher, ready for some answers.

"Is that where you were the last few days?" I ask. "With the slaves?"

He motions for me to follow him to his living area, and we each take a seat, facing each other. Watching me with a frown on his face, he looks me over, thinking something through. With a nod to himself, he finally begins to talk.

"No, Theron. I was not with the slaves. I started there, yes. But only for a moment." He rubs his chin before continuing. "Years ago—I'm talking many, many years, before the worldwide Virus—Freedom One was known by another name. It was called Sydney, and it was booming. The landscape was a little different than it is now. The land and water have been manipulated some to fit the needs of Prime Makers in the past, but from what I know, it was a beautiful place filled with happy people."

He can't be talking about Freedom One. Some might use

the words "beautiful" and "happy" in describing this place, but based on the look on his face, I think he means a different kind of beautiful and happy altogether. Something I don't know. Something I want to know, however.

"There were cars in the streets, boats filling the harbor, throngs of people walking everywhere. Sunshine, water, culture. Diversity. It was a dream."

I don't know how he could know these things, but he makes a larger population of people sound like a good thing. So different from what we've been taught since we were small Batchers. Too many people is a bad thing. Too many people means the Virus. Disease.

Catcher leans forward in his chair. "There was an underground rail system, where trains traveled at great speeds through tunnels. People rode these trains from place to place, like a deep labyrinth winding its way through the earth.

"When the Virus wiped out the population, there weren't enough people left to warrant the use of such large machines, let alone enough people to run them. So they were abandoned. Forgotten. The trains eventually fell apart or were buried in the ruins. But the tunnels—many of them—are still there, beneath us, carving paths to places outside this province."

I've never heard of such a thing, but until a few days ago, I'd never heard of surrogates, slaves, or birthing. I'd never heard of a level two stories below the Core building that extends well beyond the dimensions of the building's architecture. If there are underground cages and cells beneath us, why not forgotten tunnels as well?

"Not just train tunnels," he continues. "There's a huge network of paths beneath the surface, spanning the province and beyond. Forgotten water drains, abandoned mines, escape tunnels built during times of war. Sewer, gas, electric, telephone—at different moments in history, all of these required the use of tunnels. Some even spanned the harbor itself, underground and out of sight.

"There were even tunnels here before mankind stepped foot on this land. The sandstone beneath us is soft, and water carved endless paths a millennia ago. But Freedom One has no use for any of these tunnels—the natural or the manmade. I'm not even sure Eridian's aware of how complex the system is beneath us."

I lean forward and balance on the edge of my seat. "What do these tunnels have to do with anything?"

"I discovered them a long time ago. When I was around your age, actually." He stares out the window, watching the late afternoon sky. A few clouds move slowly in the distance. "It was an accident, really. But the timing was perfect."

There's more to his story, a lot more, but I don't think he's ready to tell me all of it.

Catcher turns back to me, and in a low voice, whispers, "That's where I've been, Theron. Traveling through those tunnels to a safe place."

"What do you mean a safe place?"

He waits. One, two, ten long seconds. "A place with the rebels."

I knew it. Somehow I knew it. "You're part of the Rise." I think of the yellow flyers circulating, the surrogates, the slaves. They're all connected somehow.

"No, Theron. I'm not part of the Rise." He slides forward to the edge of his seat too. "I *started* the Rise."

CHAPTER FOURTEEN

Catcher started the Rise? He is the one who's been circulating the propaganda? Eridian's most trusted Healer? He must be the most gifted liar I've met, yet at the same time, I trust him more than anyone I've known. I believe everything he's told me, no matter how ludicrous it sounds.

"When?" I ask. "How?"

He takes a deep breath. "When I look at you, Theron, talk to you, it's as though I've traveled back in time. You remind me so much of the man I once was."

I've thought the same thing, but it's not what I want to talk about right now.

"I started working on the Maker level twenty years ago. Like you, I began working with the surrogates, except back then, the surrogates weren't taken from the rebels."

"Who are these rebels? Is Pua a rebel?"

"It's the name we use for anyone living outside of the

123

Freedom provinces. Anyone who doesn't conform to Eridian's standard of life."

"But where did they come from?"

"They are the descendants of those who survived the world-wide Virus."

"But I thought *we* were the survivors. Our founders. That's why they started the Batcher system. So the Virus wouldn't happen again because of overpopulation."

"Our founders survived, but they weren't the only ones." Catcher presses his fingers to his temples. "Let's just say not everyone agreed with their Batch system idea."

I sit back and tap my good foot on the ground repeatedly. "So if the surrogates weren't originally from the rebels, then where were they from?"

"They were Freedom citizens."

"How can that be? You mean everyone used to know about human incubators?"

"No," he says. "The females were never brought back into the general public. Remember how I told you surrogates can birth baby after baby, for years on end?"

I give him a slight nod.

"Those women didn't know what they volunteered for when they asked to become Makers. They were basically signing their lives away."

So the surrogates were once called Makers too. Back when it was a Trade to be chosen and not a forced punishment. An imprisonment.

"It wasn't long after I started working down there that the Prime Maker at the time brought in Eridian as an adviser. She soon became the obvious favorite of his, the only one he would take direction from. And then—" He chokes on his words.

"That's when the rebels started to come. Scared. Afraid. The females were forced to birth babies, the males forced to work, and the children . . . Well, you saw what the children go through. All of it hidden from Freedom."

"You saw this transition?"

"Yes. Within a few years, Eridian was placed in charge of the rebel servant force, and she threatened any citizen with extermination if we divulged any information about these new arrivals. I was afraid. I saw what she did to those who disobeyed. Those who stood against her." He cringes. "I followed because of fear."

A look of shame crosses his face, then one of sadness. Twenty years of working down there—I don't know if I could do it. No, I *know* I couldn't do it. Catcher is a brave man for what he's done. What he's tried to do.

Catcher stands and walks to the window, his back toward me. "After two years under the new rebel system, I met her." He places a hand on the glass. "She was a surrogate, like your Pua." He lowers his head to the side, as though glancing back at me, then lifts it again to the window. "Or she was slated to become one when I gave her a physical exam and found she had a joint disease I'd never seen before. Arthritis."

"What?"

"It's a chronic inflammatory disorder that attacks the lining of the joints in your hands or feet and can cause painful swelling. She was feeling quite stiff that day. Tired. Almost feverish."

I've never heard of such a thing, and I've seen almost every ailment. At least I thought I had.

"The condition wasn't life-threatening. She seemed otherwise healthy. She explained how she'd had the symptoms most of her life. It would come and go, and she'd found a way to deal with it. Live with it." Catcher sighs. "I didn't see the problem with her carrying an infant, but I had to report it. And when Eridian came to see her, well . . . After everything I'd seen, I should have known."

"What happened?"

"This is why I didn't want you to ask Eri about saving Pua. About her traveling to the Remake facility. Because I knew it wouldn't work." Catcher sits across from me again, his knees almost touching mine. "Eridian sentenced her to die. Even after I pled a case to the contrary. Even after I suggested a Remake for the woman. Eri wouldn't relent. I couldn't live with the woman's death on my hands, so one night, I snuck her out."

"Of her cell?"

He nods. "I didn't know where to go, I just knew I had to get her out before it was too late, or die trying."

Yes. This is exactly how I feel about Pua.

"The province was already starting to fall apart. Not as much as it is these days, but we stumbled into an old passageway close to the slave housing. I heard a noise on the other side of a crumbling wall and pushed through. The place was filled with bats, and we were both terrified, but the reality of certain death for her was worse, and we somehow made it out.

"We wandered for hours that night until we hit a cavern. I left her with a promise to return. I came back to her every night for the next five days, each time with food, each time with a careful tracking of where we'd been as we tried tunnel after tunnel. It wasn't easy on her, especially with her joint condition, but we had no choice. One night we found a large hidden cavern of glass. Trees and bushes had grown along the outside, camouflaging the place. But there was a stream. Room for a garden. Light coming through during the day. It would work."

"Work for what?"

"Our new home." Catcher smiles.

"But you live here. In Freedom."

He laughs, as though that's the most ridiculous thing he's ever heard. "This isn't my home, Theron."

I scrunch my forehead, confused.

"She was only the first. I began to sneak out others. Surrogates, slaves, children. The accounting wasn't as advanced in the beginning of Eri's system, and with hordes of rebels arriving almost daily, no one noticed a few missing here or there. But a few adds up, and soon we had so many living underground in our new home, we named ourselves the Rise, always with the intent to liberate all rebels one day.

"Our numbers continue to grow, though Eridian's record keeping has improved through the years, and things can get tricky. Despite a few close calls, Eridian knows me only as the faithful Healer who keeps her dirty secret, not the leader of the force that intends to take her down some day. Someday soon."

Catcher. Leader of the Rise.

"And is that where you've been these last few days? With the Rise?"

Catcher nods. "All those years ago—when I realized I'd have to sleep at some point—I bartered for more time off than normal. Eridian readily agreed, as I had been producing healthy Batchers for her without many problems. It was a fair trade. Time to deal with the stresses of my Trade in exchange for doing it."

I stand and pace the room. "So you sneak out prisoners, surrogates. Still, to this day? On your days off?"

"Yes."

Suddenly, Pua's fate swells with possibility. "And do you think we can do that with Pua? To save her from being executed?"

Catcher frowns. "The record keeping has advanced, and Pua

is on the schedule. I have no control over that. They'll notice her missing. They'll start an investigation. You've seen what Eridian has done recently in Freedom. She'll stop at nothing to get what she wants. And a traitor on her precious Maker level? She'd want to find him desperately." He stands and places a hand on my shoulder, forcing me to be still. "I've worked too hard for too long to risk it all on a failed escape. I haven't been able to save everyone. I've seen so many people dear to me be sacrificed to protect our cause. But it's been necessary so that one day we can save *everyone*."

"We must save her. We don't have a choice. *I* don't have a choice."

He looks at me carefully, as though gauging how serious I am. "I know," Catcher says, quietly. "We'll figure it out."

My shoulders slump in relief. He understands how much this means to me. But sneaking her out, no matter how we decide to do it, means we risk getting caught.

"Wait," I say. "Is the Rise all within the confines of Freedom, just underground?"

"No. We outgrew that original glass cavern long ago." He heads to his kitchen and pulls out a drawer next to the sink. "Only some of the tunnels leading to our headquarters span beneath the province. Most of the way, Rise Central included, is outside Freedom's boundaries. Including the rebel settlement where most of our people live now."

I join him in the kitchen where he completely removes the drawer, reaching for something hidden in back. "That's impossible," I say. "You would've gotten caught the first time you left the boundaries. The Seekers would have known you'd left by your tracker."

A loud clank followed by a ripping sound comes from behind

the drawer. Catcher stands and turns to me, a small velvet bag in one hand, a tracker gun in the other. "That was easy to figure out." He removes his transmitter from his pocket. Turning it over, he unlatches the plastic cover that holds it together, and it separates in two, a jumble of wires connecting both sides.

He pulls out a tiny glass vial tucked between the wires on one side. It's about the same size as a drug capsule, and he holds it up to the light so we can both see through the clear glass. "This is my tracker. I removed it with a tracker gun many years ago and keep it in my transmitter. Wherever I go, it goes. For all intents and purposes, the Seekers are able to keep track of where I am the same as if it were installed in my head."

"But—" I spin Catcher around and look behind his right ear. Touch the fold and feel a familiar metal nub. "How?"

"I installed a new tracker to replace the real one. Only this one's a dud. It doesn't track my whereabouts. I programmed it so if a Seeker decides to test it on a random check, the light will turn green, no matter what. So long as my transmitter with the real thing is in my pocket, it makes no difference on their map."

He carefully opens the velvet bag and spreads a number of small devices along the counter. They look identical to the one in Catcher's glass vial.

"There are a number of us with replacements. Many living here, in Freedom, who are loyal to the Rise. Who help me. Who help *them*." He glances up at me, expectant.

I step away and rub the back of my neck. I know exactly what he's saying, and it takes me only a few seconds to decide. "Okay," I whisper. "I want it. Of course I do." It was never a question, really. I want to help Pua and the slaves. I want to help Catcher and the Rise. "Can you do it now?" I ask. I don't want to let myself doubt or give myself a chance to change my mind.

"Are you sure?"

I reach for a paper cloth from a roll on the counter, prepping for the open wound. "I'm sure."

Catcher smiles and motions for me to turn around. I steady myself against the counter, flinching slightly when I feel the familiar click of the gun behind my ear. It hasn't been a year since my last replacement, done just before I boarded the shuttle to my Remake. The pain is just as strong, but this time it's my choice, my decision—linked to a cause greater than me. And it feels good.

I press the cloth to my ear while Catcher gently cleans the tracker he removed. Popping it into a small vial, he secures it closed. "It's still working," he says. "Still sending out a signal. Hand me your transmitter."

I reach into my pocket and give it over, watching as he opens it and carefully places the vial between the wires.

"The tracker doesn't require organic material to function, but it does need heat. The inner workings of a transmitter are warm enough to imitate the heat of a warm body." He connects the two sides of my transmitter and hands it back. "Ready for the replacement?"

I put the transmitter into my pocket and nod. Within a few minutes, I have a new tracker in my ear, and Catcher bandages it to keep it from bleeding.

"Don't let anyone see the bandage on your way home," he says. "You can remove it in the morning, and no one will know you've gotten a replacement. Just don't forget your transmitter wherever you go."

"Unless I'm sneaking out a prisoner."

Catcher grins. "Exactly. Transmitter stays home then."

"When do I start?"

He rubs his chin. "The new surrogates arrive today. Which means new slaves as well. It's always easier to move people when the numbers are in flux. Since you don't have days off, night is best. So, tomorrow night?"

I nod. There's no time to waste. I need to learn everything I can before it's too late to save Pua. If I can see where we need to go, maybe I can figure out a way to get her there without raising suspicion. And I have to admit, I'm eager to see Rise Central. Meet the rebels.

"All right," he says. "Tomorrow night after work, head home and catch a few hours' rest. I'll come and grab you after sunset, and we'll make our first run together."

The curfew sirens begin to sound, and I touch the bandage behind my ear. I hope I don't run into any Seekers on my way home.

"Okay." I tap my pocket to make sure my transmitter is there, hoping too, that it's still working like Catcher said it would.

As I reach the door, I turn to face him. "That woman you first helped escape all those years ago—what was her name?"

"Her name is Joramae."

Is, not *was*.

"Is she still alive?" I ask. "Do you know her?"

Catcher's smile grows so wide his eyes disappear. He's happy. What is it that gives him so much joy in a place where everything is despair? I want some of it too.

"Theron," he says, "I married her."

Married.

"I don't know what that means."

"It means"—he tilts his head, as though thinking of the right description—"she's my family."

I narrow my eyes, confused and frustrated at the same time.

Everyone keeps using that word, as though it's the most powerful thing they know. How can one word hold so much within so few letters?

In a small voice, I say, "I don't know what that means either."

"You're wrong, Theron." He pats my shoulder before leading me out the door. "You do know what it means."

CHAPTER FIFTEEN

I know I should sleep. I'll need my rest before tomorrow night, but I'm so anxious about it, I can't think of anything else, and I can't get my body to relax. I keep touching the bandage at my ear. How many others in the province are on the side of the rebels? How many does Catcher have under his command?

The next morning we begin our exams of the new surrogates, and I don't have a spare minute to see Pua. I hope she's okay. I hope she hasn't given up on me. I hope . . . I hope a lot of things. I even hope there's enough hope to spare for everyone on this cracked level.

When I get home after work, my lack of sleep finally catches up with me, and I drift off. I don't wake until someone is shaking my shoulder, and I open my eyes to see a familiar bald man standing above me.

Catcher frowns. "Do you want to do this later?"

I sit up and reach for my shoes. "I'm ready. Lost track of time is all. How did you get in my apartment?"

He holds up a master key, like the ones the Seekers carry. "One of the perks of being one of Eridian's minions." He smiles. "Let's go."

I stuff my transmitter beneath my mattress. "Okay."

Once we're out of my apartment, we walk down the hall. We descend the stairwell, but instead of exiting into the lobby, we move down another level into a basement unit. Catcher's key unlocks the door there. We walk into a warm room filled with a hissing sound, like steam is escaping through a small vent somewhere. Large pipes about three feet in diameter run below the ceiling along a dimly lit hallway. We follow the pipes, walking on a cement floor and turning a corner every hundred feet or so. At the end of one hall, the pipes split into three directions, and we follow the path of the right one.

"What is this place?" I ask.

"Water filtration system." Catcher taps one of the pipes. It's so low, it doesn't take much to reach it. "These pipes run beneath the streets of Freedom, transporting water to every building in the province. The only people who come down here are the slave workers assigned to maintenance and the Seekers guarding them. And they're never here at night, so we should be good."

"Did you travel through this system to get to my place?" I thought he'd snuck out on the street or something, hidden in the shadows.

"Yes." Catcher leads me down another branching pathway. "Because it runs from building to building, it's easy enough to get around unseen."

I follow him down a set of stairs, bringing us to a lower level. It's darker, and instead of long hallways with pipes, this one is cool and moldy. There is an old computer screen secured to one wall with what I think is a map of the province, marking out the water pipes.

"And the best part about these tunnels," he says, unlocking a metal door, "is they lead us exactly where we need to be."

He opens the door, and a faint light from the other side makes the area at my feet glow, illuminating everything from my waist down. Though I can't make out what's in the room, I can at least see where we're going.

We step inside, and a familiar scent reaches my nose. It's the smell of the cages, the giant ones where the slaves are kept.

I grasp Catcher's arm and whisper, "What about the cameras?"

"We aren't going in far," he says. "And the back portion of these cages aren't monitored, just the main hallways."

I nod, trusting he's done this enough times to know what he's talking about.

"Just keep your voice down," he adds.

I stay close to Catcher, and he leads me down a metal path, the sound of our footsteps echoing in what must be a large room. When I hear the voices, a layer of gooseflesh covers my arms.

"Catcher, Catcher, Catcher," they all say. A dozen voices whisper my companion's name.

"I'm here." Catcher halts and pulls a flashlight out of his pocket. He flips it on, shining the light on several men a few feet in front of us. They stand behind a chain-link door.

I step in front of Catcher and thread my fingers through the holes, wanting to pry the door off its hinges. Wanting to help everyone out, right this second.

"Hold on, Theron." Catcher finds a lock and slips in his key, carefully swinging the door open without a sound. He looks up at the men. "I can take two tonight."

They nod and shuffle around, pushing two men to the front.

"Vishal was cut yesterday in the sawmill," one of the men says, motioning to a dark man in front. "On his hand. It didn't look serious, but they refused to let him clean it."

I reach for Vishal's hand and remove a dirty strip of cloth, revealing a red gash oozing pus. "It's infected." I wrap it back up. "We could take care of this easily in the trauma station." A good cleaning and an anti-infection patch or two would do the trick.

"Eridian allows no medical care for the slaves." Catcher frowns. "If they're injured or sick, they're exterminated." He looks pointedly at me.

If they wouldn't spare the resources for Pua or Catcher's Joramae, I shouldn't be surprised they wouldn't spare it for the slaves, but I am. Because this isn't about going to the Remake facility—it's about cleaning a wound and administering a simple drug. This is ridiculous.

"We'll get you to the Rise," Catcher assures Vishal. "You'll feel better in no time."

"Thank you," Vishal says. "My son is coming with us." He puts his arm around a younger man next to him who has similar dark skin. This "son"—whatever that means—looks to be about my age.

"My wife was taken with the surrogates," Vishal continues. "If you find her, could you tell her we're okay? And that we'll be back for her?"

I've no idea what he's talking about, but Catcher seems to know. "Of course," he says, then pauses. "We better get going."

Vishal nods. "We can never thank you enough for this," he tells Catcher, then turns to the other men in the cage. "All of you."

His words hold such reverence, and the silence in the room feels heavy with emotion, I pause for a few seconds to absorb it all.

The four of us file out of the cage, Catcher locking the door behind him, and after a short walk to the underground system, he locks the metal door as well.

"This way." Catcher leads us up the stairs to the water-pipe level, and we spend the next hour navigating endless twists and turns beneath the province. No wonder it took so long for Catcher to get Joramae out all those years ago. It must have taken forever to figure out this labyrinth.

We reach a dead end along one tunnel, a large square grate embedded in the wall. Catcher carefully removes the grate and leans it against the wall, then hands each of us a small, battery-operated headlamp.

"It's dark in here." Catcher points to the large opening. "I'll go first. We're scaling down a set of rungs embedded in the wall, then we'll have to lower into the cavern by a counterbalance system. Theron, you're last. Replace the grate behind you before climbing down."

"Got it."

When it's my turn, I slip the light over my head and lift the grate, securing it behind me as I step into the dark. My dim light illuminates the metal rungs as I climb down. "Are you okay, Vishal?" I ask, thinking of his injured hand.

"Never better," he says with a grunt. He must be in pain, and weak too, but the thought of escape and freedom from that prison must bring a form of adrenaline that can drive a man forward through almost anything.

At the bottom of the metal rungs is a small wooden platform. Square in shape, the perimeter is lined with metal loops with vertical cables running through them. Catcher kneels on one side, fastening a cable to the base of the platform. After securing several more cables along each edge, though not all of them, he tells us to stand in the center. "Hold on," he adds. Then he rotates a lever near his feet, and the entire platform begins to descend.

While Catcher adjusts the lever as we drop to control the speed, I notice the cables shifting through the metal loops, and several bags filled with what must be dirt or sand rise on every side, the counterweights Catcher mentioned. When we land at the bottom, Catcher secures the entire platform in place, and I see several more weighted bags attached to dozens of cables.

"Did you build this?" I ask.

The light from Catcher's headlamp shifts up and down in what I assume is a nod. "I can adjust the weights depending on how many people are on board. It can handle up to a dozen, though there are usually just a few of us on my normal runs."

I glance up, my headlamp illuminating the cable and weights suspended in place. "And it works to go up, too?"

"I just need to latch on the weights," he says. "It's pretty simple."

"It's brilliant," I say.

Catcher moves to the side wall of the cavern and pulls out a lighter. He lifts the flame to light something along the wall, a wick of some kind. Like magic, fire flares every fifty feet or so along the wall, one at a time. The flames stretch as far as I can see and disappear around a bend in the tunnel.

Catcher takes our headlamps and places them next to the lever, ready to go back up for another round of save-the-slave. "No more tech from this point on. That means no electric lights, either." He must see me glancing around the corridor, taking in the vastness of the space, because he adds, "It's a train tunnel."

RESIST

I can see much better in the firelight than with the bright, focused light of the headlamps. The cavern roof rises a hundred feet, the curved ceiling arching around us. Layers of paint and plaster peel from the walls, black shadows of dirt or mold scattered on top of that. This train tunnel is old and hasn't been seen by anyone besides Catcher and his rebels for a very long time.

"We need to hurry," Catcher says. "We'll have just enough time to get them to the meeting point before we have to turn back. We have to be back to Freedom before first light."

We follow Catcher through the giant tunnel. Sometimes the path narrows, sometimes it opens to a larger cavern with a platform and stairs leading up into the dark. The tunnel splits twice as we go, and at one point, a large machine sits on the tracks. It must be a train, one of the many which used to run through this underground maze, but the glass in its windows is broken, a few holes ripped right through the body of the thing.

As we pass it, I can't help but glance inside at the torn seats and bent poles lining the train. I imagine what it might have been like, traveling vast distances at high speeds, even outside the boundaries of the province. It's surreal to imagine people freely came and went all those years ago.

Along one side of a tunnel, a door is set into the wall. Catcher stops. "This is our rendezvous point," he explains. "On nightly runs I can't travel the full distance to the rebels, so this station is set up to handle the prisoners I bring. Rebels take turns at this post, so someone is always here."

He knocks on the door six times. Three long hits followed by three short ones. After a moment, I hear the gears of the locking mechanism shift on the other side, followed by the door opening. A flickering light spills out, as though from a lantern, and an older man steps out with a full white beard, his head shaved. His clothes are patched and plain, but clean and well cared for.

"Catcher," the man says, warmth in his voice. He grasps Catcher's forearm with both hands and grins. "Good to see you back so soon." He looks past Catcher to the rest of us. "Three? This is a good run."

"Two," Catcher corrects him. "This is Theron." He motions toward me. "He's joining our force in Freedom and will be helping me. Theron, this is Evert."

Evert offers a hand, and I shake it. "Hello."

Catcher introduces the other men with us and explains about Vishal's injury. "Theron and I need to get back to Freedom before sunrise. Please transport Vishal to Rise Central right away. He needs a Healer, and quickly."

Vishal leans against the wall and slides to the floor, carefully resting his injured hand on his knee. He looks exhausted.

Evert nods, wrinkles shifting near his eyes. "Not a problem." He grabs something from his pocket and flings it toward a spot deeper in the room. "Wake up! I've got a night run for you to make."

I hear the rustle of movement from somewhere inside. It makes sense they'd have two people at this post. One to take prisoners to the rebels and one to remain on duty. I wonder how many other post assignments are scattered underground.

"This one's been yapping my ear off about his girl." Evert rolls his eyes and points over his shoulder. "I'd feel bad about waking him in the middle of the night, but I have a feeling he'll be glad to get back to her and send someone else in his place for post duty."

"Is that Catcher?" A voice asks from inside the room.

Catcher's eyes narrow, and he angles his head, as though attempting to place the voice.

Evert grunts in affirmation then folds his arms. "Then again, that freckled redhead is a cute one. I'd want to get back to her too."

Catcher's eyes widen, and he turns to me. "We need to go, Theron." He pushes on my shoulder and guides me away from the door, directing me to the tracks.

"What's going on?" I ask. Not that I planned on staying and chatting or anything, but Catcher's sudden need to get moving feels odd.

He ignores me and calls back. "Get them there quickly, Evert. And Vishal, you'll be okay. I promise."

"Don't worry, Catcher." Evert waves to us. "Kai's fast. He'll get them there—"

"Kai?" I interrupt Evert, flipping around and taking several steps back toward him. Did he say *Kai*?

Catcher shuffles behind me, nervous. "Theron," he says in a whisper, a warning.

Evert opens his mouth but closes it when a man steps out from the room. "I'm ready to go. Two tonight?"

It's him. It's Kai. I recognize the black curly hair, bronze skin. He's the one who told me where to find Nine. The one who gave me her room number in the Healer building and left. The one I suspected Nine loved. Who she ran to that dreadful day in the rain.

"Where is she?" I march toward him and push him aside, out of my way. I storm into the room. Nothing more than four walls and a bed. Small, sparse. Empty. I rush back out and grab Kai's collar. I shake it, again and again. "Where's Nine? Where did you take her?"

Kai stares at me more in shock than fright, then he finally opens his mouth. "Theron?"

He remembers me, and that tells me everything.

"Where is she, you scab?" I yell in his face, my voice on the verge of breaking.

Catcher tugs on my shoulder. "We have to go, and they need to take Vishal to a Healer."

I step back. Vishal is still on the ground, but he's unwrapped the cloth from his hand, and I can see red streaks on his skin surrounding the wound. Frowning, I place my hand against his forehead. He's burning up. Catcher's right, he needs medical attention right away. But I'm not done here.

I turn back to Kai. "Is Nine with the rebels? Is she at Rise Central?"

Kai keeps a straight face, but he swallows hard, and I know I'm on the right track.

"Is that where she's been this whole time? With you?" I grab the hair at the sides of my head and pull. Nine is alive. And so close I can feel it.

Kai glances at Catcher, as though asking what he should do.

Catcher clears his throat. "I'll explain on the way back."

"You'll *explain*?" I turn to him, astonished. "Explain what? That you knew she was there?" I rub the tattoo of her name on my neck. That day Catcher asked about it—he knew it was a girl. He knew it was her. "You lied to me," I say through clenched teeth. "You used me." Of course he knew. He's the leader of the cracked rebels. "Was it all a trick to get me on your side, Catcher? Were you going to use her as bait? As blackmail? What? Tell me!"

He exhales slowly. "Let's go back."

I step away from him. "I'm not going anywhere with you." I

point at Kai. "I'm going with him. I'm going to Rise Central right now."

Catcher sighs. "Don't be an idiot. Our time's running out. We have to get back in time." He glances at my right leg, probably wondering if my limp will slow us down.

"I don't have a tracker anymore," I say, flicking my ear. "I don't have to go back. I won't."

Kai extends his hand to Vishal, helping him to his feet. They begin to walk down the tracks the opposite way from where we came.

I charge Kai, grasping his shoulders and shoving him to the ground. "You're not going anywhere without me." It's a weak threat, but if there's a chance Nine is near, if there's a chance I can see her again, I'm not giving it up. Not this time.

Kai stands and rolls his fingers into fists, his eyes piercing mine. He's shorter than I am, but more built. He'd be an even match for me in the cages.

"Theron?" Catcher's voice is soft. Careful. "You can't leave Freedom. Not yet." He pauses and sneaks a glance at Kai before continuing. "Someone needs you."

Pua.

How could I forget? If I leave Freedom now, I won't be able to save her. But I can't abandon the possibility of seeing Nine now that it's here. I don't know what to do. Pressing my palms against my eyes, I scream in frustration. I have to see Nine. I need her. But Pua needs me more.

I finally drop my hands and look at Catcher. "Promise me when I get her out, I can leave with her. That we both can go to the Rise. I don't want to stay in Freedom one second beyond that." I can hold off for a short while longer. I have to.

Catcher's eyes focus on his feet. "But all those prisoners. I need you to—"

"Promise me!" He's lied to me and tricked me, and I don't owe him anything. But despite all of that, he has, somehow, brought back the possibility of Nine. I wouldn't have that without him.

I soften my voice. "I'll continue to help you, but not from Freedom. I'm done with Eridian and her cracked province. I'm done with Seekers and curfews and drinks and gambling. I'm done with all of it. Let me help from this side."

Catcher finally nods in agreement then waves Kai off with the two others. I watch as they retreat, my heart breaking at the thought that he'll likely see Nine soon. It breaks even more knowing that once again I might be letting her go too easily.

CHAPTER SIXTEEN

I follow Catcher through the train tunnels, almost at a run. He doesn't say anything, just glances at me to make sure I'm okay. I wish I could take off without him, or linger behind, but I'm nowhere near able to navigate these underground paths yet.

It isn't until we maneuver up the counterbalance platform, climb the metal rungs, and crawl through the large square metal grate into the water-pipe tunnels that he speaks to me.

"I'm sorry, Theron," he says. "I should have told you about Nine."

I follow behind him in the small space, grateful he can't see the hurt on my face. "How long have you known?"

"From the day she arrived. Three months ago."

So that's where she went the day she left me. To join the rebels.

Catcher clears his throat. "She's the reason I found you, Theron."

"What do you mean?" I ask, confused. *I found Catcher*—in the trauma station the day I drilled a hole in his leg to save his life.

"Nine asked me about you. She knew I worked as a Healer, and she hoped I had met you. Seen you. I explained I worked with the surrogates in the Core building, not in any of the normal Healer Trades, but she insisted I check up on you. So during the last month of your training, I did." He glances at me, then turns quickly away, hurrying through the tunnel. "I observed you a number of times during your Trade tests and studied your file. You're a gifted Healer, and I knew I could use you on the Maker level. Nine was the one who convinced me I could trust you with the truth. About the females forced to carry fetuses, the slaves. She knew you'd be willing to help. Willing to join us."

A sudden flood of emotion pools behind my eyes, and I blink it away, fighting the urge to give in. Nine doesn't hate me. Maybe she even wants to see me again. "But the day you came into the trauma station—it couldn't have been on purpose." He would've died if I hadn't gotten the medicine to his bone marrow.

"No," he says. "I was about to request you as a Sublevel Two Healer with Eridian when that happened. I had just returned from a trip from Rise Central, and I must've come in contact with something I was severely allergic to. I still don't know what it was for sure. But I'm glad it happened—and that I ended up under your care. It was the perfect thing I needed to convince the Prime Maker to let me take you. You really are a skilled Healer, Theron."

I grunt and continue in silence a few minutes. No amount of praise or flowery words will make me forgive Catcher for lying to me the way he did. But at least I understand now why he trusted me so quickly.

"I was going to tell you," he says as we turn another corner. "The whole point of me recruiting you was to bring you to the Rise. It just—it takes time, is all."

Yeah. I get it. I take a deep breath to calm down. It's not his fault we ran into Kai and the truth came out before he had the chance to tell me. But he didn't have to sneak me away when he realized it was Kai behind that door. He could have told me the truth then instead of hiding it.

I think about what Evert said—about Kai wanting to get back to Nine. I wonder if Kai has reached Rise Central yet. Is Nine there counting down the minutes until she can see him too? Will she greet him with a kiss, hold him in her arms? A pang of jealousy shoots through my chest, and my eyes burn with another emotion I don't want. If Kai decides to tell her about me, will she be happy to know I've joined Catcher's cause, or upset I threatened Kai?

All I know is my life has always been about Nine, even when I didn't want it to be. It's going to take a lot to keep me from trying to get her back—get her for myself. Just a few more weeks. I'm strong enough to wait that long.

I have to be.

*   *   *

When we reach the stairwell of my building, I try to leave Catcher without saying good-bye, but his hand on my shoulder stops me. "There's something else I have to tell you," he says.

I fold my arms and wait.

"There are a lot of things you don't understand about the way people live outside of Freedom. How the rebels live—even among the Rise. About families." He holds up a hand before I can respond. "I don't have time to go into details right now, but I will. I promise you, I will. You deserve to know everything. But for now, I need you to know that Pua is a part of Kai's family. She's very important to him."

What? Pain settles into the deep recesses of my core. How can that man have some sort of claim over the only two females I've ever cared about? "I don't understand," I croak. "Does she love him?"

"Yes." Catcher rubs his fingers along his forehead. "But not in the way you're thinking. Not romantically."

"What other way is there to love someone?" My words are heated, frustrated. I hate Kai. I hate him more than anything. He took Nine away from me, and now he's taking Pua. He took her before I even had her.

"There are a lot of ways to love," Catcher says. A sympathetic smile spreads on his face. "Deeper, more meaningful ways than just romance or physical attraction. It's what family is all about."

"Stop saying that word." I want to punch the wall. Hard.

He sighs. "He cares about her very much. Not the same way you do, but he'd do anything to save her. Probably even risk his life."

Sounds the same to me. I frown. "Why tell me this now?"

Catcher steps closer. "Because Kai doesn't know she's here. And it's of vital importance we keep that knowledge from him. And from Nine."

More lies. "Why?"

"Because he cares enough about her that if he knew she was in Freedom, he'd likely come for her himself. Right away. And that would put everything I've worked to build with the Rise at risk. With our plans to attack Freedom and liberate the rebels and slaves." He grasps the air with his hands, his fists held up.

RESIST

"We are so close, Theron. So close to having the resources to do what we've wanted for so long. We can't risk that with an early, unprepared attack. We can't risk giving away our location, our tunnels, everything we've kept hidden until now. I'm asking you, please, don't tell Kai or Nine or any of them about Pua. We'll get her out, and then it will be a moot point. But until then, in case you see them before you can rescue Pua, keep silent about it. I'm only telling you now so you know I trust you. And you can trust me."

I narrow my eyes and nod. I'll keep his stupid secret. Why would I want to tell Kai about Pua anyway? So he can come in like a storm and pull her away from me like he did Nine? No, thank you.

I leave Catcher and return to my apartment. The sun has already started to rise, and I sit on the edge of my windowsill with a glass of orange juice in my hand to watch the show. I shake my head before taking another swig of my decidedly buzz-free drink.

What have I turned into? Staying up all night to save strangers. Abandoning the chance to see Nine after waiting for her for months, especially after learning she still thinks of me, worries about me. Following a man I hardly know yet who reminds me so much of myself it frightens me. All because I want to save Pua—a girl as broken as I am, who probably doesn't care for me half as much as I care for her. What's it all for?

I cringe, thinking about the Theron I am today compared to the Theron I was a few weeks ago. Am I a better person? Or just a different version of the same old scab?

* * *

When I reach the Maker level, I head straight for Pua. The halls are empty, but the cells are full with the new surrogates I began examining yesterday.

It feels like I haven't seen Pua in weeks, though it's been only a few days. She's sitting in the back corner, knees pulled to her chest, chewing on her thumbnail. When she sees me, she jumps up and runs to the door, shaking it as though desperate to get it open. After I unlock it, she pulls me in and throws her arms around my neck, her body trembling.

"Hey," I say, pushing her hair out of her face. I lean back and angle her face up toward mine. "What's wrong?"

She covers her mouth and shakes her head, fighting back tears. She forms a fist with her other hand and knocks my shoulder, her eyes accusing. "You said you'd return the next day. That was three days ago. Where have you been?" Her words are desperate. Frantic.

"I'm sorry." I think back to everything that happened since I told her I'd return. My night of drinking, the torture session with Bron and Eri, Catcher introducing me to the slaves and removing my tracker, helping Vishal and his son escape. Kai. Nine. I sink against the wall, feeling weak. I haven't had a spare minute until now, and I haven't had much sleep the entire time, either, just Lucidate and stress and travel.

"Things came up," I say. "That's all. I'm so sorry." It's a weak excuse, but if I'm not supposed to tell Kai about Pua, I probably shouldn't tell Pua about Kai. My chest aches at seeing her in so much anguish. Something must have happened. She can't be this distraught because she missed me. "I'm here now. I'm here."

She collapses into my chest, and I instinctively run my hand up and down her back to comfort her, but she flinches away from my touch. With my eyebrows drawing together, I turn her around and carefully lift the bottom of her white tank. A tremor runs through me when I see her back, and my fist clenches tight around the fabric.

"Pua," I whisper, the word strangled as it comes out. Lesions spread across her back, lines of cut flesh crisscrossing along her skin. The gashes are fresh, maybe a day or two old. It's as though she's been whipped. My teeth clench together, and I angle her face toward me.

"Who did this to you?"

She tugs her shirt down and moves away. "It doesn't matter. It's not important. I—"

"Who did this?" I ask again, struggling to remain calm. My nails bite into my palm as I make a fist.

Her gaze darts around the room, focusing anywhere but on me. After a deep sigh, she dives into an explanation, her words falling out like a gush of water. "The guards led us to the showers. I saw my chance and took it. I was so tired of sitting around doing nothing but waiting to be killed, Theron. I kneed one of the guards in the groin, stole a card key, and I ran and didn't stop until I hit a dead end. The key helped me find a room to hide in, but a Maker must have seen where I went because they came and tied me up and took me to the third floor."

"The third floor?" Seeker headquarters is on the third floor.

She continues as though I hadn't spoken because she's not watching my lips. "They put me in the prison housing. There were so many other prisoners. And the Seekers . . ." She presses her mouth closed to hold back a sob. "They did this." She points to her back. "Afterwards, one of them—Bron—told me the next time I saw the prison housing will be the last time. Because it will be in preparation for my execution. Then they brought me back here, as though everything was normal."

I'm torn between kicking the wall and collapsing to the ground, the combination of anger and sorrow making my insides twist. I reach for Pua instead, careful to avoid her injuries, and hold her as close as she'll allow, letting her be the anchor in my emotional storm.

"I'm sorry," I say softly, knowing she can't hear me. "I'm so sorry I wasn't here for you." I need to get her away from this place as soon as possible.

I step back and grab both of her hands, waiting for her to watch my lips. "I know what to do," I mouth with no sound. I don't want to risk anyone hearing me, even the other surrogates. "I know how to get out of this level—and out of Freedom. I'm taking you with me to a safe place. Tonight." I know Catcher needs my help, but we're talking about Pua's life. I can help him from the side of the Rise.

"We can't. I—I can't." Her lips tremble.

"Yes, we can." I just need to sneak in here, unlock her cell, get her out, leave my functioning tracker behind, and make a run for it. After I talk to Catcher, that is. He can draw me a map. As long as he's at work, no one will ever know he had anything to do with it.

And there's no way our escape will be tied to the Rise. I'll be a random citizen saving the life of a surrogate sentenced to death. Even Odell knows about the attention I've given Pua; he already suspects something between us. Between his and Catcher's testimonies, I'll be written off as a citizen gone rogue, not a rebel. Catcher and his plans will remain safe.

"You don't understand," she says, lifting one of my hands to her head. She presses it behind her ear. "I can't go because they came in the middle of the night and did this. To me and the new surrogates."

I feel something cold and metallic, and I turn her head to get a better look. It looks nothing like the tracker I'm used to. This one is bigger, more of a strip than a nub, and it follows the curving arch behind her ear. Small wires protrude from the sides of it, penetrating her skin along the circumference. It looks like a metallic insect, permanently attached to her skin.

"What is it?" I touch the foreign silver strip. Her skin is red with irritation where the wires enter.

"It's a tracker." She pulls her hair to one side, rolling it in her fingers, distracted. "They said it's a new kind of tracker, one that can't be removed by a tracker gun."

My eyes go wide, and I look at her again, recognize the panic, the hope being sucked away.

"The Prime Maker is the only one who can remove it, though I've no idea how." Her eyes fall. "The Seekers warned us that if we leave the boundaries of Freedom, a trigger is set off within the tracker, and a poison is released into our brain, killing us instantly."

I crouch, unable to stand anymore. I pull at my hair, my elbows digging into my thighs. "No. Not now. Why now?" I mumble to myself.

Pua kneels in front of me. "And if we try to remove it ourselves . . ."

I glance up and finish her thought. "The same thing will happen. Poison. Death."

She nods and brings her hands to her chest, collapsing into herself. I gently pull her to me. This changes everything. I can't remove the new tracker. And I can't take her if she's wearing it. I have to find Eridian. Threaten her, bargain with her, beg. Anything. I can't let this happen. Pua will die no matter which route we take. This goes way beyond doing something nice for another human being. But Pua is different. She's more. She's—

Family.

The word hides in the corner of my mind. I don't want to acknowledge it. I won't. I don't understand it, yet I've nothing else in my vocabulary to describe the way I feel about Pua. The reality of the situation hangs so heavy on my shoulders, I drop all the way to the ground, and it takes everything within me to keep from melting into the floor. It's too much. I don't know what to do, and I can't bear this feeling of misery and grief. It's a void with no beginning or end. I don't know where I'd go to start filling it up.

Pua lifts my face to look at hers, and I feel the breath rush out of me. Her eyes are soft, her touch a comfort. The warm glow of her skin, the small pout of her lips, the way the light filters through her dark hair. She's so beautiful, it's hard to remember she's in pain, injured. That she's in such a dire situation, her life vanishing like the inevitable change of seasons.

"Theron." She says my name in that amazing accent of hers, and I wish all other sounds would cease to exist. All I ever want to hear is her voice.

My heart swells so much it hurts, and for the first time I think I understand what Catcher meant about love being more than romance. More than physical attraction. Because when I look at Pua, I feel like I get the tiniest glimpse into what love could be. Oh, there's physical attraction—no doubt about that— but I know if Pua were deaf and blind, if she lost every limb, if she suffered some unforeseen tragedy to any part of her body, it wouldn't change the way I feel about her. I want to sacrifice all I have, all I am, to protect her.

Am I setting myself up for more heartache? After all, didn't I feel this way about Nine? It didn't matter how much I was willing to give her, she didn't want any of it. And with what Catcher told me about Pua loving Kai, I shouldn't want to welcome the risk. But I can't help it.

"Theron," she says again. "We still have time, don't we?" She knows she's marked for death, but I don't think she realizes it's in less than three weeks. "We'll figure something out. You and me."

"Yes." Of course we'll figure something out. We—*I* have to. Nine will have to wait a little bit longer.

CHAPTER SEVENTEEN

A rattle followed by a slam makes us both turn to her cell door, where Catcher clutches the bars. "I've just come from the slave housing." He's out of breath, like he ran the whole way. "They all have new trackers, every single one of them."

I nod. "The surrogates as well. But this one can't be removed by a tracker gun."

His shoulders fall, but he doesn't seem surprised. He looks at Pua. "Do you know how to remove it?"

She scrunches her brow. "No. They just said Eridian is the only one who can do it."

"This changes everything." Catcher leans against the door and stares at his hands, as though the lines on his palm will lead him to an answer.

The sound of stomping boots echoes down the hall, and I stand, pulling Pua up with me. I guide her behind me to block her as I face the hall, not trusting whoever's coming.

RESIST

When Odell turns the corner, I panic. A vision of Seekers torturing Pua makes my whole body tense. I want to hide her away. And Odell has already warned me about being near Pua, about working with the girl sentenced to death. I don't know what he'll do this time, when I'm standing in her cracked cell.

Odell marches straight toward Catcher. He stops abruptly and glances at me and Pua, his mouth twitching as if noticing us for the first time.

"It's okay," Catcher says. "Theron's with me."

I think Catcher's trying to reassure him that I'm allowed to be here, but the apprehension on Odell's face says something different. He glances back and forth between me and Catcher, deciding how to proceed.

"Odell!" Catcher snaps a finger in front of his face, impatient. "Talk to me." It's as if Catcher is the one in charge, not Odell. Strange.

Odell exhales slowly. "There's a mandatory tracker check in the Core lobby. I've been ordered to send all Trade workers upstairs. Right now."

I immediately slide my hand into my pocket and feel my transmitter, noticing Catcher does the same. If our trackers are checked, it will come up green, like Catcher said. We shouldn't have a problem. But . . .

"You checked mine a few days ago," I tell Odell. "Why do I need to do it again?"

"What does it matter?" Catcher rests a hand on his hip. "Odell, make sure we're in your line, like always, in case something goes wrong." He stands straighter. "But it won't go wrong."

Odell hesitates, placing a hand on Catcher's shoulder almost as if they're old friends. "You don't understand. It's not a check;

it's a replacement. We've been ordered to remove all trackers and replace them with new ones. Different ones."

Pua's hand moves to her ear, and she fingers the new insect-like tracker attached.

Odell's deep voice becomes so small, I'd imagine he were a Batcher and not a grown man if I couldn't see him standing here in front of me. "You have to leave, Catcher. I mean really leave. Now. While you still can."

"But—" Catcher begins to protest, but Odell shakes his head.

"Figure out the changes later, but if you don't get out now, you don't get out at all."

It finally hits me—Odell is part of the Rise. He's a rebel, working under Catcher's command.

Odell's transmitter buzzes. Catcher curses.

Odell picks it up and says something about the Maker level cleared, and he'll be there in a moment. He squeezes Catcher's shoulder, his face a mix of sorrow and pain.

Catcher wraps an arm around Odell in a brief hug and says, "I'll send word soon."

Odell nods and runs back down the hall.

Catcher turns to me. "Let's go, Theron."

Wait. No.

"We can't leave yet." I slide an arm around Pua's waist, careful to avoid the lacerations on her back. "I have to find a way to get her tracker out first. I have to—"

"You heard what the man said!" He rubs his bald head and speaks between clenched teeth. "We're out of time. We go *now*."

"No. You go. I'll stay. I'll get the tracker replacement, and I'll figure out Eridian's way to remove them, then I can free myself and Pua. It'll work. I can't leave her now."

"A few hours ago you didn't want to come back at all, and

now you refuse to leave. What is wrong with you?" Catcher's face is red, but I know he's not really mad at me. He's mad at Eri, at Freedom, at this broken system that has just made it one degree harder for his rebels to defeat. He'll get over my decision to stay.

Pua flinches when Catcher mentions me not wanting to come back, but I hold her tighter, assuring her I'm not going anywhere.

"I'm choosing to stay with Pua. We'll see you soon."

Catcher marches into the cell and grabs my collar. "You don't understand! You won't be getting a replacement. Because when they take that thing out of your head, they'll see it's not a working tracker. They'll know it's a fake, and you'll be sentenced to die like she is. How do you expect to save her when you're locked away in a cell, Theron? You can save Pua—you can help me save all of them—but you have to leave her and come with me now."

"He's right," Pua whispers. She turns me to her and presses her hands against the sides of my face. "Go with Catcher, figure out a way to stop Eridian, and come back for me."

I shake my head. No. No no no. I can't leave her. I won't.

"Go, Theron. It's the only way." Pua nods. "And I promise I won't do anything cracked while you're gone." She forces a smile, and I know she's referring to her attempted escape, but I can't bring myself to return the smile. Because it's not funny. None of this is funny, though it feels like someone is playing a terrible joke on us all.

This heartache—the pain in my chest—it's all too familiar. Why am I always losing the things I want to hold onto and never let go? My whole life is one endless slipping away. I'm so tired. I'm exhausted from grasping so hard and it not making any difference.

"I can't leave you." My lips are trembling.

Pua's fingers rest against them to still it, then she reaches up and presses her lips to mine, which makes them tremble again. Her kiss is a thousand things at once. A peace, a comfort, a promise of things I don't understand but hope and wish for all the same. It's an expression of love and sacrifice and . . . family. It feels like I'm meeting her for the first time, but the traitorous ache in my chest reminds me this is a farewell.

When Catcher says my name again, quietly yet firmly, I pull away from her lips and press a second kiss against her forehead. "I'll be back," I say. "I'll come back for you, I promise."

She nods against me, though I know she has no idea what I said. She feels it though. We both feel it. This thing between us that's more than anything I've felt before. It takes Catcher pulling on my shirt from behind for me to break away from her, and I don't take my eyes off her as we leave the cell, lock the door, and hurry down the hall.

It isn't until we turn the corner that I have no choice but to look away, and my eyes fill with tears that blur my vision of everything and anything.

It doesn't matter, though. If I can't see her, then there's nothing I want to see.

*   *   *

Catcher presses the button to summon the elevator.

"What are you doing?" I ask. "We can't go up there." The lobby will be filled with Seekers.

We step into the elevator, but instead of the main floor, Catcher uses his fingerprint and key to select L3. Seeker headquarters.

"Are you insane?"

"Maybe." He pulls out his transmitter and motions for me to give him mine. "But we can't leave our real trackers on the Maker level. I can't have them know we made our escape from there. If they do a thorough search of that level, they might figure out how we've been sneaking out this whole time."

When the elevator doors open, I brace myself for a run-in with Seekers, but the hallway is empty. They're probably all in the lobby or other parts of the province, performing their mandatory tracker changes. Catcher is brilliant.

He tosses both of our transmitters under a small table by the side wall. The elevator doors close. "This way they'll think we're making some kind of statement before our escape. Sticking it to Eridian and her Seeker force. A revolution."

"A revolution," I repeat. I'd laugh if that were something I was capable of anymore. But I doubt I'll find my happiness again, at least not until Pua is free and with me to feel it too.

We return to the Maker level, and I follow Catcher to the left, toward the slave housing area.

"The entire slave housing is under surveillance, so we can't go through the water-pipe tunnels, like I usually do."

"Okay." I don't know where he's taking us, but he said the province is filled with tunnels. There must be other escapes.

Catcher sighs. "There's only one other way out of this building. If it were night, I'd probably risk moving to another building first, but we don't have a choice today."

We reach a door at the end of the hall. It was once green, but flecks of paint have fallen off through the years, revealing a rusting metal surface beneath. Catcher unlocks it, and we enter a small room. I immediately smell something that makes my nose twitch. A strange, sickly sweet odor.

"What is that?" I cover my mouth with the back of my hand.

"You're not going to like this." Catcher spins a handle embedded in the wall next to a large, circular iron door. After several revolutions, the door opens, and he swings it wide to reveal a large tunnel spanning both left and right, as though we're entering it from the side somewhere along the path. The tunnel is dimly lit by fluorescent bulbs spaced just far enough apart to reveal that the shallow stream of water running along the base of the tunnel is a murky brown color.

I frown. "It's a sewer tunnel, isn't it?"

"Yes." Catcher steps into the tunnel, and I follow, cringing as my shoes become soaked in the water. "This water's been treated, though, so no risk of disease. It's flowing out of the province, exactly where we need to go."

"That's great," I say.

Catcher chuckles at my sarcasm. "Did you know workers used to ride through here on small boats called canoes to inspect the drainage? We don't have nearly the population they did back then, so the water level is much lower. We'll be able to walk the whole way."

I grunt. I'd rather ride in a boat. At least then I wouldn't have to touch the stuff. "How do you know so much about Freedom's underground?"

He smiles. "You'd be surprised how much you can learn from books."

The only books I've seen are those sold in the antique shop on Main Street. Anything else we need to read, even during our Academic Modules, are on computers. Do the rebels not have computers to do their reading? It reminds me of something Catcher said the other day about no tech beyond a certain point.

"Catcher?" I say. "Do the rebels use tech?"

He shakes his head.

No tech. That means no electricity, no lights, no transmitters. Nothing Techies would discover.

"Of course," I mumble. I don't know why I didn't think of it before. Nine and I wondered once what the Techies in Freedom were used for. They can detect technology, and if the rebels were to use it in any form, the Techies would find them. Capture them. Enslave them.

We walk the rest of the way in silence. When I hear the rush of water ahead, my excitement about getting out of the sewer is shadowed by what I see beyond the opening: the ocean. Standing at the edge of the tunnel, I look down a drop of about ten feet into ocean water below. It's not that high, not compared to jumping out of a sinking shuttle with Nine's hand in mine. But that was before I almost drowned, before the shark came and . . .

"Please tell me there will be a boat this time."

Catcher sighs. "The sewer was bad, but this is the part I knew you wouldn't like."

"I can't swim."

"You won't need to. Not really."

I narrow my eyes, confused and cautious.

Catcher points to a spot of water ahead of us and slightly to the left. "I'm going to dive down, there, to the ocean floor. There are breathing devices there. I'll bring one up for you. Then we'll swim down to a hidden door beneath the surface." He cringes at the panic on my face. "They'll find our transmitters soon enough and begin a search for us. They'll storm the streets, paying close attention to the borders. We can't go back. And we can't stay here."

I glance up and see the red walking bridge nearly above us, the one next to the concert building. We're at the northern border of Freedom, and in broad daylight like this, the Seekers will find us if they head this way.

"This is the quickest way to Rise Central." Catcher hesitates. "You can do this."

I feel light-headed, like I can't get enough oxygen into my lungs. My breathing is too shallow, and I force myself to take deep breaths, no matter the stench. "I—I can't." I look into the water. How many monsters are down there, waiting for prey?

Catcher grasps my arm. "You have to."

Suddenly a siren begins to sound, the same one used for curfew.

Catcher lets out a string of curses before tugging on my arm. "We don't have time for me to swim down and bring you a re-breather. You have to come with me. Now."

And with that, Catcher pushes me out of the tunnel opening, and I plunge into my nightmare.

PART TWO

CHAPTER EIGHTEEN

Dark and light and dark again. I can't tell what's up or down, and I forget how to move my limbs, forget if I even have any. A pressure builds in my head that makes me think I might explode or implode or cease to exist in a flash of light. Then dark. Then light. Everything is a mass of shadows and blurs. I can't remember what I'm supposed to do or not supposed to do. All I know is the water.

The water.

It's everywhere, and I know all too well what lives in water.

Someone, some *thing*, keeps tugging on me, and I tense and pull away each time, expecting to see giant rows of teeth coming at me. But eventually that something gives up, and I don't feel the tugging anymore.

Just light and dark. Dark and light. A game of chasing shadows playing out in my pressurized nightmare. As I'm about to give in, about to inhale the water surrounding me and let myself become one with it, I feel a tug on me again.

The *something* is back. And it's pressing a black rubber device into my mouth. I bite on it and focus on the something in front of me.

It's Catcher. And he has a black device too, bubbles floating out from the front of it.

He's breathing.

I inhale a desperate breath, and the need to explode disappears. When I find my limbs again and can decipher the shadows and light, Catcher pulls on me, and I kick-push-pull my way with him to the ocean floor. A light illuminates the space surrounding more black devices, and Catcher somehow opens a door in the ocean floor, helping me through.

Once on the other side, a loud screeching sounds, and the water begins to drain from wherever it is we're floating. Within a few minutes, we're left standing, dripping, in yet another empty tunnel.

Catcher pulls the black device from his mouth. He rests a hand on my shoulder. "You okay?"

I brush the hair out of my face and tear my own black device away. "I think so. No more water?"

He grins. "No more water. Come on."

I follow him to a set of rungs set in the wall, and we climb. He knocks on another round metal door above us, and after a minute, it opens, revealing a bright room beyond.

"Catcher!" A boy greets us. I'd guess he is about twelve or thirteen, though it's hard to tell for sure. I'm not used to seeing children with a full head of hair. His dark green pants are a little loose, and the scarf wrapped around his neck is filled with holes,

RESIST

but what's more out of place is the gun he has strapped across his shoulders.

"Hello, Landry." Catcher climbs into the room, turning to help pull me up behind him.

Landry runs to the side and grabs a couple of wool blankets, handing one to each of us. "What are you doing coming through the ocean entrance?"

"It's a long story," Catcher says. "And if you don't mind, I'll tell it to you another time. But for now, I'd really like to get home before it gets dark."

Landry's eyes widen. "You better get going, then." He opens a door on the far side of the room and steps back to let us through. "You still know where to change?"

Catcher rubs his hand over Landry's head with a grin. "I think we'll manage."

Landry nods at me as I walk past, then he closes the door behind me.

We're in a dark, curving hallway, the walls made of cement. Torches light the way, revealing yet another dark tunnel. I'm tired of being underground. I hope the place these rebels live isn't buried beneath the earth either. But something Catcher said is troubling me.

"Is it far to the Rise?" I ask.

"This is it."

I know he doesn't mean this particular hallway, or even where we're heading to change from our wet clothes. He means that this is a small part of a larger unit, building, community. But Catcher made it sound like we've still a ways to go.

I pull my blanket tighter around my shoulders. "But it's still morning. What did you mean about reaching your home before dark? Isn't Nine here?"

He slows his pace to fall in step next to me. "This is Rise Central. It's a series of tunnels that run underground, spanning to the opposite side of the harbor from Freedom. There are large rooms here, natural caves carved out of the earth, where refugees from Freedom can stay temporarily, where our rebel forces can meet to make plans. Combat training, rescues, mapping—all of it is done from here. It's the Rise headquarters. But it's not home." He glances up at me. "For me or Nine."

We reach a small room, and Catcher hands me a new set of clothes to change into and lets me do so privately. Then I wait for him in the hall while he changes his clothes.

I lean against the concrete and run my hands through my almost-dry hair. It's a bit stiff and grimy from the seawater, but now that I'm in a fresh set of clothes—comfortable drawstring pants and a loose knit shirt—and surrounded by the flickering firelight against the dark walls, I feel unusually tired. Or maybe not so unusual since I've barely slept the past few days. I don't know how I'll be able to travel the distance to Catcher's home if it will take the rest of the day.

Catcher leads me farther down the tunnel, and I notice several metal doors along the way. Whether they lead to more tunnels or rooms, or are exits out of this place, I have no idea. We pause at one while Catcher goes in, leaving me in the hall for a few minutes. Before the door closes, I catch a glimpse of several shelves filled with books.

When he steps out, his face seems more sullen, more defeated than it did before he went in. He forces a smile. "Just letting them know I'm back. And that I'll be staying indefinitely. At least until we head into Freedom in full force."

I nod, hoping that time is coming sooner than later—especially because of Pua. A heavy weight falls over me when I think of her. Why couldn't I have taken her earlier? One day sooner, and she would be here with me, safe. Not destined to die. Not with a deadly tracker behind her ear and welts on her back.

The cement walls soon give way to red rock—above, below, and along the walls. The tunnel feels like it's on a slight incline, and soon little pockets of light shine from the ceiling through round windows lined with plastic or glass that let in the natural sunlight. The torches become less frequent, until they disappear altogether. The tunnel curves to the left, and I see a bright light ahead. Daylight coming through an opening at the end of the tunnel. As we get closer, a barred door appears, reminding me of the cell doors on the Maker level.

"Good to see you again, Catcher," Evert says as we approach. He unlocks the gate from the other side. The sunlight creates a hazy halo effect around his head.

Catcher's smile is tight, surely wishing we were seeing Evert again under better circumstances. "Help me with the water?" he asks Evert.

"Sure thing."

The two of them fill several plastic bottles and some kind of waterproof sack that looks like it could be made from an animal skin. I strap a couple of bottles over my chest and hold another in my hand.

"I take it 'home' is much farther still?"

Evert looks between me and Catcher and frowns. He hands me something wrapped in paper, about the size of my hand. I unwrap it to find something that looks like bread, only harder and covered in seeds.

"Eat," he says, nodding to it. "You look like you're about to fall over, and you haven't even started."

I take a bite. It's a little salty, but otherwise plain tasting.

It feels heavy going down, though. I take a swig of water and another bite of the dense bread before tucking it into my pocket. As much as I want to stay at Rise Central for a day so I can rest, I'm too anxious to get to where we need to be. I'm tired of waiting, planning, anticipating. I want to be there already. The sooner we go, the sooner we can come back. Besides, Catcher said we'll be there by dark, so it can't be *that* far.

We say good-bye to Evert and walk into the sunlight. I shade my eyes, the sudden change from dark to noonday sun hurting them. But after a minute my eyes adjust, and I take in our surroundings as I hurry through the landscape, following Catcher.

I've spent my entire life in Freedom One, not counting my brief stints on shuttles and my time at the Remake facility. I've seen pictures of snowcapped mountains, lush rain forests, sparse deserts—even experienced them in the simulation machines—but a part of me always thought they were separate, apart. As though from another time, another world. And though as a Batcher I used to watch the waves and wonder what lay beyond the provincial coast, I'd never thought about what lay inland, or how large the land could be.

It was always Freedom and the fence and what we could see with our naked eye. No thoughts about how far you'd have to travel to see snow, to see trees or rivers or wildlife—all those things taught in pictures like a history in itself. But this place. I've never seen pictures like this. I've never imagined this.

From our Batch tower, I could see just beyond the harbor, which is where I assume we are now, heading farther away from the water. Back then, what I had thought were little green specks of plants among rolling, shadowy hills the color of rust turn out to not be plants or hills at all.

It's a graveyard.

The rolling hills are collapsed buildings and abandoned vehicles. But they're old, so old they're mostly buried under layers of sand. Orange and red, brown and yellow—a small range of color covers everything, hiding what really lies beneath from a distance. But up close, I see the concrete. I see the rusted metal that sticks out of the ground like thorns. The shadowy greens are weeds and thistles, smothering whatever they latch on to. Remnants of a life long past. Of a war fought a long, long time ago.

I take several gulps of water. "What happened here?"

Catcher glances around, his eyes settling on a small round stone sticking out of the ground several feet away. No, not a stone. A skull. "The Virus."

Of course. This place must have been heavily populated at one point. People living everywhere. When the Virus hit, everything faded away, people included. It couldn't have been long before the land took over again, swallowing everything back into the earth.

"So much has fallen," he says. "So much lost." He turns and squints toward Freedom, pointing at the water getting smaller and smaller behind us. "There used to be a large bridge spanning the entire harbor from that side of the water to here." His arm drops. "One of the largest in the world. But even that couldn't stand through years of abandonment."

I think of the small red bridge that spans the inlet where we jumped into the water. It's nothing compared to the kind of structure it would take to cross all of this water.

"It's a good thing for us, though." Catcher picks up his pace. "With that bridge gone, Eri and her Seekers rarely come across to this side. They don't know about the tunnel beneath the water. They don't know about the Rise sitting right under their noses. We're safe here."

I take one last look at Freedom—the water, the concert house, the small speck of the top of the Core building in the distance. I say a silent plea to Pua to keep safe. To stay alive. Just a while longer.

The fallen buildings eventually spread out until the artificial rolling hills become random hiccups on the landscape. And then, no buildings remain. The green spots really are plants, low and spiky growth hugging the ground. The shadows are black spindly trees, almost completely devoid of leaves, looking as thirsty as I feel. The layer of dirt covering me matches the rest of the landscape. Rust. We're all the color of rust, whether we're rock or sand or human. Like we're disintegrating together.

I'm relieved when Catcher lets us rest in the shade for a few minutes on the south side of a large rock formation. I rub my leg and finish off my lump of salty bread, then break into my last container of water. It's late in the afternoon, and while part of me hopes we'll reach the rebels soon, another hopes we've still a while to go. Because if where they live is more of this—hot, dense, dry—I'd rather keep walking.

It takes all of my strength to get up again, and I wish there was a way to sleep and move at the same time. I'm dying of exhaustion.

As the sun sinks lower in the sky, I begin to see wildlife. A snake. A lizard basking on a low rock. Small rodents with long ears move swiftly behind a bush and disappear as we approach. I even see several large shadows of some giant creature moving in the distance, though I've no idea what it is. I'm sure we're too far for it to notice us as well. I have no desire to find out its identity unless it's something I can ride on, because my water's out, and I don't know how much longer I can go.

When the sun hits the horizon, the rusty landscape turns to shades of purple and blue, as though the sun has beaten and bruised it. And with the changing color comes the cold. Bitter and sharp. The night is as cold as the day was hot, and I curse at the extremes. This weather is insane. I long for my comfortable bed in my comfortable apartment in my comfortable province by the tame sea.

No. The sea is not tame. I of all people know that. Neither is Freedom, where predators roam the streets, hunting for lurkers out beyond curfew. Where nothing is safe. Nothing is free.

I'll take my chances in the wild desert.

My teeth chatter in the cold, and I rub my arms, massaging life into my limbs. My good leg is as numb as my false one. I've become a master at numbness these last months. Numb, I can do.

Catcher turns to me once, his lips almost blue. "Nearly there." His words sound dusty. He's out of water as well, but he doesn't look worried.

I cling to that confidence like a warm blanket. We're almost there. Almost . . .

The sky is so big out here. I've never seen a sky so big. And the stars, the cracked stars. There are more than I ever imagined. Thousands and thousands of burning blazes in the dark. I could stand to be in the cold a little longer if I knew the stars would be here to accompany me.

I watch as one star falls out of the sky, blazing a trail across all the others. It disappears near the horizon. Or does it? I think I see it, sitting at the edge of the earth. Burning like a fire. It grows bigger and bigger the more we walk, until I see it really is a fire. Not as large as I thought a star would be, but still beautiful. Because fire means warmth. Heat.

I push past Catcher and head right for it. But I'm not the first one. Several others have found the star too, and they sit around it, warming their hands, letting the fiery reflection dance along their faces. But that's okay. There's more than enough warmth for all of us.

Before I reach it, before I can fling myself into the heat, I hear my name.

"Theron?"

My feet shuffle to a stop. Something about that voice is familiar. I know it. I—

"Theron!" A figure runs toward me, and as soon as I recognize who it is, I stumble to her instead of the star. Because she's all the warmth I need. The one thing that will heat me from the inside so thoroughly I'll never be cold again.

My legs stall. Maybe it's from our journey, maybe from feeling overwhelmed with the thought of her. Whatever the reason, I collapse to the ground, landing in a heap before she reaches me.

I feel her lift my head, brush the hair away from my face, and say my name again. "Theron." It's a mixture of happy and sad, relief and worry. But it's the most beautiful sound I've ever heard.

Just before my eyelids collapse along with the rest of me, I try out her name on my lips, welcoming it back like a long lost friend.

"Nine."

CHAPTER NINETEEN

When I wake, I think it's still night at first. The sky above me is dark, and little pinpricks of stars spot the celestial ceiling. But these stars cast thin beams across me, brightening some corners, leaving others in shadows. I'm in a room, a structure of some kind, and it isn't the sky above me at all, but a roof. Metal. Tin. It waves and bends and must be thin with all the holes that have been punched through, leaking light into the room.

And the heat. I should have known by the heat. It's daytime all right. I roll to my side and push up from my bed, which is a pile of blankets strewn along a wooden floor. The wood is gray and weathered, the planks spaced far enough apart that I can see the rusty sand below. I wonder what kinds of creatures live in sand like this. Biting ones? Poisonous?

I scratch at my head, and a shower of dust falls from my hair, sprinkling the linens beneath me. I wonder how anyone keeps anything clean here. I glance around the room. It's small, simple.

Two beds line up against one wall, a small table with three chairs against another. A tall, thin storage cabinet is tucked into the corner. A door to my left with a simple latch. Everything's made of wood. Rough and pieced together, not smooth and sanded. Not with any effort towards design of any kind.

Yet there's something different about this place. Something I can't describe. More a feeling than anything. Life. There is life here. Even though it's empty at the moment—besides me—this place has known life.

I rise to my feet and stretch, willing the tension and soreness from yesterday's journey to ease and dispense into something more manageable. I push on the door and have to duck my head to get through, stepping out into a bright morning. There's no one out here, and I'm almost glad to have a moment to myself to take everything in.

Far to my right is a series of rocks—huge, magnificent rocks that cast long shadows, which, based on the angle of the sun, will soon spread across the structure behind me and provide protection against the worst heat of the day. The stones are regal, about a dozen of them towering like buildings, with smaller ones hovering around the base. The surfaces are variegated with layers of color, dark and light, smooth and rough. They stand guard, curving away down a path, blocking the view of the other side. The only thing I see beyond them is blue sky, crowning the tops of each stone like a smooth ribbon of paint.

Several structures similar to the one I woke in are situated in the immediate area, and to my left, the land slopes downward so I can see more, all of them in clusters of four or five, disappearing into the valley below. Some are bigger than others; a few have sloping roofs, the rest have flat ones.

A number of them are painted, or were at some point, before

the desert sun baked most of it away. But all are made of wood and scraps of metal, probably salvaged from old buildings and vehicles like the ones I saw outside of Freedom. And they seem old. Like they've been here a long time.

A clucking of giggles comes from the stones, and two young girls, no more than six or seven years old, emerge from behind one, chasing each other. The first one has her back turned and bumps right into me. She twists and looks up at me, her mouth forming an "O." Then she continues running from her playmate, as though I were a tree inconveniently planted in the way of her escape.

The second girl twirls something through the air, a split length of rope with two, no, three leather balls attached to the ends. With a laugh, she sends it flying . . . right into me. The rope cinches around my legs, wrapping around me a couple of times. It doesn't hurt, but I'm surprised by its effectiveness. I imagine something similar with heavier weights, aimed at my head maybe, could do some damage.

"I was going for Bel," she says, running forward and untangling the rope from my legs. She angles her head around me to find her playmate. "Wait up, Bel!" Her golden hair is wild and tangled, almost the same color as her skin except where it catches the morning light. It looks as though strings of gold are interwoven with the rest of her hair.

When she frees her rope toy, she squints up at me, shades her eyes, and blurts out, "Sorry, Theron!" Then she bounces down the trail before I have a chance to say anything.

How does she know my name?

I follow, wondering if I'll find other people somewhere along this road. It's obvious whatever this village is—I'm assuming it's the rebel homes—there are many people here. The path continues to slope downward, but around one bend, the rest of the valley opens up, and I get a good look at it spreading before me.

Greenery is everywhere. Tall, leafy trees. Compact bushes. Grasses. It's a stark contrast to the vacant landscape from yesterday, and I almost can't believe this place exists alongside it. The deeper I get into this hidden canyon, the taller the trees become. Though the ground continues to be a sandy dirt beneath my feet, small patches of green grass pop out of nowhere, and I almost want to take my shoes off and see how it feels beneath my feet.

I kneel next to one such patch and touch the blades with my fingers. It's stiffer than I thought it'd be. And surprisingly sharp.

"Careful," says a voice behind me, high-pitched and soft.

I stand and spin to see a petite woman with black hair cropped short. A dark skirt falls to her calves on her small frame. Layers of fabric in varying shades of cream wrap around her torso and shoulders, cinched tight to fit her better.

She leans into a pair of hand crutches, like the ones we use in the trauma station for patients needing to take pressure off their legs as they walk—whether from a break or inflammation of some kind—but these have been retrofitted to span her entire forearm. They wrap around the curves of her elbows, probably to spread the pressure of her weight more evenly. I wonder if Catcher snuck the crutches out on one of his slave runs.

"Those plants may look harmless," she says, "but they have quite a bite if you get too close. Or accidentally fall into them." She smiles widely, and even when her face goes back to normal, a small smile remains, as though that's how she always looks. Her skin is smooth and brown, and she has one of those looks that doesn't clue you in on her age. She could pass for twenty or forty-two. "It's like a lot of things in this world—seemingly harmless, deceivingly beautiful. But when you look closely, you realize it does more harm than good."

"Thanks for the warning." I step away from the plant and hold out my hand to her. "I'm Theron."

She laughs softly and nods. "I know who you are. You slept on my floor last night. And you snore—did you know that?"

I drop my hand, realizing her hands are strapped into her crutches. "Yes," I say with a sigh, thinking of the times Nine made fun of my snoring. "I know."

"Joramae?" Catcher strides up the hill, finding a place beside the slight woman. When he sees me, he smiles. "Theron."

I look back and forth between Catcher and Joramae. She is the one he saved all those years ago. The one he says he married, though I still don't understand what that means. But it's obvious there's something special between the two of them. It's in the way Joramae's permanent smile deepens, touching her eyes. It's how Catcher hovers around her, like a moon to a planet. Always connected, always together, even when apart. I see it when they look at each other too. They speak words that aren't words. A hidden language only the two of them can understand.

"Are you hungry?" Joramae asks me. Her voice is so tender, it makes me want to do or say whatever will make her happy. But I force myself to shake my head.

"No, thank you." It's a lie. I'm starving, famished, but my hunger for something else eclipses whatever corporal cravings I might have. I look at Catcher, pleading with my eyes. "Where is she?" I whisper.

He nods, unsurprised. As though he was expecting me to ask. "Come on."

I follow the two of them down the red sandy path into a clearing. A large tent sits in the center, held upright by long wooden beams. Several individuals sit at tables beneath the canopy. Males and females of all ages. Children too. Some no older than two, others not quite adults, but they look completely different from the Batchers I'm used to. Boys with muscles, girls with curves. It's the strangest thing I've ever seen.

I lean toward Catcher as we walk to one of the tables. "Are there no hormone suppressants here?"

Catcher shakes his head. "No suppressants. No Batchers. No Remake."

So rebels aren't allowed to choose who they'll be. That's why Pua's hair is so long. She never had to shave it off at any point in her life. And her dark skin—the way all of the slaves and rebels look—that's how they were Made.

Catcher helps Joramae to a seat and kisses her forehead. "I'll be right back." The way he looks at her makes me think I'm getting a hint of what contributes to his perpetual happiness.

Joramae's smile deepens, and she waves to me as Catcher leads me away from the tent and down the path again. It eventually levels out, and trees cast flickering shadows across our path from the morning sun.

"I promised I'd tell you about life here, among the rebels. So when you're done with Nine, and when you're ready to get some food in you," he smirks, "come and find me."

"I will."

The main path stretches farther on, but we take a small trail to the right and stop at a small house—a shack, really. A familiar male sits out front on wooden steps, using a knife to sharpen one end of a long stick into a spear. He wears a black, sleeveless shirt, and I can see the ink of a tattoo peeking out from the fabric near his left shoulder.

"Morning, Kai," Catcher says.

Kai lifts his head and glances between me and Catcher, a small frown on his lips. "Morning."

"Is Nine around?" Catcher scratches his chin. "She was going to stop by my place this morning, but—" He gives me a sidelong glance. "I figured she'd be with you."

Kai glares at me, not shaken one bit that I'm giving it right back to him.

He returns to sharpening his stick. "Ani's washing clothes by the river." He tilts his head over his shoulder, as though pointing in the direction we should go.

"Thanks." Catcher turns to me and points along the small trail. "Continue on this path. You'll hear the water ahead. If you can't find it, or her, follow the trail back. I'm sure Kai will be more than happy to help you out." Catcher reaches out and lightly smacks the side of Kai's head.

Kai harrumphs, but I see the corner of his mouth twitch as though he might smile.

Catcher squeezes my shoulder and whispers, "Good luck."

I watch him walk back to the main road before I turn and head down the small trail, wondering why Kai called Nine "Ani." Tall grasses scrape against my legs, and the sharp angle of the sunlight cutting through tree branches gives the air around me substance, as though I can see every bug, every dust particle that floats around me. It's grounding, and strangely comforting.

I begin to hear the faint trickle of water, increasing to a steady but calm flowing sound. The path widens on both sides, the dirt at my feet covered in patches of grass leading to the water. A large basket rests on the ground at my right, a handful of wet clothing sitting inside. But no Nine.

I look out to the water. It moves so slowly, I'd guess it was some kind of lake or pond, not a river. The glare on the surface reflects into my eyes, so I shade my eyes and squint, looking farther out.

That's when I see her.

About halfway to the other side, she stands in waist-deep water, her head back as she looks up into the sun. I'm certainly not getting in the river, not when there could be hungry monsters I don't know about lurking beneath. So I open my mouth to call for her, but the sound catches in my throat, weighed down with emotion. She looks so beautiful out there. Peaceful. Content.

My legs buckle, and I lower myself to the ground, sitting with my knees pulled to my chest. I shade my eyes and watch her for a few minutes. Her hair, longer than I remember, is dark and wet from the water. Her arms stretch behind her, as though she's offering herself to the sky, the sun, the vastness. She's like a sunflower, angled toward the sun, soaking in life. I can't see her freckles from here, but I can picture them dotting her arms and face, speckling her skin like magic dust.

She's different. So different from the Nine I grew up with. Even different from the Nine who left me three months ago. Or maybe not. Maybe I've just never seen her like this, out in the open, so full of possibility. Perhaps Freedom—the only place I've really known her—is the one place she isn't free. There's something heartbreakingly beautiful about seeing her like this.

She suddenly drops her arms and raises her head, tilting it as though she heard something. When she turns to me, she mouths my name. I swear I can hear it from this distance. "Theron." A smile grows on her face, and she dives into the water, her arms rotating and feet kicking as she propels herself toward me.

She's swimming. *Swimming.* When did she learn to do that?

I stand in anticipation, but probably shouldn't have bothered, because as soon as she's out of the water she's diving into me, and we're on the ground again. Only this time I'm almost as wet as she is as she drips all over me.

"Theron." She holds me tight and buries her face into my chest. Her fingers dig into my arms, her hands shaking while she makes quiet sobbing noises.

I envelop her in my arms, pull her closer, and rest my cheek against the top of her wet hair. "Nine." It comes out like a sigh. A long, relief-filled sigh. I've wanted to see her for so long, waiting and waiting for her to return to me. I don't mind the minutes we spend in silence, holding each other. If I don't let go, she can't get away from me again.

She eventually pulls back and looks up at me, her green eyes light and alive like the plants around us. "I was worried I'd never see you again."

She was worried she'd never see *me*? I'm relieved, really I am. She's not mad I came. She actually wants me to be here. But as I recall, she's the one who left.

Nine rests her hand on the side of my face. "And then last night when you collapsed, I couldn't sleep at all because I was so worried about you."

"I'm fine." I frown a little. If she was that worried, why didn't she stay the night with me? We've slept by each other's side our entire lives. If she'd really missed me, she would have been there when I woke.

Things are different. *She's* different.

Even the way she dresses. Not that I've seen her in much else than a white tank and gray sweats, but I never imagined seeing her like this. Fitted, dark pants with holes worn through at the knees, loose threads at her waist. She squeezes the excess water from the brown shirt she wears, covered by what looks like a khaki-green vest with cords and old mismatched buttons keeping it all together. A smear of mud runs along one forearm, and her hair brushes against her stiff shirt collar made of what looks like leather or some other rough material. She looks tough.

I glance down the path that leads to Kai. My being here isn't enough to pull her away from him. Not even after we've been separated for months. I keep reminding myself it doesn't matter—that I still love her—but I don't want to think about the empty feeling in my gut that knows I'm not the most important person in her life anymore.

I once told her she's the only thing I've got, but then I think of Pua, realizing that's not true anymore either. So where does that leave us?

I push wet strands of hair out of her face. "Are you well?" I swallow hard. "Safe? Happy?"

She presses her lips tightly together and nods. "I'm okay. I'm okay." She looks away and blinks, drying the wetness from her eyes. "I'm sorry. For leaving you when I did. I didn't want to—"

"Don't," I say, interrupting her. "I don't want to talk about it."

She forces a smile. "I missed you."

"I missed you, too." I lean forward to give her an innocent kiss, but she pulls back and turns away again.

I sigh, trying to think of something to say to fill the awkward silence. "So . . . this Kai of yours. He's a bundle of sunshine."

She tosses her head back and laughs. "He's not that bad once you get to know him." There's a new glint in her eye as she thinks about him. I can't remember if she ever had that glint for me.

"Get to know him?" I say, my voice heavy with sarcasm. "I can't wait. It's at the top of my to-do list."

She giggles. "Oh, I missed this."

I grin. "Missed what?"

"The way you make me laugh. The way you . . . just *you*."

186

I want to believe her. I sigh and ask, "This is where you've been this whole time? With the rebels?"

Nine untangles her hold on me and rises, pulling me up with her as she does. "Yes. Kai and I . . . when we escaped Freedom, we came here and decided to stay to help with the Rise. We sent word home to Kai's family—the ones I told you about who live on an island in the ocean—and told them we were safe but wouldn't be home for a while. We wanted to help Catcher." She grabs her basket, and I reach for it, offering to hold it for her.

I follow her through the trail, thinking of Pua, her connection to Kai. I wonder if she's part of this family Nine speaks of.

"When this is all over," Nine says, careful to keep her eyes off mine, "we're going back." She clears her throat. "It's my home now, too."

She doesn't know about the Seekers attacking the island. About them capturing Pua and doing who knows what to whoever else was there. I want to tell her. It's obvious they mean a lot to her, but I promised Catcher. I can't risk it, not yet.

"We," I say, repeating what she said. "You mean you and Kai."

She spins around, and I pause midstride. "I need to tell you something. It's important." She looks down at her stained shoes. "I love him."

I know you do, I want to say. And I don't know what to do about that. It's not fair he won her over when I wasn't there. I stay silent and wait for her to continue.

"And . . ." She looks up at me, confirming she has my attention. "I married him. Kai and I . . . we're married."

"Married?" It's what Catcher said about Joramae—he married her.

Nine smiles. "I love him," she repeats. "And he loves me. We're going to spend the rest of our lives with each other. We

made a promise to do just that. To stay together. The two of us."
She pauses, making sure I understand what she's saying. "Only
the two of us."

The part of me that knows Nine knows her meaning without
her having to explain. She's not trying to make me feel unin-
vited or unwelcome. She's telling me there will be no physical
relationship between us. Ever. She wants only Kai. I want to ask
why we can't share her, but I tried that argument several months
ago, and Nine left me. I don't want to scare her away right when
I got her back.

Somehow, some way, I can understand her decision. Because
there was once a time I could think of being only with Nine and
no one else. To love another person so completely—it may not
be common among the citizens of Freedom, but there's something beautiful about it. A form of hope, faith, a complete trust
in another that's freeing too.

When we turn the corner, Nine speeds to a run toward Kai's
house. I hang back, thinking about this promise Nine spoke
of. While I understand wanting one person, I don't understand
how you can commit to them for the rest of your life. How do
you know you'll still love them ten, twenty, fifty years down
the line? It sounds too idyllic. I swallow hard, thinking of how
long Catcher and Joramae have been together. Maybe that's the
appeal, too. It's a quest for perfection, a commitment to make
things right, or at least as right as you can.

I wonder if I could ever make a promise like that to someone. A flash of light brown eyes crosses my mind, and my heart
skips a beat. I wonder if someone would ever want to make a
promise like that to me.

CHAPTER TWENTY

As I reach the side of the house, I hear two voices teasing each other. One of them with a distinct accent that sounds a lot like Pua's.

"You stink."

"I do not." Nine's familiar laugh echoes in the small clearing.

"You smell like crocodile pee."

"There are no crocodiles in that river."

A deep laugh. "This is Australia. There are crocodiles in every river."

"Well, I've never seen any back there. Maybe I taste bad."

A long, silent pause. Then, "You taste fine to me."

"Shh!" A string of giggles.

I turn the corner and see Nine on Kai's lap, her fingers pressed against his mouth to silence him.

Her hand falls, and she extends it toward me. "Kai, meet Theron. Theron, this is Kai."

"We've met," I say.

"Sure." Kai's eyes narrow into slits. "If by 'met' you mean slamming me to the ground while threats fall out of your mouth in a steady stream."

I should remind him we met before that, months ago when he told me where to find Nine in the Healer building, but I'm not in the mood for another argument with Kai.

Nine shoves a finger in his chest. "Be nice."

"I *am* being nice. Trust me."

Nine stands and steps back, her hand finding a place at her hip. "You know how important this is to me."

Kai sighs and stands, extending a hand. "Good to meet you," he says to me. "Again. Properly."

I shift the basket in my arms and shake his hand because Nine gives me her *be nice or else* look, though I don't want to be polite to this man. More than anything I want to ask if there's a cage in this place and have a go at him. I'd like to place a bet on that match.

Nine watches our hands break apart. "You're right," she tells Kai. "This is weird."

He raises an eyebrow as though to say *I told you so.*

"What's weird?" I ask.

She reaches for my hand. "My best friend and my hus—" She pauses, glancing at Kai as though wondering what to call him. "—Kai. You and Kai. Together in the same place. It feels . . ."

"Wrong?" I don't know why I say it. Frustration. Impatience, maybe.

"No." She shakes her head. "Having you with me never feels wrong, Theron." Her voice lowers. "Different. It just feels different."

I know. Because she feels different too. No matter how much

I miss the Nine I once knew, I know I'll never get her back the same way I once had her.

Nine wraps an arm around Kai's waist. "Theron's going to help me hang up Ivy's laundry." She glances at the basket in my hands then raises both brows, as though asking me if that's okay.

I offer a small smile and nod, wondering who Ivy is.

She looks at Kai. "I'll find you later?"

He grunts in the affirmative. "I need to help Catcher with the pulse machines anyhow." He leans down to kiss her, and I turn away, surprised at how easily she gives in to his kiss when a few minutes ago she evaded mine.

I feel a hand slip through my arm, and I move the basket to my other side. Nine leans her head against my shoulder as we walk to the main path, leaving Kai behind.

"Where are we going?" I ask.

"To Ivy's home. She's an older woman, a widow. I help her out with simple chores sometimes. Laundry. Gathering water. That sort of thing."

"What's a widow?"

She twists her mouth, deciding how to explain it so I understand. "It means the man she married has died. They have no children, so she lives alone now."

I don't understand what children have to do with anything, but as I think about this Ivy person, and Kai and Nine, and Catcher and Joramae, something clicks in my head.

I look to where we left Kai. "So you live back there? With Kai?"

Nine lifts her head off my arm. "For now. The family who built the house left on a steamship not long ago, on a recruiting trip up north."

I don't understand half the things she's talking about. "And it's just the two of you?"

"Yes."

"Is that what a family is, then? Getting married?"

"Yes," she says. "But it's more."

A series of shouts catches my attention. A few adults have gathered in a clearing, practicing kicks and punches as though training for a cage fight, though there are no cages here. Several people stand along the perimeter of the clearing, watching as two men spar in the center.

Nine notices my gaze and grins. "Does the Batchling want to volunteer to fight?"

I crack a smile, remembering the time I volunteered to be pummeled in the cage to keep Nine from fighting. It happened in another time, another world. One that doesn't exist anymore. This world is filled with truths I never knew, never wanted to know. But now it's too late.

If there's anyone who can tell me the truth in a way I can understand, it's Nine. I swallow hard, grasping for the courage to ask the question I've wanted the answer to for so long. "Will you tell me about families?"

Her face lights up, and I swear I see tears building in her eyes. "I would love to, Theron. But first I need to tell you what happened after the crash."

The practice session ends, and the two men leave with the crowd, their morning workout finished. I wonder if fighting is a sport here, or if they're training for something specific. Somehow, I don't think anyone makes bets on fights in this rebel village.

Nine watches my face for a minute, then grabs the basket from my arms and walks toward the empty clearing. She drops the basket and spins around, motioning with her hand. "Come on."

I stand there, stunned. Not knowing whether to walk to her or laugh or scratch my head in confusion.

Nine unfastens her vest and shrugs it off, then ties her hair back with a simple string. She rotates her arms as though to stretch them, then sends a few kicks high into the air. Whoa. I've never seen her do that before. After bouncing on her toes a few times, she rests her hands on her hips and tilts her head at me. "What are you waiting for?"

I enter the clearing. "What are you doing?"

"Hands up," she orders. "I want to show you something."

I'd rather fight than do laundry any day, but not against Nine. The idea is absurd. "I'm not going to—"

Suddenly her back leg spins forward into a side kick that comes dangerously close to me. No, not dangerous. Controlled. I've no doubt she could have made contact—serious contact—if she wanted to.

I jump back, my mouth falling open.

She laughs, and her cheeks flush. "I've been training every day since we got here. For months now." She sends a double punch toward my chin, holding her right arm suspended in the air. "All of the rebels train under Catcher's orders. We're getting ready for an attack on Freedom."

I swallow hard. Nine participating in an attack is the last thing I want. I never would have considered it. Yet seeing her here, like this, I wonder if I never gave her enough credit.

I reach forward and grasp her fist, guiding it to her side and moving it out in a punch again. "You want to twist it," I say. "Palm up at your side, palm down when extended." I make sure her first two knuckles are aimed at her target, lining up with her wrist and forearm. "Good."

She mimics the motion again and again, her face determined to get it right. I watch her carefully. The clothes she wears are barely damp, the heat and sun doing a quick job of drying them. The freckles across her face are so familiar, I feel as though I could close my eyes and I'd still know exactly where every one of them is. A part of me wants to lean down and kiss each one. Another part of me says I made a mistake leaving Freedom and coming here to the rebel camp. I have a feeling both parts are wrong, and they'll need to find common ground. Soon.

"The crash?" I ask, reminding her what she wanted to tell me.

"Remember how you told me to kick away?" she asks, practicing her double punch in the air.

I don't have to answer. She knows I remember.

"I did exactly what you asked." She brings her right leg up into a front kick, followed by her left. "I kicked and kicked. All night long. And more. I don't really remember; it's kind of a blur. I woke on a beach, and Kai and his father found me there."

"What's a fath—"

She stops and stands straight, resting a hand on my arm. "I'll explain everything, I promise."

I nod and she continues.

"They took me into their home where they lived with their family—father, mother, children. Hemi was there. And Kai's twin, Puangi. We call her Pua for short."

I take in a sharp breath; I can't help myself.

She folds her arms across her chest, tilting her head in confusion at my reaction.

I know she promised she'd explain everything, but I have to say something to cover my gasp. "What's a twin?"

She twists her mouth as though thinking about it. "Kai and Pua were . . . Made at the same time."

"Like us?" I ask. "They are from the same Batch?" I think of Pua's bronze skin, black hair, and light brown eyes. She does look like Kai in the same way most Batchers look like each other.

"Not exactly," she says with a laugh. She goes back to practicing her kicks.

With her leg outstretched, I clasp her foot and rotate her ankle forward so her foot points in line with her leg. I bend her toes back a little, pressing the heel of my hand to the ball of her foot. "This is where you make contact," I tell her. I stand in front of her with my legs bent, extending my hands out as targets. She alternates kicks, aiming for my palms each time. "Good."

I think about Pua living with Kai. Have they known each other their entire lives? I guess if they were Made at the same time, they have. Again, it reminds me so much of me and Nine.

"They all lived together in the same building," Nine continues. "No Fosterers, no Farmers, no Seekers, no Makers. They kind of did the jobs of everyone themselves. Like *all* of them, helping and contributing and sacrificing. It was nothing like Freedom, Theron. Children weren't isolated or living in Batches. They lived with, and were taken care of by, their family."

A completely different society. A different way of living. It doesn't seem like the smartest or most efficient, but I can see the appeal of being around adults and learning from them one on one.

"They didn't have electricity." Nine pauses and takes a few deep breaths. Long enough for me to absorb that piece of information. "Like, at all," she adds. "No dish machines or vehicles or ways to communicate. Not even simple lights."

"Because of the Techies," I say.

She nods. "They were hiding from Freedom. From Eri." A shudder goes through her when she says the name. "They went to a lot of effort to become invisible, to protect the ones they cared for. To live how they wanted to live."

Living together in these family groups doesn't sound like much of a threat to me. How could they be a danger to Freedom? Why doesn't Eri leave them alone? Why bring the rebels into the province? Visions of surrogates behind bars and slaves in cages pull at the edges of my mind, and I think I do know why they are brought here, though I still don't understand it completely.

"I've learned so much from them," she says, moving into a knife hand attack. "How to work and clean and cook." She cracks a smile at me before extending her forearm and stopping her hand an inch from my chest.

We used to make fun of Nine and her inability to cook, but then I remember the night before she left and how she made pasta in my apartment from scratch. I'd never thought much about how she'd learned that.

"Kai even taught me how to swim and catch fish in the ocean."

Kai taught her to swim. My mouth clenches together with a tight jaw. I bet Kai taught her a lot of things. Things that should have been for Nine and me to figure out together after our Remake.

I focus on her outstretched hand, lining up her fingers and tucking in her thumb, making sure her fingertips are flush. I tap them against my palm to show her where to make contact. But all I can think about are how many things I missed during our months apart.

"I thought you had died, Theron. In the ocean. I thought about you every day on that island. Every minute. But I'd finally gotten to a point in my life where—I don't know—I could live without feeling crippled by the memory of you."

I turn my head away. Is she saying I was easy to give up? My mind knows she's not. She admitted it herself—it took a long time. Wasn't it that way for me, kind of? When I thought she had died? It felt impossible to move on at first, but eventually, living day after day wasn't crippling. I didn't feel sad all the time and could live a life. Maybe not a full one, but a decent one. It wasn't until Nine returned months later that I realized how much she meant to me. That I wanted to hold her and never let her go again. Too bad it wasn't enough.

"I fell in love with Kai." Her arms fall to her sides, and she clasps her hands together in front of her. "I fell in love with him. And his family. And the way they live, and that's why I married him."

"But I love you." It's out before I can stop it. And though it may have changed, transformed into something less distinct, less sure than it used to be, it's still true.

"I love you, too, Theron. But I love you like a brother."

With a frustration I can't contain, I say, "I don't know what that means."

She thinks for a minute. "It's the way Kai loves Pua."

My heart twists, thinking of the two of them having any kind of relationship. If Kai is going to be with Nine and only Nine, why would he have feelings toward Pua? I don't understand.

"It's not a romantic kind of love."

My eyebrows shoot up. This is what Catcher was trying to tell me.

"It's caring about someone so much, you'd do anything for them. Sacrifice for them. Protect them."

Nine hasn't explained anything because I don't see the difference. The same pang of jealousy shoots through me when I think of Kai and Pua as it does when I think of Kai and Nine.

She smiles with a sigh, bringing her leg up into a round-house kick, stopping just short of my shoulder. "I know this is very confusing." She holds her fisted hands up. "Think about our life together as Batchers. How close we were."

I close my eyes and imagine Nine young, bald, and clinging to me. The way I held my fists up against those who picked on her. The way she'd help me with my academic work.

"Now imagine if we'd never had our Remake. No . . ."

I open my eyes to see her biting her lip, thinking of another explanation.

"Think about us always as children, always under the hormone suppression. Never becoming male or female. Never maturing."

I narrow my eyes. "What about it?"

"Wouldn't you still love me, then? We wouldn't need a romantic love to care about each other, to sacrifice for each other. Just the fact that we felt the other person was more important than ourselves is enough. That's how I care for you still. What it's like for Kai and Pua. What it's like for Catcher when he looks at those slaves and surrogates, and how it tears his heart out to see them imprisoned. It's because he loves them. Even when he doesn't know them, he loves them."

She knows about Sublevel Two and what happens down there.

I take a deep breath. "It sounds so complicated."

"Then that's my fault." She sends another roundhouse kick into the air. "Because it's not complicated. It's simple. It's the simplest thing, to care for another person so much you forget yourself. That's what family is all about."

"Family." I think about the word while I adjust her base leg, showing her how far she needs to turn it to get the right angle for her roundhouse.

"That's what I want with Kai. I want to have children together with him and grow old together and—"

I step back. "Have children together?"

She smiles shyly up at me. "Yes. I want to get pregnant and have babies and—"

"Whoa." I run my fingers through my hair and pull at the ends of it. "How do you know about pregnancy and babies?" I thought that was a Maker level secret. Did she say she actually wants that to happen to her? For all of Catcher's efforts to rescue the surrogates from the Maker level, I wouldn't think anyone would want that to happen to them. I must have heard her wrong.

She frowns and wipes the sweat from the side of her face. "Birthing babies is nothing like it is in Freedom. They've got it wrong. It's not all pain and anguish and imprisonment. It's beautiful."

I slowly walk backwards to the side of the clearing. I can't believe I hadn't thought of it before. There are children here. If people get married, the way Nine described, and birth these children . . . then are there surrogates here too? A way embryos are made? Surgical rooms for them to be implanted? How else could they make this happen?

"This is why they don't use electricity," she says. "This is why they hide. Because Eri and her cracked Seekers find them and kidnap them and take them to Freedom to be used as surrogates."

"And as slaves," I add.

She nods. "When I was still on the island, my tracker started beeping. I thought the Seekers would find me there. If they did, they would find Kai's family too. So Kai and I left the island." She glances up at me, sorrow on her face. "We went to a camp south of Freedom, but it was horrible. They kept the people locked up, shoved together without proper food or clothing or living conditions." She shudders with the memory.

I think of everything I've seen on the Maker level and nod. This doesn't surprise me at all.

"They were sorted and taken away to be used by Eridian in her sick and twisted idea of a perfect society. They are used to Make us. To sustain us. And those they didn't need, they . . ." Her voice trails away, but I know what she'd have said: They were killed, because they were no longer needed.

Like Pua.

"It's all wrong," she says, pushing loose red hairs away from her face, a sheen of sweat on her forehead. "And Eri has kept it from us. From everybody."

"And that's what the Rise is fighting for." I think of everything Catcher has told me about a better way to live. A better way to be free.

"Yes. She needs to be stopped. And we're gathering together to figure out how to do it. How to fight back. How to save the ones we love."

I wonder how many of these people know someone trapped in the slave housing. Know one of the females forced to birth Freedom citizens. After seeing what was happening, I knew

I wanted to help Catcher. We have to go back and save them somehow. Save those children. Save Pua.

I still don't understand something, though.

I step close as she slips into her vest and begins fastening it closed again. "Nine, how could you want to carry a fetus? Do you not understand what that entails?" Before she can answer, I add, "And how would you get an embryo in the first place? Do the rebels have a way to implant it in you?"

"Oh, Theron," she says with a glint in her eye. "This is the best part."

CHAPTER TWENTY-ONE

That doesn't make sense," I say, shaking my head. "No way."

Nine has just finished telling me sex—or *making love* as Kai calls it—is how babies are made.

"It's true," she says. "You need a male and a female to create life."

As we walk along the path, I remember the laboratory Catcher took me to, where the back room held the containers labeled EMBRYOS. Refrigerated columns and doors stood in the front room. I bet if I looked again, they'd be labeled sperm. And eggs. Items Nine says are needed to produce embryos.

"But why does no one get pregnant in Freedom?" We both know it's not because there's no sex taking place.

Nine's face clouds over, and she turns away. "They do something to us during our Remake so we can't reproduce on our own. Only the Makers can do it."

"That's why they still made me go," I whisper, "even though I didn't choose anything different for my Remake."

She nods slowly.

I have no desire to create life in the way Nine explained, but it's strange Freedom took the choice away from me—from all of the citizens—in secret.

We reach Ivy's home and walk around back to where ropes are tied between trees, held taut. Nine shows me how to hang the wet clothes we brought from the river along the ropes so they'll dry without a drying machine. The fabrics are the same simple earth colors I've seen on the few rebels I've come in contact with so far. I wonder if they don't have access to finer fabrics or vibrant dyes, or if they prefer to not call attention to themselves like people do in Freedom.

As I secure the last piece of clothing in place, I feel Nine behind me. Her hand slides into my hair, fingering its length. She tugs on my collar, and her fingers touch the tattoo of her name. She traces every letter, reminding me of when she gave me the temporary version. It feels so long ago. She finally drops her hand and leans back against a tree, bracing one foot on the trunk.

I face her, my eyes drifting to her stomach, envisioning a life growing inside her. I look away. "Why is it so important for Eri to take that ability away? So they can control the population? So they can avoid another Virus?"

Nine shrugs. "That's what Eridian told me."

There's something more, but I can't put my finger on it. "That's why they divide the rebels," I say. "Separate the males and females. So they can't reproduce. Because they still have the ability."

Nine gives me a sad smile. "That's what a family is, Theron.

One female and one male get married. They make a promise to be together for the rest of their lives. And they have children together. They teach them and raise them and love them."

"And Freedom takes it all away." No wonder the rebels want to fight back. To rescue those captured. To stand up for their way of life. They want to save their families. "Is this how all rebels live? In these families with one male and one female?" I think of Pua and wonder if that's what she wants someday too.

"Mostly." Nine smiles. "When they marry, you call the female a wife, and the male a husband. When they have children, the wife also becomes a mother. And the husband a father. Pua and Kai have the same mother and father—their parents—which makes them part of the same family."

"Is that why Kai doesn't love Pua the way he loves you? Because they come from the same parents?"

"Yes. When you have the same parents, you're siblings. The males are brothers and the females are sisters." She laughs. "You can't marry a sibling."

Brother. That's what Kai is to Pua—her brother. "You mentioned others in their family. Back on the island."

"Hemi and Tama." She smiles. "Both of them brothers. But family is more than blood, Theron. I'm part of the family too, even though I'm from Freedom. There's a bond between us that is hard to define. It's how I feel about you, too."

"Having a family," I say, more to myself than anything. "This is important to you. This is how you want to live." They aren't questions. I already know the answer. She's already chosen it.

Nine nods. "I want it so badly, Theron. And Freedom, Eridian—all they do is take it away. We have to stop them."

"Do you think Pua wants to have a family?"

She makes a funny face. "I'm sure she does."

I gulp and push down the blush beginning to spread on my face. I can't let Nine know I've met Pua. That I know where she is. What will happen to her if I can't save her?

Nine sighs. "I miss Pua. I consider her my sister. She's taught me so much." She gives me a teasing look. "And she's very beautiful."

You have no idea.

Her smile fades. "I know this is a lot to take in at once." Nine slides her hand into mine. "About sex and babies and families. The rebels, the slaves, the surrogates. The Rise. But I want you to know I'm here for you, whenever you have questions. Okay?"

I nod.

"And Kai will be glad to answer any questions too."

I scrunch my face. "Yeah, that's not going to happen."

She giggles and rolls her eyes. "He's really not—"

"—that bad once I get to know him," I finish for her. "You told me."

The freckles on her face dance as she grins. "He knows how important you are to me. So you're important to him."

It's my turn to roll my eyes. "Yep. A real charmer that one. I think from now on he'll lie awake at night imagining ways to kill me. I don't know what you see in him."

Her eyes sparkle as though she's thinking about him, and I regret bringing it up.

"Why does he call you Ani?"

"It's the name I chose for myself," she says, her eyes glancing to my tattoo. "Nine is who I left in Freedom." She probably thinks it's who she left behind with me. It doesn't really matter, I guess. To me, she'll always be Nine.

"Can I kiss you?" I ask, interrupting her thoughts.

She releases a small gasp. "No, Theron. I'm sorry, but no. And you need to stop thinking about me in that way."

"What way?"

"Romantically."

"I don't understand how showing you how I feel makes any difference to this marrying thing you've chosen. I'm not trying to steal you away from him." I know it's not what she wants.

"But the way you used to touch me and hold me," she says, "it's different now."

"I know," I mumble. I want to change the subject. Talk about anything but the fact that Nine doesn't want me the way I wish she did. "You're an amazing fighter, by the way."

She grins. "You think so?"

"Yes." I ruffle her hair, pulling it out of her tie and watching it flop wildly around her face. "We should have practiced together, as Batchers. I could have taught you to fight back then."

"Well, you're teaching me now," she says. "You should help teach the others, too. We could use another fighting instructor."

"I'd like that," I say. Fighting I can do. "Though I admit you make it easy."

She tucks her hair behind her ear. "We always did make a good team, didn't we, Theron?"

I press my lips together and give her a tight smile. "Yeah, we did." How I wish neither of us said it in the past tense.

*　*　*

We crowd around the small table in Catcher's home, sitting on stools and buckets. Nine sits between me and Kai while Hattie stands on my other side, shifting closer and closer with each passing minute. Hattie is the golden-haired girl who snagged me with her rope toy this morning and, as I've just learned, is Joramae and Catcher's child. That's how she knew my name.

"You probably haven't had any decent food for a while," Joramae tells me, switching my empty plate for another full one. "Maybe ever."

I'm stuffed, but I can't get enough of the roasted root vegetables and slabs of steak she's cooked up. I've never had anything that tasted so rich and delicious, especially for breakfast. And the fried bread things doused in sugar—it's like I have tongue sensors in my mouth I never knew existed until now.

Catcher stands and forces Joramae to sit at the table. "You've made enough food to feed the entire village," he says. "Now sit and enjoy some of it while I clean up."

She opens her mouth to protest, but he silences her with a quick kiss. She blushes and turns to the rest of us, dishing out a conservative portion of food for herself.

Hattie's fingers tug on the back of my collar. "What does your tattoo say?" Before I can answer, she keeps talking. "It doesn't look like Kai's tattoo. His covers half of his chest and stomach and a little bit into his shoulder but it's not even words at all but these weird swirls and lines but not like a picture of something more like just a pattern and—"

"Hattie." Joramae's voice is soft but piercing. Scolding.

Hattie dips her head in an apology, but her eyes are still trained on mine, waiting for my answer.

I sigh, trying to keep my face from turning red. "It says *Nine*."

"Like the number?" Hattie tugs on my shirt again to get another look, as though she doesn't believe me.

Nine laughs a little. "It's my name."

Hattie scrunches her brow and looks at Nine. "But your name is Ani."

"Yes," Nine says. "But it used to be Nine. When I was a Batcher. Your father used to have a Batcher name, too."

Hattie's eyebrows shoot up. "What was it, Daddy?"

Catcher keeps his back turned as he cleans the small kitchen area, but he answers over his shoulder with a laugh. "I was Three."

"Three," she repeats, thinking hard. "Like our family. You, Mom, and me. Three of us." She turns to Nine. "Ani, does that mean you and Kai are going to have"—she counts carefully on her fingers before her face lights up—"seven children?"

Kai chokes on his bite of food, but Nine grins and takes it in stride. "You never know."

Hattie giggles and presses her hand against my face. "What about you? What was your number-name?"

I cringe. "Fourteen."

Her eyes go wide. "You better find a wife quick, then. You're going to be busy."

"Hattie!" Joramae breaks her usual quiet tone. "I think it's time for you to go out and play."

Hattie leans over and gives her mother a quick kiss on the cheek, oblivious to what she said that was so wrong. After throwing her arms around Catcher's waist and squeezing as tight as she can, she bats her eyelashes at me then bounces out of the small house. Nine's laughter fills the space, and Catcher's shoulders shake more than they did before.

"I'm so sorry about that, Theron." Joramae's face is pink. "That girl has no filter."

Nine nudges me in the side. "And I bet she wishes she were a decade older, because that girl's got a crush on you."

I swallow hard. The only experience I've had being around children was either giving hormone shots during my Healer training, or when I was one. It's amazing how unabashed they can be. Innocent. Yet honest about things. What Hattie said about having children makes me think of what Nine told me this morning.

I clear my throat and speak loud enough for Catcher to hear, though I look at Joramae as I speak. "This morning, Nine told me how children are Made among the rebels." I glance at everyone around the table. Kai and Joramae seem a little embarrassed, but Nine nods slightly, a smile on her face. "But she also told me our ability to reproduce is taken away during our Remake. So how is it Catcher has a daughter?"

Joramae slides her hand over mine and pats it. But before she can answer, Catcher steps to the table. "What they did to you during your Remake to prevent you from reproducing . . . it's reversible."

I pull my hand away and rest it in my lap under the table. "Reversible?"

He nods. "It's not complicated, either. When you're ready, I could do it for you. I've helped many former citizens who've escaped Freedom over the last two decades. Male and female."

Citizens? I thought Catcher only helped slaves and surrogates get out. And he said *when* I'm ready, not *if* I'm ready. As though I would automatically want the ability to have children. To have a family.

I shove my chair back from the table. "Excuse me." I stand and nod toward Joramae. "Thank you for the food." Then I turn and leave before I start punching the walls of her home in frustration.

I head toward the large stone towers that mark the start of this rebel village. Winding through the maze of rocks, I find a quiet, shady corner and drop to the ground, leaning against a low boulder. I rub the back of my neck and think about my tattoo. It represents not only a person, but a lifestyle. Where Batchers become citizens and where the right to choose everything is the norm. Not husbands and wives and birthing children outside the boundaries of the Core building. Not families.

Of course in Freedom they've taken away that choice. No one knows it was once a possibility. Why would Eridian keep that secret? What's wrong with reproducing on our own? What's wrong with having families? No matter how foreign and strange it sounds to me, it doesn't mean it shouldn't be an option for people who want it. And it's obvious a lot of people do want it. Including Nine.

But there must be something wrong with it. Some kind of danger to Eridian or to Freedom. Something more than over-population. But I've no idea what. I just know my brain can only take so much new information, and the thought that I might be able to reproduce—have children and a family of my own—is overwhelming.

The sound of shuffling feet comes from around the corner. I glance up and slide my hand through my hair, expecting Nine to come into view. But it's not her. It's the last person I want to see. The one person I wish I'd never met in the first place.

Kai.

CHAPTER TWENTY-TWO

I hold up a hand to stop him before he starts. "I'm not in the mood for a lecture." *Especially from you.*

"Don't flatter yourself," he says, kicking a small spray of dirt in my direction. "I'm just walking through to get to the pulse machines on this end."

"Pulse machines?"

Kai rolls his eyes before turning the corner and disappearing from view. A whole minute passes before he peeks back around the stones, scrunches his forehead, and mumbles, "You coming or what?"

I stand up and dust off my pants, then follow the path through the giant stones until I see a large stretch of desert expanding before me. I have to shade my eyes from the sun. I see Kai about a hundred feet ahead, walking seemingly to nowhere, and I hurry to catch up, falling in step beside him.

"Where are you going?"

He doesn't answer, just keeps walking. I've been around the guy a grand total of two hours, and I'm already used to his indifferent attitude about everything and everyone. I was half kidding when I asked Nine what she saw in him, but seriously, who would want to be around someone like him all day?

When we're about a quarter of a mile out from the rock formation, we stop in front of two large manmade cylinders resting on the ground. Each is as long as I am tall, but one is composed of a thick opaque plastic while the other is clear. I can't see much beneath the clear plastic, though, because the dirt and sand has rubbed the material into an almost pinkish-white.

"Is this a pulse machine?" I ask, though I know Kai won't answer. "What does it do?"

He removes a panel from one end of the opaque cylinder, checking to make sure wires are plugged in where they need to be. "I don't know much about electricity," he says, his voice gruff, "but I know these things destroy it."

"Destroy electricity?" I crouch and peek behind the panel he fiddles with. "How?"

He sighs and points to a black panel bent over the center of the cylinder. "This takes energy from the sun and makes the gears or whatever work in the tube." He replaces the panel and makes sure the bolts connecting both cylinders are secure. "There's a timer, and every so often the wire coils in this one are triggered." He drums his fingers along the top of the opaque cylinder, making a low, echoing sound. "It blasts out an electromagnetic pulse that destroys any form of tech within miles."

I know the rebels don't use electricity, so this must be a weapon to use against someone else.

"It destroys any Freedom devices."

Kai nods. "If they can't get their computer screens or

transmitters up and running, they can't communicate out here. Or navigate for that matter."

I picture the Seeker guns in my mind. They run on electric triggers and connect to digital readouts. I bet these pulse machines take out their weapons too.

"And this has kept them away all these years?" I ask.

Kai shrugs. "Catcher says they've had to move several times in the past, but for the most part Freedom devices stop working miles away, and those idiots don't know why. I've never seen them near this place."

I dust a layer of sand off one of the tubes. "How many of these pulse machines are there?"

"Twenty-four," he says, standing and squinting toward the south. "Spaced evenly around the perimeter." He starts walking again, and I follow without being told this time.

We pass the remains of a fire, ash spread among broken bits of charred wood. Several seats made of tree stumps and logs surround it. It makes me remember something that could have been a dream.

"Last night," I say. "Was there a fire? Out here beyond the village? I think I remember a fire, but I'm not sure if it was real."

He grunts, which I take to mean *yes.*

"And Nine, was she—"

"Let's get something straight," he says, stopping me. He glances over my shoulder toward the stone pillars in the distance before staring at me with his usual sour face. "Things are different here. With the rebels. With families. And whatever you think used to be between you and Ani isn't—"

I lift my hand to stop him. "She already gave me the 'I'm going to be with Kai and only Kai' speech, all right? She made it clear there will not be a physical relationship between the two of us. You don't need to worry about her."

A smile tugs at the corner of Kai's mouth. "Oh, I'm not worried about Ani. She can make her own decisions and take care of herself."

I think of the Nine I used to know. It was always *me* taking care of *her*. I was the one she'd turn to when she needed help or someone to confide in, to find comfort in. When she left me, I convinced myself she found a new someone to take care of her—Kai. It never occurred to me the person she replaced me with was herself.

"Then what is it?" I ask.

"It's *you* I don't trust."

"Like you said, Nine can make her own decisions. I don't know what that has to do—"

"Ani's told me a lot about Freedom," he says sharply. "About the way you people live there. Even within your Batches as children, you slept together, showered together." His expression sours even more. "She told me some of what goes on in Freedom Central. The kinds of lives you lead with brothels and gambling and drinking and partying. I don't care if you don't buy into the way we live here. I don't care if you're done hearing about *family*." He sizes me up. "I can't stop Ani or Catcher or anyone else from trusting you and welcoming you here, but I won't put up with any of your Freedom habits that threaten our way of life. And I won't apologize for holding you to that, whatever it takes."

I may not be ready to embrace the rebels' lifestyle, but I'm certainly over anything and everything having to do with Freedom and its ridiculous Prime Maker. "That won't be a problem," I say, keeping my voice steady despite Kai's thinly veiled threat.

It's the most he's spoken to me since I arrived, and I know if I want to have anything to do with Nine, I'll have to get along with Kai. Not that we're going to become best friends or anything, but having him acknowledge me in a room or conversation would be a start.

Kai nods, satisfied with my answer. "Good. With that out of the way, I'm supposed to tell you someone's waiting for you at Catcher's house to take you to gather water." The corner of his mouth twitches, and I raise one side of my mouth in response.

"Thank you," I say, my mood lifted. I step back and pause, my chest tightening for a moment. I make sure I have Kai's attention before adding, "For everything." I take a deep breath. "For saving Nine. For taking care of her. For teaching her how to take care of herself. For bringing her back to me." I swallow hard. "And for letting me have her now. Though it's not the way I always wanted, it's more than I expected I'd get these last months. So, thank you."

I wait for a response this time; I'm not going to let him get away with ignoring me.

He waits. He looks at me as though really seeing me for who I am and not as a threat to be handled. Then he lowers his head in a nod and continues to walk away toward the next pulse machine on his list.

Coming from Kai, it's as good of a concession as I'm going to get.

I'll take it.

* * *

I find Nine in front of Catcher's house, two buckets dangling from each hand. She twirls in a circle, the buckets catching air from the force and gliding up and down through the air. If she could spin fast enough, I wouldn't be surprised if they propelled her straight into the air. She looks more free than I've ever seen her in Freedom, and it confirms to me everything about that place—the choices and the equality and the freedom—are good principles applied in a cracked way.

"Hey, you." I reach up and grab two buckets from her freckled fingers.

"Theron!" She jumps in surprise and giggles. "I didn't see you." She glances over my shoulder. "You didn't kill him, did you?"

It's my turn to laugh. "No," I say, ruffling her hair. "In fact, you were right. Kai isn't so bad once you get to . . . well, you know."

She laughs harder, and when it gives into a sigh, she says, "Thank you. For not completely writing him off."

I can tell it means a lot to her that the two of us are getting along—relatively speaking. So I will make an effort, because I know it's important to her. Like Kai knows I'm important to Nine, which is why he's making an effort, too.

I nod and hold the buckets in the air. "Where to?"

Nine leads me past several clusters of homes. Many have small garden areas surrounding them, but we also walk past a fenced-in area where a dozen people work in a field of crops laid out in rows. It reminds me of the fields on the other side of the red bridge. But instead of slave children working the fields, it's rebels. They are not forced to work, they do it out of necessity. And by choice. These people make me view choice a lot differently than the way I've always known it, because there are consequences for what they choose to do. And those consequences aren't hidden two stories below them.

We pass an orchard, followed by a small cluster of boulders.

On the other side the grass is smooth and lush, and it runs up a small incline to a pool of water. It's only about five feet in diameter, but it's nice and clear. A small spout of water pours directly out of a rock above the pool, feeding the pond.

"It's a natural spring," Nine says, positioning one of her buckets below the flow of water. "We do our washing in the river—clothes, dishes, bodies—but that water's not good for drinking. We do have a well in the center of the village." She waves her hand over her shoulder. "But this stuff tastes much better. Almost as good as the water on Mahawai."

"Mahawai?" I exchange an empty bucket for her full one.

"It's the name of Kai's island. Where I washed up after the crash."

I swallow hard. "And where his family still is?"

She smiles. "Yeah. His sister and brothers. Their parents. I miss them so much. We plan on going back as soon as the rebellion is over."

I think of Pua and what she told me about Seekers attacking their island. About them taking her away and how she has no idea what's happened to the rest of her family. If they're even alive.

"Have you heard from them?" I ask, my voice cracking.

"Not yet," she says. "But we sent them a message. Even if they do send something back, it could take months. It takes a while to travel by steamship."

I wonder if there's anyone left on the island to receive her message. What if her family was stolen like Pua, taken to be slaves? Or worse, killed because they weren't needed or because they were having children without permission from the Prime Maker. I've seen what Eri's capable of within our province; I don't want to see what she's capable of outside Freedom's boundaries.

"You have to know something, Nine." I switch places with her and begin filling one of my buckets. "Eridian is looking for you."

Nine nods as she watches the water pouring out of the spring with deep concentration. She's not surprised.

"No," I say, trying to get my point across. "She's *really* looking for you. As in completely tearing the province apart to figure out where you went."

She looks up at me, eyes wide. "What?"

I wonder why Catcher hadn't told her, but then I realize I'm the only one who knows Eri's motivation behind her behavior. "Things changed the moment you left." I swallow hard, pushing the memory of that awful day deep down. "She started a province-wide curfew. There are random apartment searches. Frequent tracker checks. Interrogations." I squeeze my eyes tight, the bucket of water in front of me reminding me of another, larger basin of water and the torture I went through. I put the bucket down and glance at her. "The Prime Maker has become so desperate, people are disappearing." I think of Setia. "Dying."

Nine drops to the ground and brushes through the hair on the side of her head. "I had no idea," she whispers. "I know she's crazy, but I didn't think she'd take it out on everyone else. Even the citizens?"

I drop to my knees in front of her. "Why does she need you so badly?"

She snaps her mouth closed, and her eyes dart to the side. "I . . . I don't know."

Doesn't she realize I know when she's lying. "Nine?"

She looks back at me, her eyes watering. Her bottom lip trembles as she speaks. "She told me I was an experiment."

I scrunch my brow. "What do you mean?"

Nine sighs, defeated. "My freckles, Theron. My red hair." She pulls at her hair. "I was Made this way on purpose. I wasn't an accident."

I told her that, too, when we were Batchers. I've never seen her differences as something to be mocked, something to question. But I've always been curious about why her Maker would have Made her that way. And now that I understand how infants are really Made, how embryos are formed, I wonder who Made Nine.

As though answering my question, Nine says, "Eridian used to be male. She became female during her Remake, and she used some of her own sperm to Make me."

I force myself to swallow the gasp that wants to escape. Eridian is Nine's . . . father?

Nine pulls my hand into hers and grips my thumb and pinky like two handles keeping her in place. Grounding her. "She said she wanted to Make someone different from everyone else, so instead of being my own person when I was finally Remade, I'd want to be like everyone else. To belong. To become . . . like her."

Her hands shake in mine, and I pull her into an embrace, rubbing her shoulders to still her shudders.

"She was right, at first. All I wanted was to be like everyone else, but after the crash and the island and Kai—" She hesitates. "I just want to be me. And I definitely don't want to be like Eridian."

"You're nothing like her."

Nine sniffs and looks up at me. "She's got to realize that by now. I left and I'm not coming back. It's almost as if . . ."

I give her a moment, but she doesn't finish. "As if what?"

"She told me there were others. People watching me,

watching us. Waiting to see what would happen with me. She acted so relieved when she found me. As if there's something more to me. To her experiment." Nine pulls away and grips one of the bucket handles. "Did she say anything to you about me?"

I think of what Eridian said—Nine is the only one who can save us, that she's the key to everything. And I think she's right. There's something more than Nine being tested as a social experiment. If Nine's at the crux of the survival of Freedom, there's something much more going on, but I've no idea what it could be. As much as it scares me, I don't want to frighten her either.

"She's just been looking for you," I say, keeping Eridian's words to myself. "She knew we were close and so she asks me about you all the time, thinking—" I look away.

"Thinking what?"

"Thinking that I was important to you. That you might come back for me some day." I can't disguise the uncertainty in my voice. We both know she was never coming back.

"You *are* important to me, Theron." She rests her palm against my face. "That's why I had Catcher look for you, teach you. Bring you to me."

"I know." But it's not enough. It never will be. And there's nothing I can do about it.

CHAPTER TWENTY-THREE

When we reach Catcher's home, he's standing out front, talking to Kai.

"What's going on?" Nine asks as we get close, resting our water on the ground.

Kai extends his hand, and Nine grasps it, stepping close to his side.

Catcher rubs his forehead. "Two of the pulse coils are busted." He glances at his wife, standing inside their door. "And we're out of supplies to fix them. I want to take Kai and a couple others to Rise Central to gather what we need."

"Can't it wait?" Joramae says quietly. "You just got back."

Catcher frowns. "I don't like having that big of a hole in our defenses. Not even for a day." His expression softens. "And I can't send someone else." He says it as though anticipating what her next argument would be. "I want to see what's going on in Freedom with the aftermath of Theron and me leaving. And

221

maybe find out more about those new trackers they're putting in everyone."

Joramae steps out and leans in close to her husband. "Be careful," she says, worry written across her face. She's spent so many years away from him, waiting for him to come back as he has basically been undercover in enemy territory. The way she looks at him now, it's obvious he's everything to her. I can't imagine the worry she must feel every time he leaves. I glance at Nine, at her spotted nose and fire red hair. Maybe I *can* imagine it.

"I will," he says. "I won't even go into the province. I'll just meet with my runners. They'll fill me in. Then we'll grab the supplies we need and be back within a day and a half. It'll feel like no time at all."

"Catcher," she whispers. "It always feels like a lifetime."

He pulls her close and kisses her as though she's the only one here with him, as though she is the most important person on this entire planet. It makes me think of someone else.

I clear my throat. "Catcher?"

He finally breaks his kiss and turns toward me.

"Can I come?" I ask.

He frowns. "No offense, Theron, but we'll be moving fast." He glances to my busted leg.

I curse this cracked injury but swallow my pride. "I understand." I pause, wondering if I should wait until we're away from the crowd, but finally say, "Can you . . . Will you check on—" I steal a glance at Nine and Kai, swallowing hard.

"Yes." Catcher gives me a look. He knows who I'm talking about. "I'll check on her too."

I nod, and my shoulders relax. I hadn't realized I'd been so tense.

Nine looks at me funny, as though wondering who I was

asking about. Then she looks up at Kai. "I'm going to stay here. With Theron."

Kai nods. "We won't be long."

Joramae sighs. "Well, can you at least wait until morning? It gets too cold out there at night, and I don't want you freezing your fingers and toes away."

Catcher looks conflicted, surely thinking of the broken pulse machines. But it's two devices among twenty-four; it can't hurt to wait a few more hours. He relents.

"Okay," he says. "But we leave before dawn. Kai?"

Kai nods. "I'll let the others know."

* * *

I dream I'm standing at the edge of a lake, feet firmly pressed into dry ground. The water is so still that it looks like glass, and I think I might be able to walk along the surface. But when I take a step forward, my foot sinks below the water. It's not too deep, and my wet foot feels as solid as the one on dry land, but it still scares me. Because I can't see below the surface. I can't see where my foot has gone. There could be monsters living down there that bite, strange creatures that slither and strangle.

But as I'm about to pull my leg back, the ground begins to rumble like an earthquake. The trees along the bank shift unnaturally, and the dirt at my feet separates and gives way, forming new lumps and crevices, changing to something less solid. Less sure.

It's as if I don't know this land anymore like I once did, and I want to escape. But the only place I can go is into the water. And I'm afraid of what's in there. I'm afraid of what I don't know. So I stand there, hesitating, deliberating between the shaking ground and the still water.

Something flies in front of my face, a tiny fluttering of iridescent wings. It's a butterfly, turquoise-blue and black wings waving in front of me.

Which should I choose? I ask it. *Water or land?*

The butterfly hovers in the air for a fraction of a second, then flies right into my face, making me flinch and duck, my hand swatting in front of my face. In that moment, I realize I have lost my balance, and I'm falling to one side, directly into—

"Theron!"

I sit up quickly, my hand swiping across my nose to swat something away.

A pile of giggles sits on the floor in front of me in the form of a little girl.

"Hattie?"

She twists her lips and raises one brow. "Do you know you snore?" She holds up a large brown feather from who knows what kind of bird and giggles again.

I rub my nose, wondering how long she'd been tickling it while I slept. I glance at her other hand where she holds fast to a small wooden toy in the shape of a girl, complete with a miniature dress and hat. Now I realize what I'd seen in Catcher's apartment. He must have been making a toy for his daughter.

Joramae walks in through the front door with a wide basket strapped to her back, her hands fastened to her crutches. "Hattie! I told you to let the poor man sleep."

"I was bored," she says, standing from the wood floor. "And Daddy left hours ago. I want Theron to take me to the coop."

Joramae glances at the feather in Hattie's hand. "Looks like you've already been. Besides, you go to the coop most mornings by yourself."

"This one's from yesterday." She swoops her hand through the air, as though the feather turned her fingers into birds and they can fly. "And Daddy promised he'd take me today. But—" She glances at me on the floor, tangled in blankets.

Joramae opens her mouth to say something, but I stand and stretch, glancing at the morning sun through the cracks in the walls. "It's okay," I say. "I'll take her."

Hattie grabs my hand and leads me out the door, Joramae whispering a quiet "Thank you" as I leave.

We hurry down the path past the central tent and several houses. But before we reach the community garden area, Hattie pulls me to the left, away from the main path. This trail is narrower, waist-high fences running along both sides. The fences are made of wood, wire, slabs of plastic—whatever material the rebels could find and repurpose. And on the other side of the fences are animals. A few I've seen before, the cattle and pigs. Others I've seen only in pictures, the goats and sheep. Several of them I can't identify at all.

"Do you farm these animals?" I ask Hattie.

"Of course not. I'm only seven."

I suppress my smile and clarify my question. "No, I mean the rebels. The community. Do they raise these animals for food?"

"Yeah," she says, swinging our arms between us. "Pig for pork, cows for beef, chickens for . . . chicken." She giggles. "But some of them we don't eat. Like the lambs."

"Lambs?"

"Yeah. The little fluffy ones. Aren't they cute?" She points to our right, and I glance over the fence to see a few dozen sheep in a wooden pen.

"What are they used for then?" I ask.

"To look at," she says, matter-of-fact. "Because they're so darn cute." Her voice rises at the end, and it makes my smile grow.

I have a feeling I'm not getting a proper education on the farming of animals here among the rebels, but from what I can see, I get the gist of it. The rebels are completely self-sufficient, doing the unwanted Trades alongside desired ones. Though by the way Hattie bounces and hums on her way to the coop, I think sometimes it must be hard to tell the difference.

We reach a long building framed in wood and covered in a mesh wire so the chickens can't escape. Hattie grabs a cupful of some kind of grain from a canister with a hinge and hands it to me. She unlatches a door on one end of the coop and walks right in, waiting for me to follow. The coop ceiling is high, but I still have to bend my head to fit through.

Hattie reaches into her pocket and pulls out vegetable peelings, scattering them on the ground of the coop. "We give them our leftovers sometimes, but mostly they have their feed." She points to the cup in my hand. "Your turn."

"You want me to feed them?"

"Yeah, it's easy. Just toss it."

I hold the cup above my head, like I'm about to throw the whole thing across the enclosure in one swoop.

"No!" she yells, her eyes wide. "Not like that." She dips her fingers into the cup and tosses the grains evenly in front of her. The birds flock to where the food goes, and she nudges me to try again.

"But they don't know me," I say. "How can they trust I'm feeding them the right stuff?"

She raises an eyebrow. "I don't think they're picky."

I press my lips together. I like how honest Hattie is,

unabashedly so. She doesn't care what other people think, she just says it like it is. I wonder if all children are this way.

I crouch a little lower, hunching my shoulders, and stick my neck out like a chicken. "Bwak, bwaaak." I toss a little grain to the ground and continue to cluck while darting my head in and out, ruffling my arms like feathers. "Bwak."

Hattie giggles. "What are you doing?"

"I'm becoming one with the chickens."

"What?"

"In case they're afraid of me." I bring my hand in front of my face and shape my fingers into a beak, pretending to open and shut it as I cluck again. "They'll trust me more if they know I'm an innocent chicken too, right?"

She shakes her head but continues to giggle.

"I think it's working." I cluck, ruffle, and toss. "Try it."

Soon we're a couple of farm birds content with telling anyone who'll listen about our chicken lives.

"I'm going to eat this worm now. Bwak!"

"There's an itch in my feathers. Ba-bwak."

"I stepped in my own poop. Bwak, bwak."

Even when we're out of feed, we continue to stomp our way through the chicken coop, though I don't think these birds laugh half as much as we do.

A voice calls from outside the coop. "Did you stumble into the wrong house, Theron?"

I drop my cup and stand tall, hitting my head against a wooden beam above me. "Ow." I rub my head and bend over again, getting a good look at Nine standing outside the wire mesh.

Hattie grabs the cup, runs to the door, and pushes it open.

"We're becoming one with the chickens," she squeals, depositing the cup back in its spot. "It was Theron's idea."

I follow her out the door and secure it behind me, my face surely turning a bright red.

"Oh, really?" Nine presses her lips together to keep from laughing.

Hattie tugs on Nine's shirt. "This way they won't be scared of him." She tosses her hand in the air as though it makes perfect sense.

"Of course," Nine says, stealing a glance at me. "I totally understand. Theron can be quite frightening."

Hattie pulls Nine down to her level and whispers into her ear, though loud enough even the chickens could hear it. "Especially when he snores."

Nine loses it and bursts out laughing.

My palm goes straight to my forehead, and I close my eyes briefly. I can't believe she said that. I drop my hand, open my eyes, and say, "Hattie?"

She looks up at me, all big eyes and innocent expression. "Huh?" How can anything be wrong in the world when a face like that is in it?

"I think you've got bird poop on the bottom of your skirt."

She looks down and makes a face. I take advantage of her distraction and lift her up, throwing her over my shoulder.

"Ah!" she screams, flailing her arms and legs. "What are you doing?"

"I'm taking you where you belong." I march down the narrow path between animal pens and plop her into one in particular.

She clutches the fence, afraid of whatever animal awaits her, but when she sees a trio of sheep waltzing her way, she makes a run for them, scattering them as she does. Her laugh fills the morning air and deepens my smile at the same time.

"Why'd you do that?" Nine asks beside me, leaning against the railing.

"Because she's so darn cute." I laugh at my inside joke.

Nine scrunches her nose at me, figuring me out. "I should have known you'd be good with kids," she finally says. After carefully looking me over, she gazes at Hattie running wild through the pen. "You'll make a great father someday, Theron."

My smile falters, but instead of bolting and freaking out like I did yesterday at the thought of having a child of my own, I force myself to consider it seriously. "In Freedom, we don't ever see children. Unless you're a Teacher or a Healer giving hormone shots, you could live the rest of your life without seeing a child ever again."

Nine sighs. "It feels strange, doesn't it? To think of never being a part of this." She doesn't elaborate, but she doesn't have to.

I think of what my life was in Freedom. Nightspots and gambling, drinks and cage fights. The pleasure those things brought was nothing compared to making a little girl laugh in a chicken coop out here in the middle of nowhere, and for the first time, I think I'm getting a glimpse, a tiny insignificant sliver, of that love Catcher was talking about. Beyond a romantic kind of love. Beyond a self-fulfilling love.

"It's what we're meant to do, Theron. As people, I mean." She wipes a tear from her eye. "We're meant for this kind of life. Can you feel it?"

Yeah. I feel it.

CHAPTER TWENTY-FOUR

They should be back by now." Joramae paces the small space inside the house. Her joints haven't bothered her much today, so she's been able to get around without her crutches. The sun is setting on the second day Catcher and Kai and the others have been gone, and Catcher promised they'd be back earlier this afternoon.

"I'm sure it's nothing," I say, reassuring her. "Maybe it was harder to salvage the supplies than they thought. Maybe someone was sick at Rise Central, and Catcher needed to help. It could be any number of things."

She bites a nail and nods. "You're right. It's fine. He's fine."

Hattie's already asleep on her parents' bed, her small snores creating a lullaby to her sleep. I hope I remember to tease her about it tomorrow.

"If they're not back by morning," I say, "I'll go out beyond the boulders and see if I find anything."

Joramae clasps her hands together. "Okay." She blows out the lantern on the dinner table and climbs into bed with her daughter.

I step outside into the dim light, the big sky turning darker by the second. It's true what I told her; Catcher could be held up by any number of things. But the one I'm worried most about is Pua. Is she okay? Is she safe? The longer they take to return, the longer it will be before we head back and get her out of there. My worry over what the rebel plans are in terms of infiltrating Freedom keeps me awake until I get tired of swatting the bugs that fly around me, and I head inside and fall asleep on my pile of blankets on the floor.

*   *   *

When I wake the next morning, they still haven't returned. After breakfast I venture out past the stone pillars and walk to one of the pulse machines—the same one Kai checked on the other day. Joramae gave me a goggle-like contraption called binoculars. I hold it to my eyes, and it magnifies the image so I can see much farther than I would with my naked eye.

I see nothing along the horizon. Nothing but sand and dirt and brush. And sky. Blue, cloudless sky. A flock of geese fly across my field of vision, the land beneath them wavy and glimmering from the heat baking on the surface. I spin slowly, taking in the view from all angles, but I see no one until the blurry cluster of boulders marking the village comes into my field of vision. I see a red smudge in the middle of it all. After spinning the adjustment nob on top of the binoculars, Nine comes into focus, her hand shading her eyes as she looks out at me.

I lower the binoculars and let it rest on my chest, the cord attached keeping it secure around my neck. I raise my hand in greeting, and she picks up her pace to a light jog, reaching me within a couple of minutes.

"What are you doing?" she asks, out of breath.

I lift the binoculars. "Just seeing if anyone's coming."

"And?"

I shake my head.

"I'm not worried," Nine says. But the way she bites her bottom lip makes me wonder if she's trying to convince herself more than me. "Kai's the most capable person I've ever met. He'll get them home in one piece."

I bat my eyes and bring a hand to my chest. "Yes. Kai is everyone's hero. He's likely taking down the entire enemy force with one swat of his hand, summoning the sky to rain down food to feed the hungry, and breaking hearts of women across the land by declaring his undying love for the one and only Nine."

She rolls her eyes and rests a hand on her hip.

"Oh, sorry," I say, raising two hands, palms facing her. "The one and only *Ani*. My mistake."

"You're so funny," she deadpans. "I can't believe I actually missed your teasing."

I grin and glance down at the pulse machine, thinking about what other defenses Catcher has hidden in the rebel village.

Nine nudges my shoulder. "What about you? How many hearts did you break by leaving Freedom when you did? Are there a number of girls mourning Theron's disappearance?"

I frown, thinking of the only girl I care about back there.

"Hey." Nine lifts my head to look at her. "Sorry. It was a joke."

I sigh heavily, crouching next to the machine.

She follows suit. "There is someone, isn't there? Is that who you were talking about when you asked Catcher—"

"Do you know how these things work?" I ask, interrupting her.

She hesitates, probably debating whether or not to press me. But I can't talk about Pua with her, even if I wanted to. Catcher made that clear.

She finally gives in. "I have no idea."

I nod. "Kai told me a little about it and what they do, but I don't think he knows any details."

"What are you thinking?"

We stand and head back toward the village. "Do you know what Catcher is planning in terms of an attack against Freedom?"

"We've made some weapons of our own, but mostly we've been collecting guns. Catcher has a connection on the Seeker force who's obtained guns and such from the Freedom armory." She shrugs. "We've all had intensive training on them."

I nod, thinking about Odell. I wonder if he's the only Seeker on our side or if there are others.

"We disable the electronic connections associated with any guns before bringing them here or into the weapons storage at Rise Central to keep them hidden from the Techies."

"I assume they store ammo as well?"

"Yes. We've been learning hand-to-hand combat too." She grins. "Of course you already know that."

I mirror her smile, and we walk silently for a few minutes. "You said you've been *making* weapons?"

"Yeah." Nine waves her hand through the air. "Bows and arrows, fighting sticks, spears, bolas. We've got quite the mix of cultures in camp. Everyone pools their resources and knowledge to teach the others. It's kind of neat, actually."

I remember Kai carving a sharp tip onto a long stick and wonder if he was making one of these spears. "What's a bola?"

Her eyes widen. "Oh, you're going to love this." She grabs my hand and speeds to a jog, dragging me behind her toward the towering rocks and into the village. A wall I hadn't noticed before stands near the practice clearing. Practice weapons of all kinds, mostly wood, hang from hooks along the wall.

Nine reaches up for something that reminds me of Hattie's toy, a length of rope weighted with three balls on the ends. "This is a bola," she says. "These two cords are the same length, about the length of your arm. The third one's a little shorter, and the ball on that end is heavier too."

I lift each ball to gauge the weight. "You throw it at a target," I say. "And the rope wraps around it, incapacitating or injuring the victim."

She raises an eyebrow. "Yeah. Have you used one before?"

"Not exactly." I chuckle. "Will you show me?"

Nine holds the cords with the weights hanging below her fingers. "Spin it above your head like this." Her right arm rotates the bola above her head. "Make big arcs, so it doesn't tangle. Aim it at your target, and throw it hard."

She lets go, and the bola flies across the clearing to an unsuspecting tree. The ropes spread wide apart in flight—the difference in weights must cause that—and a whipping sound breaks through the air as it wraps around the tree trunk.

"Wow," I say. "I want to try."

Nine retrieves the bola from the tree and hands it to me. I toss it again and again, surprised something so simple could be so effective.

After a while, she pries the bola out of my hand and hangs it on the wall. We try several other weapons, and Nine carefully shows me how to use the guns.

When we're done, we glance at the rebel weapons hanging along the wall.

"Do you think it will be enough?" she asks.

"The weapons?"

"Yes, the weapons." She slips her arm into mine. "The guns. The rebel force. The training. They've never fought before, not for real. Most have never seen a Seeker let alone a province full of buildings and people and electricity. They don't understand how streets work or about transmitter communications. They don't know any of it except for what the few of us who've lived there have told them. I'm not sure it will be enough."

It's true. It sounds like insurmountable odds. The only thing I can think the rebels—we—have going for us is that we fight for a reason. A purpose. We fight for freedom, the right to choose for ourselves, the peace that comes without the constant threat of Freedom soldiers. We fight for love and family.

"It will be enough," I say. We haven't much time left, so it has to be.

*   *   *

Joramae is a mess. She swings her crutches through the air or pounds them on any surface within reach. "Four days. Four days! If that man isn't already dead, I'm going to kill him when he gets back."

Nine drums her fingers on the kitchen table. "I'll be right there with you. Kai is so dead."

Feeling just as frustrated, I stand from the table. "I should go look for them. I'll head to Rise Central and see what's going on."

Joramae aims a crutch in my direction. She's going to break

something in this small space. "Sit down, Theron. You don't even know how to get there."

I slowly lower into my chair, but I'm not ready to give up. "I'm sure there are a dozen people in this village who do. I'll take someone with me."

Nine threads her arm with mine. "If something happened—if something's gone wrong—I don't want you in danger, too."

"But if something's wrong, we'll never know unless someone goes to investigate." I want to help, but I've no idea what to do.

"If something's wrong," Joramae says, "we'll know soon enough. Someone will come, either from the Rise or from the Seekers."

Seekers coming here to the rebel village? The only way that could happen is if Rise Central is completely overtaken. With two pulse machines down, Techies will find this place eventually. I shudder at the thought of Eri's influence reaching this far beyond Freedom.

"Of course if Catcher is the one who finally walks through that door," Joramae says, pointing her crutch at the house entrance, "I might have you drill a hole into his other leg."

I let out a chuckle.

"You saved his life, Theron." Joramae smiles. "And he's been praising you ever since."

Nine nudges me. "Who's everyone's hero now?" she teases, referencing my joke about Kai.

I'd normally say something arrogant, like "Was there ever any doubt?" But I'm no hero, and my stomach feels uneasy at the thought. "It's something anyone would have done," I mumble.

Joramae rubs her sore wrists. "No, Theron. It's more than most would have done. You saved more than one life that day."

I think of Joramae and Hattie. He loves them more than

anything, even when he's apart from them. Distance doesn't change how he feels about them. He provides for them. Protects them. I understand how you can care for someone from a distance like that. Because of Nine. Because of Pua.

Then there are the rebels. The entire Rise force is kind of Catcher's family too. He has a lot of responsibility but doesn't show regret or remorse for shouldering it.

"Has he always been like this?" I ask. "Catcher, I mean."

"Like what?" Joramae scoots back on her bed and leans against the wall for support. "Bullheaded?" She cracks a smile.

I grin. "Taking on the world without a thought for himself."

She sighs. "Did he tell you how we met?"

"You were a surrogate," I say, stealing a glance at Nine. I need to be careful not to bring up Pua. "But you were declared unfit to carry a child."

Joramae nods. "Because of my arthritis."

"You were his first escapee." I picture Joramae behind bars, sitting in the corner of one of those cells. Dark hair, brown skin, twenty years younger than she is now. So much like Pua.

"He found a way to leave his tracker behind, and we traveled for hours beneath the province through endless tunnels." She closes her eyes as she remembers. "He'd leave me to return to Freedom during the day and come back for me at night. Then we'd walk some more. He brought me food, drink."

I remember what Catcher told me that day in his apartment about how he returned again and again to find a safe place for Joramae.

"Some nights I could barely walk at all, and Catcher would carry me." Her voice cracks with emotion. "When we finally found a suitable place for me to stay, he came back often, even started bringing others he helped escape. I honestly don't know when that man slept."

I think of all the times Catcher said I remind him of himself, and I realize he's wrong. So wrong. He's stronger, braver, more capable than I am. He's completely selfless and doesn't hesitate to do what's right no matter what. I am nothing like him, but I realize now, I want to be.

"He formed the Rise and established this village a few years later. We eventually fell in love. Got married. Hattie came many years later. Our little family is the best thing that's ever happened to me, and it's all because of that bullheaded man."

Nine leans her head against my shoulder. "It's a beautiful story, Joramae."

Joramae opens her eyes. "I'm blessed to have him. And you're right, Theron. Catcher takes on the world with no thought for himself. He does it because he thinks of me, of Hattie. He thinks of you, Ani, and Kai. He thinks of the surrogates and the slaves. He thinks of every citizen in the province because he knows what their lives could become if they knew the truth about families. He organized the Rise to fight back, to rescue our people from imprisonment, yes, but he also organized it to liberate those citizens who think they are free, but are bound in chains of ignorance. They need him too."

"They need all of us," Nine whispers.

The door swings wide, and Hattie runs in. "They're back. They're back."

Nine runs out the door while I help Joramae from the bed. She doesn't bother with her crutches, just stumbles to the front of the house, me close behind. I see Kai right away, walking toward us from the boulders. Catcher is at his side, along with the other two rebels who went with them. They carry rolls of wire

238

and other heavy equipment on their backs, lowering it to the ground when they see us waiting for them.

And that's when I notice several more people behind them. Did Catcher bring them from Rise Central?

Nine screams in elation, but she doesn't run for Kai like I expect her to. Instead she heads straight for a woman with long brown hair and fair skin who looks to be around Catcher's age. The woman pulls Nine into her and holds her so tight, there's no doubt they know each other. The rest gather around them and reach for Nine as well. An older man with dark skin who looks like an older version of Kai, and a young boy not much older than Hattie. Nine reaches for a small child—the youngest I've seen outside of a Batch tower—around a year old I would guess. How does she know these people? Did she meet them at Rise Central when she first escaped Freedom? Or perhaps they're from this village, returning after a length of time away.

I'm so caught up in watching Nine interact with these strangers, I don't notice Catcher break away and hurry to Joramae. He lifts her and kisses her as though he hasn't seen her in years, not just four days. I grin at the way she kisses him back as though she hadn't just been threatening to punish him for being away so long.

When Catcher finally pulls away, he turns to me and says, "Thank you for watching my family."

I nod distractedly, my eyes still trained on Nine and the strangers. "Who'd you bring with you?"

Catcher leans close, hesitating.

"What is it?" I ask. Something must be wrong.

He rests a hand on my shoulder. "They arrived via steamship from the Pacific."

I've no idea what that means, and my patience is wearing thin. If they're not from here, then—

"It's Kai's family, Theron." He makes sure I'm looking right at him. "Pua's family."

I suck in a sharp breath. How will we keep our secret now?

CHAPTER TWENTY-FIVE

D o they know?" I whisper.

He shakes his head. "They know she was taken by Seekers, but beyond that, they've no idea if she's alive or not. They don't know about the surrogates or the slaves in Freedom."

"And Kai?" I ask. He knows about the surrogates. I wonder if he's mentioned them to his family.

"After learning what happened on his island, he asked me privately about Pua yesterday. If I've seen her on the Maker level. I don't think he wants to tell his family anything until he knows for sure."

I wait for him to continue, to tell me what he knows.

"I told him I'm not sure if she's down there." He pauses. "But it won't be long until—"

"Theron!" Nine waves me over.

Catcher squeezes my shoulder before letting me go. We'll have to finish our conversation later, though I'm sure I can complete his sentence on my own. It won't be long until Nine starts wondering about Pua. Until they start asking me about her. Until they realize Catcher and I have kept this from them the whole time.

Catcher said telling Kai about his sister would ruin plans for the rebellion, because Kai would likely infiltrate Freedom too early. But I'm not sure that's true. If anything, it would give us motivation to ready our forces to face Eridian and her Seekers for good.

I desperately want to ask Catcher what he found out about Pua. If she's still okay. Alive. As I walk toward Nine and Kai, I glance behind me. Catcher gives me a nod, as though he knows what I'm thinking. Pua's fine. But any more news will have to wait.

I'm surprised by the expectant faces of Kai's family. The woman—the one I assume is the mother—steps forward and presses her hand against my face. Her hair is braided, and little wrinkles form at the corners of her mouth. There's something about her that reminds me so much of Pua.

"Theron," she whispers. Her accent isn't as strong as Pua's or Kai's, but it's there. "Oh, Theron." She pulls me close and embraces me as if we know each other. "Nine's told us so much about you."

The others pull me into their arms too, and we're suddenly in the most awkward group hug ever. I finally step back and get a closer look at them. They look a lot like Kai. And Pua.

The older man, Kai's father I assume, squeezes my shoulder. "We were so relieved to hear you survived that terrible crash."

The crash? Nine told them about me while she was on the island? Of course she did. Kai had to know who I was before he found me and told me where to find Nine that day in the Healer building. But if they've known about me this whole time, that means the whole family knew.

Including Pua.

I pull away, press my fingers against my temple, and think

back to that first day when I met her on the Maker level. When she first heard my name. She seemed surprised, relieved even. She knew me! This whole time she knew who I was. Maybe that's why she trusted me so easily, because Nine told her about me. But why would she keep that from me? Why didn't she say something?

Nine furrows her brow. "What's wrong, Theron?"

I drop my hand and look up. "Nothing," I say too quickly. I force my shoulders to relax. I have to shove Pua out of my mind before I mess this up. "This is your family?" I'm not sure if I'm asking Nine or Kai, but I don't think it matters.

Nine throws an arm around the woman who embraced me first. "This is Miri, short for Miriama." She points to the older man. "And her husband, Arapeta, or Ara."

I nod at him. The facial hair on his chin and above his mouth is more gray than black, though the cropped hair on his head has only a few gray strands.

"This is Hemi." Nine rests a hand on the young boy's shoulder and pushes him forward a little. He reaches out a hand, and I shake it.

"Nice to meet you, Hemi."

The black curls on his head fall into his eyes. Though I've seen several children since I've been in the village, I'm not sure I'll ever get used to seeing people so young without shaved heads or wearing white tanks and gray sweats.

Nine leans close, lifting the infant into her arms. "And this is Tama."

He's mostly bald with small tufts of dark hair sprouting from his head. His skin is lighter than Kai's and Hemi's—his brothers. He reaches for my face and grabs a fistful of skin. I'm surprised by his strength, but the curiosity on his face shocks me more than anything. He's taking me in, forming an opinion of me.

When he finally blinks and a smile forms on his chubby little face, I swear something inside me melts, transforms into something soft and pliable, and I realize I've never seen anything so precious as this little life in front of me.

"Do you want to hold him?" Nine asks.

I open my mouth to protest, but Tama reaches both arms toward me like he expects me to grab him. What choice do I have after something like that? I grab him under his arms like Nine is and hold him suspended in the air. He's much lighter than I expected, but it's awkward, his legs kicking the air.

Nine presses him closer to my chest until I feel him settle against me. He claps as though applauding me for a job well done, and I can't help but laugh in reaction. Tama stops clapping and looks at me, eyes wide. Then he flings his head back, laughing with me.

I take a moment to make sure he isn't going to fall out of my arms, then we watch each other again. Everything else falls away. Background voices go mute, faces blur. The only thing my mind focuses on is this infant. This child. Here he is, surrounded by people who help him, who take care of him. Who are there when he needs them. Who teach him, who love him.

It suddenly hits me, like a solid punch to my face, a kick to my gut. Only this hit is a good thing, and it's something I've been waiting for a long time, I just never knew it.

I want this.

I want this so badly.

To have a child of my own. Someone to care for, love. Someone to look at me like this every day as though I'm the only person in the whole world with the right—no, the privilege—to raise him. Not a hundred different strangers. Not random people hoping to earn enough points in their Trade. The responsibility to love someone so unconditionally—how could it be wrong?

I take in a large gulp of air. I blink, my vision sharpening. Everything is sharper, stronger, warmer. My world is suddenly clear in every sense, and I realize this is something worth fighting for. The rebels have always known it; it's why they're building arms against Freedom. Because Freedom takes away the ability to create life. It's the greatest gift we've been given, I think. And we need to protect it. We need to make sure everyone has the right to choose this gift too.

When I look at Nine, I see tears falling from her face. It brings me back to the present, and I quickly glance at everyone else. They are watching me as though seeing me for the first time.

I clear my throat and hand Tama to Nine, suddenly embarrassed. I can't imagine what I was doing that made them look at me like that. But as soon as he's out of my grasp, my arms start shaking, and not because he was too heavy or uncomfortable. I clasp my hands behind my back to keep them still. They ache with a desire for something more than my life has been thus far. I want a family.

And I know who I want it with.

On cue, Nine turns to the others. "Will you tell me where Pua is now?"

Ara rests a hand on her shoulder. "The Seekers came," he says. Then his words come out in a rush as he begins to explain the invasion on their island.

Listening to him talk about Pua and her capture is the last thing I want right now. I also don't trust myself to keep my secret around them, so I quietly slip away and head straight for Catcher's house, not bothering to knock. As soon as the door is closed behind me and I'm sure no one can hear me from outside, I ask, "How is she?"

Catcher sighs. "She's alive."

My knees shake, a flood of relief filling me. I hadn't realized how anxious I'd been until now, and it makes me think of Pua's family. Does Catcher realize how cruel it is to keep this information from them?

Joramae steals a glance at me before turning back to her small stove.

I wait for Catcher to continue, but he doesn't. I walk to the table and sit across from him, my feet tapping impatiently. "How much time?"

He rubs his chin. "I received a message from Odell while in Rise Central. She's got three days."

"Three days?" I push back from the table, suddenly feeling claustrophobic. "That's sooner than we thought. What happened?"

"I don't know." Catcher's hand moves to the back of his neck, and he steals a glance at his wife, worry in his eyes.

"We have to go back," I say. "Now."

"Theron—"

"Don't *Theron* me. There isn't an option. We have to go." This should be obvious. I don't know why he's resisting.

"The security has tripled since we escaped. The whole province is on lockdown. Forget curfew, no one's allowed to leave their homes except for work. No nightspots. No cages. No gambling. The entire place has turned into a prison. And even if we could find a way in, we still don't know how to remove or disable those new trackers without killing her."

Joramae turns abruptly, her expression upset, but she doesn't say anything. She tosses a plate of food on the table and heads to the opposite end of the room.

"So I take her somewhere within Freedom," I say. "Hide her. Until we figure it out."

Catcher reaches for a roll, but doesn't take a bite. He turns it in his hand as he continues to talk to me. "It's a tracker. They will find her no matter where you take her. That's kind of the point."

I grit my teeth at how cavalier he's being, but do my best to keep my cool. "Then we move in with our rebel attack. Right away."

"I want to. You know I want to." He hesitates. "But we aren't ready. I feel like we're missing something important. I don't want to move until we're sure."

He's not getting it. "We don't have a choice." I slam my palm on the table, and Catcher's plate rattles.

"We're short on manpower," he explains, keeping his voice level. "Short on weapons. With me out of the province now, things are complicated. Most of the citizens on our side couldn't escape before their false trackers were discovered. They were killed, Theron. Executed on the spot. We have to wait until I can figure out—"

"You've been waiting twenty years!" I stand from the table, unable to sit still any longer. "I don't believe you. You *are* ready. Nine told me you've been training the rebels, making them practice with the weapons. I don't believe that you don't already have a plan in place. You're just afraid."

"Theron," Joramae says softly from the edge of her bed.

I spare a look of apology for her, but I narrow my eyes at Catcher and wait for his response.

"You're right. I *am* afraid." He scrubs a hand over his face. "I don't want anyone to get hurt. On either side. We want to free the rebels, yes, but we want to free the citizens as well. Free them from Eridian. Not kill them."

"This is a rebellion," I say. "People will get hurt. People will die. You can't avoid that."

"I know. It's just . . . I've witnessed so much death, Theron. I'm tired of it. And I don't want to be the cause of it any more. Give me another day. I promise I'll—"

"She's dying!" I grit my teeth. "Every second we sit here and do nothing, you're putting those slaves and surrogates in more danger. Your hesitation is costing lives."

He sighs. "There's something else. Odell told me there's something brewing in Freedom with Eridian, and it has to do with those new trackers. He's not sure what. Let me find out what she's up to first."

"She's insane." I lift my fists to the sides of my head, emphasizing her erratic frame of mind. "She's been insane from the start. Whatever she's up to now is no different than what she's been up to this whole time. All of it's wrong, and she needs to be stopped." We don't have time to wait for more information.

"Theron." Catcher speaks through a clenched jaw, slowly. "I'm not refusing to go. I'm saying we need to do this smart."

How can he just sit there as if they aren't digging Pua's grave as we speak? As much as I wish it wasn't true, I can't do this without him. "What if it was Joramae sitting in that cell right now?"

"That's not fair," he says. "You're putting Pua's life in front of every other."

"That's right. I am." He'd do the same. He has to realize that.

Catcher picks a small piece from his roll. "It's not what she would want."

"Don't you dare tell me what she would want." I point a finger at him and begin pacing the room. "You don't know anything."

He stands and reaches an arm toward me. "I'll do everything

I can to find a way to leave as soon as possible. I know she needs us—needs you." He drops his arm. "But going in now would be suicide."

Doesn't he realize *not* going in would be a form of suicide for me? Not to mention we're pretty much killing her ourselves by not doing anything. I can't sit here and do nothing. We're out of time. Catcher says he wants to find a way, but why should he? He's got everything he wants right here.

I yank the door open and storm out of the house.

What am I going to do now?

*   *   *

It's already cold out, the sky dark. The stars light up the night, revealing our secrets. All our wrongs and mistakes. I've never wanted a buzz drink so bad in my life. Not even during my lowest moments missing Nine. Maybe it's withdrawal. Maybe I want to pretend none of this is happening. I wish I could hide away, pretend everything is perfect. But that would be a lie, because everything is cracked. It always has been, and I'm tired of it. I want it to be right for the first time and every time. I have to make it right.

I head down the village path and find myself in front of Kai and Nine's small home, my feet leading me here without knowing it. Solemn voices escape through the windows, the reflecting light of candles and lanterns creating shadows along the wall. They've anticipated this reunion for a long time, I think. Months. What a bittersweet moment.

I thought I was ready to tell them everything. Convince them to help me get Catcher to agree to a rescue, but I hesitate. These people aren't my family. No matter how well they may know me because of what Nine's told them, I don't know them at all.

I'm sure they'd welcome me inside, but they may not like what I have to tell them, and the bravery I thought I had in a heated moment with Catcher is sucked out of me.

I'm about to head back to the main path when I see a flickering light toward the river. Curious, I venture down the small trail. Several feet inland from the water, a small fire is set into a clearing. A chill blows through the air, and I rub my arms. A shadow of a person stands in front of the fire, but I've no idea who it is. Either way, the thought of a little heat sounds really nice right now, and I take a few more steps toward it.

"Theron." The voice is male, deep, with a strong accent. It's Ara.

"Hello," I say, stepping to the opposite side of the fire and holding my hands out to warm them. "Do you mind?"

"Of course not." He looks up at me, the waving firelight catching the wrinkles on his face. "You're always welcome with us. Understand?"

He says it almost like a command, but not callous. It's a kind of directive, as though he wants to make sure I know he's serious.

"I understand."

He nods and looks back to the fire. "You mean a lot to Nine, so you mean a lot to us. Family is like that."

"Yes," I say. "I'm starting to understand that."

"Good. I hope one day you not only understand it, but you feel it so much the truth of it makes a mark on your heart. Like a testament of something certain. Real. It's a great blessing to know something with such surety."

I think today might be that day. The moment I held Tama in my arms something was written on my heart. As sure as the tattoo on my neck. "What happened to Kai's sister?" I ask, taking a chance. "Why isn't she with you?"

He exhales. "After Nine and Kai left, it wasn't long before Seekers found our island. It was a matter of time, I suppose. Still, we weren't ready for it."

I glance down at the rogue embers jumping away from the fire. "How did they find you?"

"It wasn't Nine, I know that. Her tracker wasn't working at that point. I think it was chance. The Seekers had gone to a nearby island not long before. Their search must have been a little farther this time, that's all." He looks up at the sky, the smoke creating a haze over the sharp pinpricks of stars. "We ran into the hills. It was late afternoon, and Pua wasn't home. She'd been visiting cousins a few miles away when they came. I sent my wife and the younger two inland with a plan to meet at a certain grove of banana trees while I stayed behind to look for our daughter.

"I never found her, but a friend witnessed the Seekers take her away. She had been walking home, alone along the road." His voice cracks. "We should have been more careful. Kept a closer eye on her. She can't hear, and they probably snuck up on her easily because of her disability. It's my job to love and protect my children. To protect Pua. I failed her."

I swallow hard, thinking about how terrifying the experience would have been for Pua. "It's not your fault," I say. "It's no one's fault but theirs."

He nods, but I don't think he believes it. "I've no idea what happened after she was captured. Was she sent away? Was she killed?" He brings a hand to his mouth. "What if we never find out what happened to her?"

I know he doesn't expect me to answer, but something inside me longs to give this man some kind of assurance.

Tell him.

He clears his throat. "It'll be okay," he says, as though convincing himself. "We came here to find Kai and Nine, and now we have them back. We found you too. Today is a good day." His voice is solid, his words sure. Even his stance and expression say he's fine, but I know he isn't. Because I think I know what he means when he says he loves his daughter.

I want to protect her, too. I want to take care of her. It's more than a romantic kind of love. It's a yearning that's beyond any kind of physical attraction.

Freedom expects us to live our lives according to superficial desires. What will make me happy in this moment? What will bring me the most pleasure? They teach us we are slaves to our desires, but we're so much stronger, so much greater.

I want to tell him about Pua; I do. And I will. But nothing is going to happen without Catcher's help. I need to find a way to convince him we're ready as a rebel force to go in right away. I have to convince him the Rise will have the edge in a potential attack. And I have to figure it out fast.

CHAPTER TWENTY-SIX

It takes me a while to fall asleep, but when I do, a familiar dream greets me. I'm standing at the edge of a quiet lake again, one foot in the water, one on land. But this time, as soon as the ground rumbles, I don't hesitate, and I step completely into the water to escape the quake. The water is calm despite the churning earth around it, and I walk toward the center of the lake, the water getting deeper with each step until it's up to my neck.

I glance around the perimeter of the lake. The entire landscape has become unrecognizable in its chaos, while the lake remains impossibly silent. And though I still don't know what lurks beneath the surface, it doesn't scare me. I slowly lower into the water, submerging myself completely.

But I don't drown.

Instead, I feel like I've taken my first breath.

My eyes flick open. It's still dark, the barely-there hint of dawn teasing the horizon. I step into the cool desert air outside

Catcher's home. When I reach the small house near the river, I hesitate. I don't want to barge in, but I also don't want to wait one minute longer. I need to get to Pua as soon as possible.

I carefully open the front door, cringing as it squeaks in the otherwise silent early morning. A movement in the shadows startles me, and I release the door from my grip, catching it before it slams back on the frame. A moment later it opens, and Kai steps out.

"I couldn't sleep," he says, as though he was the one needing to explain his strange behavior.

"Me neither. I need to talk to you."

"Not here."

I follow him to the main path and into the open commons area. Taking a seat beneath the large canopy in the center, I inhale a deep breath and decide to go for it.

"I know where Pua is," I say. "She's in Freedom, on the Maker level. She—"

Wham.

I stumble forward from my seat, the right side of my face on fire. After standing straight, I smooth my hand over my cheek and glance at Kai, who is standing a few feet away. He shakes out his left hand.

That scab.

"You done?" I spit at him.

He flares his nostrils once. Twice. Closes his hands into fists and releases them again. He finally relaxes his shoulders and says, "Yeah. I'm done."

"Good." Because I'm not.

I shove him and follow it with a punch to the gut before he has a chance to react. When I go for him again, he dodges left and sends a fist into my side. The back of my hand gets a piece of his jaw, and I manage to grab a clump of his hair and yank his head down to meet my lifted knee. He bounces backward and stumbles to the ground, spitting out a fresh dose of blood from his quickly swelling lips.

I wait for him to get up again before rushing him with my right shoulder, my body tucked into itself. We both fall to the ground, and I feel a kick to my groin. Oy, that kills. I roll onto my back. Kai stands, then kicks again, aiming for my side. I roll away and jump up, swinging a roundhouse kick into the side of his head. I miss, but it rattles him. I take advantage of his wavering and grab the front of his shirt and shove him backwards into one of the poles holding up the tent.

"What are you doing?" Nine yells from the main path. She rushes to where we are, in the middle of our fight. "I could hear you two all the way down the road." Her jaw drops when she sees us, her eyes taking in the lump on my cheekbone, her fingers touching Kai's swollen lip, edged with blood.

He winces, then narrows his eyes at me. "I trusted you."

I take a step back, glowering at him. "Why do you think I came to see you this morning? Because I trusted you too."

"Ani told you about my sister a week ago." He steps to the side and begins to walk away, his arm around Nine's waist. "You've lied this whole time. To me. To Ani."

Nine pulls from his grasp, spinning to face me. "Lied about what?"

I sigh. "Catcher wouldn't let me tell you."

Kai's brows furrow, and he glances up the path that leads to Catcher's house. He looks back to me. "Last time I checked, you were free to do as you choose. I thought she was more important to you than this." He tilts his head toward Nine at his side.

I know he's talking about how I should have told Nine as

soon as I connected her with Pua. As soon as I realized what Pua meant to her, as a sister. I can't help but think of Pua sitting in her cell. She's more important to me than keeping Catcher's secret. I wish I'd realized it earlier.

"Will someone please tell me what's going on?" Nine glances between me and Kai.

I should be the one to tell her, but Kai spits it out before I have the chance.

"Theron knows where Pua is."

She looks right at me, disappointment in her eyes. "What?"

I slump my shoulders. "She's on the Maker level. With the surrogates."

A visible chill travels through Nine, and she pulls her arms into her chest. "Why didn't you say something before?" Her voice is soft, sad.

"Because Catcher didn't want me to," I repeat, feeling impatient. I glance at Kai. "He thought you'd go after her and might expose the Rise while you were at it. He knew the rebels weren't ready, and he couldn't risk anyone going in."

Nine steps close to me and tilts her head forward, as though wanting to keep what she's about to say private, though Kai is right here and can hear everything. "I just . . . I never thought there would come a time when we'd keep secrets from each other."

Something inside of me heats up, like a gust of air feeding a flame. "Are you serious? So the day you up and left without telling me where you were going, what you were doing—that was some misunderstanding on my part?"

I regret the words as soon as they're out. Nine's face reddens, and she steps toward Kai, whose hand tightens into a fist. He's going to punch me again, and I'm not sure if Nine will stop him.

"Listen." I hold up a hand. "We can finish this later." I motion between me and Kai, referring to our fight. "But we're running out of time to save her."

"Save Pua?" He steps closer. I've got his attention now. "Is she . . . pregnant?" He makes a face somewhere between pain and worry.

"No," I say. "When they discovered she couldn't hear, they decided not to use her as a surrogate because they thought it might affect the infant she carried."

Kai visibly relaxes. "Then what do you mean *save her*?"

I swallow hard. "Because, since she's of no use to them as a surrogate, they're going to kill her."

Nine gasps, then looks at Kai. Something passes between them. A shared thought or memory, I don't know.

Kai reaches for my shoulders, but instead of shoving me like I expect, he grips hard to keep himself upright, his legs starting to give way. "What?" he croaks.

"They also installed a new tracker in her, and if we tried to take it out with a tracker gun or left Freedom boundaries, she would die. We had no choice but to leave her."

"Pua," Nine whispers. A hurt look crosses her face. "How long?" She doesn't have to elaborate. I know exactly what she's asking.

"Two days."

Kai squeezes harder, pain shooting through my shoulders. "Two days?" He curses and shoves me away, shaking his hands out and attempting to get control of himself. "I have to get my father. I have to break her out of there. Now."

I step close. "Kai, we have to do this smart," I say, repeating Catcher's words.

"We?" He spits at me. "There is no *we*. You voted yourself out of this the minute you decided to lie to us." Shaking his head in disgust, he adds. "I don't care what Ani says, you're not the great hero she makes you out to be."

Nine cowers from his words, but I don't know if it's because she thinks he's lying or because she knows it's true. Either way, all of this drama is getting us nowhere.

I want to hit him again. So hard he might not get back up. But I've thought this through enough times to know we're going to have to work together. "Kai, you cracked scab, listen to me for one second."

His brow wrinkles as he glares at me, but at least he's not interrupting me or walking away. I'll take what I can get.

I take a deep breath. "The only person who can remove Pua's tracker is the Prime Maker. And it'll be impossible to get to her without going through her throng of Seekers. This isn't going to be a simple rescue attempt. Eridian's gone psycho with her security forces. Armored vehicles, weapons, soldiers." I pause, scratching the facial hair along my jaw. "This will have to be an all-out attack from our end. *The* attack." I let that sink in.

"You mean the Rise," Nine says. "This will have to be the rebellion we've been waiting for."

"Yes." I step forward. "If we want to save Pua, we have to stop Eridian. Once and for all. And we have two days left to do it. Catcher is hesitant about sending in the rebels. He says we're not ready, that we need something more."

Kai curses. "I don't care what Catcher thinks."

I nod in agreement. "Unfortunately, the rebels do. They won't go in without his order. And we need them."

"What do you propose?" Nine asks.

I frown. "Convince Catcher we're ready."

"How?" Kai studies my face.

"Where are the supplies you and Catcher brought back yesterday?" I ask. "The ones to fix the pulse machines?"

Kai leads us to the animal pens. A small lean-to out front serves as a storage area for tools and other farming equipment. Piled on top are the wires, switches, and molded pieces of plastic scavenged from Rise Central.

"Do you know how the machines work?" I ask.

"A little." He frowns. "I mostly know what I'm supposed to do to fix them. Catcher showed me." His face sours when he mentions the rebel leader.

I don't blame him; I'm frustrated with Catcher as well. Catcher wants to attack Freedom, but he has a family too, and it's more than Joramae and Hattie. It's all of us—all of the rebels. He wants to make sure we're doing this the right way, to spare as many lives as possible. I can't imagine what the burden of that responsibility would be like.

"Will you show me?" I ask.

After walking out to the first broken pulse machine, Kai removes the side panel. "There's a metal cylinder here, in the center." He points to a black core suspended in the middle of the apparatus. "The power comes in through these panels that connect to the wiring."

My eyes follow the exterior panels to the coil of wire I remember seeing the last time I was here with Kai. There's an open space between the core and the wires.

Kai points out a switch on one end of the unit. "The entire thing is on a timer. Electric current runs through the wires—"

"—creating a magnetic field." Nine shades her eyes and leans closer. "Right?"

Kai nods. "A really intense magnetic field. A fuse lights some kind of explosive material in the core, creating a sort of explosion traveling as a wave through that core." He kneels and moves his hands through the air as he explains. "The core then comes in contact with the wiring."

"That would short the circuit," I say.

"Exactly. The wire is temporarily cut off from the power supply and in turn compresses the magnetic field."

"Is that what makes the pulse?" Nine asks. "What sends out the burst of electromagnetism?"

"Yes," Kai says. "The whole thing resets itself to do it again and again." He starts unwinding some of the wire, areas where it's been corroded, so he can replace it.

I glance at the other supplies we brought from the lean-to: solar panels, capacitors to store energy, plastic to repair the outer shell, and endless lengths of wire. While Nine helps Kai with the installation, I pace back and forth in front of the machine.

"How heavy is it?" I ask. Before either can answer, I step to one end and attempt to lift it, trying to gauge its weight. It doesn't budge.

"Heavy enough to sit through the rain and wind any storm throws at it," Kai says, his eyes focused on his task.

The thick exterior plastic must defend it against the blazing sun, too, which is a feat in itself. The morning sun has cleared the horizon, and I squint toward the east. Toward Freedom. "Can someone get hurt if they stand in front of it when the pulse goes off?"

"Nope," Kai says. "It's not that strong. They probably won't realize anything happened."

That's good. "Why can't the Techies detect the electricity pumping through the wires?"

Kai knocks on the metal casing. "This shielding blocks their devices somehow. Makes the whole thing virtually invisible."

It's lead. Or some other heavy, impenetrable metal. I suppose the rebels could technically use electricity within the village if they could block the wiring with more shielding, but I don't think they mind living without power. It'd be more work than it's worth, and this way, they can reserve the supplies they do have for protection.

I brush the side of my nose. "For someone who grew up without electricity, you sure know a lot about it."

Kai shrugs. "We've been here for months, and this is my main job. I learn what I need to survive. We all do."

I pick up the rest of the tools and follow him and Nine to the next cylinder needing repair, studying each pulse machine as we walk past. "What are the second cylinders for? The ones sitting next to the main unit?"

Kai holds up a bag of capacitors. "Energy storage. Sun doesn't shine at night, so power is collected during the day."

I nod. The cylinders aren't portable, so there's no way we can take them into Freedom. But it's good to know they'll still work when the sun isn't shining directly on them. If I could take that idea and—

"What are you thinking, Theron?" Nine runs her fingers over a crease between my eyes. "You've got that super-focused concentrated look. You always had it when you brainstormed ways of sneaking us through the Batch tower at night." She smiles, and a relief I hadn't realized I craved settles through me. We're okay. We may keep secrets from each other, we may not be inseparable or read each other's minds the way we used to, but we'll be okay.

"I have an idea." I stop and point toward the rebel village. "When you two are done, come find me at the lean-to. I think I know how to convince Catcher we're ready." I turn and run for the stone pillars, not bothering to wait for their response.

CHAPTER TWENTY-SEVEN

I quickly sort through the materials in the storage pen and find a large sheet of paper and something to write with. I start sketching my design: a simple explosive core, the tight and compact wrap of wiring, a centrifugal force generator. The paper dangles from my hand as I march to the chicken coop. The mesh wire used to enclose the birds could be molded into the shape we need, creating the space necessary for the magnetic field to form. The wool from Hattie's sheep would give us all the rope we want. Utilizing the pulse machines, we should have enough supplies to build everything we need. I hope.

I finish with my sketch just as Kai and Nine return. Without saying anything, I spread the sheet so they can both get a look. Their eyes study the page, taking it in.

"How large is this?" Kai asks.

I grin and hold out my hand, palm up, as though I'm holding a small fruit.

Nine takes in a sharp breath. "This is brilliant, Theron." She snags the paper and darts up the road.

"Where are you going?" I yell after her.

"It's time for Catcher to wake up," she calls back.

Kai and I laugh at the same time and hurry to catch up with her.

*   *   *

"Bola grenades?" Catcher's face wrinkles in concentration as he bends his head over the paper spread along his kitchen table.

"Sort of." I tap the page. "They're bolas like the rebels have been training with, but the heaviest ball at the end of the ropes will be a pulse grenade—a miniature version of the pulse machines you've been using to protect the village. The radial design of the ball will send the pulse in all directions instead of a single focused one."

"How do you activate it without a power source?"

I stand and twirl my arm above my head in a large arc. "When you spin the bola, the centrifugal force will activate the generator, sending electricity through the wiring. When you let go," I extend my arm, mimicking the action, "the bola will spin toward the target, whether it's a Seeker or a post or whatever. Once the rope cinches tight and the weapon is motionless, the centrifugal force is cut off, shorting the circuit . . ."

"And sending out the pulse," he finishes for me.

"Exactly," I say. "It's a dual-purpose weapon. We can use it to injure or entangle enemies, the same way the rebels have practiced, but it will also take out power in the surrounding area, rendering Freedom weapons useless."

"How far will it reach?" he asks. "The pulse, I mean."

"We can't know for sure until we test it, but based on the size ratio to the original unit, my guess is about a five-hundred-foot radius." I study his face. He's cool as stone.

He studies the diagram a little longer. "There are no lead shields to block them from Freedom's Techies."

I nod quickly. "We won't activate the generators until we're inside Freedom boundaries. They won't be searching for rogue use of electricity within the province."

"What about the village?" he asks. "We'll have to take apart all of the pulse machines to retrofit these grenades. My people will be left unprotected out here without them."

"Yes," I admit. "There will be nothing to prevent the Seekers from coming out here. But there will also be nothing to attract them. No electricity. No questionable activity. We're talking about two days. And the Seekers will be a little too occupied with the Rise during those two days to worry about doing any exploration. After that, we won't need to protect the village anymore, because Freedom will no longer be a threat."

Catcher narrows his eyes, doubtful.

"Look," I say. "Send a message to Rise Central. Have them set up extra watches. They can be an extra layer of protection should Seekers head this way for any reason." I pause. With a low voice I add, "But they won't. It's two days, Catcher."

He sits back and folds his arms across his chest. I glance at Nine and Kai across the table to see if they have a better read on Catcher than I do, but they also seem unsure. I look back at Catcher, his forehead crinkling deep in thought.

He reaches for his leg and rubs a spot below his knee, the place I drilled into not long ago. "That's Theron," he says slowly. "Always thinking outside the box."

Hope rises in my chest, but Catcher's face doesn't change, and I still have no idea what he's thinking.

"Please," I whisper so softly I may have imagined saying it. I glance at Joramae, leaning against the wall with her crutches at her side. I can't help but think of Pua when I see her. I miss Pua so much it hurts. Like my heart is forgetting how to beat, and every time it does is a struggle. This is our last chance, and her fate is in Catcher's hands.

When I look back at Catcher, he's watching me. And he's torn. I know he is. When his eyes finally soften, I kneel next to him, and he places a hand on my shoulder. I feel like a student at the feet of his master. Except it's more than that. Because I know Catcher cares for me beyond what you'd expect from a coworker. Or even a good friend.

I think this is what it feels like to have a father.

I reciprocate the action and squeeze Catcher's shoulder. "This is what you've been working toward. The rebels are ready. Once we neutralize the Seekers' electricity and weapons, we'll have the advantage. The pulse grenades will guarantee more lives saved. It's the missing piece you've been waiting for. You didn't want anyone to get hurt, and these devices will get us as close to that as possible. The province is already falling apart." I think of the abandoned buildings, elevators out of order, crumbling walls. "They won't see this coming, and it will rattle them. We can do this."

Catcher turns to his wife, a question in his eyes. Something passes between them. A shared thought or feeling I can't read, and Catcher turns back to me. "Okay."

I sit back on my heels, relief flooding my chest. I tilt my head toward him in gratitude, then beam at Nine and Kai, their expressions mirroring my own. "Okay," I say.

*   *   *

Catcher sends scouts to Rise Central with the message to be on extra alert the next couple of days and to prep forces to infiltrate Freedom soon after we arrive. Nine and I work on retrofitting a prototype pulse grenade while Kai shows a group of rebels how to take apart the large cylinders and salvage the parts we need.

Catcher has some kind of wave machine he uses to test the large cylinders. It can read the output of the pulse, and we risk activating a bola grenade to test it out. My estimations were off by a hundred feet, but we should still have plenty of bolas to cover most of the ground in Freedom One.

Once we're confident in the prototype, Nine and I show others how to build the grenades while Catcher makes sure we have all the rope and counterweights we need. The village has put off everyday chores in order to focus on the task, and soon we have an assembly line of sorts forming under the central tent. We work well into the night, lanterns lighting the work surfaces until we have no supplies left, just a large pile of pulse grenades tied to bolas, waiting to be used.

"Get some sleep," Catcher tells everyone. "We've got a big day tomorrow. Meet here in the morning. We'll hike to Rise Central and brief the others on our plan. In a couple of days, we'll be bringing back a lot of friends and family, so those of you staying behind—get ready for a party."

His words are met with cheers from the crowd, and I can't help but smile, anticipating the relief everyone will feel when their families are together again. When their people are finally free.

* * *

"How do you get the electricity going?" Hemi asks, lifting the grenade and squinting at it. The early morning light creates a soft glow around the device.

I point to the rope hanging off the end. "You twirl it like you would a bola. The generator takes the energy you put in by spinning it and turns it into electrical energy."

"And to make the pulse?" He brushes a lock of curly hair from his forehead.

"When the spinning stops," I say, wrapping the rope around his torso as though he were caught by the bola, "so does the power, and the pulse shoots out."

"Won't you explode?" He raises an eyebrow.

"Nah. It can't hurt you." I unwrap the rope from around him. "At least the pulse won't hurt you. The bola is another story."

"Doesn't look that scary to me."

Miri rushes over to us, out of breath. "Hemi! I've been looking for you everywhere." She snags the grenade out of his hand. "You're going to get hurt fooling around with that thing."

"Theron said it can't hurt me," he whines.

Miri looks up at me, and I shrug an apology. "Well," she says, "Theron isn't used to the trouble eight-year-old boys can get into." She hands me the pulse grenade and winks. "Yet," she adds.

I grin and watch as she wraps an arm around him.

"Now run home and find your father." She ruffles the hair on his head. "He's getting your baby brother's stuff ready for Joramae and will be taking you there soon. Don't disappear again."

"Yeah, yeah." Hemi runs off toward his family's house by the river.

"You're not staying?" I ask. I assumed she'd stay and watch the two little ones.

She shakes her head. "I think I'll be more useful in Freedom." She swallows hard, as though she's nervous. "I'm not terribly familiar with the province, not outside of the Batch tower at least, but I know more than most people here. And I know how those people think." Her voice cracks. "And I want to be there if—when—we find my daughter."

Of course. I know enough about families to not doubt that. "You said you're familiar with Freedom . . ." I glance at her dark brown hair and fair skin, answering my own question as she does.

"I'm like you, Theron." Her voice is soft. "And Ani and Catcher. I'm from Freedom."

"How—"

"I escaped as a Batcher. Through that hole in the ocean I heard you had the pleasure of swimming through not long ago." She smiles, but she drops it before adding, "You'll be okay, Theron. This life outside the fence, it's worth it. It's worth fighting for. Thank you for having faith in that." She pauses. "Thank you for recognizing how important she is to us to fight for her, too."

I swallow the words that want to escape. I'm not doing it for Miri. I'm doing it for completely selfish reasons. Because I love her daughter and can't live any longer without her. Instead, I say, "You're welcome."

She nods and begins packing her supply bag with her share of grenade bolas, others within the village trickling in and doing the same. Men and women, old and young. People who have trained for months and years. As they strap on their packs and gather other weapons—knives, tech-free guns, spears, bows—I know they're ready. This will work. It has to.

"Are you ready to head back there?" Nine sidles next to me, elbowing my side.

I frown, wishing there was a way I could make her stay in the village. I know she's been training and her skills and her knowledge of Freedom will be assets, but the thought of her in danger makes my stomach churn. I can't help but think of Eri finding Nine and whisking her away for good. At the same time, I think Nine might be the key to getting close to Eri and figuring out how to get the trackers out of everyone.

I take a deep breath. "I'm ready. I haven't been gone long, but it feels like forever."

She nods. "I often wonder if I imagined my time there. Made it up, you know? It just doesn't seem real sometimes."

I don't want to feel like it's made up, because that would mean I wouldn't have lived a life with Nine. No matter how cracked that place is, no matter how wrong they are about the way things work, I wouldn't trade away our time together.

She must see the hurt on my face because she adds, "You're the only good thing to come out of that place." She lifts my chin. "It's because of you I survived long enough to regret having to go back now." One side of her mouth rises. "I don't think I'll ever be able to thank you enough for that, Theron."

"You won't," I say, attempting to lighten the moment. I don't want to talk about regrets or what could have been. I just want to find Pua and start moving forward. "You'll be forever in my debt. My evil scheme is unfolding exactly as I planned."

She punches me in the shoulder and then rests her head on the same spot, whispers a soft "Thank you," and leaves to help Kai with his pack. She doesn't look back.

When everyone's ready to go and good-byes are exchanged among families, I walk to Catcher's house to let him know we're ready. His front door is halfway open, and I take one step into the small room, then pause. He's kneeling on the floor, his wife on one side of him, his daughter on the other. They form a small circle, hands held tight between the three of them, heads bowed.

Catcher mouths words I can't make out, though there is a reverent, hushed quality to his speech. I don't know what he's saying or who he's speaking to, and it feels like a private moment for him and his family, but I can't help but watch as the three of them remain so still, so humble. When he's done, he pulls both of them into his arms, whispers words into their ears, and embraces them for several long moments. When I see tears on Catcher's cheek, I step outside silently and wait for him out front.

Despite how much time Catcher has spent away from his family his entire life, the feelings they have for each other remain strong. It's amazing how you can love someone so much though you can't see them. I loved Nine. Even when I thought we'd be separated forever and I'd never see her again, even when I thought she was dead, I still loved her. I love Pua. Distance doesn't take that away.

After several minutes, Hemi walks up the path, his baby brother in his arms. He pauses next to me and twists his mouth, as though carefully deciding what to say. "Promise me you'll find my sister."

"I will." I've never said truer words.

I hear the door squeak, and Catcher steps out, his face dry. "Theron," he says, all business.

I offer him a smile. "Ready for this?"

He nods and pats my back, leading me toward the central tent. I glance back to see Joramae welcome Hemi and Tama into her home. She wipes her face with the apron tied around her waist and gives me a small wave before closing the door again.

PART THREE

CHAPTER TWENTY-EIGHT

The day is long and hot, and my leg is already killing me, but there's something about being surrounded by people you care about, people who share the same hope, no matter how small, that bolsters you and makes you capable of doing things you never thought you could.

I glance down at myself and smile, realizing I look like the other rebels. My dark green, conservative cargo pants with several patches, my black knit shirt with a hole in the side. The gun strapped to my chest, worn boots, and a bag full of bola grenades over my shoulder. I've never been one to dress outrageously in Freedom, but I don't think anyone in the province would recognize me like this.

We remain silent for most of the journey, saving our energy, keeping our thoughts on the battle ahead. When we finally reach Rise Central, we're welcomed into a large common area where food and sleeping accommodations have been arranged. After

Catcher gives us brief directives of what will happen tomorrow, Evert shows us where we can retire and rest up for the next day.

I lie on the floor, the pack beneath my head a makeshift pillow, and stare up at the ceiling. The room is dark, only a few torches left to light the perimeter, and I can't tell if the shadows shifting across the ceiling are a result of their smoke or my imagination. I don't think I'm tired, I'm too amped for tomorrow's invasion, but seemingly a second later someone nudges me awake and Catcher is there, crouching next to me. I must have fallen asleep without realizing it.

"I need to talk to you."

I follow him out of the room, carefully stepping around hundreds of sleeping bodies. We enter the tunnel-like hallway, and Catcher leads me to a room several doors down, a lantern already lighting the space. A large map is secured to the wall, patched with smaller, overlapping pieces.

"I've been reviewing the tunnel system," he says, his voice scratchy.

"Have you slept at all?" I ask, noticing the bags under his eyes.

He ignores my question and points to the wall. "The water tunnels are our best bet. They lead to every building in the province, and they're large enough to fit us. I think the main force needs to be at the Core building and surrounding area, since that's where the slaves and surrogates will be. But once word gets out we're there—which it will even without their transmitters—Freedom forces will be pouring into the area."

I place my palm against the map. "What if we start here, in the center beneath the Core building? We take out the power. That should negate all surveillance equipment so we can get into the slave compound without being seen on those cameras. A team could start slipping them out through the tunnel system without anyone noticing. Another team will go for the surrogates—"

"I have to lead the surrogate team," he says, his voice hard and worried. "I'm the only one who'll know how to get them out safely."

"Okay." I hesitate. There's something he's not telling me, but I don't push him. "But I'm going for the surrogate holding cells first. Maybe Kai or someone else can get the slaves—"

"I need you in charge of the slaves," he interrupts again. "There are several members of the Rise who can fight their way through the hallways in the Core building without having an intimate knowledge of the place. But you've been in the slave housing. You know where everyone is. The children. The sick. You know how to get them out."

I shake my head. "Surely you have countless former slaves in the group. They'll know that place better than I do. I'm going for Pua first."

He steps toward me and grasps my collar. It doesn't matter that he's so much shorter than I am, the look he gives me makes me feel like a small child.

"I agreed to do this for you, do you understand?" His nostrils flare, and he looks back and forth between my eyes. "I wanted to wait. I wanted to make sure we were ready, but I'm risking my people to help you. You're like the son I never had, Theron." He chokes on his words. "You are family. And I would do anything for family, no matter how cracked it may be."

He lets go of my collar and shakes out his hand, getting control of himself again. "I need you with the slaves first. Once they're out, then you go for Pua. Do you understand?"

I nod. "I understand."

He moves back to the map and slides a hand to the east. "Our main goal needs to be getting our people out. Second, we make sure the holding facilities and surrogate machines are destroyed. We can't let them start collecting people again. Without the capabilities to impregnate surrogates or control the slave force, it will at least slow them down. Once we manage that, then we take control over the entire province. When the slaves are secure and I have the surrogates out, we'll split up our forces and work our way out from the center point, covering ground radially."

This has been his plan all along. Using the water tunnels to bring in the rebel forces. Freeing the slaves. Destroying machines. Securing the province. It's a well thought-out strategy, but with the grenades, we can improve our tactic. "What if we have people stationed throughout the province to begin with?"

"What do you mean?"

"We won't need everyone in the Core building for the initial attack. Not only will people stand around with nothing to do, but they will clutter the escape routes, perhaps causing more chaos than anything. What if we set them up at key points underground in the tunnels? They can set off some of their bola grenades from there."

Catcher rubs the back of his neck. "From below ground?"

"Yes." It makes sense. "The pulse waves travel through walls. The grenades will take out everything within a radius of four hundred feet, including vertically. The pulse will travel up into the buildings through several stories. When the electricity is out, then we make our move, using the rest of the bolas and whatever other weapons are needed. We'll take the Seekers by surprise."

"I think that will work," he says, "but we need to set up a timer system. If the power goes out all at once, we'll have every Seeker running for the Core building to get status reports and commands from the Prime Maker." He stares at the center of the map. "We start at the Core building. Several minutes later, we set them off in the next street. Then the next. That should give us enough time to rattle outside forces enough for our people to take them down by hand. The few who get away and head for Eri can be handled by the Core building force, because by that point, everything will be secure."

We stand still for a moment, absorbing this new plan.

I tilt my head. "How will the groups know when to set off the grenades and head up top?"

"Next to each door that leads above the water tunnels is a clock for regulating heat and flow." Catcher begins to pace. "We'll instruct each team to move forward according to those clocks, though once their grenades go off, the clocks will stop working." He talks quietly, as though to himself, sorting through his thoughts. "I suppose the water will stop working too, since it's run on timers and electrically operated levers. I hadn't thought of that." He scratches his head and looks up at me. "It shouldn't be a problem. We'll get the water working as soon as the fuses are replaced. As soon as Freedom is under Rise control."

I'm sure he's right, but it makes me wonder what else we haven't thought of. What else is run on electricity that we've forgotten about? Something that might be a whole lot more important than keeping the water pipes running.

"What about Eridian?" I ask.

Catcher frowns. "She'll have an entourage. I don't know how we'll get close to her."

I do. "It doesn't matter if we get the surrogates and slaves out. They can't leave Freedom with those new trackers in their ears. Maybe we need to find Eri first thing." With Nine's help, we might have a chance to get close to Eri. I have a feeling the Prime Maker will do anything to get Nine.

"But if she knows we're there, the entire province will be on alert." Catcher shakes his head. "Surprise and stealth is our advantage. We can't waste it."

He's right. I lean against the wall and fold my arms. "Then we help our people escape, but keep them somewhere close to the Core building so we don't create suspicion on the tracker boards. We keep them safe until we've figured out how to disable the trackers."

"Where?"

"I think I know of a place, but I have to be sure first." I step close to him. "I'll get the slaves out. When your surrogates are free, meet me at the holding cells. I'll know by then where to take them. Once they're all secure, and the rebels are moving in on Freedom, we find Eri."

Catcher narrows his eyes but doesn't question me further. Because he trusts me. "Okay."

I nod. It's a messy plan with too many variables, but it's all we've got. And most importantly, it will lead me to Pua.

"I've already sent a scout to tell Odell about the bola grenades." Catcher runs a hand down his face. "He'll make sure the Seekers on our side will disable the electric components of their weapons the same way we have so the pulse won't affect them. We need every able-bodied Rise sympathizer in the fight today."

I nod. "What time is it?" I ask.

Catcher blows out the lantern and opens the door into the hallway. "It's time to go."

*   *   *

With the rebels awake and ready, I glance around at our group. Large in number, intimidating. I certainly wouldn't want to stand against us. Some rebels in the group have painted their faces with simple lines and dots—war paint. Others, like Kai, have a black tribal design on their chins, which I admit, makes them look more threatening than usual. When Kai leads the group in a war chant and dance that involves stamping feet and rhythmically shouted war cries, I get caught up in it, feeling fired up and making vicious facial expressions of my own.

I'm grateful we can head back through the standard tunnel system and not through the ocean. As thrilling as swimming through the water and walking through the sewer was—not really—I'm glad to stay dry as we enter the province.

The counterbalance platform works perfectly, even having to move up in several small groups. Within half an hour, we're travelling through the water tunnels in a single file, keeping quiet as Catcher leads us through the maze by memory.

At each strategic stop, he gives instructions to those we leave behind about when to activate the grenade and move up top in ambush. We make fifty or so stops, leaving five to seven rebels at each one. The rest follow us to the Core building.

Catcher leaves me with a group at the door that leads to the slave housing. He'll continue on to the surrogates using a different entrance.

"Remember," he says. "I'll meet you at the holding cells, and we'll find Eri together."

I nod and watch as he leads away half of our group with him.

I watch the clock at the door as though it might disappear if I turn away. I clutch a bola in my hand. I make a silent plea for all the grenades to work. The Seekers are more numerous than we are, more skilled with guns. I adjust the gun strapped across my chest. I've practiced with it, but hope I won't have to use it. I glance around the dozens of faces with me and wonder how many of them will still be alive in a few hours. I see Vishal among them, and I angle my head in a small bow of respect; he knows exactly what we're about to walk into.

"Stay close to me," I tell Nine.

She rolls her eyes. "I can take care of myself."

"I know." She's more capable now than she's ever been, but that's not why I say it. "I need you close; I can't lose you." I don't tell her it's because she might be the key to finding Eri. It's a form of lying, I know. But what good will it do right now when the truth might frighten her? Though looking at her determined face, I'm not sure anything frightens her anymore.

"Theron," she says, her voice softening. "I'm not going anywhere." I know she means more than this battle, this fight. She means she'll never leave me again. And I believe her.

I go over the plan one more time with our crew, then count down the last seconds. "Ready?" I ask no one in particular. I catch a few nods, and my heart beats so fast I think it might go out along with the rest of the power when I start to spin the bola above my head. I swear I feel the buzz of electricity as it flows through the grenade, a slight vibration in the rope I might be imagining. Then I take a deep breath and stop it abruptly, mid-swing. The quietest thump of an echo sounds, and everything goes dark.

I pull the latch, and the door opens to a dark room. The same one Catcher and I entered all those nights ago to get Vishal and his son out of the cells. Only there are no dim lights illuminating the space. There are no red blinking lights indicating the use of video cameras or sound sensors. It's pitch-black, and even when I think my eyes have adjusted, I don't see much. A couple of small lanterns are lit among our group, and Kai leads us down a long hallway.

I think I hear shuffling feet in the distance, but no one speaks. It's too early in the morning for the slaves to have been sorted and sent to work. Perhaps they think we are Seekers, come to do harm. "Are there any Seekers in here?" I call out.

"No," a few answer. Then one male voice says, "Is that Catcher?"

"Not Catcher, but we are the Rise, and we're here to get you out." I pause, the silence in the room so sharp I could break it with one breath. "All of you. Everyone is going home today."

A series of cheers sound, and I cringe for a moment, hoping no Seekers are nearby to hear the noise, but it's impossible to stop their celebrating. I send a dozen of our force through the slave cells with instructions to break everyone free and gather them back in the water tunnel to await my orders.

I lead another group, including Kai and Nine, down to the sick bay. "Get these doors open," I say. "These people will need medical care, and I've got a plan for that, but for now, just get them to the water tunnel like the rest."

When we reach the end of the hall, I see flickering lights behind the windows in the double doors.

"The power is still functioning on this end." Nine takes a bola out of her pack and spins it, activating the circuit, then she drops the whole thing to the ground. The lights go out.

I open the door to a large room of cells filled with children, several of them crying or screaming in fear in the thick darkness.

"It's okay," I shout. "We're here to help you. We won't hurt you. We're taking you home to your families."

The sobs die down as Kai lifts a lantern, his face ashen. "They're children."

I nod, no time to cushion that blow. I turn to Nine. "You and Kai get them to the water tunnel. I'll meet you there in a few minutes."

She grabs my arm. "Where are you going?"

I focus on her face, hesitant to leave, but know I have to do this alone. I'll only be a few minutes. "I'm going to find us a place to hide." I run down the hallway without turning back.

CHAPTER TWENTY-NINE

I leave behind the sick bay and hurry through the slave cages. I glance to where the metal landing ends in darkness, knowing that path leads to the main hallway of the Maker level. It's the way to Pua, to the holding cells. I wonder if the power in that area is out yet. If any Seekers are suspicious because of broken lights and disabled weaponry.

A part of me is tempted to ditch the plan and go after Pua, but I force myself to stay on the path that leads to the water tunnels. I'll see her in a few minutes. I can wait for a few more minutes. Besides, the outward spiral of grenades throughout Freedom will start soon, and I need to get where I'm going before that begins.

When I'm in the water tunnel, I close my eyes for a second and recall the map I studied last night, remembering where I need to go to reach the trauma station. I turn left, pass two right turns but take the third, then another quick left. There are no rebels stationed by the door, and the clock still ticks, which means the power is still running though the hallway is dark.

I push open the heavy door and run up the concrete stairs, two steps at a time. When I reach the main floor landing, I press my ear against the door but don't hear anything. I'm not sure how much I'd hear through the thick material even if there were noise on the other side, though. I grasp the latch and pull it open, revealing daylight and a street . . . and an armed Seeker in a black jumpsuit who falls backward into me, as though he'd been leaning against the door.

"What the—" He spins quickly, reaching for his gun, but I step close and grab him by his collar, pulling him into the stairwell, quickly making sure there are no other Seekers on duty with him out there.

I shove him against the closed door, cringing at the loud thump it creates, and hold his arms to his side so he can't grab his firearm. He attempts to butt my head with his, but I turn away and his forehead catches my nose instead. He uses my distraction to kick my shin, and I shout in pain. Curse this bum leg of mine.

A quick knee into his groin makes his legs crumble, and a fast jab to his jaw makes his eyes roll to the back of his head. He groans and sinks to the floor, still conscious but completely useless. First thing I do is pull the gun away in case he has some miraculous recovery. I should have set off a grenade to disable any nearby firearms. The Seeker blinks his eyes open and slurs some threat I don't understand. One more solid punch to the face and he's out, likely for the rest of the day.

With him sprawled on the floor, I think about my next move. How could I be so cracked? The door was supposed to lead me to the trauma station, not straight into a Seeker. I must have taken a wrong turn, but I've no idea where so I can't go back. I'll have to go out in the open to get there.

I glance down at my dark shirt, cargo pants, and stained boots. Nothing flashy, nothing special. Which is exactly why, if I head out there looking like this, I'll stick out compared to the rest of the citizens.

But maybe I can make this work.

I size up the Seeker. He's shorter than I am, but I can't be picky. I unzip his black jumpsuit and ditch my own clothing, climbing into his. The legs come up short, and my arms stick out beyond the sleeves too far, but I'm not going for fashion here, just stealth. It'll have to do.

I strap my gun to my back and place my gear over it, hiding it from view. I grab the Seeker's weapon, his transmitter, and his portable screen. I'm running out of time, but I slide his finger across the screen to log him in, and I tap my way to the tracking board on the display. The lights aren't red anymore; they're blue. Likely indicating the new tracker. A large congregation of blue lights hover around the Core building—the surrogates and slaves. Nothing looks suspicious. Yet.

I tuck the screen away, take a deep breath, and open the door to the morning light. The trauma station is across the street. I must have gone too far, and now I'm in the side stairwell of the small cinema that sits across the road. With my shoulders back and my steps sure, I stride through the street without looking around. I'm not going to draw attention to myself, and the more I appear I'm doing exactly what I intend to, no one will look twice at me.

When I enter the trauma station doors, a strange sense of familiarity comes over me. I hadn't worked here very long before being reassigned to the Maker level, but I still feel like I belong.

And as I turn the corner and see Iden behind the glass typing at her keyboard, I realize it isn't this place. It's the people. The anticipation of seeing her and Gray. It's a good feeling.

Her peach-colored hair is tied up, a single braid wrapping around a simple bun. Black designs weave across her forehead and down her nose, reminding me of the temporary tattoo I gave Nine on her bald head all those months ago. The tips of Iden's fingers are black with the same temporary ink, as though she dipped her fingers into a vat of ink, staining her skin to the second knuckle of each finger.

I tap on the glass with the back of my hand, and her head shoots up. She tenses at first, seeing the Seeker uniform, but then her eyes find mine and they widen in surprise. She mouths my name, the metal studs in her cheek shifting, then she reaches for a button beneath her table that opens the door to my right with a click.

I slip through and close the door behind me.

"Theron? What are you doing here? And what's with the Seeker uniform? The Prime Maker sent out a search for you when—"

"I'm sorry, Iden." I glance nervously to the clock on the wall. "I don't have time to explain, and I have to ask a favor. A huge favor."

Her eyes scrunch with worry. "Are you okay?"

"Theron?" Gray walks toward us, and while Iden doesn't drop her gaze from me at his approach, I startle for a second. I'm jumpy right now, and I need to calm down.

"Gray. Iden." I take a deep breath. "I need your help. I've got a lot of people I need to hide, and I want to bring them here, to the trauma station. We've got the space, medical supplies for the injured, and a way to lock this place down." I point to the quarantine system. "There's a chance the power might go out, but light from the skylights should be enough to see by while you administer to anyone who might need help."

I head to the back, passing two patients along the way. They don't look seriously injured, but they're in for a big surprise. Gray and Iden follow close behind me.

"What people?" Gray asks. "And why are they hurt?"

"Only some of them are hurt," I say. "The rest . . ." I don't know how to finish. I don't have the time to explain it properly anyway. "Just keep them safe. Keep them hidden until I come for them. It should be about an hour or two."

I step through the utility door in back. In front of me is the door to the stairwell I should have come through. I turn back to see their faces. Both unsure, Iden with a frown on her face.

"Please." My plea is short but clear. "Do this for me." Their expressions become determined.

Gray's stance straightens. "Whatever you need."

I breathe out with relief. "Thank you. I'll explain later. Just secure all entrances and set a silent lockdown routine. No Seekers. Not even the Prime Maker gets in. Do you understand?"

Iden nods. She glances over her shoulder into the trauma station. "No one will get through."

"Thank you. Keep this door propped open." I step forward, but pivot back, reaching for Gray. "Actually, will you come with me? I could use your help."

He doesn't hesitate and slips past me into the stairwell.

Iden jams the door open with a heavy metal box. "Go. I'll set up the lockdown."

I hurry down the steps to the water tunnels, Gray following close behind. I can hear people before I see them, their voices traveling through the maze of tunnels like a buzz of quiet insects.

We turn the final corner, and I see Nine, both of her hands holding those of small children on each side, a crowd of prisoners stacked behind her.

"Kai and his parents are in back," she says, "making sure we've got everyone."

I rest a hand on her shoulder. "Stay here with me." I turn to the large man at my side. "Gray's going to lead the group back."

Gray swallows hard.

I raise an eyebrow, as though asking if he's all right.

"Yes," he says. "I'll take them."

"Good. When the last of them are through, secure the door behind you. We'll likely have more for you in a bit. I'll be back."

His eyes widen, then he swallows again before leading the people to the trauma station. Someone takes the children from Nine's hands, and my voice shakes when I tell Nine and Kai, Ara, and Miri, "Let's go find her."

We run to the slave cages, eerily dark and empty. When we reach the main doors that lead out to the hallway, I crack the doorway open. I'm still in a Seeker uniform so if someone sees me, it should prevent them from automatically calling for help. But no one's there, so I open the door all the way, and we move quickly through the hallway. I check around each corner to make sure it's clear before we hurry along each stretch. When we reach the main elevator that leads to the lobby, my heart races, knowing at any time someone could walk out of those doors.

I debate whether to set off a grenade. Disabling the elevator would be ideal, but I don't want to call attention to confused Seekers whose transmitters might die before we absolutely need them to. But after glancing around the next corner, I see three Seekers on the far end, one of them armed. The other two laugh at some casual conversation they're having.

RESIST

We have no choice. I motion for Ara to engage a grenade, and after spinning the weapon above his head, he sends it flying their way. After a grunt and a curse from one of the Seekers, the distant buzz of electricity zaps. Everything goes dark.

We hurry down the hall as quietly as we can, our hands running along the wall to guide us. I can hear the Seekers fumbling with their flashlights, cursing when they discover they don't work. Between their rustling and our stealth, we might get past them unnoticed, but then I feel someone step on my foot and trip in front of me.

"Who's there?" a voice calls out.

Ara lights a match in time for us to gauge where the three Seekers are. I kick out at the one in front of me, knocking him into the wall. I'm surprised yet not surprised to see Nine kick the gun out of another one's hand—not that it would have fired anyway—and I restrain him while she sends her elbow into his face.

I can't tell what's going on with the third, but I drag the two downed men together and tie their arms behind them with the bola ropes. I tie their feet together as well so if they wake, they can't go anywhere to warn someone.

"Let her go!" Kai yells.

I look up in time to see the third Seeker holding Miri by the neck. Ara's match burns out, and I hear the distinct *thunk* of Kai knocking the butt of his gun into the Seeker.

Ara lights another match and kneels next to his wife, slumped on the ground.

Kai pulls his mother into his arms. "Are you okay?" he asks, his voice shaking.

Miri grips her neck, running her fingers along a pink line left behind by the Seeker. She nods and takes in a labored breath. "I'm fine." After glancing at her husband, she adds, "Really."

289

After tying up the third Seeker, I say, "Let's go." We need to keep moving. We're already wasting too much time.

I feel my way along the walls, familiar with the path to the surrogate holding cells. In the last ten feet before the entrance, the lights flicker. The power is still on here. It can't be more than two hundred feet from where we set off the bola grenade, half the distance we estimated. Hopefully it's an anomaly, and the rest of the pulse grenades will work as anticipated.

Around the bend in the wall, I find one woman on guard duty. Holding my hand up to let the others know to stay back, I walk toward the woman, who appears unarmed. When she sees me, she gives me a nervous smile. But I think it's because she thinks I'm a Seeker, not because I mean her harm.

"Good morning," I say, pausing at her side.

"Good morning." Her eyes roam over me, and the corners of her lips fall into frown. "Do I know you?"

She either doesn't recognize me and is suspicious, or she does recognize me from my time as a Healer here and is still suspicious. Either way, I don't want to give her time to reach for her transmitter.

I lift my gun. "Hands up," I order, motioning to her pocket. "I'm going to grab your transmitter. Don't try anything."

She nods, her eyes wide with fear.

With my gun still aimed at her, I grab her transmitter and pass it to Nine, who's rounded the corner, the others close behind.

The guard glances at us, her lip starting to quiver.

"You have cell keys?" I ask.

She glances to the wall behind her where a single key hangs from a hook. It's a master cell key, just what I need. I reach for it and know I can't contain myself any longer.

"Ara?" I turn to Pua's father. "Bring this one in behind us, will you?" I motion to the guard and lower my gun as Ara raises his, taking my place. That's enough answer for me. I run into the cell hall, the others following.

I hear Miri gasp and see Nine and Kai stop by a cell to get a better look inside. They weren't expecting these conditions, or maybe the sight of all these women at once is too much. But I don't have time to console them. I run full force to the back of the room, through a maze of halls and bars, until I come to the last one. I'm moving so fast, I slam into the bars to stop myself, the noise startling the girl inside.

The girl who isn't Pua.

CHAPTER THIRTY

No. No no no.

I grip two metal bars and shake them, frightening the girl on the other side, her eyes wide, her fingers pulling the blonde locks of her hair in front of her face to hide.

"Pua," I whisper. I'm too late. We're too late.

No, I won't accept that.

I spin around and peer into every cell, one by one, to get a good look at each girl. All of them frightened. All of them nervous.

All of them *not* Pua.

Kai steps around the corner, continuing to look in each cell. "Where is she?" he yells at me.

I turn and collapse backward into a set of bars. I grasp the hair on my head as I slide down. My shout is agony and despair and the sound of hope being sucked right out of me. She can't be dead yet. *She can't she can't she can't.*

"Where?" he yells again. "She's not here!"

I don't answer. Instead I look up at the ceiling. I don't want to be here anymore. I don't want to live like this. I want this nightmare to end.

Some part of me notes that Ara opens an empty cell in one corner and forces the guard inside. He locks her in and steps to me. His face is broken. He's on the verge of losing it too. "We have to free these women."

I know. But what's the point? None of them are Pua.

I feel a sting on my cheek and realize Kai slapped me across the face.

"Kai!" Nine shouts.

Kai ignores her and shakes my shoulders. "Focus, Theron. We need you."

My eyes drift up to his, but I can't seem to concentrate. What is he saying?

"Think." He crouches next to me and shakes me again. "Where would they have taken her?"

"It's too late," I mumble. "She's gone."

Kai grabs my chin violently and makes sure I'm looking right at him before saying, "She could die in the next few minutes, and we won't be there to save her because you're being a cowardly idiot right now. Man up and think. Where could she be?"

I blink one-two-six times and let his words sink in. He's right. I have to think. If she were about to be executed, where would they take her?

"The prison housing," I say. "She said they'd take her there before . . ." I summon every ounce of energy I have to get my feet under me and stand straight again. "That's where they take the prisoners who are supposed to be executed."

Nine swallows hard. "Do you know where that is?"

"Yeah." I point to the ceiling. "Three stories up. No, five. Five from where we are."

"Okay," Kai says. "Let's go."

Ara and Miri are deep in conversation. Miri nods then turns to us. "Your father and I will stay here. We'll release these women and take them to the trauma station with the others and wait for you there." Tears pool in her eyes, and I know she's desperate to see her daughter.

"Okay," I say. "We'll be there soon." I glance to the clock on the wall. We have to go quickly.

The three of us run out of the surrogate holding area and into the dark halls, running right into a group of rebels.

"Catcher sent us to meet you," one says.

They're members of the group he led when we split up. Doesn't he need their help with the surrogates?

Kai nods. "You can help my parents with these women."

The rebels hurry past us into the surrogate cells while the three of us maneuver to the elevator. A functioning elevator somewhere else on the level would be ideal, but we can't risk running into any Seekers, and I think the dark halls are more likely to be empty.

At the elevator, Kai helps me pry open the doors and remove a small ceiling panel leading above the elevator unit. Nine and Kai boost me up until I'm standing in a dark tower with cables extending from the elevator and disappearing into the dark. A set of rungs run up along one wall. This might work.

I help them through the opening, and they follow me up the ladder. We climb five stories, but the faint glowing light above the elevator doors indicates the power is still on. I make a plea no one is on the other side and pull open the doors with Kai's help. We boost Nine up, and she in turn helps us maneuver onto the third floor where the halls are lit, but empty.

With a bola ready in my hand, we rush in the direction of the prisoner housing and slam right into a Seeker, practically running over him. I pull Nine away and hear Kai's gun engage, but when I recognize the narrowed expression of the Seeker and the scar running through one eyebrow, I hold up my hand.

"Kai, wait." I drop my hand and place it strategically on my own gun, not entirely sure I won't have to use it. "Hello, Odell."

His face relaxes slightly, and I notice a new scar running along the left side of his jaw, pink like it's still healing. I wonder how he got it.

He glances over his shoulder to make sure we're alone.

I see his ear as he does. He has one of the new insect-like trackers. So even the Seekers have them.

Odell turns back. "What are you doing?" he whispers. "This place is crawling with Seekers."

I raise an eyebrow and look behind him. The halls aren't exactly hopping.

He sighs. "We've been summoned downstairs because of power outages in certain spots in the building. This elevator's not working, so most guards are on the other end of the floor. Those the pulse grenades?"

I grip the bola in my hand, trying to trust him the same way Catcher does. "Possibly."

Odell nods. "Catcher is in the surrogate wing but said I should meet him in the holding cells. That I'd find you there."

If Catcher was heading there, why would Odell be on this end of the floor? Was he planning to climb down the elevator shaft?

Doesn't matter. We don't have time to waste.

"We need to find Pua," I say. "Where is she?"

His eyebrows come together, but he knows who I'm talking about.

"Is she here?" Kai spits out, impatient. "With the prisoners?"

Odell takes in Kai and Nine, then looks back to me. "Follow me," he says.

We hurry through the halls. I'm grateful to have sunlight coming in through the building's windows. If we have to use a grenade up here, at least we'll still be able to see. I can tell when we've reached the prisoner wing because the carpet gives way to tile, and the doors have barred windows installed at eye level.

Odell stops in his tracks and maneuvers us out of sight behind a wall partition tucked beside a window. He must see something or someone ahead, but I don't know what. He takes out his transmitter, and after hitting a few buttons, holds it to his mouth and says, "Kathan and Shields. We need you in the lobby right away."

The transmitter buzzes, followed by a male's response. "We're on prisoner guard and were told we couldn't—"

"Right away," Odell interrupts. "It's a unit one emergency. All posts abandoned."

"Order set," the voice says, and Odell's transmitter shuts off. He bends his head around the partition, waiting for what I assume is sign of Kathan and Shields abandoning their post. After a moment, he waves us forward, and we're running down the hall again. We stop at a door marked with the number 342, and Odell unlocks it, swinging it open.

I hear a female shout in surprise as Odell steps inside the door. I see a brief flash of dark hair, then I hear her voice, crying with relief. "Kai?"

I hang back, letting Kai and Nine rush in front of me to greet their sister. The anxiety I'd felt melts right out of me. She's okay. All that matters is she's okay. I watch as the two of them embrace

Pua in their arms, making sure she's whole, healthy. I smile at the way they lift her face to theirs when they ask her questions to make sure she can understand their words.

"Are you in pain?"

"What did they do to you?"

"You're too skinny."

"Can you walk?"

"Did they hurt you?"

Pua leans into them, as though they give her the strength she needs to be brave. To come back. To escape. "I'm okay," she says over and over. "I'm okay." She holds on to Nine. Pats her brother's face. Leans her head against his shoulder and smiles. As though she's the one comforting them. She's so good at that.

"Mom?" she asks. "Dad? Hemi and Tama?"

"They're fine," Kai says. "They're all fine."

She lets out a sound of relief. It's a happy sound. The sound of hope and faith. She's safe. And she's here. That's all that matters.

I'm torn between joining them and standing outside the room to give them space. I can't take it much longer, and as I'm about to say something, Pua looks up and sees me standing in the doorway.

"Theron." Without taking her eyes off me, she pushes her way forward and runs to me, jumping into my arms. I fall into the door frame and slide to the ground, Pua gripping my shoulders as she settles on me. She looks at my face, tears pooling in her eyes.

"You came back." Her voice shakes, and she bites her lower lip to stop it from doing the same. "You came back for me."

"I promised you I would," I whisper. "I didn't stop thinking about you for one minute while I've been gone. I was so worried . . . ." My voice cracks. "So worried I was too late. That you . . .

I—I didn't want to lose you." I reach up and run a hand through her hair.

"Theron," she says, her eyes staring at my mouth. "You won't lose me that easily." Her lips turn up into a smile before they're pressed against my lips, kissing me.

I pull her close, returning her kiss and saying a silent thank you to whatever force or being brought us together again. I don't ever want to let her go.

"I've missed you," she says against my lips.

I pull away and grin. "Even my pig noises?"

She tosses her head back and laughs. "Especially your pig noises."

I move in and start oinking into her neck, nuzzling my nose and mouth along her skin. I know she can't hear it, but she can feel it, and it makes her laugh louder. I don't think I've ever heard a sweeter sound. That is until she brings my lips back to hers and kisses me again, a long moan deep in her throat. *That* sound would make me drop to the floor if I wasn't already here, but the moment I realize she probably doesn't know she's making the sound—well, that makes my heart race so fast I moan right back, determined to let her kiss me as long as she likes.

When she's done, she leans her forehead on mine and presses her nose against mine, and takes a long, deep breath. "Thank you," she says. "For coming for me."

I sigh, the sound of her accent making every part of me relax when I've been pulled tight in constant stress since we've been apart. "Why didn't you tell me?" I ask. "You knew who I was from the first day we met, didn't you? When you learned my name. Why didn't you say something?"

She presses her palm against my face. "I was afraid," she whispers. "I didn't know if Nine and Kai were still alive. Where they were. I didn't want to give you a false hope, and I . . ." She lowers her head and looks up at me with her big brown eyes. "I was being selfish, I guess. I wanted you for myself. I didn't want to share you. It's ridiculous, I know."

I pull her hand from my face and place it against my chest. "Nine may be tattooed on my neck, but you . . . Pua, you're tattooed on my heart." I think of what her father told me, about feeling truth so deeply it makes a mark on your heart. "I'm yours. All of me."

She smiles, letting a few of her tears fall.

I want to kiss her again, but someone clears his throat, and I look up to see Kai glaring at me. Nothing new, of course. I'll add this to the list of things he despises about me. I don't care about what he thinks, but I do care about . . .

Nine's mouth hangs open, pure shock evident on her face. But I still can't tell how she feels about me and Pua together like this. I look at her, a question in my eyes, asking her, without saying anything, if this is okay. Her mouth closes, and her freckles shift as a smile grows on her face. Crinkles appear at the side of her eyes, and her hand shoots up to cover her mouth, waving in the air in front of her like she can't contain whatever emotion bubbles inside.

When she finally drops her hand, her lips press together to keep holding in her emotions. She links her arm with Kai's and nods at me. Telling me she's okay with this. Saying, without saying anything, that we're okay. We're still okay, and she's happy for me. For us. I hadn't realized how worried I'd been about it until my shoulders relax in relief.

"Oh, wipe that stink off your face, Kai." Pua scowls at her brother. "I'm not going to let you ruin this for me."

Nine bursts into laughter and leans her head against Kai's

shoulder, the movement making him relax instantly. Pua turns to me and wraps both arms around my neck, feeling behind my ear to make sure I don't have a tracker. I reach for hers and feel the insect-like device behind her right ear.

But she's still alive. That's what matters.

Kai folds his arms across his chest. "This is fun and all, really." He rolls his eyes. "But I think it's time we find Catcher in the surrogate wing."

I stand and help Pua off the ground. She slides her fingers into mine and squeezes tight. I'm totally okay with that.

In the hall, we all turn to Odell, expecting him to show us the way, but he shakes his head. "I think you should return to the holding cells and wait for him there."

Something's wrong. "Do you think he's done freeing the surrogates?" I ask.

Odell pauses. "No. But I still think it's better to wait where he said—"

I cut him off. Pua is alive, and I need to make sure she stays that way. We don't have time to waste. "More electricity will go out through the province, and we need to get all of the rebels out of this building before more Seekers come investigating. If we can help Catcher get the surrogates out, we should."

Nine shivers beside me. "Maybe we should do as he says, Theron."

Pua leans closer to me. "I think we should help Catcher." She glances to the prisoner rooms along the hall, lost in thought.

I turn to Kai to see what he thinks. He glances at Nine, then back to Pua and me. "Let's save them," he says.

I nod in agreement, and Odell finally sighs. "All right. But remember I tried to keep you away."

CHAPTER THIRTY-ONE

The power is still on as we walk into the surrogate wing, but some stubborn lights flick on and off, as though they can't decide whether to hold on or give in. We enter a set of doors marked SURROGATE UNIT to the right, and I prep myself to hear the familiar buzz of women talking. I guess a part of me expected cells like the slave housing and surrogate holding area, but there's no talking where we are. No sounds but the humming of electricity as it fights to stay on, beeping monitors that remind me of the trauma station, and the shuffling feet of a frustrated man.

"Catcher?" I ask. His bald head is covered in a layer of sweat.

He spins around, his face a torturous mess. "I can't wake them up," he says, on the verge of tears. "They . . . they did something to them. They won't wake up."

Kai steps forward. "What are you talking about?"

"The surrogates," he cries. "I've tried everything. Usually they're kept under until two weeks before their gestation is up.

That's when we prep them for delivery. We give them the sentient serum and within ten minutes they are fully cognizant. But they're not waking up!"

"What do you mean 'kept under'?" I ask, though I'm afraid I know exactly what he's talking about. I walk toward a long line of white fabric tents—I've no idea how else to describe them. At one such tent, I move one panel aside to reveal a patient beneath it. Female. Unconscious. Tubes and wires connect to her arms; leads placed on her temples and neck read vital statistics. Her stomach is large; I wonder if that means she is close to full term. She's someone's daughter, maybe a sister, a wife. I glance at the long line of tents. Is Vishal's wife here somewhere too?

I turn back to Catcher. His hands drag down his face in frustration. "I don't know what to do."

Nine stands behind Kai, clutching his arm, in obvious fear about something. Kai gently peels her off him and walks to another white tent. I'm not sure how many are in this room, the wall curves around a corner making it hard to tell, but I do know how many females are kept as surrogates. Hundreds. My stomach churns, realizing with horror there are hundreds of women here, kept unconscious while they grow babies inside of them.

I thought they'd be kept in cells, awake. It never occurred to me they would be placed in a coma. Air flows in and out of their lungs, blood flows through their veins—but what kind of life is this? I gag, thinking about what Catcher told me once, how after these women give birth, they are impregnated again and again, carrying babies for years down here. This is worse than what my imagination let me believe. This is madness.

"I saw one once." Nine grasps her elbows across her torso as though she is holding herself together. She's nervous. "I came down here and saw one of them giving birth. Before our

Remake." Her eyes shoot up at me. She never told me about this. "The woman was screaming in pain. I was so confused. I didn't know what was happening."

She takes several steps toward Kai. He pulls aside a white curtain to see who or what's hiding behind it. "It wasn't like Miri," she tells him. "It wasn't family and love and joy. It was pain. She was awake just to give birth. Just to experience that pain." She brings a hand to her mouth. "Is that all these women know?"

I thought the surrogates were unconscious for their implantation procedure because they didn't want to carry an embryo in the first place. I didn't realize they were sedated for their entire pregnancy. For the majority of their lives.

Catcher spins around and begins pacing. He covers his ears as though he doesn't want to hear what Nine is saying, though he knows it's true. He's lived it every single day for the last twenty years. Caring for these women is what's kept him going, what's kept him here. What made him start the Rise in the first place. Because he wanted to get them out. And now that he's here, now that the day has come, his hands are tied. For some reason, they won't wake up. He can't free them, even when there's nothing else to stop him.

"They are kidnapped from their families," Nine spits out through gritted teeth. "Thrown into cages. Put under to become slaves to their nightmares, only to wake to experience inexplicable pain as they give birth. The babies are taken from them, and then they are impregnated again. It's like a torture chamber." She inhales as though through a cry. "We should have come here first. Months, years ago."

I shake my head to clear it. What's done is done. What matters is what we do now.

I turn to Catcher. "How many have you given the serum to? Maybe it was a bad vial. Or maybe something's wrong with those particular females. Maybe we should try—"

"Why do they have trackers?" Kai shouts from across the room. "Behind their ears—why do they have them?"

I walk closer to see what he's talking about.

His eyes narrow. "It's not like these women are going to get up and walk out of here. Why would they need trackers?"

Odell walks toward Catcher and makes sure he's got his attention. "This is what I was telling you about. Eri's got something planned with these new trackers, and I don't know what it is. The citizens have them." He touches the new tracker behind his own ear. "The slaves and surrogates, too. Maybe," he eyes the small white tents spread evenly along the walls, "maybe the part we don't know is why these females have them too. Maybe that's why you can't wake them up. Because it's interfering with the serum somehow."

Catcher's lips tremble. "It doesn't matter *why* right now. All that matters is that these women are hooked up to life-support machines. Do you understand? *Machines.*"

I back away from the surrogate and watch Catcher carefully.

"In a matter of minutes," he says, "all of Freedom One will be without power. And we have no way of postponing it or communicating with our rebel forces to call it off. When the power goes out for good, these women will be cut off."

The reality of the situation hits me in my gut.

Catcher's face goes ashen. "And if we can't wake them up, they're going to die!"

Nine starts running through the room, glancing at each tent, desperately trying to find who knows what. A hidden switch? A secret vial? Anything that will clue us in to how to wake these women.

My voice is low when I say, "Maybe when the power is off, whatever is keeping these women under will be disengaged, and the serum will work then."

"Even if that's true," Catcher says, "the serum takes ten minutes. They might not last ten minutes. I don't know. We've never disconnected a female without her awake first."

We can't lose these women. There are hundreds of them. And hundreds more lives growing within their bellies. I feel like I've been stabbed in the chest—because it's my fault. The thing that might kill them is the lack of electricity, which is my invention, my doing.

"We have to find Eri," I say. "She'll know how to fix this. And how to disengage the trackers."

Kai folds his arms. "And tell us what they're for besides tracking."

"There's no time," Catcher cries. "The rebels are going to set off the grenades."

I shake my head. "They're going to set them off, yes, but not in the Core building. We're the only ones assigned to this area. We won't use any more bola grenades while we're in the building. We'll buy you some time. You keep trying to wake them, and"—I pivot around, figuring out the best scenario—"Odell will stay here to hold off any Seekers that may come this way. He'll guard you and make sure you can keep them alive."

I glance at Kai. "Can you find your way back through the tunnels to the trauma station?"

He nods, his face uneasy. "I think so. Why?"

"Take Pua with you and wait there."

"Wait? For what? For the other rebels to fight Seekers when I should be with them? I don't think so."

"Did you see how many slaves we freed?" I yell. "They must be protected at all costs. If the trauma station is infiltrated, everything we've done here today is for nothing. We keep them safe until we figure out how to disable those cracked trackers and then we get them out of here."

His nostrils flare, thinking about it for a moment. "You said me and Pua. What about you and Ani? Aren't you coming with us?"

I glance at Nine, my eyes locking onto hers. "I need you," I say. "We have to find Eri. We need to convince her to talk to us, to tell us how to disable the trackers. Wake the surrogates. See what else she's been planning." I pause, swallowing hard. I feel like I'm using her—I am—but it's the best shot we have right now. I instinctively rub her name on my neck. "Eri says you're the key to stopping this madness. I don't know what it means, but I think you're the only one who can get close to her."

"Yes," Nine says, resolute. "You're right. I need to go with you."

Kai throws his hands in the air. "There's no way I'm letting you get close to that woman."

She ignores his words, stepping up to him and kissing him hard on the lips. "She won't hurt me," Nine reassures him. "Trust me. I have to do this."

He grinds his teeth, as though wanting to force her to stay with him, but at the same time knowing she makes her own decisions. Knowing that she's strong enough. Brave enough to do what she thinks is right. I never felt that strongly about her, and there's a comfort that comes with knowing he's exactly who she needs.

My eyes flick to Pua, and her face falls.

"I just got you back," she says.

I promised I wouldn't leave her again, but I need to keep her safe. "Go with Kai," I plead. "He won't let anything happen to you."

She glances at her brother and bites the inside of her cheek. "I'll go with him, but not to the trauma station."

I watch her without blinking, silent, trying to understand what she's saying.

"We're going to release the rest of the prisoners," she says. "From the prisoner housing where you found me. We'll take whoever's willing to fight with us and let the others go."

"No." I lean toward her. "I won't let you risk it. We can get the prisoners later."

She closes the distance between us and wraps her arms around my neck. "I'm going for the prisoners. Most are Rise sympathizers, and with an intimate knowledge of Freedom, their allegiance will only help."

"I agree, but . . ." I pause, thinking through my argument. We can get them later. When I can go with her. When I know she won't be risking her life just when we earned it back. I open my mouth to say so, but she leans her forehead against mine, and my words stall.

"Trust me," she says.

In the corner of my vision I see Kai talking to Odell. Odell gives him his card key. Kai can use it to release the rest of the prisoners. He's already accepted this new plan. He trusts Pua. Nine. He trusts me. It's time I do the same.

I breathe out the word. "Okay." I lean back and say it again so I know she sees it. "Okay. You go with Kai and get the prisoners. We'll see you in the trauma station."

Pua smiles, and in that moment I know she's more than just a pretty face. She's brave and strong, and it makes me love her that much more, even when we're apart. Distance can't change the way we feel about each other. I've learned from Catcher that you can love someone when they're not with you. Even when they're gone.

I catch Kai's attention. "Don't forget," I say. "No grenades."

He glares at me. I guess that's an affirmative.

I don't add it should be no more grenades at all costs. Above their own lives. Because it's one or two lives to save hundreds. Who's to judge whose life is worth more than another's? But I'm too much of a coward to ask them, ask Pua, to sacrifice themselves if need be. Hopefully no one will need to make that choice.

I kiss Pua before her brother pulls her away from me and toward the door. He aims a fierce look right at me. "I'm trusting you," he says. Then his face softens, surprising me. "Bring Ani back to me."

I watch as they hurry out the door, Pua's face a combination of determination and love. *I'm trusting you, too*, I think to myself, hoping Pua will be okay.

I turn to Odell. Catcher is rifling through a file cabinet in the corner, probably looking for anything that might help him with the surrogates.

"Where is she?" I ask Odell.

He sighs. "Unless they've sent forces into the province, Eridian will be in the lobby. Or . . . or there's a conference room on the south side of the main floor. It's where she gives instructions to the Seekers before our nightly curfew run. She'd be using it in an emergency like this."

I glance at Nine. We can't walk out in the open like this.

Those Seekers will have functioning weapons. I glance down at my small jumpsuit, then at Odell's.

"Nine," I say while looking at Odell. "Do you think you can fit in this Seeker uniform?" I tug at the black fabric on my chest.

Before she can answer, Odell sighs heavily and begins unzipping his jumpsuit. "Fine."

With Nine hiding behind one of the surrogate tents for privacy, we all play a game of changing outfits, and soon Nine and I look like we're a couple of Seekers, our uniforms both fitting just right. As long as no one recognizes our faces, we should be able to slip past most of Eri's force without suspicion. I hope it will be enough to get us close to the Prime Maker.

*　*　*

When we pry open the doors to the lobby, nobody cares that we're walking out of a dark elevator shaft instead of an elevator unit, or maybe they just don't notice. Everything is chaos. Several Seekers force a crowd of citizens outside through the main lobby doors.

"The Core building is off limits," one shouts. "If you continue to force your way in, you'll be taken to prison housing."

Many retreat from the threat, knowing what Seekers have been capable of the last few months. But others continue to shout at Eri's men.

"The power is out in our entire building!"

"I can't get the water to work."

"There are fights in the street."

"Something's wrong with my tracker."

"I'm injured, and the trauma station is on lockdown."

That last one makes me nervous. Though, in truth, it all

makes me nervous. We've taken too long. The grenades are already going off, and the power outage is spreading.

One of the Seekers fires his gun in the air above the crowd. The fact that Seekers still have working weapons shakes me, and I hurry through the lobby to get away from them, head lowered.

"We'll look into your concerns soon." The Seeker's voice fades away the more distance I put between us. "The Prime Maker is doing everything she can to—"

I don't hear him finish. Nine keeps up with me, her steps sure, her stride strong. Her head is lowered as well, eyes clear on our target. We need to get into that conference room on the south end. We need Eri.

There's one guard on duty outside an open door, but he's focused on what's going on inside the room more than he is on guarding the entrance. His stance is slightly askew, his body angled toward the door.

I keep my head down and move in past him, doing my best to come off as a capable Seeker. Nine is close behind me. I resist the urge to grab her hand and hold on to it. We get in without incident and stand at the back.

I almost can't breathe, the mass of black jumpsuits making me feel claustrophobic. How many Seekers does Eridian have on her force? She must have recruited more over the last months because this is ridiculous. Mostly men, some women. All of them armed.

A familiar voice speaks in front, addressing the Seekers. It's rough and deep with a hint of a sneer. It's Bron. I remember the welts on Pua's back, and my limbs shake with rage. I chance a look to see Eri standing next to him, her hands behind her back, her eyes scanning the room. I sidestep to stand directly behind another tall man and lower my head. We can't let her see us. Not yet.

"The attack we've been anticipating has arrived," Bron says.

"The rebels are within our boundaries now, hiding in the shadows. Seek them out. Stop them. Kill them. We must not allow them to take over."

They know we're here? How? All they've got are a few downed power lines. No one's seen us. No one knew we were coming. It feels way too soon for them to reach this conclusion.

"We're sending a minimal force to guard the slaves and surrogates," he continues, "since one of their main goals will be to free those captured there. From our own intel, we know they're staging an all-out attack. Use whatever force is necessary to stop them."

Eridian steps forward. "They will not be in uniforms so it might be hard to tell them apart from Freedom citizens." She pauses, shifts her lower jaw left to right, then continues. "If you suspect someone, anyone, whether they claim to be a citizen or not—or if you know them to be a citizen yet there is still cause for suspicion—stop them at all costs. Kill them. This is war, and lives will need to be sacrificed to protect the cause of Freedom."

She's crazy. The Prime Maker doesn't care about anything besides maintaining her power and the functioning of her precious Freedom One. I carefully scan the crowd of black jumpsuits. Every Seeker is armed with a weapon, and I realize if I set off a grenade now, it would disable all of their weapons in one shot. It's tempting, oh so tempting. I could save so many lives. Both rebels and citizens.

But we're just above the surrogates. Above Catcher and Odell and hundreds of females. A pulse grenade would mean we'd lose so many others. My fingers grip the bola weapon resting in my front pocket. Tightening and loosening. I want to stop these Seekers while I can, yet I'm not willing to sacrifice those women and their unborn children to do it.

Bron rattles off other sets of instructions, but I can't concentrate anymore. The red stars in white circles on each jumpsuit blur, and my stomach squeezes tight. So many will die today, and it's all because of me.

Nine's elbow in my side brings me out of my daze. The Seekers are moving out. I don't see a clock, and without a transmitter on me I can't check the time. I just hope most of the rebel grenades don't go off until the Seekers are in their assigned stations throughout the province. We'll do no good against an armed enemy. The thought makes me swallow. We're surrounded by armed Seekers, and there's no room for any more mistakes.

The crowd clears, and our first bit of luck finds us. No one is left in the room but me, Nine, and Eridian. Not even Bron remains. Eri has her back turned to us, her palms resting on a table against the far wall, elbows locked. Her head is bowed, shoulders raised. She's tired and worn.

She doesn't notice as we step close, or as I engage the gun across my chest. She must not hear our footsteps, feel our presence behind her, smell us, sense us, anything, because it isn't until I have the barrel of my gun pressed into her waist that she stiffens. She automatically reaches for her transmitter, but it's not in her pocket like she expected.

Nine holds it in the air and, her voice shaking slightly, says, "Looking for this?"

Eridian spins around, eyes closed, lips moving as though in a silent plea that what she thought she heard isn't her imagination. She opens her eyes slowly, taking in a sharp breath when she sees us. Sees her. Eri's mouth falls open.

"Nine," she whispers.

It sounds a whole lot like hope.

CHAPTER THIRTY-TWO

I look around, sure at any moment some Seeker is going to walk into the room and ruin this.

"To your office," I say. "Quietly."

Eri doesn't look at me or give any indication she heard me at all. She reaches a hand for Nine, her fingers stretching to touch Nine's bright red hair.

"Not here," Nine says between her teeth.

I dig my gun deeper into Eri's side, and she finally flinches from the pain and turns her face to me, dropping her hand.

"Now," I say.

She leads us out of the conference room. The lobby is eerily vacant, though crowds of people are gathered beyond the front doors. I see them through the glass pacing and yelling though I can't hear them. The entire building must be on lockdown because no guards are left to defend it or its Prime Maker. At least there are no guards on this level. Any minute they'll discover their slaves and potential surrogates have gone missing. I cringe, thinking of Catcher and the surrogates in their white tents. I hope Odell is everything Catcher gives him credit for.

I don't even have to hide my gun as we walk behind the front desk and move into Eri's office. She heads straight for her own desk, but I yank on her shoulder and force her into one of the chairs on the opposite side. I don't want her triggering some kind of alarm hidden in her desk or computer. I lean back against her desk, my weapon still pointed at her.

"Nine," she says, sitting on the edge of the chair, her attention completely focused on Nine, who walks around the desk and sits in Eri's chair. "Where have you been? Where did you go? When you left—"

"Shut up." Nine turns Eri's transmitter on and places it on the desk so we can hear the communication between Seekers as they search for our rebels.

Get the Batchers back in their tower, a voice says, crackling with disruption.

Nine leans forward. "How do we disable the trackers?"

Eri's face twists into obvious confusion. "The trackers?"

"The new ones," I spit out, impatient. "The ones you gave to everyone, including the slaves."

"And the surrogates," Nine adds. "Tell us how to disable them."

"You can't disable them." Eri shifts in her seat.

"That's a lie," I say. "Odell said you could do it."

"Odell?" Eri's eyebrows shoot up, her lips twitching.

I'm such a scab. I just gave away our biggest insider. How could I be so stupid?

"Tell us," Nine says, returning the conversation to what's most important. "Now."

The Prime Maker clears her throat. "I told you the truth. You can't disable them. You can't remove them, either. Not without releasing—" Her words stop.

"Releasing what?" Nine shouts. "An electric shock into their brain? A poison? Tell me."

"Poison." Eri says it so softly I barely catch it.

The Seekers report that the citizens are in an uproar at the gambling centers.

"A poison," I say, standing tall. Pua mentioned something about a poison.

Eri nods. "If you try to leave or if you try to remove the tracker, the toxin is released."

Something in her choice of words catches my attention. The rise in pitch, her gaze turned away. She's lying. Or not quite giving us the whole truth.

"What sort of toxin?" I ask.

She doesn't answer.

"No way to remove it?" Nine asks, bitterness in her voice. "How convenient. So everyone who has one is destined to stay here forever? In Freedom One?" She pauses, gauging Eri's expression. "I don't believe it."

"There's an antidote," Eri says, matter-of-fact. Her eyes roam up and down Nine. "I'm not an idiot."

Nine snorts. "Where is this antidote?"

Eridian remains silent.

With a heavy sigh, Nine mumbles, "We're running out of time." Then she turns to the computer and begins typing at the keyboard.

Take them out. Take them all out.

I cringe at the words on the transmitter. I don't know who

they're taking out, but the Seekers obviously still have electricity if they're able to communicate through their transmitters.

"If she's not going to give us anything, I'll find it myself." Nine looks up at me. "I need her print to log in."

I press the gun to Eri's forehead. "You heard her," I threaten. "Unless you want me to cut off your finger and hand her that. Your choice."

Eri narrows her eyes at me and stands from her chair.

"Don't even think about doing anything cracked," I say.

She walks to the desk and reaches around to run her finger along the computer screen. Nine visibly cringes at her proximity, but as soon as Eri's back in her seat, Nine is fast at work on the computer.

"See if there's a tracker map," I say over my shoulder, not willing to take my eyes off Eri.

Looting. The citizens are looting shops on Main Street.

After a moment, Nine says, "They're okay. The slaves are still okay."

Eri shoots to her feet. "What have you done—"

"Sit down," I yell. "You only speak when we tell you to speak."

She slowly lowers to the chair, her eyes glued on Nine scrolling through the computer screen.

"Theron?" Nine's face glows from the reflection of the computer, her forehead wrinkling. "Come and look at this."

I move behind the desk to see what she's talking about.

"It's some kind of data chart." She stands, motioning for me to take a seat in the chair. "It might have the answer to the tracker problem. See if you can make sense of this."

Nine takes my place in front of Eridian, engaging her own weapon, ready to shoot the Prime Maker at a moment's notice.

Nine questions her about the surrogates while I attempt to deci-pher the chart.

"Why won't the surrogates wake up?" Nine asks.

Eridian guffaws. "Why are you trying to wake my females?"

"They are not *your* females," Nine says. "They don't belong to you. And neither do the children they carry."

"Of course they belong to me. I Made those infants. I gave those women a purpose. I own them."

"You can't own a person!" Nine's hand trembles. "Whether they're a surrogate, a slave, or a citizen of Freedom One. They are free to choose for themselves. Their life. Their happiness. Their family."

"Family," Eri spits out. "That choice will destroy us all. Because it means breeding without regulation. It means—"

"You don't care about overpopulation!" Nine counters. "You just want everyone to be under your control. Do things your way. Because you're a sick, crazy person who never should have become leader of anything, let alone a whole society of innocent people."

"It's not my way," Eri whispers.

"What?"

"It's not *my* way," she says again. "Not anymore. Can't you see I'm trying to get it back?"

Nine snorts. "You're not making any sense." They both fall into a sullen silence.

There, the rebels. What's that in their hands?

The voice cuts short, and I stare at the transmitter, hope ris-ing in my chest. The rebels are fighting back. The grenades—they're working.

I sit taller and study the file on the screen. It's a green, three-dimensional chart with the words EMBRYO RECORDS on the right side. By sliding my finger across the screen, I can make it rotate right or left, up or down, exposing different sections of the chart. It reminds me of a tree, with a pair of numbers connected to each other that branch out to several more. Where the numbers connect, more branches are formed so what started as two numbers at the base eventually becomes hundreds, thousands.

They have to represent Freedom citizens. Each pairing has both an M entry and F entry. Male and female. Both contribute to an embryo, repeating over and over again. It's a record of every Batcher ever Made.

I zoom in and notice a smaller set of numbers beneath each entry. A date. The date the embryo was created? Curious, I focus in on the first numbered pair. The one from which all other paths branch.

I read the date and estimate on my fingers, counting how long ago the date represents. I repeat the calculation four times, the last time pulling a pen and paper from Eri's desk and doing it by hand. I reread the number on the screen over and over again, making sure I'm seeing it correctly.

The armored vehicles have stalled. The transmitter crackles. *Communications are out in all sectors but three and six.*

I toss the pen on the desk and push my chair away from the computer like it has a disease. I shiver at the metaphor, my hands shaking with uneasiness. I press my palms to my eyes, trying to chase away what I've realized. Dread finds every corner of me.

The Virus spread throughout the world and wiped out almost everyone on earth. The few to survive decided to Make humans in limited Batches. That way, the population could be controlled and we wouldn't risk another Virus. Batches were started in response to the Virus by the very first Makers.

Why then, no matter how many times I calculate it, does the date on the first pairing listed—the first embryo formed—precede the date of the Virus?

"What's wrong, Theron?" Nine's gun is still trained on the Prime Maker, but her eyes are focused on me.

I stand and walk slowly to Nine's side. I can barely look at Eridian when I say, "I know what the toxin is in the trackers."

Eridian's lips curl into an insolent smile. "Catcher was right about you," she says admiringly. "You're very smart. Too bad you left when you did. I could've used someone like you on my force."

"What is it?" Nine's forehead creases with worry. She can read the look on my face, and she knows it's something bad.

"The Batches weren't Made in response to the Virus," I say, swallowing hard. "They started before the Virus even happened."

"What?" Nine's gun lowers slightly, her arms faltering.

"And Eridian . . ." I stare at the Prime Maker, wondering if she could really do it. If she is sick enough, deranged enough. Unfortunately, I've no doubt she is. "Eridian's going to release it again."

Nine lets her weapon fall completely. "The trackers contain a virus? *The* Virus?" Her face freezes for a minute, then she steps forward, pointing a finger into Eridian's chest. "Freedom was never about controlling the population. It was just about *control*. That's why the Batches were started before the first Virus was released. So you could build a society completely under your control. So you could produce these so-called perfect beings who choose what they look like and what they act like, but all of it was to be under your control."

"No," Eri says. "It's always been about peace. From the very start."

"Is this what you call peace?" I say. "Making your people believe they are free and equal, while others slave away below them."

"It's not my people I've tried to impress," she says.

"Then who?" I ask. "Whose opinion is so important that an entire group of people live as slaves or surrogates, who labor for the false security the rest of the citizens think they have?"

Eri pauses. "It doesn't matter anymore. They aren't important anymore."

Nine raises an eyebrow. "If you don't care about impressing whoever these people are, why release the Virus? Why kill the rebels to make those people happy?"

I interrupt Nine as I realize something. "But you're not just killing the rebels. The citizens have the new trackers, too. You're going to spread the disease among your own people. Why?"

"It's not the rebels I'm trying to kill. It's not Freedom citizens either." She sits with her hands in fists. "It's *all* of them."

This game is tiring. "Who?" I ask again.

"The other Prime Makers and their precious Freedoms!"

Nine tightens her grip on her gun, shaking herself out of a daze. "Have they received new trackers too?"

"No," Eri says. "But it doesn't matter. Because they're coming. Freedom One is where it will start, but not where it will end."

"Who's coming? The other Prime Makers?" Nine covers her stomach as though she'll be sick. "Why are you doing this?"

"Because," Eri says, sighing. "They're going to shut me down."

"What do you mean?" I'm so confused. Are they going to replace her? Find a new Prime Maker? Is that why she's been acting so desperate? To protect her position? It's ridiculous to think she'd kill everyone to preserve her power. Then again, after everything she's done to the slaves and surrogates, what she's done to her citizens, I wouldn't put anything past her.

"I had to bring in the rebels," Eri mutters. "None of the citizens were choosing less-desirable Trades like working in the sewers or the crop fields or the factories. Our province was on the verge of collapse." Eri glances up at me, as though convincing me of her sanity. "I handed the rebels over in exchange for citizenship. In exchange for my freedom. They became slaves. They became surrogates. I brought them in, all in the name of freedom. And this is how the other leaders repay me. They're going to take away all I've given them."

Eridian started this. Catcher told me she had been an adviser to the previous Prime Maker and was put in charge of the rebels. He didn't realize she was the one who brought them here in the first place. All because our so-called *free* society was failing. Of course it was. Because this isn't freedom at all.

"Is that why you Made me?" Nine asks. "Is that why I was an experiment? To replace you should they shut you down?"

"I Made you to save a dying system."

"What system? This place you call Freedom?" Nine waves her hands in the air. "It's been dying since it first started. From the first time the Virus was released. From the very first Batcher ever made. This is not how people should live, and you know it. You came from the rebels. You knew about families and fathers and mothers, but you turned your back on them. So why am I surprised you're turning your back on the other Prime Makers now? You're selfish, and nothing will ever be good enough for you, will it? You can't kill everything and start new when things go wrong."

How does she know Eri lived with the rebels? Nine has a bigger role to play than I realized.

"I don't understand." I fold my arms across my chest. "If Nine came back earlier, or if she had never left, what difference would that have made? Why did you need her so badly?"

Eri tilts her head toward me, but her focus is on some distant spot. She is looking past me, or through me, at something I can't see. "I told you. I Made Nine to save a dying system. I didn't have a choice. They were going to shut me down. And not just *me*. All of it—my entire province—unless I could prove to them I could make it work. I started with the rebels—used them to keep us going, keep us functioning—but it wasn't enough." Eri blinks several times, her eyes finally focusing on me. "It wasn't enough to prevent our citizens from escaping."

Like me. And Nine. Miri. Citizens who joined Catcher's cause. I wonder how many have managed to run away from this place. How many want to?

"That's why I Made Nine. She was supposed to *want* to stay, to belong. I hoped to show them that she did everything in her power to fit in with everyone else, the way I once did. But she ended up running away too."

Nine's voice is quiet. "We're ending this madness today. We'll find the antidote. And when we're done with you, we'll go to every Freedom province and put a stop to their Batches and their twisted idea of equality. We will teach them about families and the real way to live—the only way to live that will bring true happiness. Lasting joy. Because this"—Nine motions to Eri—"is the furthest thing from it."

Eridian tosses her head back and laughs. Actually laughs. "You have no idea what's going on in the world, do you? You haven't scratched the surface of our secrets. You think *I'm* crazy? I hope, no, I *want* you to meet the Assembly one day. Then maybe you'll learn you're more like me than you realize."

The Assembly must be the ones Eri's been trying to impress. A chill runs through me thinking that if they really are worse than the woman in front of me, what will it mean for our world?

Eri leans forward, resting her elbows on her knees as they bounce up and down, restless. "We wanted a world free of pain," she says, almost like a chant, as though convincing herself. Making herself feel better for the chaos she's created. "To have peace. Don't you see? I can do that. Start fresh. With a new world. A new people."

I grind my teeth together. "Where is the antidote?" If we can't stop the Virus from being released, we need to know how to heal those who become infected. We have to stop it before it spreads.

Eridian waves her finger in the air and frowns derisively. "Tsk. Tsk. I'm not giving away my best bargaining chip. I value my life you know."

I step forward and grip the Prime Maker by her hair, ripping it out of its bun, forcing her to stand. I shove her toward the door.

She brings one hand to her chest, the other smoothing her hair down. "Where are you taking me?"

I catch the hint of fear in her voice, and I'd be lying if I say I don't feel a sense of satisfaction about it. "To the surrogates," I say, hoping Catcher has a better idea about how to stop the Virus. "You're going to wake them up. And you're going to give us the antidote to the Virus. Unless you want to see what it's like to be the one on the operating table for a change."

"Sounds like a plan to me." Nine grabs the transmitter from the desk. It's been silent for a while now. I'm glad to know our grenades are working as planned. We might come out on top today after all.

CHAPTER THIRTY-THREE

The elevator doors open to Sublevel Two. The halls are dark, a faint light flickering where the surrogate wing is. I don't understand. This place hadn't been touched minutes ago when Nine and I left. Who would have set off a grenade in this section? Unless Catcher . . .

We run through the hall, forcing Eridian to move quickly in front of us. There are no signs of Seekers anywhere. It doesn't make sense. I heard Eridian assign men to this post. We should have encountered at least one or two by now.

When we get to the surrogate wing, I tell Nine to stay back with Eri while I investigate, just in case. With my back against the wall, I slowly step into the surrogate room. The lights are out. The machines are silent. But a lantern has been lit. The one Catcher brought with him. But no Catcher.

If the power is out, then that means . . . Oh no. The surrogates.

I hear the faint sound of someone in pain. No, not

pain—discomfort. It's a long moaning, aching drawl of breath. I walk through the aisles of white tents until I realize it's coming from one of the tents. What the—?

I hurry to the source and unzip the white casing, revealing a dark-skinned, dark-haired woman. Her high cheekbones are pronounced in the slight, weakened state of her face. She turns her head to the right, then the left. Slowly, her eyes blink open, and they're staring up at me.

"Are you all right?" I ask, not sure if she's a ghost, or if I am seeing a surrogate wake from unconsciousness.

Her eyes widen, and she starts flailing on the bed, her body shifting back and forth as she tries to escape. She pulls on her arms and legs, and for the first time I notice she's strapped down. She's not going anywhere.

"Shh," I tell her while I figure out how to loosen the straps. "I'm not going to hurt you. Please, stop."

"Not again," she wails. "I don't want to do it again." Her cries echo in the room so loudly, I don't notice Nine and Eri come up behind me.

"What happened?" Nine asks, startling me.

I spin around. "The power is out. But this one woke up."

"Where's Catcher?" She looks around the room, but he and Odell are nowhere.

Another moan comes from a few beds down. Nine rushes to check on that surrogate, so I hold up my gun and force Eridian to kneel. "Hands together," I say. After cutting a length of rope from one of the bolas, I tie her hands to her feet so she can't go anywhere.

Eri watches Nine, then diverts her attention to another white tent where the surrogate inside has started to move around. "It's because of the electricity," she says.

"What do you mean?" I narrow my eyes at her. "What's because of the electricity?"

"The surrogates waking up. The thing keeping them under was a computer program sending a signal to their brain to remain in a comatose state. When the power went out, the signal was disrupted. So now they're waking up."

So it *was* something electric keeping them under. "But why wouldn't the serum wake them?"

She winces and adjusts her wrists. "We changed to an electric-based system the day we installed the new trackers. They don't take minutes to wake anymore. It's instantaneous once the signal is disrupted."

"So it doesn't matter that they're on the life-support machines," I say. "They become conscious at the same time it shuts off, so the life support is negligent." They can breathe. Their hearts can beat. But if waking is an immediate response, then the power must have barely gone out. I glance around again, wondering where Catcher could be.

"All of them are awake," Nine calls to me. "Or they will be soon. Now what?"

I rub my jaw. "We have to release them. Get them out."

Eridian laughs out loud. "Good luck with that." When neither of us respond, she rolls her eyes. "They've been kept like this for months, years. Their muscles have atrophied. You'll be lucky to get them to sit up and eat on their own. There's no way they're going to walk out of here."

She's right. Why didn't we think of this? Why didn't Catcher . . . No, he must have thought it. Maybe that's why he insisted on coming here himself. Maybe he never planned on returning with us to the rebel village. Not yet anyway.

Nine stomps to Eri and gives her a threatening look. "Then why the straps? Are those just for fun?"

Eri flinches, and I think she's taken aback by such a strong and confident Nine. "A precaution," she whispers. "So if something like this happened—if the power accidentally went out—they don't end up hurting themselves or falling off the beds. I need to protect our unborn Batches at all costs."

"Who cares about these females," Nine spits at her, "as long as the babies inside them are thriving? Right?"

The Prime Maker presses her mouth closed. She's wise enough to not antagonize Nine any more than she already has.

The transmitter at Nine's side crackles, and a voice comes through.

Communications are back up. All units report.

The transmitters are working, but how?

Weapons secure. Vehicles operational.

Rebels are weakening.

Minimal losses.

Seeker weapons are functioning. Rebel forces are fading.

Nine throws the transmitter against the wall in frustration. It breaks into dozens of pieces, littering the floor, while cries from the surrogates continue to permeate the room.

"Haven't you realized it by now?" Eri tilts her head up at me. "You can't stop me. Even with your family principles and true freedom and whatever other ridiculous notions you tell yourself matter. Even with your adorable rebel forces and your cute little grenades. I. Can't. Be. Stopped."

She knows about the bola grenades. How could she know about the grenades?

"We even disabled the electric components of our guns so they wouldn't fail when your little pulses shot out."

How did she know to do that?

"You might have managed to take out our communications," she continues, "but only temporarily, obviously."

The pulses weren't strong enough to destroy the tech in the province. Only render them useless for a short time. How could I be so cracked? We didn't have time to test the grenades properly. I was too eager to get to Pua; I was blinded by what could go wrong. And everything has gone wrong. Everywhere we turn things are going wrong.

"Let Eridian go."

I turn to the voice coming from the doorway. Low and solid. It's Odell, and he's got his gun trained on the back of Catcher's head as he pushes him forward.

No.

Odell shoves Catcher farther into the room, and I can see the pain of betrayal on Catcher's face, even in this low light. Odell says it again. "Let her go, or I blow a hole into your precious rebel leader."

Odell betrayed us. Betrayed Catcher.

My mouth falls open. "You told Eri about the grenades. About our attack. About—"

"About everything." Eri yanks on the rope around her ankles and wrists, but it holds tight. "You, your little girlfriend in the surrogate cells, Catcher and his valuable Rise. All of it. After you escaped with Catcher, we interrogated my Seekers and forced Odell to confess. Some people will give anything to spare their own lives."

Odell's new scar.

"After that," she continues, "all I had to do was have Odell send word to Catcher that Pua was dying right away. I knew you'd come. Now I have *all* the rebels within my grasp." She

328

licks her lips. "I didn't know Nine would be with you, though. Now that was a pleasant surprise."

"Drop your weapons," Odell yells. His blond hair has come loose from his ponytail and flaps wildly as he speaks. He tosses a used bola grenade to the side of the room. He must have stolen it from Catcher and set it off earlier—or maybe Catcher was forced to use it in his defense. Either way, now I know why the power is out in this wing.

I glance at Nine and know neither of us will give in easily. We both keep our guns trained on the Prime Maker.

"Drop it now," Odell says. "Or I *will* shoot him." The barrel of his gun knocks against Catcher's head.

I meet Catcher's gaze, and he shakes his head slightly.

In answer to Odell, I engage a bullet and bring the gun to my shoulder, ready to shoot.

Odell shoves Catcher forward so hard he stumbles to the ground, and Odell pulls the trigger. At first I think it's a warning shot, meant to scare us into submission, but when I see Catcher fall flat against the floor, blood staining the back of his shirt and running to the ground beneath him, I realize he shot to kill. Or at least injure.

I am running forward to assess Catcher's wound when Odell's booming voice stops me.

"Weapons down!" His face is red, and I don't doubt he'll take us all out if it comes to that.

I slowly lower my weapon to the ground and see Nine in my peripheral vision doing the same. With my arms in the air, I stand tall again, making it clear I won't try anything.

Odell points his weapon at Nine. "Untie her."

Nine crouches and does as he says.

Eridian jumps to her feet and hurries past us, taking her

place behind Odell and his weapon. A smile tugs on her face, as though everything is working out exactly as she had planned.

"If only you'd come back sooner," she says, looking at Nine. "You have the power to stop this. But I'm afraid it's too late."

Nine frowns. "What do you mean *I* have the power?"

"The cure. The antidote." Eri sighs. "You're the only one who has it, my little experiment."

Catcher rolls onto his back, a line of blood dripping from his mouth. His breathing is labored. I have to stop the bleeding before it's too late. But Odell is trigger-happy, and I can't risk it.

Nine steps forward. "I don't have anything. Please tell us where the antidote is."

Eri purses her lips. "The antidote," she whispers. "It's you, Nine. *You* are the antidote. You are the cure. But you weren't here in time, and now the world is going to unravel around us, because you left me." She clicks her tongue, and the sound of it sends a shiver down my spine.

Nine freezes in place, studying Eridian. A loud wail comes from one of the surrogates.

Odell shifts his feet. "I need to get you out of here, Eri. It's not safe."

Nine holds up a hand as though to stop them. She addresses Eri. "You said it was too late, but the Virus hasn't been released yet. No one with a tracker has left Freedom. No one has tried to remove it. It's still contained." She offers a hand toward the Prime Maker. "I'm here now. I can stop this. Tell me how, and I'll do it."

Eri stares at that hand as though it's the treasure she's been looking for her entire life but that turned out to be a mirage. A false hope. Her eyes glaze over, darkness shrouding them. Almost as if she's saddened, defeated.

"But the Virus *has* been released," Eri says.

No. It can't be. "How?" I ask.

She smirks. "The new trackers that are in every slave, surrogate, and citizen are run on tiny batteries that keep the Virus from being released into the host. Disable that circuit, and . . . oops. Contamination." She steps toward the doorway. "Thanks to your little stunt with the pulse grenades, you and your rebel force have injected the Virus into every person in Freedom One. Because of you, the world is going to disappear. Bravo, Theron."

My legs falter beneath me, and not because of my weakened leg this time. I collapse to the ground. A pain shoots through my stomach so violently I feel bile rise up my throat in reaction. I force it down, but sweat builds on my forehead and neck. It's my fault. Everything that has happened here today—everything that is about to happen—is all my doing.

"Looks like you won't be saving anyone today after all," Eri says as she reaches the door. "And you came all this way . . ."

She slips through the door, Odell closing it behind them.

Nine reaches for her gun and hurries to the door. I don't know if she's planning on going after them or making sure they stay away, but I don't care. I rush to Catcher's side and apply instant pressure on his wounds. I check his pulse and breathing, searching for other injuries, making sure I don't miss anything.

"Theron," he mumbles, coughing up a fresh round of blood.

"Shh," I say. "It's going to be okay. I'll get you patched up and out of here in no time." I swallow hard. He's lost a lot of blood and is bleeding internally. I need to get him to the trauma station right away. I look up at the surrogate beds. Maybe I can find an empty one, lift Catcher on top, and then wheel him out through—

Catcher grasps my forearm. "A drilling attempt isn't going

to save me this time." He manages a small smile through his expression of pain.

How can he smile at me when the whole world is falling apart? When he's about to—

No. I have to think. Maybe there's a dermastrap or atomizer I can find with meds to keep him stable. I think through our lists of patches that might extend his life long enough to—

"Promise me you'll get them out," Catcher says. "Promise me you'll find a way to get them all out of this place."

Does he realize they're all infected and can't go anywhere?

I shake my head. "No. No, you're coming with us. You're going to make it." There's no way I'm leaving here without him at my side. "Think about Joramae and Hattie. They're waiting for you."

His grip tightens. "Promise me you'll take care of them, too. Make sure they're okay. My Joramae . . ."

"No!" I can't believe this is happening. I wipe my face on my sleeve to dry the tears I didn't realize were falling. "Don't give up, Catcher. Please, hold on."

"Theron," he says, his eyes glazing over. "Promise. You have to promise."

Nine kneels next to me. She places one hand on my shoulder and one on Catcher's leg, pain etched on her face.

My shoulders hunch, my body caves. "I promise," I say weakly. "I'll make sure they're all okay." If this is all I have to give Catcher, I'll make sure it happens or die trying.

He winces, his pain overwhelming him. "The R-Rise. I want you to take my place. You are their leader now."

"I can't." He doesn't understand what he's asking. He doesn't realize it's my stupidity, my impatience, that has brought the world to its doom. If he did, he wouldn't be asking me this. "I'm no leader. I can't be the hero." I've killed innocent rebels here today. I've killed the world with the release of the Virus. I've killed Catcher. I'm the last person in the world with the skills, or the right, to lead a rebellion against Eridian and the Freedom provinces.

Catcher lifts his hand to my face and rests it against my cheek. He looks at me like . . . like a father. He's my father, and as his son, I've let him down. I've failed.

"Theron," he whispers. "Courage isn't always about grand feats achieved by grander champions. The bravest are those who know what's right, and who don't give up defending it."

I feel Nine's hand squeeze my shoulder. She's not a stranger to bravery. Maybe . . . maybe I can find it too.

Catcher clears his throat. "When great people fail—and they usually do—they try again. And again. Because you can't stop truth."

I think of the words on that yellow flyer I found outside my apartment. The one that spoke of family and a call to fight for it.

"Remember what this is all for," Catcher says.

"I do," I say. "I will." I lean over, and Catcher's arms wrap tightly around me, his strength surprising me. And not surprising me. I will continue to fight, and protect, and lead. If there's one thing I want my life to be, it is to become like this man who taught me that I could be more than I was. There's nothing better I could ever aspire to.

The responsibility he feels toward the rebels and his family—it's because Catcher knows freedom doesn't come from resisting responsibility, but acting upon it. Our accountability is a gift. We are meant to be free men and women. Free to work. Free to be independent and gain self-respect. To lead. To help and protect beyond ourselves. It doesn't mean it's easy, but it's the key to breaking out of bondage. Catcher knew that, and he sacrificed his life for it. It's his happiness secret.

"I believe in you," he whispers in my ear. Then his arms go slack.

The pain that shoots through me is tangible, measurable, as though I could cast a net and catch it. Observe it. Count the hundreds of ways I caused it. Count all the ways I must learn to let it go.

"Theron." Nine tugs on my shoulder, tears streaming down her face. "You heard what Eri said. We have to tell the others. Everyone in the trauma station."

I pull back from Catcher and sit on my heels. "The slaves all have trackers. They all have the Virus now." I wipe at my nose, my face. "Everything we did to get them free is pointless because we can't bring them back to their families."

She bites her lip. Nine doesn't have the answer either. She stands and glances around the room. Whimpers continue to sound from the waking women. "We'll have to leave the surrogates here."

My face falls. "I promised Catcher I'd—"

"Just for an hour or so. Until we figure out what we're going to do about those infected."

I glance at the white tents. "Okay," I say, knowing we have no other choice. "But I'm not leaving them here in fear. We can spare a few minutes to say we're not abandoning them. That help is on the way."

Nine nods and hurries to the first bed, unzipping the white covering. I do the same on my side, wondering how I can offer these women hope when I don't have any left to give.

CHAPTER THIRTY-FOUR

*A*s we walk through the water tunnels leading to the trauma station, I think about all the people I've let down. Catcher. The rebel forces engaged in a dying fight. The slaves I'm about to face. The surrogates. Something catches in the back of my throat as I picture those women, still strapped to their beds.

I knock on the metal door, and soon Gray is there with a gun. He exhales in relief when he sees it's me.

"Finally," he breathes. "These people have been filling me and Iden in about who they are. Where they're from." He swallows hard, empathy on his face. "How they are Made. About everything. I can't believe this was happening right under our noses."

"I know." I spare a thought for my own ability to reproduce, or lack thereof. With Catcher gone, I don't know how to reverse it—for me or any other citizen we manage to liberate. Of course it won't matter if no one lives through this pandemic. That needs to be our focus right now.

Squaring his shoulders, Gray continues. "The Seekers are out front, trying to break in. The lockdown security measures are keeping them out, but I don't know what to say to get them to back off. I don't think they know the slaves are here, but the whole situation is getting more and more suspicious the longer we don't respond."

I walk into the crowded room, hundreds of hopeful faces looking at me. My heart nearly stops when I realize Pua and Kai aren't back yet. Iden is in the far corner, rifling through Setia's unorganized files. Nine runs to Miri and Ara, embracing them and diving into an explanation about where we've been. It's something I'll have to tell all of these people in a minute. The power is out, but the skylights provide more than enough light.

"And another thing," Gray continues. "Something happened to my tracker when the lights went out. I felt a small pinch, like a bug bite." He looks around the room. "It happened to everyone."

It was the Virus releasing into his system. I run a hand through my hair, my tongue frozen in my mouth. How can I tell him he's infected? That they're all infected?

I steel my expression. "Tell the Seekers there's been an outbreak of an unknown contagion, and you've had to quarantine the area. The lockdown will be removed once the outbreak is contained."

His eyes widen. "That's brilliant. I should have thought of that." He hurries toward the front room to convey the message through the glass reception window, a smile on his face. Unfortunately for Gray, the outbreak isn't a lie.

I desperately want to leave and look for Pua, but I can't avoid this any longer. I raise my hand to get everyone's attention. "There's something I have to tell you. Those of you with trackers, those who've been captive here in Freedom One, unfortunately there's been—"

"Theron!" Iden yells from her corner of the room, holding a file of papers in the air. "You're going to want to see this."

I open my mouth to say this isn't the best time, but Nine stands beside me and locks her arm with mine. "It's okay," she says. "Go ahead. I can do this."

I rest the side of my face against her head. I know she can do this. She can do anything. It's a blessing and a relief that Nine can step in and take care of me when I need it. She's family, and that's what we do.

"Thank you," I say. I walk toward Iden at the back of the room.

Iden slaps the folder onto the table with her inky fingers. I flip it open, running my fingers through dozens of pages. I don't know what I'm supposed to look for. I sigh, attempting to maintain my patience in an already terrible day. While I hear Nine's speech in the background about the Virus, trackers, and pulse grenades, I do my best to focus on Iden. "Tell me," I say.

She nods. "So remember how Setia was working on some secret project for the Prime Maker?"

"Yes."

"Well, according to her files, it was a virus. But not just any virus. It was *the* Virus—the same one that wiped out Earth's population all those years ago."

I glance over my shoulder at Nine who's talking about the very same thing, then I turn to Iden, my shoulders slumping. "And?"

She ignores the despair in my voice. "And . . . she conducted tests on patients in a highly secure lab in the Core building. Most patients were those held captive, like these people here. But some of them were citizens. Those captured by Eri and her team of Seekers."

Setia had too much on her shoulders, too. I should have asked her about her secret project. Listened to her. Been there for her when she needed it before it was too late.

But she kept these paper records. Was she trying to hide certain information from Eridian by not posting it on the province-wide network? Could it have something to do with the blood sample she was working with the day I helped her with the centrifuge?

Iden continues. "Everyone tested contracted the disease—rebels and citizens alike. We were Made after the Virus had already gone dormant, so we are all susceptible."

No, I think. *Not after*. The rebels are descendants of the first generation to survive, but we citizens were started before the Virus was even released. But we certainly weren't exposed to it. Neither were our Makers, the founders of the Batch system. I picture some scientists safe in a tidy lab, protected from the disease while the rest of the world rotted away, all in an attempt to build a perfect society.

"But take a look at this one." Iden pulls out a sheet of paper and hands it to me. "This subject received the same tests, but the disease didn't take hold—no infection. The experiments were done on a child. A Batcher." She leans over and points.

There, written along the bottom of the page: Batch #1372; Member #9. That's my own Batch, which means . . . I look back at Nine. She's finished talking and is trying to answer questions from the fearful crowd.

"Whoever this is," Iden says, "this person is immune to the Virus." She turns the page over and taps it with her finger. "This person could be the key to finding a vaccine."

"Or a cure," I add. A vaccine would prevent the Virus from spreading, but it takes time to produce. But a cure—an antidote—can help those already infected. And Eridian said Nine is the key.

Nine the experiment.

I grip the papers in my hand and march toward Nine, Iden following close behind. Doing my best to ignore the slaves arguing and talking, I get Nine's attention. I pull her to the side. It's as much privacy as we're going to get.

"Eri was right," I say, giving her the papers. "You're immune to the Virus. You have the secret to the cure."

Her eyes widen as she glances at the papers.

"I don't know if it's coded in your DNA or something else, but"—I voice what I've already decided, what I made my mind up about the second I knew the Virus had been released—"but whatever it is, we need to stay and find it. Save these rebels. Save Freedom citizens."

She shakes her head. "If it's true, then I'm immune—not you. You still have time to get out. Take Kai and Miri and anyone else without a tracker. Warn the others."

I glance to the back door, hoping to see Kai and Pua. *Where are they?*

"But I promised Catcher—" I pause. What did I promise him? That I'd find a way to get these people out. Get them safe. I promised I'd take care of his family and make sure they're okay. I promised . . .

I promised I'd take his place as leader of the Rise. I think of Catcher's words: *Remember what this is all for.* I'm done with resisting what's right. Because the brave don't give up defending the truth.

A calm settles over me. I know what I have to do. Despite the chaos and the terror and everything that has gone wrong, I feel a sense of peace. The path I've chosen and the path always intended for me have converged. It may be for a small moment, but for now, it's enough.

I face Nine. "I promised Catcher I'd make sure they're all okay. Every last one of them. I'm not leaving until we find the cure." This is all I have to give Catcher, but I think he would agree it is enough.

"But, Theron . . ." Nine's voice shakes.

I give the papers back to Iden and grasp Nine's shoulders. "It doesn't matter if a few of us get out now. We'll only be postponing the inevitable. I'll be more use here. We'll stop Eridian and her Seekers, find a cure, and save everyone." I glance toward Miri and Ara, who have stepped up beside us. "Besides, we don't know that we haven't already been exposed. The Virus could be airborne and have already entered our systems. We can't risk anyone going back to the rebel village and infecting those there."

"Hemi," Miri whispers, bringing her hand to her mouth. "Tama."

Ara pulls her into his arms. "They're okay. They're safe. Joramae will take care of them."

Joramae. Who's going to tell her about her husband? She'll be so worried, waiting for Catcher.

I swallow hard, and my shoulders cave. "We can't let anyone leave Freedom." Will Eri try to send Seekers to the rebel camps knowing the people we've left are exposed? "And we can't let any of our families enter the province boundaries either."

"What about the Prime Makers?" Nine says. "Eri said they're coming. How do we keep them out?"

"I don't know." I turn to face the crowd. I continue to address Nine, but I raise my voice so everyone can hear. "All I know is we can't give up. We need to continue to fight and do everything we can to find a cure."

I glance at the faces in the room, sorrow eating at the insides of me.

I'm sorry for what I've done to you, I want to say. *I'm so sorry.*

A few in the crowd nod. The rest are silent—either in rage or despair.

"We'll assign border patrols," I say. "Others to care for the surrogates. We'll make sure the slave facilities and surrogate machines are destroyed so the Prime Maker can't use them again. It's the first step in liberating the citizens who have been kept in the dark far too long."

Nine wrinkles her brow. "There will be no one to liberate if everyone is dead. Start testing me right away. We'll find a cure to this Virus." She looks at me, determined. "We will save these people. We have to."

I think of the citizens fighting in the cages, drinking at the nightspots, doing all the things I once did. They don't know life can be more than a futile existence in the pursuit of a happiness that never fully satisfies—just like I didn't know. They deserve a chance to change their lives too.

As if she knows what I'm thinking, Nine adds, "I want them to have the freedom to choose this life."

The same way Nine did.

The same way I have.

Because you cannot stop truth.

Nine meets my gaze, and I can sense everything she's feeling in that moment, just like when we were Batchers. Fear, hope, love. The kind of love that makes you willing to sacrifice all you have, all you are. The greatest love there is.

"Okay," I say. "We'll start testing you right away." I glance at Iden. "But we need to find out more about the Virus. Duration, severity. How it's transferred. Symptoms. We know nothing about this disease."

"That's not true," a voice sounds from behind me, weak and soft but with a distinct lisp.

I turn around and see Pua first, though it wasn't her voice I heard. Her eyes latch on to mine, relief filling both of us, knowing the other is safe. She and Kai hold a prisoner between them, supporting her weight. A dozen other prisoners fall in behind. They are bruised, beaten. Tortured.

They made it. They rescued the prisoners and made it back.

Pua is swept up by her parents, who are crying in relief over the daughter they thought they'd lost.

I take a good look at the prisoner, now supported only by Kai. Cuts and gashes in various stages of healing cover her arms and legs, bruises of every color spread along her face, and dried blood mottles the formerly orange hair on her head.

The paper files fall from Iden's hands. "Setia?"

"You want details on the Virus, Theron?" Setia taps her pierced tongue against her teeth. "Now *that* I can definitely do something about." She cracks a smile, and I can't help but mirror it, a small sliver of hope finding its way into my chest.

ACKNOWLEDGMENTS

In late March 2012, around three o'clock in the morning, I sat at my computer and cried. It was an ugly cry, the kind where fat tears fell in a deluge onto my keyboard without my permission. I couldn't seem to catch my breath, awkward sounds coming from somewhere deep in my throat as I tried to keep myself under control. I'd just finished the first draft of *Remake*, and my heart felt betrayed by what I'd just done to my all-time favorite character—Theron. When I finally pulled myself together and crawled into bed, I promised to make things right for him. I vowed he'd get a chance to tell his story and enjoy a happier ending than the one Nine left him with. So I would love to thank everyone who played a part in helping me fulfill that promise.

Thanks to my agent, Katherine Boyle, for being my advocate, cheerleader, support, and level head when I needed it. Also to everyone at Shadow Mountain for making this book possible, including Chris Schoebinger, Karen Zelnick, Sarah Shepherd,

ACKNOWLEDGMENTS

Heather Ward, and Malina Grigg. I especially want to thank Lisa Mangum and Heidi Taylor for kindly (and bravely) convincing me to throw away the 100,000 words I'd already written and start again from scratch. It was probably the hardest thing I've ever done with my writing, but I'm so proud of how much stronger Theron's story became and am grateful for your brilliance.

A heartfelt thanks to my critique partners: Kathryn Purdie, Robin Hall, Emily Prusso, Kelley Lynn, and Christy Petrie. I'm so blessed to be on this writing journey with you, and I can't thank you enough for kicking me in the rear or offering a shoulder to cry on, depending on what I need most at the moment.

And thanks to my family who support and inspire me every single day, especially my daughter, Emma, who reads all of my drafts and brainstorms through plotting issues with me. It's been amazing having teen readers in my home, and I will miss it when they're grown. (Hint: Stop growing. Seriously, stop.)

Finally, I want to thank my husband, Daniel. When my sisters-in-law first read *Remake*, they said, "You realize Theron is our brother, right?" From his humor, arrogance, and fighting skills to his leadership and desire to sacrifice and help those around him, Theron is so much like my husband—and probably why he's my favorite. So a great big thanks goes to Daniel, who not only supports and encourages my writing, but inspires me and so many others with all the good he does. I love you so much.

DISCUSSION QUESTIONS

1. At the start of the story, Theron is still mourning Nine's absence and turns to fighting and drinking as a way to cope with it. What might be a better way to deal with sorrow or loss? Have people ever hurt you emotionally before? What have you done to get past that pain?

2. Theron has always been a good fighter, but in this book he discovers something worth fighting for and utilizes his talents for a worthy cause. What talents do you have? Have you ever used your skills to help others? If not, what are some ways you can use what you know to serve those around you?

3. Eridian does all she can to keep Freedom One running smoothly. Name a few things she changed in the province since becoming Prime Maker. What signs are there that show that Freedom is falling apart regardless of her patchwork solutions? Is there anything she can do to keep the society from collapsing?

DISCUSSION QUESTIONS

4. How would you define the word *family*? Do people need to be related by blood to be considered family? Are there things about living in a family unit you sometimes take for granted? Does distance or time apart change how you feel about your family? Theron thinks of Catcher as a father by the end of the book. Name a few characteristics of a good father that Catcher demonstrates.

5. Theron is riddled with guilt by the end of the story, believing everything that has gone wrong is his fault. Do you think the rebels should have waited before infiltrating Freedom, or was going in right away the correct thing to do? What would you have done? Have you ever done something to help an individual in need only to have your actions hurt them or make the situation worse? What are some ways to overcome guilt?

6. Theron enjoys being a Healer. It brings him a sense of peace to help others who otherwise can't help themselves. How does this thinking translate to how he helps the rebels and families later in the book? Have you ever had a job or responsibility that is both enjoyable and helpful at the same time? How can working hard and acting selflessly make you happy?

7. Originally, Odell is devoted to Catcher and the Rise, but eventually he switches sides when tortured by Eri and her other Seekers. What would it take for you to give up on a cause you believed in? Would you be willing to risk your safety, your life, or your family for a noble cause? If a person gives up on something because the sacrifice is too great, do you think they were never truly devoted in the first place, or are there limits to what we should be expected to give?

DISCUSSION QUESTIONS

8. A number of characters in the book deal with physical disabilities, including Theron, Pua, and Joramae. Some of them struggle with their limitations while others refuse to look at it as a disability at all. Can you think of a few examples of how different characters view those with disabilities? What physical trials have you dealt with in your own life? Have those experiences hurt or helped you? How much does a person's ability factor into their self-identity, if at all?

9. Despite being locked in a cell for most of the book, Pua shows the reader she can be strong even as a prisoner. Can you name one example of this? How has Nine become stronger since Theron last saw her? Did his opinion of Nine change because of it? How does this affect his attitude toward Pua and her strength?

10. Catcher tells Theron there are a lot of ways to love someone. What do you think are some of those ways? Originally, Theron believes that love is purely a romantic emotion. Do you agree? Is his belief reflective of the self-important nature of his society? Can you think of ways Theron shows love to others, or ways others show love to him, that don't involve romance? How about in your own life? Can you love others without knowing them?